The Education Of Black Dickey

Kenneth Wayne Bowens

ISBN: 0-9653447-6-2
ISBN-13: 9780965344760

Dedication

My daughter Chanika and my son Kayin, you guys supply me with my daily bread for living. Momma thanks for a lifetime of patience, tolerance, and love. My siblings, Karetha, Fred, Donald, Danny, Jackie, Febra, David, and Mary, thanks for always validating what honesty and hard work looks like. My heart ruptures whenever I remember all the brothers and sisters that were killed violently and suffered through slavery and Jim Crow; and all the brave white people that were murdered and cast out of white society for doing the right thing. Thanks, you've performed all the heavy lifting, and your tormented lives made it possible for me to feel free to write this book. Lisa Newby, a white woman that has assimilated and bonded with African American culture, you're one of the few white friends I have in Oklahoma. Thanks for spending weekends working tirelessly editing. The GRITS, ABLE and Bridges book clubs, you guys have made reading every book an animated adventure and me a better writer and storyteller. Thank you. Tamara Moore thanks for holding my hand, and black womanly...pushing me across the finish line.

Bibliography

These books and materials were priceless resources.
2001 Final Report of the Oklahoma Commission to Study The Tulsa Race Riot of 1921: Research provided by The Oklahoma Historical society
African American newspapers: (Tulsa Daily Star and The Black Dispatch)
The Tulsa World and The Tulsa Tribune
Black Indians by William Loren Katz
Black Indian Slave Narratives by Patrick Minges
American Apartheid Segregation And The Making Of The Under-Class by Douglass S. Massey, Nancy, and A. Denton
The Shaping of Black America by Lerone Bennett, Jr.
And still the waters run by Angie Debo
An Oklahoma I Had Never Seen Before Edited by Davis D. Joyce
Riot on Greenwood by Eddie Faye Gates
Black Wall Street by Hannibal B. Johnson,
Journey toward hope by Jimmie Lewis Franklin
The Blacks in Oklahoma by Jimmie Lewis Franklin
The Germans from Russia in Oklahoma by Douglas Hale
The British and Irish in Oklahoma by Patrick J. Blessing
The Czechs in Oklahoma by Karel D. Bicha
The Poles in Oklahoma by Richard M. Bernard
Black heritage of Oklahoma by Gene Aldrich
The Germans in Oklahoma by Richard C. Rohrs
Oklahoma City African American discovery guide by Kendrick Moore
Acres of aspiration: the all-Black towns in Oklahoma by Hannibal B.Johnson
Tulsa race riot: From Wikipedia, the free online encyclopedia

Chapter One

"Get out the vehicle niggers!" The white policeman yelled the degrading term in a fierce old nasty southern twang. Wounded by his assault, in the dim light of dawn, I squinted through pouring rain and was able to detect freckles on the face of the white officer. But what captured my attention and held my eyes swollen with panic was the shotgun the cop had aimed at my head.

There we were four young black men of the hip-hop generation; our hands were locked in cuffs at the back. We were shoved to the ground and forced to bathe in Oklahoma City's autumn windy showers. As we laid face down, muddy polluted water dripped across our lips. Black Dickey soaked and shriveled inside my boxers.

Why did these two white policemen hate us? Why did they want to kill us? And right there lying in the chilly waters of fall the question that had dogged me all my life made me shudder. "Why had it been impossible for me to live in this city this long without ever forming a single intimate relationship with a white person?"

***

The leaves had been dying again. They had blossomed into golden browns, russet red oranges, and lemon yellows. The sun had sucked the green life out of them and now the autumn's rains had blazed through Oklahoma City with sweeping winds that shook every tree's foundation. Dead leaves were spread like blankets all over the yards in our neighborhood. At an eye's glance one could see the dead foliage had assembled into artistic exquisite patterns. Then the winds would blow, sweeping the crusty leaves into poetic crackling sounds, destroying one piece of art for another.

Despite the fact that they don't pack the brisk cold punch of Chicago's winds there's a resiliency in the super force of the Sooner State's often hundred-mile per hour gust. Hundred's of blustering tornadoes blow through the state injuring and killing people and causing millions in property damages annually.

That night gigantic thunderbolts had knocked the power out in our home three times. On the last occasion the electricity stayed off. I navigated through darkness and found a flashlight. Since 1 AM I'd burned the twenty-first century's mid-night oil with this miniature spotlight. Flipping through my notes and my psychology textbook pages was becoming more of a task of my will than it was to improve my mind.

According to the battery powered digital clock the phone began ringing at 5:50 AM.

"Hey Dawg! What's-up?" It was my cousin Danny and I knew he wanted something from me to be calling this early.

"I've been busting my brains all night for an early morning exam." In a drained tone I informed him of the frustrating details of last night. I was hoping he would make our conversation quick. I didn't want whatever he wanted to disturb my recall memory for the test.

"Ah...bro"—

The *ah and* the *pause* from my dear cousin was the hint that he needed my help. Since childhood our bond as best buddies had matured into a caveman of '*ahs and pauses.*'

"Uh hey bro I gotta get to this gig! You gotta hop over here and drop me off downtown." Danny sounded desperate. Aunt Betty must be on his back. I checked the time on the clock again.

The answers to what might be test questions had been rehearsed inside my head for twelve straight hours. All night intermittent lightening and gigantic blast of thunder mysteriously enchanted me. Somehow the noise and the outburst of illuminations had intermingled with my learning in a way that was invigorating. Thunder and lightening, these two entities had developed a cozy relationship with my thoughts and as we traveled through the darkness together we'd become friends.

According to the Jewish humanist psychologist Abraham Maslow human beings have a hierarchy of needs and these wants must be satisfied for that person to function at full speed. Folk's physiological requirements should be met. People need to feel safe and every human being needs to feel like he or she belongs somewhere. After those are achieved a person is capable of feeling good about themselves and their lives and familiar with what feeling *good self-esteem* truly feels like. Self-Actualization happens to people when they are able to achieve their full potential. If people are given those basic freedoms they are able to achieve peace with themselves and are at liberty to give lovingly to the world.

The first twelve years of Danny's life he was always hungry and afraid. Brought up by an alcoholic drug addict prostitute Danny had been left alone on several occasions with grown-ups that had shady morals. Some of their street instincts were absorbed into Danny's blood. Maslow believed a person had to acquire certain psychological attributes from one level to ascend to the next. Wherever Mamma and I ranked on Mr. Maslow's echelon, we whole-heartedly embraced Danny with all the love we had.

I calculated that my good deed, delivering Danny downtown, would take approximately an hour. Afterwards a sixty-wink nap would give me thirty to forty minutes to rehash the exam and the drive to CSU was twenty minutes.

A gush of Oklahoma's autumn's wind spurted through the weary pores of my warm night owl skin. The downpours and all-night gentle steady drizzles had soaked the earth. I walked to my car squashing into dead brown leaves and golden grass.

I rolled off in my silver Camry with the exam notes on the top of my brain ready for regurgitation. With Snoop Dog's latest CD as background, I supplied myself with mental test questions and answers.

I sped through drip drops of rain and daybreak's murkiness down Prospect to 36th street, turned east and hopped on Interstate 35. Five minutes later I arrived on the lower eastside of Oklahoma City. I exited on Northeast 16th and Douglas Boulevard and drove down an incline street that ran parallel to the highway. At the bottom, a puddle of dirty water doused the Camry's fresh wax and the windshield.

Blinded, I stopped at the four way stop sign and turned the windshield wipers on faster. Suddenly out of last night's leftover rain, shallow echoes turned into rumbling beats and those rhythms became a resounding crescendo of thunder blast. The noise appeared to alter into a flash that illuminated across the skies and the glow melted the moisture from the clouds into a ferocious downpour.

All alone, wrapped in the cozy warmth of the defroster, I was feeling safe in the car from nature's savage conditions. I became enthralled with the rap-tap-tap prattles of water that bounced against the armor I was in. Intimately, autumn's wet weather snuggled and shivered up my spine and the warmth of deja vu curled up beside me and became my private passenger. From the grave I heard the cultivating hymns of my Grandmother and briefly saw the loads of moles caked on her red tanned face.

"Boy you have the prettiest big brown eyes." Glaring into my soul, with a grand smile she would hold my chin in one hand and many times repeat those words.

I was four years old and I was in her lap that day when we stopped at the same four way stop sign. Wiped slowly into my view were portions of what use to be one in a handful of the nations black owned hospitals—*Edwards Memorial.*

She'd told *Walter Edward's* story many times and I began hearing Grandmother's captive husky cadence.

"Walter Edwards made his first fortune selling scrap iron to the United States government during World War II. In the spring of 1945 his wife, Francis, fell ill and was taken to the basement of one of Oklahoma City's best-segregated hospitals. Off in some cryptic vault—that's where the doctors tended to the coloreds!" Her frown would scrunch the tiny whispers underneath her nose. "In the cellar ain't no place to be when you're sick." Twisting her big-bronzed lips she would complete this cycle of her physical aggressive outrage.

"In those days, that's how white folks defined equal." Her story had an ache in it. Whenever she spoke of the old days it was like she was pulling the scab off an unhealed sore. Mean and nasty things had been done to her and the old woman was still hurting, those old days were still slapping her upside the head. Grandma would wave her finger in my face, clarifying her feelings of racism for a four-year-old to understand. When her eyebrows relaxed I knew some of her ancient anger had dissipated, and we both knew she'd made her point. Rolling her sugar-sweet cinnamon eyes down on me, they assured me she was right and blacks had been mistreated and in many offensive ways.

"Without delay he removed his honey from the second class conditions. Walter flew her straight up north to the Mayo clinic and they treated her with dignity and cared for her in livable conditions and Francis recovered.

"The rich black couple knew everybody didn't have money to go north when sickness comes on the family and that there was a need for a first class caring hospital for blacks in Oklahoma City. You had a great uncle, while he was going blind he traveled over two hundred miles from Paris, Texas on a buckboard wagon to be treated right here. Uncle Ed could sing a song prettier than an eagle could soar. The doctors here did their best but the old black gangly blues man lived a long time as blind man." He was wearing dark shades and I saw the long legs of the sightless man float calmly through her ancient eyes.

"In April of 1948, *Edwards Memorial hospital* was built for the black community. It was three stories high and had 105 beds."

Today the old Edward's structure serves the community as a nursing home. The answers to why blacks were segregated in the first place haunted me in my fourth year of life. I still shake my head, bewildered and ask segregation, why? Even though I was living in the remnants of the actual full blown concept of Jim Crow, what blacks endured then was as foreign to me as the idea of surviving on Mars.

Across the street from Edwards Memorial were *"The Projects."* As I headed towards them, fear jumped on my back and rode with me.

On the governmental subsidized apartment's premises, brutal murders, felony assaults, drugs, and prostitution, were as steady and as gruesome as the morning's downpour. Along with Danny and my aunt, other unfortunate poor people lived there. I always said a silent prayer for all of them and myself when I entered and exited the downtrodden dwellings

I entered the parking lot and avoided most of the potholes but not all of them. I had often thought of asking my cousin if he'd meet me out on the street, I didn't consider this suggestion in this rainstorm.

I parked in the middle of the complex on the side that faced I-35. In the shadows I saw Danny huddling under a staircase, the steps ascended to my aunt's apartment. But Danny wasn't alone there were two other men with him. Obviously they had found a way to keep dry as they waited.

The three dark silhouettes jogged the short distance through the haze of water over to the car and I roll the window down a smidgen.

"Hey Bro." Leaning towards the window Danny greeted me. Water splashed off his brim and swilled over his face. The face-bath and his grimace gave his genuine smile a cynical street-smart smirk.

"What's up?" My quirky smile was an innuendo that Danny understood. I was asking for an update on his situation—why two other men were with him.

Twisting away from the window he tipped his hat in the direction of the two mystery men behind him.

"This is Buddy and Jarvis." Through blurred daybreak's light and webs of water I could see Buddy was husky, he resembled a shorter condensed version of Danny. Danny was six feet two and was two hundred thirty-pounds of stout thick muscles. Buddy was a yellow fellow with a mole smeared on his nose. Jarvis was charcoal; flimsy thin and maybe his skinny frame stretched him into barely five feet and nine inches. They both gave me a-hey-brother-man nod.

"Drop us off downtown. We're all going to unload warehouse trucks today."

"Cool." I nodded.

A large murky cloud parted and behind the smoke was a glare of daylight. Briefly it revealed the age of the autumn day.

I headed down Grand Boulevard. As I drove, peering through the rainstorm, I was able to see obscure images of wild dying golden weeds and shadows of rotten trees. Once upon a time on those soggy vacant grounds a section of a hard working pulled-up-by-bootstraps and almost self-sufficient black community had existed.

Somehow riding in the downpour and morning's murky dimness became eerie. Mysteriousness crept into the Camry and I began dreaming.

***

James Stewart played the character George Bailey in the famous Christmas movie 'It's A Wonderful Life.' Over a half century ago Walter Edwards was this real life personality personified. Stewart portrayed a man who owned the Bailey Buildings and Loans. He was able to offer reasonable home loans to working class citizens in a small town. Walter Edwards showed the same compassion for African Americans in Oklahoma City. Mr. Potter, the villain/antagonist in the adorable Christmas story was a rich and powerful businessman. He wanted to own everything in the tiny township. In real life, FHA/VA government loans, banks, real-estate agencies, neighborhood associations with restrictive covenants, home loan companies, KKK, and racist whites embodied the fairytale Mr. Potter. They were not and had never been in the business of getting along, supporting or graciously giving home loans to Black people. All his life, George Bailey had sacrificed his dreams in order that others could live the American Dream. In a society that detested the sight of African Americans, against all odds, racism, discrimination, segregation, redlining by financial institutions, Mr. Edward's journey was much more problematical. After investing his money in this vacant section of the city he hired craftsmen and they trained African Americans and the Edwards Edition was built. That's when the brother decided to test the 14th Amendment. Did blacks have the same rights as whites? He had to fight with city, state, and federal officials and finally the door was opened for blacks to receive government home loans. In a time of degradation and second classed citizenship most blacks were not able to have a 'Wonderful Life' but because of Walter Edwards they had a better life. To them he was their George Bailey in the flesh.

***

Snapping out of the daze I continued gazing through the hazy weather. Far across the baron field I believe I began to hear undertone echoes of hammers tapping.

I turned west at the light on N.E. 10th street and realized this old section of the Edward's Edition was gone forever.

"Put some new jams on man!" Danny said, he snarled semi-agitatedly. He turned the CD volume down and began searching through my CD's. His guest remained silent. I tuned him out and practiced answering test questions in my head.

I coasted pass our old al amateur, Douglas High School. The two-story campus was spread across at least two blocks.

A stoplight and a left twist of the steering wheel and we were on Martin Luther King. Danny slid in a P Diddy CD.

The raindrops were making their own beat on top of the Camry. The competing rhythms caused a disruption and I began to wander away from mentally masturbating test questions.

Whenever they traveled on the road every black person I'd ever known had developed a six sense. They could always detect when a cop was nearby. Was it the suspicious folklore we were all brought up on the reason we'd developed this third eye instinct? Were we more afraid of the law than whites? Was my cultural bias brainwashed upbringing only a symptom of the black/police relationship? Was paranoia of the police transmitted at conception in every black person's DNA? Are cops the real gang-bangers, the original OG's? Without a clear comprehension of how and why law enforcement had set off a second sense in African Americans I knew that the instinct and the police was part of the reality for all the blacks that I'd ever known.

When I made a right on N.E. 8th Street none of us visibly looked for them but I felt the whole groups eye's scrutinizing through the violent streams and spot the squad car. Were the cops sheltering themselves from the storm at the old abandoned Phillips 66 service station or were they hiding? Were they waiting on us?

Black Dickey shuddered and in a whisper said, "We're four young black men of the hip-hop generation driving in an African American economically challenged area. This is dangerous!"

"Oh shit! There's the man." Buddy the biggest one of the two back seat travelers blurted what our African American nature sensed.

An assassin's thunderbolt and flashes of lighting lit up the skies. The powerful surges splattered more water out of the skies, drenching the window shield. I switched the wipers on even faster.

I peered through the rearview mirror and spotted some murky headlights following us. Suddenly a red light swirled on and

Black Dickey sank between my thighs. I drifted to the curve and parked.

The churning cherry flashes in the dark of dawn and the turbulent weather gave the appearance that a deadly accident had occurred.

"Get out the vehicle niggers!"

Two white cops stood over me and I was drowning under heavy raindrops, and another frightening reality rushed in. Nationally one out of three African American men, sooner or later, ends up in prison and this state ranked third in the country for doing the dastardly deed.

Kaboom! Suddenly, the skies let loose another resounding thunder blast. If someone was watching me it may appear to him or her that the roar of the weather, the eerie shadows of the morning, or the chilly downpour was the cause of my shivers. But it was something much more insidious. A shrieking overwhelming humiliating feeling was beginning to make me believe I was less than human.

I'd heard the old horror stories of segregation but I hadn't lived long enough to understand the after affects of Oklahoma's eighteen Jim Crow laws.

In the first half of the twentieth century, this red state danced the Jim Crow jingle. In every slow rhythm step as the good old white folks of Oklahoma hooped and hollered, square danced to these orchestrated savage synchronized sequential beats, they tore into the heart of United State's Constitution. The laws they created restricted and isolated blacks for years. These handed-down inhumane institutionalized devices along with white superior demeanors have devastated and demoralize blacks. They've denied African American their civil rights.

These American Constitutional privileges were originally conceded way back in 1868—in the 14th Amendment after the end of slavery. This added revision in the constitution was suppose to guarantee that the ex-slaves would be treated as equals under the laws and as citizens of the United States. At the beginning of twentieth century, Oklahoma, a new state, would start the process of instituting the illegal segregation Jim Crow Laws. Those white lawmakers wanted to make sure that equality for blacks would never happen in the latest settlement in the country. In 1964 the federal government passed another civil rights law that defeated most of the Jim Crow Laws, and again, this legal process was suppose to officially end segregation. But just like the Constitutional law approved almost a hundred years earlier, the dominant culture in Oklahoma still didn't recognize African Americans as equals. Only God knows the amount of inequalities and the magnitude of the transgressions that have been committed against the dignity of African Americans and the amount of misery perpetrated on the soul of the world.

The stream of water that's beginning to invade my nose does not bother me. Instead my mind is flooded by questions I'm afraid to ask. Back in those days what were white people thinking? Were they stupidly ignorant, selfishly evil, or were they afraid of black people?

The water starts strangling me but I barely cough. I'm afraid that if I move too aggressively the white cops will blow my damn head off. As far as I could see the influences of those earlier decisions were still affecting my life.

Blacks and whites in Oklahoma treat each other like they're from different planets. I wish we had more of a loving relationship. I don't believe we really know each other.

***

(Blacks stood in lines for four and five hours in order to vote for Barack Obama and he lost all of Oklahoma's seventy-seven counties. Oklahoma was the only state in the country that John McCain won every county, making the state reddest of red states.)

***

It seemed as if it was only yesterday when Mamma was teaching me the ABC's and quizzing me on multiplication tables one through twelve. As I stood outside the police car the taste of filthy water from the puddles began to settle in with my saliva. And as the rain doused my face a sudden realization hit me; *a black man's childhood into manhood happens almost overnight!*

As I bathed in autumn's wind and rain the days of my yesteryears began to pass through my life.

Chapter Two

The word "*Oklahoma*" means *red person*. Why white Oklahoma educators are proud to point out this simple basic fact about the state's Native American history has always seemed weird to me. Even though Native Americans have never profited from the state's rich oil treasures or been apart of the power structure that would give them a voice in politics, the portrayal of Oklahoma as a "*red person's*" home this tidbit of information is extremely deceptive. The people preaching this one pony sermon forgot to emphasize the lawless murders and the devastating destruction of indigenous culture that occurred when the land was taken. All these annihilations have affected the crimson people and these events are not enthusiastically part of the state's public education. They certainly won't tell you in a school textbook that African explorers were the first visitors to arrive on the native's land. You won't see this on the evening news and there are no documentaries or movies in the works to enlightened Oklahoma or America of this fact. Only a handful of historians and authors, like Lerone Bennett JR, Ivan Van Sertima, Ceclia Klein, and David Hurst Thomas, write about the African skeletal bones that were dug up in Oklahoma, and the African artifacts that were found throughout Central and South America. If white folks knew the truth about this part of Oklahoma's lost history, I wonder, in an African language, what would be the term for "*black person*?"

Only ten years after the 13th Amendment would officially abolished slavery, in 1875 when Oklahoma was still Indian Territory and when ex-slaves and freedmen had become Buffalo Soldiers, the brave militiamen were riding sweaty old horses over the crimson soil. Back then tumbleweeds drifted, buffalos roamed, coyotes howled, bears growled, rattlesnakes crept, and all were king of the wilderness. The black warriors protected the Natives' land, keeping white homesteaders, the boomers, from invading and steeling what was left of Native terrain in America.

First, they took half of the territory. Then they took it all. Six, God-grab-it-while-you-can land runs occurred from 1889 through 1892. And then, beneath the hot sun and under grueling conditions, in saddlebags the wooly haired warriors hauled the *"Industrial Revolution"* into the newly formed townships. The Buffalo Soldiers would assist in erecting telegraph and telephone lines for the soon to be new state.

Lucky or unlucky, my mother was my personal historian. At times growing up I disliked and discounted her unpleasant and cruel observations about the history of white people. But according to her "When 200 black folk arrived in Oklahoma City, part of the first 1889 land run; they were forced to settle in a small section of the city called Sandtown. Later when Oklahoma became a state in 1907, that's when they made illegal alienation and unconstitutional segregation from African Americans legal. Black people were legitimately set apart from the rest of the world.

"These good old boys of the city's first counsel set out to destroy the freedoms, aspirations, hopes, and dreams of the ex-slaves and their descendants. The laws gave them legal permission to treat African Americans different and less than other humans. The legal authorities dealt with them harshly and black people could only work in low paying service jobs and were cajoled and threatened and not allowed to integrate with decent white people."

Under the cherry flashing light I began to hear Mamma go on to say, "We'd been working for free; building this country for almost 300 years and instead of rewarding us they banished us from their sight."

I was only four when I first recall hearing the first version of her proclamations. I didn't know if Mamma was teaching me the ways of white folks or teasing me by telling evil horror stories.

"You don't even treat a mule like that." Sometimes her opinions and words were different but I could always feel the pain and anger in them. Mamma could be giving me a bath, cooking dinner, or she could be outside with her friends, I'd be playing with mine. I'd hear sadness and see her hurt eyes and she'd be testifying again. And as I caught a ball, learned a new video game and came of age I'd wrestle with accepting her historical narratives. I didn't and still can't understand how other humans could be so cruel to people because of the color or their skin?

"During and after all those land runs, whites even embraced po' ass immigrants that was fresh off the boat. Germans, Italians, Czech, Jews, Polish, of course the English and Irish, their own precious bloodlines, all were brought into the fold of '*whiteness*.' They welcomed them into their neighborhoods. Although there were resistances—adjusting to each other's customs and traditions—soon the white society flourished like one big happy family. They all attended the same schools, given the privileges to vote and run for public office and pursue the American dream. These shared commonalties and vegetated intimacies and understandings, caused them to see everything white as human so having sex among the different groups became accepted..." And Mamma's sermons on white folks would go on and on.

I was also four years old when Urban Renewal came a-knocking at our door. Mamma said our family was among the last few survivors of what use to be a vibrant black neighborhood. "African American teachers lived their whole lives to educate. Your children were their children and the whole community was one big family." She would say.

Vibrant! Huh. Wood rats as big as possums crawled in the ceilings in the day and the critters crunched on the walls for snacks at night. Scared of a flood of them gnawing through the foundations and munching on me I would usually fall asleep with my eyes wide open. I could hardly believe there was ever anything dynamic about our little shabby framed house. Chips of white paint were all the cover that was left on our weather beaten decaying home.

The neighborhood had been half-torn down, and abandoned houses and businesses were everywhere. Some buildings and homes had been removed but their concrete foundations were left still intact. And there were samples of use-to-be dwelling's wreckage; bulldozed piles of rubble were right beside homes where black families still lived. Weeds and trees and uncut grass grew sparsely over blocks on deserted lots. There were streets with potholes big enough for a child to hide and never be found.

Inside our shotgun built home, on her hands and knees, Mamma was unable to scrub the huge black corrosion off the old linoleum floors. My bedroom was in the living room on the couch and on the opposite side we had a gas stove that heated the whole house. For privacy Mamma would use a bedspread or a sheet as a door to enclose the next room for her bedroom.

Blocks up the street in every direction white families were buying up land. They were building the kind of brick houses that you see on TV. And new constructions for businesses were springing up daily. *Gentrification* is what Mamma called it. "Across the tracks," that's what white folks called where we colored folks had lived; this was the property most blacks had once owned or rented. It was near downtown Oklahoma City. The area was once the cheapest real estate in the city, and now with the new construction, and since most blacks had been relocated, the price of this land was off the charts." The sage that rested in Mamma's grit persona validated her sentiments as if African gods were guiding her gradual head nod.

"Back in the day most black folks never could get private or government home loans. If you were white you officially qualified for a mortgage." Gnashing her teeth and rolling her tanned eyes Mamma would express her frustrations.

Watching white folks with families or any families while I was growing up often disturbed me. I often daydreamed what it would've been like if my Dad had lived, if I had been afforded the opportunity to have a real family. My dad was killed in a car crash when I was two years old. I keep an old photograph of him in my wallet. Like me, he was tall but he had golden brown features. Mamma and I have more of a reddish tan.

The owner of our home sold the shabby shed to the city. It was our good fortune that Mamma had recently graduated from Oklahoma University's Nursing School. Because she had to take care of me, it had taken her eight long agonizing years to get her degree.

During that time I only remember Mamma busy working, studying, and being a nurturing and sometimes neurotic mother. The only time I saw her calm and excited about her life was on Sunday's in church.

When she received her baccalaureate, Reverend Melvin Stokes had Mamma stand before the whole congregation and share her blessing. I'd never seen her smile so big.

That day in May the sun appeared to shine brighter. Mamma wore a satin Easter canary yellow dress and her glad-to-be alive beaming grin illuminated the whole chapel. Tears flooded her eyes when she stood at the podium and gave homage to Mrs. Ada Lois Sipuel-Fisher.

"God thank you for giving Ms. Ada the courage to stand up against the racist Jim Crow Laws. Ms. Ada broke down the color line. Under malicious conditions, in 1949 she was the first African American in the south to ever enter a white University." Mamma paused and sluggish raindrop tears ooze down her cheeks. Mrs. Ada's spirit appeared to be weeping underneath Mamma's skin causing an emotional tremble.

After a round of amen's from the flock, Mamma acknowledged Mrs. Nunley. She was the first black woman to enter Oklahoma University's nursing school.

I was only four and I didn't understand the significance of Mamma's joy of graduating from a predominately white school or the awe that the parishioners bestowed upon her for achieving the task. Starry eyed, they gawked as if she was Jesus, as if she'd performed a miracle, like graduating from a white college was the same as walking on water.

As a child I didn't know that the adorable Ada, whose gentle face and perfectly trimmed body, fit more in a man's sexual fantasy, or as a pin-up in *JET*'s beauty of the week, or that this pint sized woman was a pound of dynamite! The delicate little lady didn't look like your typical revolutionist. But Ms. Ada was more than a black man's vision of a beauty queen. I found out she was a woman of steel, a black superwoman. And her mission was to rescue every black child's dream out of the torturous hands of Jim Crow. The mild mannered sweet young woman was part of the strategy the NAACP used to set up a showdown for the history making 1954 Brown vs. Board of Education decision.

All summer long Mamma was decked fashionably in linen whites. Faded bloodstains were on her uniform as she played Florence Nightingale in St. Anthony's emergency room. The eviction deadline drew near and Mamma worked double shifts, she was busy saving lives and money to pay down on our first home.

On a windy autumn day in Oklahoma City, our family finally began living the American dream. At four years of age I remember being strapped in the front seat of our Chevy as we escaped the old tarred bumpy potholed streets in our neighborhood. I knew we were close to our new home when the riding became soft and easy.

As I strained my neck and peeped through the window, I began seeing houses similar to the ones I'd seen on TV. But I didn't see any white people like I'd seen on TV. Most of the homes were brick. They were different sizes and all of the homes had garages. On a smaller scale, we were moving into an African American version of my TV America.

It was like we were driving right into a scene right, into one of my favorite movies, *The Wizard of Oz*. The street we drove on was Springlake Drive, this was our Yellow Brick Road, and the neighborhood, Park Estates, our Land of Oz.

We passed a manicured park where children were swinging, climbing up and down a slide, and running around making wild faces. Kids hopped out of sandboxes and chased one another. There was exhilaration and joy in the Land of Oz. From living life in the dingy black and white photographs of the ghetto I was now observing clear color even in the form of grimy knees.

The bricks to our new home were like fudge ice cream that had melted into a rich vanilla. Two chocolate posts held up the extended roof and as the top sloped over to the ground level cement porch, it also gave shade to a three foot raised stone flower garden.

Mamma pulled the car up to the dark auburn one car garage door. I hopped out on the driveway and trotted a trail that fitted into our first walkway and the concrete magically transformed into a porch. The front door and the windows were all trimmed with the same delicious dark chocolate as the posts. Mamma unlocked the door and barefooted I darted across an orange rug that tickled my toes and made my feet bounce. Our home had handles that rolled the windows out instead of us using our hands to raise them. And God blessed us with central heat and air. All I had to do was turn a knob to warm or cool myself. Even though Mamma and I never used the dishwasher we had one. Mamma said it was too slow and we would end up cleaning everything twice but when Mamma wasn't at home I use to sneak and turn the electronic washer on and listen to the engine run.

One bedroom for Mamma and one for me and our car lived in the garage with our new washer and dryer. Yip-pee! No more trips to the Laundromat.

Our backyard had two tall oaks and one pecan tree. It was tiny but we had our first patio and the Bermuda grass on the plot of land was a rich dark green. A nightlight hovered above the patio and our storybook home had a six-foot tall picket fence. I would later install a basketball goal.

I had my own bedroom and I was euphoric that first night. I believe this was the first hours of darkness in my four years of living that I was able to close my eyes and coast into a deep sleep. I didn't worry if wood rats would eat me alive. A gentle peace guided me to sleep and slept beside me all night.

Mr. James Green had a friendly smile and perfect teeth. His pearly whites were almost hidden underneath his un-even salt 'n pepper mustache. He was our short dark pot bellied next-door neighbor. His wife Essie was also chubby and also had a smoky glaze and her wide nose articulated her African features. The Green's didn't have any children. He had been an airplane mechanic and after twenty years of service to his country he'd retired from the Air Force. Mamma said he was lucky 'because back then they didn't let many black men in that branch of the service and that was during the Viet Nam War'.

The Greens had lived in the neighborhood for years. Mr. Green always wore a clean but oil stained auto-mechanic uniform, I presumed he dressed this way because he used his driveway to repair all the neighbors' cars. Frequently well into the night, shadows from a droplight would appear through my back bedroom window, it was Mr. Green working. Later when I became a teen-ager the droplight from the mechanic's driveway would shine on his protégé's face, me.

Lavender was the color of her family's two-car garage and a golden trim traced the top of their fiery red brick home. Five years of age, Trisha lived in the house across the street and her home was twice the size as ours. She had two long jet-black wavy Native American ponytail braids. As she trotted up and down the street, waggling down her backside, the threads would do an exotic dance. Her eyes were big and spry. She had cute pink kissable baby-doll lips and when I first laid eyes on her my four-year-old body had its first instinctual sensations. Trisha had a peach complexion and I was in awe of this older thin girl's physique and her polite impish accent.

Her father was a tall man roughly built and lived in brown skin. His head was completely gray. He drove tractor-trailers across country to support his family and I believe he was years older than his yellow-layered wife.

One year older, Trisha was two inches taller and her long legged strides carried her quicker around the neighborhood than mine. She introduced me to all the children near our ages in the area. In the summertime we swam and played baseball at the park, rode bicycles, and explored the creek in the woods right outside the neighborhood. Our pick-up unsupervised basketball games lasted well after sundown, and Oklahoma City's best basketball players were created in those backyards. On rainy or snowy days Trisha and I watched TV together, played board games, and sometimes I would introduce her to my wonderful world of video games.

On a warm summer night when I was eight and my Cutie Pie was nine, Trish seduced me. It was a Friday night and Trisha's parents had dinner plans and Mamma was working a double shift. We were left alone to take care of each other. After watching some TV and playing video games, the little Cinderella face girl said, "Do you want to f...?"

Her language didn't shock me; Trisha had always had a bad mouth. The invitation made me nervous. How was I going to handle her tender body parts in a gentle way? I had had a crush on her from the moment I'd laid eyes on the fairy-tale angel. And I was astonished that the princess of my heart was asking a mere peasant like me to do the nasty!

But she was the leader so I followed her precious polka dot panties into my bedroom. She pulled back the bedspread and fluffed the pillows with some quick hard pats and mashes. Then she slipped out of her brown skirt, yellow blouse, and her chocolate spotted panties. She leaped on the bed backwards, removed her training bra and ordered me to come on. Two bumps the sizes of large grapes were on her chest. A line of tiny hairs prickled down from her naval to the top edge of her pooh-nanny. As she lay on her back with her legs spread, gazing at her pooh-nanny she let out a ticklish giggled and then glared at me.

"Come on get on top of me!" with a devil-may-care smile, impatiently she ordered.

The olive veins on her wrist showed up in the inner sides of her elbows and were engraved in her neck. The streaks I'd seen with Trisha completely dressed were under her armpits and now I saw the jaded stripes on top of Trisha's private parts. Fascinated by her nakedness I carefully crawled on her. I didn't want too hurt her.

"Stick it in—stick it in!" She begged.

I can always remember being fascinated with my genitalia. Even at three years of age I was amazed how my secret dong-dong would become hard as steel without me even playing with it.

I raised my bootie and guided my pre-puberty limp penis down on top of her. Trisha used two fingers to spread her sacred spot open. When we came together, gradually we both began gyrating, imitating what we thought were sexual motions. At this critical time when I needed penetration my penis demonstrated to me again it had a mind of its own. It wouldn't get hard. I was unable to pierce between Trisha's lips. Flimsy, it constantly slid against Trish's gap.

"Whoa! That feels good." Trisha said, beaming up at me.

I humped and rubbed up against the cherry brown outsides of her cavity for five minutes. Then—

"—Ok that's good. Now get up!" Trisha was done feeling good so she ordered me to remove my naked body off her sleek little frame.

We were done with this activity of play. We didn't speak of our night of curious sexual exploration, that night of naked naughtiness, for years.

Girls mature sooner than boys do and I was a year younger than Trisha. When you're a teen-ager, a year younger than a female is akin to living time the way a dog experiences living life; girls are aging like dogs.

For a while she was faster afoot until her grapes grew into round juicy melons and her butt puffed shapely into pre-womanhood. I was busy swelling into premature manhood. In fact when I was thirteen I shot up to six feet. And that's when I discovered I could fantasize and visualize Trisha naked. Upon seeing her womanly butt and huge juicy breast, my penis would turn into steel. And as I played with it, this amusing experience took me on a fantasy trip that produced unbelievable pleasurable orgasmic seizures. The first journey would leave my whole body jerking in happy-land, un-controllable spasms for more than a minute.

I was still playing with my penis and video games when Trisha began riding off into sunsets with older guys that drove sports cars. My heart would weep when I'd see her arriving home in a brother's car at 3 in the morning. The motor would be running, cold smoke piping out of the exhaust—she would hop out and flee to her front door and each time I would think, had she asked him to f...her?

***

Over the years I've had hours upon hours of moral lectures on life delivered by Mamma. She cooked, I sat at the breakfast table; she barbecued while I shot hoops; during any and all activities she constantly preach her ethics on sex, respect for your elders, and of course her favorite was educating me on the immoral behavior of white folks.

She told me our brand new nice home and this neighborhood was part of society's hand-me-downs. It was built in the 1940's for white folks. "That's when a black person couldn't buy a home in this area." She would say.

"Even though the Supreme Court had said that the Oklaho-ma neighborhood segregated law was unconstitutional there was and are sections of this city just for blacks and then places for the rest of the folks in the city. The NAACP led the fight against the rac-ist law. And in 1917 the Supreme Court declared the segregated law illegal but for years and still today neighborhood associations are using restrictive covenants to get around the segregated hous-ing laws. In 1948 the Supreme Court declared integrated neighborhoods unenforceable. Damn stupid Supreme Court! They can send men to the moon but let us want something and they can't piss straight." Mamma would shake her head and raise her eyebrows in disgust.

"Unenforceable?" Snarling, and justifying her scowl she would add, "Congress didn't put any money into an agency that would allow an organization to investigate and prosecute the violators. The government didn't create an atmosphere that would allow an intimate relationship for blacks and whites to flourish. Instead the Veterans Administration, Federal Housing Administration, and all the banks participated in redlining. In the late 1940's while white GI's were receiving home loans the government began building the projects in the black community." The older I got more details were added to some of the same stories.

When I was younger hardly any of Mamma's reasoning made sense. Even though in our neighborhood all I saw were black people. It scared me to believe that so many people were against children of my color. Anyway, all I saw on TV were good white people. They made me laugh and appeared friendly.

Chapter Three

Months before our move to Oz, the city had hired a demolition company to tear down the boarded up half-abandoned apartments over on N. E. 30th and Prospect. Police dogs had been frequently used to bust drug dealers, and it seemed like every Saturday night there was a murder, or a shooting on the apartment's premises. This was why, Mamma said, they finally destroyed the apartments and replaced it with a school.

"Thelma Parks Academy…it's about time they named a school after a black woman!" Mamma exhaled and the words rolled out as a relief. This was her answer to a long vigilant prayer. After she read the newspaper, she strutted over and opened the refrigerator door, grabbed the pitcher of cold water, poured a glass full and guzzled.

"We've had to fight to have schools that we attend named after us. Woodson, Dunbar, Edwards, Page, Douglas and F.D. Moon, they are all names for black men. It's about time an African American woman was given her due! " She placed the pitcher back inside the refrigerator and a grave worried pause took over her face. "It should've been called Clara Luper. She performed most of the heavy lifting during the Civil Rights era." The bothered gaze quickly vanished. "Don't let me catch you drinking out of this water jug and spreading germs young man." With a stern face she winked.

There was a list, another list, and another list; black parents had registered their children and wanted to get them into the brand new school. Finally, only days before school started, "You made it son!" Mamma read the letter from the school board with a prize-winning smile that lit up her face. We had won the lottery.

On a stormy September morning Mamma had us up early and we were waiting on the steps for the first day that Thelma Parks Academy opened its doors.

Fast forward, I skipped right through Kindergarten and first grade! Since Mamma had already taught me the ABC's and how to spell one-syllable words and she'd read me most of Dr. Seuss's books, I was far ahead of the other students. Naturally I became the teacher's little helper.

By the third grade a lot of the other students had caught up with me, and we were equal in our educational abilities. During the first nine weeks, half of the grades I received were 3's, the other half were 4's, equivalent to B's and A's in grown up language.

My disappointed and intolerant Mamma glared at the report on me and said, "I'm not raising a lazy good for nothing dummy in my house. You'd better do better! No...No. You're going to do better! Go and get me every assignment you've had this year." Mamma slowly meticulously started hovering over me like a mother hen, teaching me discipline and how to study.

Through other boys I was introduced to the art of peeping under little black girl's skirts. As they sat at their desk we'd sneak and take a peep at their panties. In the mornings it became a game for us. Who could find the best views and try and find the girl that was wearing the prettiest colors. And of course whoever found the view of the prettiest girl's underwear was the winner hands down. This devious activity became a bonding experience for us, part of playtime, a recess in the classroom for the guys.

In the fifth grade I had my first white teacher, Mrs. Byrd. She had reddish-brown hair, was young, thin, and for some reason I thought she looked good, especially in pants.

"Hmm. Used to be against Oklahoma law for any of us to be taught by a white person." Mamma said, as she shook Mrs. Byrd's hand and gazed on the young pretty teacher with suspicion.

After Mamma had embarrassed me on the first day of school, I decided to confront her.

"That was a long time ago Mamma. I know you've had white teachers."

"Yes son I have, and none of them in this city understood black culture." She frowned. "Most of them were afraid or condescending. It's hard to communicate with or have respect for folk that think their ways are always better than yours. Plus they don't have a clue and most of them don't know or care about how their laws and ways have hurt black folk. Therefore I've never met a white person in this city that believes they need to offer us an apology and that means I don't believe we can have an honest relation-ship."

Mamma was making me paranoid of the white race so I didn't trust her at least where Mrs. Byrd was concerned. My physical instincts were developing and I began to experience secret desires to see my teacher naked.

Often in class I found myself staring at the educator. I studied her pointed nose; it was sharp and narrow, it was different from most people of my color. I noticed whenever she became frustrated she'd bat her blue eyes and the nerves in her jaw would quiver. I watched her tiny lips articulate perfect white southern Okie accented sounds. Little white hairs grew under her nose and over her make-up. Embarrassingly, I secretly watched Mrs. Byrd's tits wiggle around in the flimsy bras that she wore. Shamefully, when she wore pants, I found myself gazing for the split in her hips and on the sly I'd glance for crinkled panty seams. Automatically I would avert my eyes down on the upside triangle imprint made in the front of her slacks. My cousin Danny had exposed me to naked female photographs from magazines. As I ogled those obscene pictures I would ponder this question: When a woman wears pants, the outer imprint creases in the material that formed an upside down triangle around the pubic area, was this image a sampling of the shape and mass of her pubic hair? Was this inflection directly proportional to what was hiding behind the material? That's when I began to imagine my teacher naked. Were the hairs over her vagina long or short, straight or curly, cherry or black or brown?

Whatever lay on the other side of her cotton or nylon panties I was beginning to sense it had to be a bag of goodies!

***

My cousin Danny was husky, dark red, a shade darker, and two inches shorter than I was. He was Mamma's only and younger sister, Aunt Betty's son. He was born a month before I was. And for the first twelve years of his life he lived in horror hell with a crack head prostitute alcoholic Mamma.

Mamma would get calls at 2 AM from the police station; I was beginning to believe that the cops had our number on speed dial. Under many dark skies we had to ride downtown and get Danny at the station before he was turned over to child services. Usually there'd been a raid at a crack house or his mother was out on the streets selling her body, she'd have him with her and an undercover officer would bust my aunt.

"You need to stop taking or leaving this boy with those street punks when you go out whoring. Bring him over to my house." Mamma would condemn the actions of her addict alcoholic sister. Sometimes before Aunt Betty went out whoring she'd call or bring Danny over to our house and then other times she'd forget. But I guess when you're talking to an addict you can't expect consistency.

"What is fellatio?" Out of seven-year-old Danny's mouth he would ask Trisha and I these and many other sexual questions? After seeing us baffled Danny would school us and always answer his questions. "It's when a man gets his thang sucked." Trisha would frown and call him nasty but I knew she was secretly fascinated by his advanced sexual knowledge. She was always asking me where he was when he wasn't at my house.

As we grew older a lot of girls seemed to like the bad-stepping-explicit-carnal-conversations Danny's persona offered. With his hip-hop swagger Danny perfected his nasty talk to girls and ended up doing the nasty with a lot of them.

One wintry freezing day, when Danny and I were nine and Trisha was 10 years old, we all stood in my backyard puffing on a cigarette. Breathing in cloudy cold air and exhaling out smoke, we wheezed. We choked. I got ill. Danny got addicted…and so did Trisha.

***

Women's underwear, bras and slips use to be a female's private affair. I grew up watching girls out in public almost naked. Cotton and silk flimsy colorful Jezebel's bustiers, camisoles, tanks, tees, and use-to-be negligées were transformed into arousing sexy blouses and skirts now openly worn as outer fashions. I had a bird's eye view scrutinizing nipples and booties as girls formed into women.

In Jr. High my tender innocent eyes were wide opened. I witnessed camisoles woven in delicately fine fabrics generously exposing large sections of budding breast. I saw exotically pierced belly buttons and from that point my imagination was lead spiraling downstairs by trails of frizzled pubic hairs. On the sly, and rubbernecking, I gawked at teenage girls wearing pants so tight, so firmly fit, the material would look like it was glued between their hips. And most of their britches hung so low I could see large parts of their panties. G-strings flashed and I saw half-naked hips. That was the style.

This was also my first experience of being in classes with white girls. Soft red heads, chilled plums, electric blacks, funky cherries, iced coffees, copper blasts, red pulses, red copper spritzs, lively auburns, and they had a rainbow of other stylish hairdos. Tender pink tits began sprinkling pixy dust in the air and magically enlarging my penis. I had unbelievable urges to touch, fondle, and squeeze the pale skin. It was an exciting titillating time for me to be changing into a man. I experienced a ton of unrestrained indiscriminate urges and extraordinarily involuntary hard-ons.

Back in grade school, black girls had flirted with me, girls such as Shanika, Chandra, Teressa, Jopaz, Belinda, and Robin. On separate occasions these fine little dark skin goggled-eyed girls had merrily swayed my hand, batting dreamy eyes at me, and bashfully requesting, "Would you be my boyfriend?" I was becoming aware of how I appeared to females. As I gazed in the mirror I considered myself to be an attractive guy. Since these girls also thought that I was I began to believe I really did have *it going-on*! I began to walk around Thelma Parks Academy with my head up and full of confidence.

In Jr. High my penis was on a nonstop hard-on. Obviously living with this condition, I was more than motivated and was driven to fulfill my instinctual desires. I appreciated the X rated magazines my cousin had previously offered but I wanted to know and experience more. On the Discovery Channel there was a documentary on the mating habits of peacocks. The female peacock would spread her colorful feathers to show her sexual affection to the male that she'd selected to mate with. In Jr. High I observed some of those fine colors light up as shy affectionate smiles appeared on some of the black girls. But none of the little southern belle Oklahoma City white ladies shined a single tinted feather on me. Their constant rejection began to make me feel hideous. I'm sure un-appealing people must feel this hideous sensation from the world all the time. At least I had the approval of the people that looked like me. But still hideous is a weird feeling to absorb into your skin.

From the time I boarded the school bus in the morning until the time I stepped off the bus, waving good-bye to my friends and returning home, I had to frequently hide unsolicited indescribable embarrassing hard-ons. A glimpse at a white girl dressed in some-thing slinky exposing her breast and the thought of sliding in be-hind a black girl's shapely booty, at puberty my penis didn't judge what color the female was.

I'd lie in bed with grease, lotion, and occasionally if neither were available I would use only my bare hands. I'd fantasized my penis penetrating luscious precious nookie. Black, White, Asian, Latino, Native American, we'd do it doggie-style, missionary, and sideways. Acrobatically I would flip flop them on top and we'd have sex until I saw the veins in their neck stretch. I heard their pleasure moans grow into orgasmic screeches as I gazed into the gawk of their hysterical eyes. My ecstasy juice would explode over the sheets and drip down the chokehold of my hand.

But I was one of the few miserable guys that suffered all the way through high school without ever getting any. I'd like to say remaining a virgin was my choice or blame it on my obedience to Mamma's strict Christian teachings and the tons of medical infor-mation she'd freely passed on. I was a virgin venereal disease free and baby less. This was not because my penis picked this lifestyle.

The young ladies I dated always made the choice. On every occasion I tried hard as hell to get them naked in order to get some real satisfaction. Desperately I wanted to release the rage stored inside my penis deep into a coochie. I served them dinner and fine wines, underneath full blue moons I tussled with sisters in cars and we wrestled on top of covered beds in secluded motel rooms. We shared sensuous kisses and I had a few bumps and grinds and as the evenings would come to an end often I was left with puked sperm stuck in my boxers, gluing them to my pants. Frequently as I touched and stroked my rhythms into and against a woman's body and as I felt and sensed her passions rise, every time when I believed I was on the verge of getting some I'd always hear, "Stop!

Stop!" The gentleman that I was trying to become would reel in the fierce desires inside my penis. And to my penis' heartbreaking dissatisfaction I'd take the young lady home. My ding-dong wouldn't get wet inside of a woman until my second year in college.

With nothing better to do I hit the books hard. And I ended up receiving scholarship offers from colleges all over the country. Mamma believed my best bet as a black man for success and actually graduating was staying close to home. Central State University was a twenty-mile drive and the school had the largest assembly of black undergraduates in the state. "You'll have a support system there." Sincerity mired with worry Mamma would tell her son.

I had known Loretta Graham since seventh grade. Back then I had an eagle's eye gaze that meticulously observed inches of baby-fat falling off by the pound on some of the chubby girls. I vigilantly gawked at even the thin girl's bodies as their booties puffed and their tits protruded. I saw their physique's budding into curvaceous ripe women. I ogled breast and juicy compressible hips and the combinations together easily energized and super-sized my genitals. Loretta never wore two and three inch pumps. She always dressed down in clothes that were unassuming, like flat Oxfords, Mary Jane's, and charming Hush Puppies. Colorful turtlenecks discretely hid sneak peek previews of her tits. Silk embroidery blouses were bashfully buttoned to the top emphasizing her character's essence. Clever and classy she hid behind outfits offering silhouette images to the horny guy's imagination. Behind the sheltered garments I assumed her mid-size perky breasts were splendidly plumped at about 32 inches. I had never heard her swear or impolitely yell at another person. She was always gracious. We'd never had a real in depth conversation, only civil chitchats, at school, football games, parties, and whenever we ran into one another at the local markets.

Loretta Graham was a deep dark creamy chocolate sister and she lived only eight blocks away from the lonely bed I'd spent puberty choking sex's ache out of my penis and splattering excessive sperm all over my bedding.

Still a virgin my sensitive sexual desires were similar to a bloodhound's instincts, I was always on the hunt. I began to sniff at Loretta our freshman year at CSU. I believe that's when we both spotted and saw the lover in the other for the very first time. Weeded out of our social sights was the clutter of folks we'd hung with separately since Jr. High.

In a *College Algebra* class that was the original time my penis' passions began to desire Loretta's petite package as a splendor for pure sophisticated pleasure. There were only four blacks out of forty-four students in that group. Out of that four I was the only Electronic Engineer major and she was the only one preparing for a degree in Computer Science.

We began studying together, and discussed programming, the Internet, and how we were going to make money in the new age of the computer world. African culture and African American history were branded on Loretta's heart. Video games, basketball and football were still my fixations. Art exhibitions and dramatic plays we appreciated together and we agreed and argued on their themes. With my superficial senses and her rich sensibilities our beloved journey had begun.

We spent over a year of exhilarating explorations in tongue dueling. Always completely dressed, the body heat from those explicit inquisitions would always lead us to humping in many forms of sexual impressions. But these erotic actions were still leaving me lingering as a tortured soul. If I got lucky with Loretta, able to walk away with samples of sticky semen in my underwear, I considered the quest for sex a success.

We watched the others intellect digests several textbooks, regurgitate the fine print and score high on tests. I rubbed against her tits for support. And sometimes when she was exhausted she'd fall asleep in my lap for comfort. For over four semesters, nineteen months, we'd finally bonded as one. I could feel her exhaling the air that I breathe. When we were drained form studying and when I begged for sex making her weary, she'd satisfy me with passionate kisses and cuddles and often we'd fall asleep in each other's arms.

Maybe it was my aggressiveness for sex; did my countless solicitations finally ware Loretta down? Did she decide she should just give in to get me off her back? I didn't know and at the time my carnal appetites didn't care.

It happened in the springtime, Spring break. It was the early days of April and a week earlier Loretta had taken me out to dinner to celebrate my 20th birthday. That day as Loretta sucked on a hot saucy Texas barbeque short rib, she licked her lips; surprisingly she offered her body up to me as a birthday gift.

"You're twenty and a man Kayin...my man!" Staring dead at me she batted her eyes with the naïve purity of an angel. But Loretta's tone was strong and I could feel the presence of a woman's promise coming at me.

"I want to give you the gift a woman gives her man. I want to make love to you." Her words seemed to soar from heaven—from God almighty. It was an overdue answer to a long vigilant pleading prayer. Finally I'd gotten a response! And I could see and feel it! She and it was sitting right in front of me.

I gobbled down dessert, homemade apple pie. I don't recall if the pastry had a sweet taste or even if it had a delicious flavor. I was stuck with a mouth-watering appetite for the menu that sat across from me. Hot barbeque sauce was smudged on the edges of her mouth and suddenly I had a fetish, a craving to lick Loretta's mouth inside and out.

Chapter Four

Loretta was like a lot of young people I had grown up with; she was being raised under the old school morals of her grandmother. Only thirty years old, Loretta's mother had died of sickle cell when Loretta was at the untainted age of five. Since her grandmother grew up in the pre-Civil Rights era and before all the revolutions of the sixties her sensibilities on raising children were steeped in stringent old school philosophies.

Loretta worked part-time for the post office and I was a thirty-eight hour almost full-time slave for Wal-Mart. School and work ate up most of our lives. We needed quality and personal time to christen our new adventure. We wanted this treasured experience to be special. We made up our minds to escape and put some distance between the ethics of our childhood, get away from the two iron-fisted matriarchs that had raised and ruled us. And it had to be a get-away place far from the grinding pressures of school and work. Our natural maturational instincts as mammals were desperate to express lust anywhere—at least mine were. But as compassionate sophisticated humans we needed a secret private place to do our business. And although Loretta had placed the sex proposal on the table I agreed our first time should and would be treated tenderly with much love. I needed her to feel safe and at ease.

The foothill of a mountain is where I was to become a man. The wooded area that rented cabins was located eighty miles southeast of the city.

Loretta had begun taking birth control pills months earlier and even though we both knew we were virgins we had long ago supplied each other with the results of the HIV/AID's test.

"Don't forget the prophylactics?" When we spoke on the phone that morning and as I listened to her last minute precautions I imagined seeing distress on Loretta's face. Afraid, maybe she was, but I knew beneath her concerns that there was a composed woman that didn't forget how to pronounce the medical term for a rubber. Birth control pills plus a condom—Loretta didn't want to have an accidental pregnancy and neither did I.

Old Chi-Lites and Stylistics CD's romanced us during the quiet hour and half drive. Loretta was frigidity. Frequently and briefly her stares upon me were serious. Occasionally her vacant daydream gazes carried her eyes out the window over the countryside. We avoided discussing our mission.

Hilltops jam-packed with mountain rocks hid our hide-away cabin site from the main highway. The valley was populated by newly, ripened green trees and spring's bounty blossomed in colorful wild flowers, and fresh country air sung a happy song to our lungs.

We'd arrived early on a clear sunlit morning. We unpacked and inspected the accommodations. The usually meek Loretta boldly swept and brushed the winter's nest of spider webs off the ceilings, in shadowy corners, and behind the cabin's doors.

I caught Loretta nonchalantly peeping at the shine on the fine chocolate that glazed over the grandfather headboard, the place where we were going to do the nasty. I studied the old style frame and wondered if the headboard, mattress, and springs were sturdy to suit our purpose. Playfully—I shoved Loretta down towards the mattress and to brake her fall instinctively she snatched my arm pulling me on top of her.

Nose to nose gazing into each other's eyes Loretta broke our tense silent conversation. "We have clean linen and plenty of fluffy pillows." She said. And like a prude she began sniffing the sheets and politely lifted my hands from her waist, hinting for me to get up and off her.

Young dandelions and wild flowers sprouted, butterflies danced and baby honeybees buzzed on the side of us as we strolled side by side over the dirt trail around the lake. We veered off the path and laid a pallet under a huge cedar tree. The spanking new leaves flourished us with shade while we relaxed and lazed and picnicked and as we gathered in the seasonal fragrances.

Dusk brought with it gust of left over winter winds. With wood orderly stacked by the old fashioned fireplace I started a fire. I was bending down, kneeling in front of the fire and was almost hypnotized by the wavering sapphires as they blended into the golden blazes, when suddenly Loretta primped out of the bathroom wrapped in a towel, and it covered only her precious private parts. Enthralled by her ready-to-do business forwardness I dropped the logs and met her endearing gaze. In a trance our bodies became like magnets. We began to move in slow motion—and without breaking the spell Loretta without hesitation unleashed the towel. And the unveiling of her body, it was aesthetically engaging and gratifying and the most incredibly delicious painting I'd ever laid eyes on.

Water beads dripped between her wet chocolate breasts and as our bodies got closer, the dribbles were also moving in slow motion. The stream trickled down and circled her navel. In my mind I drew a square that was fixated on how precisely and compactly plumped her 32" tits were and how well they fit on top of her dark slim waistline. My appetites raged. At the bottom of her figure a massive gleaming patch of moist curly jet-black vaginal hair dissolved the drips. The upside down triangularly shaped bush took my gawk along and I spotted a smidgen of her vaginal opening. Whoa! I could feel my entire body emerging into an erection.

Loretta's nakedness was pleasurable to my eyes but my gawk made the bashful dark brown beauty droop her head.

In one move I was standing close to Loretta and with my middle finger I guided her chin up until our eyes reunited. We embraced and our skins sunk into one person. The friction of my stiff penis against her vaginal hairs sent tiny muscular shrills into my nerves and sent my protruding organ into an uncontrollably vigorous frenzy.

Swooping all 110 pounds of Loretta's bare flesh into my arms I carried this bundle of sex and laid her self-disciplined assets across an old secure mattress.

Outside the bedroom window of the house made of logs I was startled by a night owl's hoot. I became awestruck by the streams of the moon's blue light that poured through the open curtains. The beams covered Loretta like a transparent blanket and gave the impression of her innocence in a radiant angelic glow.

I joined the suspense of my fascination. Suspended over her bare flesh I relaxed my chest muscles into the squishiness of her breast. Our private manes became entangled. My penis brushed against her vagina and rested between her inner thighs. This snuggly position my penis found itself in seemed to have automatically produced an action that made her hips flex and her legs to spread wide.

Faint whispers of deep breaths were breathed into my ears when my penis began tugging into the tightness of her hole. Although my penis was covered with plastic I was invigorated by the trickle of her vaginal cream. The tip of my penis' head jerked impulsively and plunged into her affectionate heated waters. The thrilling glide was full of enchantment and it was a joy ride into what appeared to be a bottomless pool.

This was heaven—the dream meeting the reality of every inspirational fantasy I'd jerked-off to. But those visional baptisms didn't prepare my solid rock organ for this joyous New World it had entered. If my life never ever got any better and if I had to die that moment it would be okay. I had felt, seen, and entered the Promised Land.

The deeper I penetrated her, the volume and the intensity of her ekes and ahs shifted and became dramatically brazen. She grabbed a tight hold on my back, bent her knees and swung them up even with her head. The acrobatic curl of her body into a round ball appeared to widen her vaginal walls. I snatched up her hips with both hands and drove in deeper.

A slight rhythmic wiggle of her hips and I lost the reins of my penis. Spastic spurts of ecstasy seized power. Jerking convulsively I began dousing what seemed like an ocean into the pregnancy inhibiting, disease protecting bag. I could feel semen overflowing the edges of the rubber into her sexual pond and dripping against her vaginal walls.

My dwindling manhood was ejaculating when Loretta yelped, "Did you come already?" I flopped alongside her reeking in my first bad after sex funk. My shame slid in as a shield between us.

It was the quietest and longest fifth-teen minutes in my life. Secretly under the sheets I rubbed my penis like it was a magic lamp. I wished for my rod too posses the urgency I felt. I needed a quick redemption of my manhood and that meant an instant hard-on! Laying with my back to Loretta the seconds lingered and the humiliation howled at me like a lone wolf in the woods. Pre-mature ejaculation was destroying the perfect dream I'd envisioned for our first time. Finally the wish came true. I was hard again and ready to redeem the dream.

A second, third, fourth, fifth, again, again, again, again, and again—with every entrance into the Promised-Land semen was squirted before Loretta was given adequate pleasurable satisfaction. During one intermission Loretta dashed into the bathroom and I heard water running. I assumed she was wiping any of my access juices off. As I lay alone, lying in the company of guilt and shame and silence, I began to hear the sound of faint baby cries echoing from the closed door.

We tried several more times that weekend, until Loretta finally complained that she was sore. I had flunked sex education 101.

"It's ok Kayin. I never thought sex would be fun anyway." She lied to make me feel better but I still felt like a deviant wimp.

I counted how many revolutions were made on the Camry's 14-inch tires on Sunday night's lonely eighty-mile drive home. Some of the displeasure of the sexual nightmare that I believed Loretta experienced seemed to have faded underneath the dark shades of her chocolate skin. And other pieces of the horrid experience were expelled out and through the night black car window that her blanked face stared into.

Instead of gawking at the sensuous pictures in the magazines that Danny had given me it was time for me to begin reading the articles and researching and studying all the nasty, educational publications I could find. I needed a cram course in sexual techniques. I ended up downloading multiple sex videos from the Internet. Some were instructive but others were just freaky. As I listened to women squeal and watched the grimaces on their orgasmic faces I began taking photographic memories of the moving physique of the men that brought them to that joyous place. I had to absorb all the sex information I could find and figure out how to simulate them in order for me to stimulate the female anatomy. I was desperate and needed get an "A" on the subject.

Weeks would drift through our lives before I was given another opportunity to see Loretta naked again.

I rented a room at a motel off of Interstate 35. *Liquid Love* was sensuously carved on the bottle and the greasy substance had a doodled drawing of a vagina twinkling; the aphrodisiac had made the sex organ come alive! It tasted like chocolate covered cherries; the potion was a warming massage lotion. I held the plastic bottle up and showed it to Loretta while she rolled out of her bra. She gave me a wry smile.

This time the experience would be different. I would take my time before I came. That's what I hoped for and what I had promised her.

Self-consciously she slipped out of her panties. She lay on her back exposing her jet-black curly vaginal hair and I was gawking again. I tried to slyly disguise the look into a natural glare. She arched and spread her legs. Her luring explicit image added fuel to my already excited appetites. Suppressing my penises' urges, those intense desires that begged to immediately plunge into her, I tried to think about something else. I wanted to approach the situation differently. I decided to examine Loretta's vulva as if I was her private gynecologist.

I dropped samples of the Liquid Love on the edges of two fingers. Loretta's pubis was covered with dark thick curly hairs. With the fingers I grazed a single wave of her hair. I lifted and released the hair and then frisked my fingers through all the fur.

Smut was the color of the outsides of her outer labia. Applying my thumb and middle finger, I held Loretta's outer labia opened. The top of Loretta's hood was charcoal and the insides were dark pink. With my eyes almost touching her vulva I lifted her hood and spotted her clitoral gland. I made a mental note—*her clitoris was there, somewhere in the background*. Her charcoaled inner labia was wrinkled and resembled the noodle on a turkey, the insides of it were pink and moist. The urethra was a tiny hole near the top of the vaginal opening. And there was a slither of skin that stretched to Loretta's anal opening. This must be her perineum I reasoned.

Drenching my fingers with Liquid Love I performed as the videos had instructed. I stuck my index finger inside Loretta and began making small circles around the top of her hood. Loretta's hips immediately flinched and soon her vagina was rolling slight rhythms with my finger. Soon she'd arched her legs in a leaping frog stance and her butt began slightly gyrating, adding a more upbeat tempo. Wow! Gazing at her squirming flesh made my hormones shoot into overdrive.

"Eke-ah!" The sensuous sound eased between Loretta's lips. Casually Loretta reached one hand down and guided my finger to a spot that was higher and closer to the top of her hood and she shoved it deeper inside. She was setting the pace motioning me to touch her with gentle larger circular strokes. Loretta had been a virgin but obviously she'd had experiences with an object or maybe, like me, she'd used her own hands. She knew her body well enough to know what made it feel good.

"Eke-ah! Woo-whoa-woo!" Loretta intensely controllably squealed. I believe what I was doing was new to her body and the good-girl was trying to muzzle what she was feeling. Uncontrollably her knees leaped up to her head and her vaginal rhythms increased. She was making love to my fingers.

"Ah—shit!" After five minutes of my fingers screwing her the Christian girl let loose a slow kinky sinner's screech. Inside the nerve endings of my fingers I began to feel Loretta's clitoris enlarging. Her vaginal walls swelled, her hole shrunk and the heart-beat of her eager organ had a suction choke hold on my fingers. Loretta's eyes tweaked and she propelled my touch even deeper inside. Her hips started thrusting out of rhythm and her legs flung spastically.

"Eke-ah! Woo-whoa-woo! Oh-my-god-she-it!" As my Christian lover's body pulsated with pleasures, she exasperatedly shouted. I watched her breathing gradually dwindle into weaker sighs, her tit trembles ceased, and her pounding heartbeats eased. Her legs slowly drooped into limpness. Finally there it was, the after sex glow was painted on her face. She had that satisfied radiance. Her moans and seizures were sequential flashes of the ecstasy scenes I had seen in the videos. But this was real and I'm sure this was a Divine gift that had been given to both of us.

Since Loretta had gotten off, my confidence as a man was almost restored. I wanted to see if my fingers could escort her to that magical place again. I explored and located more sensuous spots inside her. I made her moan and come again, and again, and again. As I began to beat my chest for being better in bed this time around, the guilt and shame of pre-ejaculation was fading.

Entering me was a newborn courage. It was time for me to release the monster inside my stiff penis. I had to take another chance and place it inside her manhood-eating seductive juices.

I mounted my six four frame over my ladies' five foot four inch body. Whoa! Her virginal walls were already pre-energized, orgasmic and juiced with electricity and I was able to easily slide inside and experience the extreme potency of her vagina's magnetic vigor.

Loretta began to wiggle her hips and the slippery wet sensations fast started my ass into an uncontrollably shudder. And when I felt her black sleek body slithering against mine I became hysterical. It felt like I was rubbing against a serpent's skin. Her moist malleable tissues were launching an array of sensual impulses. All of her simulating highly charged sliding motions instantly filled my whole body with a blissful rage!

But this time I had to manage my penis and prevent premature ejaculation. I pulled up and almost out of her sea of pleasures. Shifting down to a lower controllable gear I changed the direction of the beat. My penis's heartbeat slowed and I began to measure the enjoyment of every intense wave of satisfaction. If the gratification got too intense, once again I modified the rhythm. Often in powerfully passionate moments I had to switch the entire track we were boogying to.

As I navigated inside her my penis slowly started exploring Loretta's vaginal parts. By its sensitivity, I located her clitoris. I flirted with the organ with gentle jabs and sporadically switched my rhythms. Loretta squealed when I moved with her passionate clitoral thrusts. When I felt her vagina tighten and sensed a muscle forming in her clitoris, I knew it was time to plunge into a faster speed. Loretta's legs began wobbling into convulsions. I opened my eyes and saw her eyes tweak and roll. She tossed her head back as if the magnitude of the pleasures were too strong for her tiny body to contain.

"Eke-ah! Woo-whoa-woo! O-o-o-god-damn-K-a-yin!" A spastic Loretta screamed.

Later as we lay side by side I got excited watching large sweat drops glide over her naked body. She gradually eased in one sustained deep breath. Releasing the air brought a big smile that consumed her face. It was the afterglow again.

After we laid motionless in silence, an invigorated Loretta began snaking her body down the side of my torso. She arrived at my genitals and she sat up in the bed with her legs crossed. Switching roles from how this episode of our sexual exploits began that evening, with her thumb and index finger, Loretta began to examine my wilted organ.

"Look! The size of your red and olive veins resemble muscles." I tilted my head and it looked floppy to me.

A new sense of wonder and mystification was what I saw in my lover's eyes, as she glared at it.

"Your penis is twilight black at the shaft then underneath this scraggly black hair next to your testicles your natural caramel color reappears." Now I was beginning to understand some of her awkward gawks. My penis was two-toned.

The soft sensitive way Loretta held my rod between her two fingers was beginning to arouse me. The object she held in her hand was obviously a new discovery to her eyes. As she groped her fingers up and down the length, twirling it in her hand, squashing it, feeling its durability and thickness, unintentionally she was stimulating my pole. I could sense ounces were being added and magically right before her pretty little oval eyes my Jackal and Hyde transformation took place. As she observed my penis' metamorphosis, the characteristic features of her curious exploration changed and she became the face of a happy little camper.

"Everything and everyone needs a name. I like the black part of your penis. It's closer to my color." She shrugged her naked shoulders and sheepishly smiled. "How does **Black Dickey** sound?" Loretta had a neurotic compulsion to classify and organize anything and everything. And I believe she got off on massaging this obsession. I also thought it was her profound appreciation for the object that introduced her to the wonderful world of *intercourse orgasm* that she decided to name her guru.

Loretta and I began to have lusty musty sex just as much as we hit the books and that was whenever we weren't in class, working, or sleeping. We found ourselves craving each other between classes and seeking out nearby vacant halls on campus. I would pin Loretta in a corner and Black Dickey learned how to sniff out Loretta's clit while she was fully clothed. If the gratification became overwhelming for me while we were dry humping I could always switch the dip and the tempo, and even if I soaked my shorts, pre-ejaculated, I would continue grinding into her clit until her body squirmed into seizures. And in bed cuddling, after she was drained of multiple orgasms, frequently my baby would burst out crying. I believe they were tears of joy. I became a sex-pert on every inch of Loretta's skin that was erogenous and we learned that was most of her.

Chapter Five

I'm a junior, a college student in this community—I wanted to scream! With his aim still beaded on us I was afraid to even breathe. If I moved a faction I was sure his fingers would flex and I'd be shot with both barrels.

As we lay on the side of the road he rotated a pinpoint aim on us, and without my permission, I saw the other cop ransacking the Camry. We were being treated like America's most wanted terrorist, and I felt like I was Ben Laden.

Maslow. Maslow. Maslow. This was a direct attack on my security and as a 21 year old black man growing up in Oklahoma's America, I was already experiencing developmental issues.

My attention drifted from the dark roadside and funky tasting water to the lit up clean decency of the university's classroom. "*Professor King, sorry I'm missed the test; I was uh…uh…*" How could I begin to explain to him my humiliation? And was it even possible for a white man to understand my situation?

"Hey!" The cop in my car kneeled on one leg in the back seat, leaned out the door and held up a plastic bag. "Here's the drugs!"

Drugs? What? Gritting my teeth I gently screamed. I gawked up at the forty something pudgy white cop and saw he was pleased with his discovery. An ugly sneer of hate towards us seemed to give him pure enjoyment and his contorted frown let us know he was getting ready to inflict even more misery into our lives.

"*Drugs*'! What the hell was going on? Like a bag of manure I was snatched to my feet. The freckled-faced policeman shoved me hard and I stumbled up against the squad car. What in God's name had Danny gotten me into? Danny vigorously shook his head, denying any association with the drugs.

Buddy and Jarvis were placed in the back of the patrol car. Danny and I waited in the wet weather. The thunder and the raspy interference sound of the police radio entertained us. After fifthteen minutes, finally, a transport patrol car came for us.

Black and white cars were all over the station's parking lot. My guts twisted and an alarm went off. Why was I experiencing overwhelming dread when I was surrounded by an army of police vehicles? And it hit me! All me life, all the conversations I'd ever had with people in our community concerning race, they all echoed one fact. In the daily lives of a lot of Oklahoma City's African Americans it wasn't the religious Islamic fanatics shouting Jihad that we were afraid of; it was the people that we paid to protect and serve that were our terrorist.

Handcuffed, in custody, I began to think of myself as a prisoner of war and I believed I was at the headquarters of the enemy.

As Danny and I were escorted up on the wretched aged elevator for booking, I glared at him again with disgust.

"I'll get us out of this mess!" Danny mumbled under his breath after reading the fury in my gaze. The cops separated us and I wouldn't see my cousin for a while.

The civilians that worked at the station gawked at me like I was a nasty piece of shit. I was fingerprinted, photographed and lead to a cell.

It was called a holding tank. The large stone room was like a modern day dungeon and the place reeked with filthy stale liquor, dried urine, and fecal matter.

In a space with fifteen rock slab beds I was jammed in with thirty-six other bodies. Drunks were passed out in passageways and one inmate was using the trunk of the commode for a pillow. Connected to the top of the stool was a push button drinking fountain, the fumes alone were enough to pollute the water. Dysentery and cholera, and dying from some disease flushed through my mind.

The stench and dying from an illness was only a distraction. Being beaten to death was my major concern! My intestines felt like they needed to shed some feces. If one wrong word uttered from my lips was misinterpreted or if I mistakenly had inappropriate eye contact that challenged an inmate, I could easily be killed. Black Dickey snuggled between my nuts for safety.

Some of the sober inmates lay across the brick beds, some played cards or read tattered books, while others strolled back in forth and mumbled secret troubling conversations. I joined in the private walks.

I finally slid into a corner to sort out what I'd say to Mamma. Another hour passed, and lunch was served. I skipped the milk and tossed the stale bread with the chunky peanut butter into the trash—that was lunch.

A few hours later I overheard a group of inmates informing others that since it was already late Friday afternoon we would all have to wait until Monday to be arraigned. No judge to set bail meant I was there for the weekend. Black Dickey's three nights and two days expectations of ecstasies with Loretta were thwarted. For the past six weeks we'd skimped and saved and schemed at spending this weekend together. Easy inexpensive, accessible, affordable, getaway sites were becoming a way of life for us.

Over the course of the next three days two brutal fights broke out right in front of me. A gash on the side of one man's head spewed blood on my white shirt. Blotches of red were absorbed into the material that had already dried and semi-shrunk. In another battle, the prisoner had his right eye clawed out of the socket and he had to be rushed to the hospital. There were several all night treats of brawls, constant arguments, and I listened to stories even more pitiful than mine.

I had pulled an all-nighter preparing for a test and even though I was dog-tired for the next three days fear kept my eyes wide-opened. Dead-tired, under devastating circumstances, I was living wide-awake in a hellhole and forced to observe the worst of human behavior.

On Monday morning Mamma was in court for the bail hearing. She saved me from further madness by promptly placing up our home in the *Land of Oz* for collateral.

Depleted from any signs of sanity I stared out the window speechless in a stupor while Mamma drove me home.

"My Lord, my Lord, my Lord! My sister and her son; they're delivering our entire family to the wicked white oppressors on a silver platter. My Lord, my Lord, my Lord!" Mamma shook her head in disgust and eyeballed a horrifying stare in my path. The gawk gave me a mental spanking. Her puffed gape opened my wrecked depression and splattered guilt into my blood stream. The situation was partly my fought and I should have used better judgment. But was it bad judgment? Was I responsible? If I was white helping out a relative and his white friends would I even be in this situation? Would my mother or I be questioning my judgment? Still, I wrestled with whatever measurable accountability I may have had for the predicament I was in.

As she pulled in front of the house she noticed my Camry was missing, "Damn they've got your car!" I was still traumatized by all the drama and Mamma had chaotically rushed to my rescue; we'd forgotten to get my car from the pound.

"You stay here. Go get some rest. I'll get Mrs. Green to drive your car." Mamma took pity on me and as a nurse I'm sure she'd diagnosed I was suffering from PTSD (Post-Traumatic Stress Disorder).

"You take a bath before you crawl into bed." She coiled her face to emphasize my obvious odorous jailhouse funk.

As the warmth of water showered my skin, I tried to scrub the whole filthy experience of jail out of and off my life. Already dazed, water beating against my body seemed to hypnotize me and I began reflecting.

*Watershed moments: Before moving into Oz, I was incapable of using that adjective to describe my previous short life experiences. As I palmed my genitals in one hand, graciously and generously, I began massaging suds all over Black Dickey. As I held my organ I became sensitive to his disappointments and triumphs. Aware that I had a snowball's chance in hell of ever getting some from a white girl in Oklahoma. And for years the sum of all of my begging from a sister was zero, each day that passed without soaking my penis in a vaginal hole had brought him more gloom and despair. I acknowledge that High school graduation had been a proud moment for me. Getting a scholarship and into a college nearby had been a dream come true. Those private achievements were expected, all products of hard work and a demanding mother. Neither could compete with my habitually starved carnal desires. I wagged Black Dickey and thought, oh how elusive and heartbreaking sex had been for him! Loretta had given me sex and that had been my second **watershed moment.** She gave me this precious gift and her world changing endowment had Black Dickey weeping with joy! Marinating Black Dickey in her juices and becoming the meat sandwiched in the middle of her womanly but-*

tered bread, palming and squeezing her tight muscular smoked thighs, in these riches I'd found my pot of gold—my nirvana!

I held my face up, turned the pulsating speed on high and allowed the water to thrash down. *Shea butter* was massaged into my hair. And in an uncontrollable frenzy I scratched deep into my scalp. I was trying to remove the affliction of being in jail.

Watershed moment: *Walking, talking, and eating, were normal learned human behaviors. And as far back as I can remember, woven into Oklahoma City's black community, I'd heard cops were ruthless and notorious. As the white cop held that huge double barrel shotgun at my head, when I saw the hate in the white man's gawk and felt him wishing I'd make a false move, when I knew he wanted to blow my damn head off...that was another **watershed moment**! His community had taught him it was ok or a good thing to kill a black man. In my brief existence I had witnessed acts of violence and I had engaged in some fistfights myself, I'd never been locked inside a cage with constant bizarre aggression. In jail I was trapped, vulnerable, exposed to indiscriminate unrestrained explosive brutality. The state, the police had the power to do anything they wanted to do with my life—I concluded, and that was a reality and another **watershed moment.***

I stepped out of my spell and from the tub and I was the walking dead, a zombie. I headed to my bedroom.

On edge in the privacy of my own space and inside my skin and on the outer shell I was naked as a jaybird when I dove towards the bed. And in mid-air I was snoozing before my head hit the pillow.

For fourteen hours I lay in bed dead to the world. Tuesday morning I staggered awake and unsuccessfully tried to shake off the nightmarish weekend. The aroma of bacon let me know I was back in Oz. And getting to school on time buzzed ahead of the dread I was feeling and this was the impetus that steered my ass into gear.

I found a plate of eggs, bacon, and toast that Mamma had placed in the microwave. The nurse had already left to save lives.

Physically nourished and alert I was ready to feed my brain. I marched outside and was shocked when I spotted that my car had been beaten-up. The sleek Camry resembled a hoopty. The hood was buckled. Already traumatized I carefully inspected the inside of my car. The front and the back seats were shredded. Electrical wires were yanked and left dangling underneath the dashboard. It was as if a band of crack-heads used butcher knives searching for dropped hits. I remember watching TV detective programs and cops always used the term, *"tossed the vehicle"*.

Vinyl seat covers would take my measly savings. Then to re-wire the signal/lights, air/heater, radio/CD Player, windshield wipers and…just thinking about all the cost was causing my head to hurt. Do it myself! I decided. I'll buy new wires and spend the whole weekend on my back under the dashboard. I popped the key in the ignition; the motor was fine.

The insolated life I had once known had been violated and that day in all my classes my concentration drifted. Repeated flashes of the evil cop and the shotgun barrel; an open eye socket, globs of blood, streaming funk from the jail, and a plucked eyeball rolled around in my head. These frightening videotapes were vividly replayed and relived all day.

Briefly interweaving these nightmares, inside the corridors of the clean learning environment, I began to stare at each white student with suspicion and envy. How did these reds and blond-headed people spend their weekends? Was all their worries consumed with passing college courses? Did they wonder if a shotgun would be pointed in their faces when they left school? Were the pink people living in fear of an upcoming trial and the prospects of facing prison time? Did any of them have these extra pressures?

At the end of the day, the only way I figured I could halt the haunts from the horrible watershed weekend was to replace it with my most important wish that came true. If I had to beg for it, I had to get some of Loretta's loving!

Without crushing my ego further by my anxious pleas Loretta was ready and willing to console and give me her special treats. My queen broke her strident restrictive schedule and we both skipped work that night.

Loretta's grandmother had one of few rarely framed houses in the neighborhood and it was down the road from ours on the southeast edge of Oz. A stairway of crimson brick led to the porch and pasty, wooden rails decorated it. On the wooden deck there was an old fashioned swing and in the spring and summer exotic potted flowers surrounded it. Before Loretta gave me some, out in night's darkness, we use to bump and grind fully clothed on the old swing. The rickety squeaks would echo the rhythms our bodies made.

Loretta's grandmother was like many elderly black Oklahomans. They had migrated from Texas to escape small Jim Crow towns. When she arrived with her husband in the prairie town in 1955 they found an already established segregated Oklahoma City. Most of the jobs available for black women were private housekeepers for white women and bed making clean-up jobs in the downtown hotels. She chose the latter. With the revolutions of the sixties and by the sweat of her brow life did get better for Loretta's grandmother. She was able to retire as a factory worker. She and her diseased husband bought their modest three-bedroom house in the Land of Oz in the mid-seventies.

That night under autumn's orange slice of the moon the winds blew easy and the relationship between Loretta and I eased into another phase.

Loretta's cozy faintly lit living room was adorned with African Art. Photographs of Black Eve and queens Nofretari, Hatshepsut, and Tiye, rocks and miniature artifacts from Mt. Kilimanjaro and the pyramids, these African relics gave the area an imposing mystique. And I was in awe of their majestic spiritual meanings.

"Is that you Kayin?" Loretta's grandmother hollered from the rear, she was in the den. In the midst of the culturally royal scenery I had my pants unzipped; my hands were under Loretta's dress gripping her ass, while Black Dickey was rolling with the rhythms of Loretta's clitoris. An ebony laced trim silk skirt; the soft material had made it easy to feel Loretta's sensuousness and to dive into her vibe. But our excitedly energized bodies caused us to stumble and the noise had gotten Loretta's grandmother's attention.

"Yes ma'am!" I shouted. I released Loretta's butt, we gazed at each other intently, exhaled, and our salivating erotica slowly eased away.

"Come on back and visit!" Even though I suspected the old lady knew I had been intimate with her granddaughter I prepared myself to respect her request. I zipped my pants and assumed the innocence of an angelic studious college boy.

To get to the den I had to pass through the kitchen. Collard greens, black-eyed peas, meat loaf and homemade cornbread, the southern tangy flavors spiced the air and gave me a rush. The scent felt like it was full of nutrients and the odor had the effect of smelling sauce being administered. Ah!

"Hi Kayin! Have you had dinner? We have plenty." Mrs. Graham was swallowing the last of her meal. After she gave the festive invitation she fiddled a toothpick to the side of her mouth. Always wearing her fashionable purple robe the old lady shoved her serving stand to the side and leaned, relaxing in a brown leather recliner at a 90-degree angle. A blanket was folded on her lap. The TV was on CNN. Beside the empty plate on her serving table there was a giant cup of sweet ice tea and her thick granny bifocals.

"Hi Mrs. Graham, thanks, but I already had supper. Woo! Whatever it was you ate, it sure smells like it tasted delicious!" I rubbed my tummy and proceeded to drop a kiss on the old woman's charcoaled forehead.

As she picked her teeth she gave me a hard inquisitive gaze.

"Now tell me what did those blue and gray clad evil Klansmen do to you?" Elderly black people have a unique way of expressing what they mean without any apologies. She flexed the chair into an upright position and flicked the TV off. I explained my situation and then spent the next amicable half-hour listening to the trials of the black men of her life and how abusive they'd been treated by Oklahoma City's Police Department.

"I'm getting sleepy." She yawned. Once again I kissed her on the forehead. I extended a hand and helped her to her feet. Mrs. Graham grabbed the cane that leaned against the side of the recliner. We walked side by side to her bedroom. "Now you gone and visit with Retta." With a sly eye the old woman winked.

A guest bedroom separated the two ladies private spaces. As I leisurely walked down the hall Black Dickey began to worry. Would Loretta have her head buried in a book or could he pick up where he left off in the living room?

With an ear pressed against my baby's door I gave it a light tap. Sada's sexy lyrics were barley audible. Loretta cracked the entrance. Under an indigo lamplight's dimness I glanced down and became a captive of her tiny slinky rose negligee. She widened the door, gracefully offering me her hand Loretta curtsied; it was a classy southern invitation, one that I readily accepted. As she tilted I was exposed to her round firm dark mocha tits. I was amazed that my sneak around lover had asked me into her boudoir and was seductively nearly naked.

As I glided through the entrance, behind me I heard a soft click. I peaked back and, Loretta mischievously was quietly squeezing the door shut. Are we still tiptoeing into love making, I surmised. I quickly summed up our discrete, secret-from-our-guardians, love affair: Sneaking and hiding away on the mountain; and creeping away on weekends as if we were only best buddies; sneaking around experimenting in interstate motels; humping in bump-n-grind quickies in deserted halls between classes. Our sexual relationship had been hush-hush, kept underground from my mother and her grandmother. Had we advanced all the way to the inside of my bashful baby's home?

I quickly removed my canary yellow v-neck sweater and dropped my trousers and boxers in the next stroke. Whirling Loretta up into my arms I laid her face down on the bed. The negligee flounced up and exposed a large portion of Loretta's creamy chocolate thighs. Awkwardly, Loretta's ass had perched upward, and in this unnatural pose and the way the sheik red fabric fell above her bootie, to my already horny gaze, the posture was a perfect photographic expression of eroticism. Black Dickey robotically snapped the shot and turned-on.

I mounted her doggie-style. Reaching underneath her I embraced the firm and squishiness of her tits. Loretta eased her hips into half and double shift rhythms and feeling safe in the comforts of Loretta's bed I added corresponding cadency wiggles. Black Dickey slide up and down sides of her ass-hole and he was unexpectedly splendidly stimulated. "Eke-ah…! Kayin." Sensuousness radiated off the strip of skin between Loretta's vulva and her ass, her perineum. Stroking the area had also aroused her. The sudden increased feeling impulsively jolted me into slamming Black Dickey into Loretta's twat. She quickly scuttled the rhythms of her hips into spasms. Electrified by her swift passionate seizures, with long thrust, I soon followed. This was the quickest she'd ever came.

After she disposed the rubber Loretta, crawled between my legs. She hugged Black Dickey with one hand. With the eyes of an angel she winked a devil may care lure up at me and then in the direction of Black Dickey.

Loretta slipped a fresh condom on Black Dickey. She slid her moist tongue up the side of Black Dickey and when she reached the shaft he was back, hard as a rock.

"My friends said this is a *special gift* a woman gives to the man she loves." Imitating a bad girl's smile Loretta plunged Black Dickey between her smoldering smokey lips. The friction of Loretta's jaws plus her saliva as a lubricant gave her tongue slick wiggles, a power that sent a scream of new original ecstasies into Black Dickey.

I knew Loretta hadn't read a book on *oral sex* and I doubt if she'd previewed any other how to instructions on the topic. If any classes were offered on the subject in the Bible belt of Oklahoma, I was certain she hadn't enrolled in any of those courses either. She was a rookie oral sucker not that I could tell what an experienced penis licker felt like but Loretta made a mistake when she began nibbling on Black Dickey. Her teeth nicked a nerve near Black Dickey's head and the pain for him was similar to my fear when I gazed up the barrel of that shotgun. Instinctively I snatch her head off my penis!

"Damn!" The stinging ache caused me to cuss.

"I'm sorry...did that hurt?" The shame-faced angel asked. I nodded. Loretta began to puff soothing tiny breaths all over Black Dickey. She whistled soft air over my balls and then licked and sucked them. Then she placed a rejuvenated effervescent Black Dickey into her mouth. I began to feel the actual rhythms of love-making and her whole orifice started to have reflexes like a vagina.

Newness brings interesting reactions and old comparisons. The way that Loretta would grab my ass and hold it in place with an ironclad hand while she was coming, I began to have a similar response. Consumed in passion I embraced the back of Loretta's head until her tongue performed like a clitoris and allowed the snake slitters to wrestle the juices out of Black Dickey.

The entire evening was an unsullied episode and a spiritual experience for Loretta and me. She'd offered me an oral intimacy and her new warm sensitive loving was exceedingly pleasing for Black Dickey. I was extremely needy that night and by her unselfish actions I knew she'd sacrificed her Christian beliefs. But that night I felt Loretta's faith was changing. Without hesitation she'd allowed her tongue to touch my soul completely. Her generosity was soothing to my injured psychic and Loretta had trusted our relationship to advance, we'd entered into the solitude of her sacred bedroom. And even more imperative for Loretta's sake, since she'd paid half the bills for years, she'd finally exposed our secret sex life to her grandmother. The simple changes that Loretta put forward that night nourished my convictions in our relationship. Her support moved our connection to more than just two horny student-lovers I believe we were beginning to live our lives as grown-ups.

"Get up Kayin! Kayin get up!" I struggled to get an eyelid opened. I awakened and a butt naked Loretta stood bowed over the bed slinging her chocolate crispy round firm tits above my head.

"Honey get up you're going to make me late. I have early classes this morning." Meekly and with a stern tone my baby pleaded. Being aware that I was awake, Loretta quickly threw on a robe; she grabbed a make-up kit, some bathing lotions and stuck them into a plastic see-through bag. I believed when she hastily hiked out of the door she headed to the bathroom.

No alcohol was served last night but after our new sexual liberation I was druggy. Still tripping between the horrid weekend and the substitute cure of last night, I tried to make sense of what had happened. Was our honeymoon over? Was Loretta my new unpredictable sinning lover back to being the uptight Christian, and the up and coming black professional businesswoman?

I heard pulsating morning fresh water splashing down the hall and the image of a stream beating against her naked body drove flashback yearnings to have more of last night's delights. Black Dickey sprung into action!

Since the two women had shared this household for years I figured they probably hardly ever locked any of the inside doors, including the bathroom—and I was right.

When I silently slid opened the shower door water was splattering on the face of my petite piece of gooey dark chocolates. I gazed upon Loretta's wet nakedness and again I was mesmerized. Water rushed over her nipples and down on her trimmed feminine hips. Steady streams rolled in and out of her naval as if this part of her body's structure was a waterfall. Her thick vaginal bush looked like trees absorbing water in a rain forest. And the way rain forests are a lively green the wetness gave Loretta's vaginal hairs an alluring rich dark wavy appearance.

Butt naked I stepped inside and under the sprinkles.

Startled and shy by my unexpected entry into her privacy, Loretta cautiously, involuntary, folded one arm to cover her breast the other hand shielded her vaginal hair.

Batting her eyes as if they were dismissing her surprised panic, her gawking eyes were immediately drawn to the dangling of a gloved Black Dickey.

"Oh! You are going to make me late. Tehehe!" Loretta delivered a halfhearted appeal and then let loose a spunky little girlish giggle.

As water bounced between our bodies I moved quickly and was up on Loretta's girly gaze. I lifted her legs up and pinned her against the linoleum wall. Loretta sprouted her legs around my waist and her arms formed a tight seal that circled my body—she fit into me like a missing piece. The full-throttled massaging water swished across the rhythms that my naked ass made and Loretta's passionate squeals were muffled under the splash of water beats.

Chapter Six

"I love you." There was no more than an inch of air between our lips when Loretta whisked that old poetic stanza into the wind and into our world. Through a tiny space and with the molecules of a magnet, the verse heaved us together. We kissed and said our good-byes outside in her driveway.

I drove off and repetitiously the vibe *I love you* rode with me like a god. Other than my mother and grandmother, Loretta was the only other woman who'd shown real affection for me.

After school I got on *Goggle* and searched for a local attorney.

Mrs. Lora Mae Williams wasn't the cheapest and probably not the best lawyer but on the phone she was the best salesperson. She had worked in the D.A.'s office and had an intimate relationship with the prosecuting attorney's staff. She planted that idea in my head and that's why I chose her. It was comforting to believe I had someone white that had a personal bond with my persecutors.

Mrs. William's had time available that evening and I made the appointment. As soon as I hung up reasons to fret pounced on me. *"You're a college student and you don't have any money to hire a lawyer."* My misfortunes had already placed our home on the chopping block and now I'd have to ask Mamma to co-sign on a loan. Damn!

There's nothing in this world like a mother's love. On the drive to *Tinker's Credit Union* Mamma's only question was how and why I'd chosen Lora Mae for a lawyer, not once did she ask how much.

Only blocks away from the filthy institution where I was held hostage in the city jail, Lora Mae's office was on the first floor of an old building that demanded remodeling or demolishing.

Lora Mae Williams was a squatty mid-forty something woman that looked extremely white. Her blond hairstyle was highlighted in ginger and the black roots gave it an exotic gleam. Like most white women in Oklahoma City Mamma thought all of them overdid it in the make-up department. With a slanted nose Mamma would say, "Too thick on the eye-shadow and too heavy on the face powder! Why do Okie white women insist on dressing like clowns?"

Stacks of books, pamphlets, loose papers, tacks, and a roll of clear tape cluttered her desk. Either Mrs. Williams was a busy lady or she was a sloppy pig or maybe a little of both. She wore an out-dated navy blue Brooks Brothers business suit. The pants she wore were too short—wade-waters. Her most assuring and endearing credentials continued to be her familiarity with the district attor-ney's office. "I know those guys…" She said, nodding, adjusting her glasses. In a southern matter of fact way she was saying she could handle them. We left her office almost convinced that she could persuade the authorities of my innocence.

Cool misty breezy nights were the forecast for the weekend. Cuddling under the covers with my sweetheart Loretta is what Black Dickey had designs to do, but on my back under the dash-board repairing the Camry is what I did.

I was under the weather that was the reason I gave Professor King for missing his test. I did the make-up exam. It was probably a more complicated examination. Ninety-five percent, that was my score. *"There are no excuses for missing a test."* This was the motto of the slim beaked nosed dictator. The King had already delivered his rules at the beginning of the semester and if for some God for-saken reason one did ignore his warning the highest grade a stu-dent could receive was a "C". I was lucky the tyrant gave us the opportunity to throw out our lowest score.

The following week Oklahoma's autumn winds blew heat through the rustling leaves and the sunny temperature was a balmy eighty degrees. The robins, redbirds, scissor-tails, jay-hawks, and a variety of warm weather birds had already flown further south, only small swallows and a few other colorless birds circled the skies and waited on the harsh winter weather that lay ahead. A jailbird I had known for all the seasons of my life called me collect—it was Danny.

I had known this man all my life and there was never a day I hadn't thought of him, this was true when I was locked up and cer-tainly since I'd been out. Hateful and angry reflections illuminated the thoughts and images I had of my cousin. Neither my aunt, nor any of his friends had money for bail. And even though I wanted to break his neck, I hoped and prayed my cousin would find his own way out of that hellhole.

"Hey bro, what's happening?" Danny had been gifted or at least had nurtured and perfected a slick cool whisper in his voice. As a teenager when he spoke on the phone he'd use this soft sensuous undertone to get girls into bed. I was jealous because I couldn't imitate the sound and I was unable to bed a girl. This time I picked a muddled anxiety in his polished tone. Living life in that dungeon for three whole weeks is an existence I couldn't phantom. Danny had spent at least six months in the county jail before and he was fearless in a fight, maybe it wasn't so bad for him. I wanted to believe that idea.

We joked, laughed, spoke of old times growing up and the high school years. Then I began to ask him about the drugs—

"Shshsh, not right now bro!" Danny shushed me as if he knew someone was ease dropping.

"Can you get hold of some money and bounce me up outta here man?" Danny's hip-hop swaggering tone had an undercurrent; I felt his desperation and sensed the dribble of a little boy's cry. I felt powerless. I had no money or assets and I didn't know any rich black folk. Because of his record his bail was more than mine.

"I'll see what I can do man." Yeah. I gave Danny false hope, clinched my fist, bit my tongue and regretted that I'd suggested an impossible promise. The truth, I knew of no one who could help him. I'd never seen a wealthy black man in Oklahoma City. And since my arrest I was beginning to believe God had only blessed a few of us in the whole world with the riches and accesses that I believed ordinary white people could have or had.

"Man I know those brothers and they weren't carrying when they got in your ride. Man that was a whole goddamn pound those cops lifted! Man where were we going to sell that much stuff at six in the morning, it was raining cats and dogs, you were taking us downtown! What black person do you know is doing business downtown right under the man's nose in this cow town? Man I don't know why but these mother's are setting us up!" I imagined Danny's head sneaking and ducking a look-see on the other side of the receiver, if the phone was bugged, then he could hide, and no one would be able to hear us. My cousin used that sort of logic sometimes.

Growing up in a southern city where many blacks had a hate-on for the police, and experiencing the bone curling repulsiveness in the white cop's eyes—I almost believed Danny's account about the drugs being planted.

The best I could offer Danny was to supply his cigarette habit. I carried him a carton of *Kool's* on my weekly visits.

A week before Thanksgiving ice formed in the clouds and dropped deadly icicles all over the Prairie State. Huge deadly frozen pointed particles hung from rooftops. On the limbs of weak withering wintry trees, the frost appeared to be part of a weird winter harvest. Some of the frost snapped the frail limbs quickly while other icicles lingered and the heavy weight gave the tree a weeping willow swaying posture, but finally the gravity of the massive loads would snap the helpless limbs like twigs. Cars skated through the streets and swerved off into ditches and into each other. The freeze snapped telephone and electrical wires. Entire communities were without power. Mother Nature spared Mamma and I and most of the black folks of Park Estates, but down on the lower eastside where Danny's mother resided, that neighborhood was one of the electrical casualties.

Aunt Betty spent the next bitter cold eleven days with us. For her convenience I converted the garage into a din. She slept on a rollaway bed and used a space heater to stay warm and cozy.

On day four we gathered at the breakfast table and Aunt Betty divulged her discontent for being second class.

"White folks are going to get their shit turned on first." She perched her lips like a child and sipped through the steamy smoked swirls of black coffee. A dark crucifix scar was branded in the middle of her crimson-yellow forehead, a left over war wound from her drugging, drinking, and prostitution days. The mark appeared to come alive whenever she was angry. Still possessing a tight petite figure at forty-one, the blemish was the only imperfection I could see she had. And even though Aunt Betty had begun taking college classes at Oklahoma State's extension center in Oklahoma City, and had been sober almost eight years, she had never allowed herself to believe the illusion her existence could ever be as precious or as equal to Caucasians in Oklahoma City.

Hip-hop grew up in America's ghetto streets and Aunt Betty had lived the street life. When I was a budding teen-ager, Aunt Betty was in her early thirties. She was a wiry party-girl, and her lean body paraded in mini, and wildcat skirts, silk camisoles and low rider pants. She exposed her slender crimson sexy tummy and tender tits. In my pubescence, silently and without me wishing, Black Dickey had had incestuous erotic passionate daydreams of a naked Aunt Betty.

"Girl you know that's the truth." Mamma chewed on her bacon and confirmed her sister's protest. Always the big sister in many ways, Mamma had a tinge of bulk in her stature.

"Hurry up and eat! I'll quiz you on your mid-term Organic Chemistry exam." Mamma sucked up a mouth full of grits and made the suggestion to Aunt Betty. Her little sister was studying to become a nurse like her. Both sisters still had housecoats on, rollers in their hair and I was eating breakfast in my burgundy robe.

I dressed then I entered the living room and saw the two ladies had moved from the dinning table and were lodged at the living room table. Mamma had a book propped in her lap and I assumed she had asked Aunt Betty a hard question because Aunt Betty appeared bewildered.

"I bet Danny-Boy's freezing his buns off!" Aunt Betty leaped from her chair and rushed to the front door. She parted the three tiny purple curtains at the top and stared through the glass. Her gaze became frozen into the outside weather's coldness.

Mamma rose from her chair, she placed the textbook on the black octagon marble coffee table and followed her sister to the door. Mamma began massaging her fingers on top of her little sister's shoulders.

We were middle class, a family that used most of our income to pay monthly bills. We hadn't planned on the disaster of an arrest. There were no monies set aside for bondsmen and lawyer fees. It was hard to watch huge tears drip form Aunt Betty's maimed defeated eyes.

That was our morning before our lives entered the world and Thanksgiving was three days away.

***

Although I received most of the same information and I sat side by side with white students in classrooms, I always felt they had a cultural advantage. Like hip-hop, soul, blues, spirituals, and slave songs were steeped in black codes, most of my instructors, teachers, and professors were white, and they had their own innuendos. I believe these cryptograms were unintentionally and intentionally easily communicated to my white classmates.

"You've got to work twice as hard and be twice as smart as the white students." This was the Black folk's Declaration of Independence, and throughout my life, Mamma had repeated that handed down coded policy principal. This affirmation was born in America and became the standards whites set up to judge African American achievement. The forefathers who wrote the United States Constitution had laid down the gauntlet. Legally, originally and officially the document said a slave's life was worth only three-fifths the value of a white person's.

The semester ended ten days before Christmas and an upcoming trial was sizzling inside my head like a fuse on a lit bomb. To pass finals I had to man-up and muster strength from African American ancestors and use their old handed down mantra.

After two and a half years of burning the mid-night oil, practicing the *twice better than* rituals, at the end of the term I was more than a four point student. According to the evaluations of their customs, I was almost equal to a white person. More than an average Negro—more than three fifths of a person, at least I wanted to be seen this way in the eyes of a Oklahoma white judge and jury.

Preparing for the *Baby Jesus'* Christmas holiday, I found myself immersed in a mixture of moods. Parts were inspirational, there were bits of melancholy, and a bunch was erotic horniness.

Since last spring I'd been hustling to pay for a finely woven camel coat for Momma, and I was thrilled I was able to get it out of lay-away on time.

A corduroy Jacket and matching purse was the natural pimp-down style Aunt Betty was shooting for in her new life. I got the set at a Nearly New Shop—it was fun to see my despondent aunt beam with Christmas merriment.

I delivered Danny his regular carton of cigarettes plus I placed money in his account for special goodies. I received the usual depersonalization mean and nasty stares from the staff at the police department.

"Empty your pockets." With a spiteful scowl and a pig's face the white woman blurted. Her glower overshadowed the wrinkles above and below her skeleton lips. The detestable grimace had silently added *Nigger* to her demand.

"Put your belongings in here!" She slipped a manila envelope through an opening underneath the protective glass.

I placed my wallet and keys inside and she slid the package back to her.

"Write your name on it!" She snapped, obviously irritated at my stupidity.

Even though I'd never considered striking a female, I wanted to haul off and bitch-slap her. But the visitor's room of a jail wasn't the best place to exercise criminal conduct. I imprisoned my emotions.

In only a week's time Danny's creamy skin was a shade darker. A bumpy rash had grown across his cheeks. Since Danny's incarceration his stout physique had lost at least twenty pounds. His cool style had changed to edgy.

"Bro you know I appreciate the gifts. A man has got to have candy bars and something to read up in this shit house." Danny managed to show gratitude through his tortured frown.

Sitting across from the man behind bars in the orange jump suit, I shook and bowed my head, knowing I couldn't give him what he wanted most—freedom!

Driving away from the house of pain, I was suddenly filled with an overwhelming horror. Danny was street tough and he was withering. If my green ass was in a cell I'd be eaten alive within a week.

***

I rarely dressed up in a suit and tie and since high school I usually wasn't a regular at church services, but with a trial looming I needed all of God's loving care to carry me into the New Year.

Since Loretta and I belonged to different churches, she went her way and I was Mamma's escort to our mid-night candle-lighting service on Christmas Eve. Our congregation, close to three hundred faithful, was made up of the neighborhood's working class. I grew up knowing every member. I knew all of their peculiar habits and most of their imperfections. This was the church that I freely swam under the waters in baptism and graciously gave the spirit my pubescent heart.

In the same manner as we'd done before I'd become a visitor, Mamma and I sat in the sanctuary in our usual middle row mid-section pew seats.

The children's choir sang *Away in a Manger*. Their innocent harmonies whisked me off into dreamland. Deja vu! I use to be one of them. I became soothingly wrapped into the romantic idea of being a child again.

The adult gospel singers crooned a soulful *"Silent Night"*, *"Noel"*, and *"Hallelujah."* There were a lot of old-heads among the adult vocalist and I had a rush of imposing memories. I recalled when some of the men had hair and when it was darker and when the women were a few pounds lighter. I thought of occasions when several of them had disciplined me for running in church or for talking during a sermon. The first time I read a verse at the podium Sister Frazier adorned a gleaming smile on me and her spirited glow gave me the feeling that I belonged up there. When the minister announced all the scholarships I had received, with everyone in the congregation applauding, my eyes were drawn to Brother Ervin. His wholehearted claps caused his whole chubby body to wobble. There were more recollections of personal intimate conversations and incidents with individuals in our fellowship and I became serenely absorbed by those good old days. I believe I finally had a clue of the meaning *"It takes a village".*

The temple was quiet as a mouse when my childhood Sunday school teacher Sister Mary Robinson, appeared at the podium.

"The light of hope..." With perfect diction that's how she began. Strangely the title of her message slammed against my heart like a ton of bricks. I desperately needed hope in my world.

Reading from the book of Matthew, she began eloquently telling the story of *The Three Wise Men*. With precise articulation, her opening testimonials floated off her tongue into the air sprouting wings and the words appeared to soar straight to heaven. Always solemn, the biblical theatrical storyteller narrated Isaiah 40

1-5—*The Prophesy* of the coming of Jesus. She skipped to Luke and read, while in the background the congregation saw the children pan amine a performance as Mary and Joseph and how the baby Jesus was born in a manger.

And at midnight it was an amazing sight to witness a church full of black folk, each holding a lit candle in the darkness, singing *Joy to the World*. Caught up in the moment, I reflected—we're not even seen as equals in this state; yet, here we stand singing in harmonious bliss. ***Feliz Navidad.***

Outside, underneath a harvest moon, as I stared up into the clear crispy black skies, I saw sprinkles of the Big Dipper. Under the glare of the parking lot light Mom huddled with a group of her fellow Christian women friends. I propped my butt against the fender of the Camry and maintained the amazement of being seduced by the winter's chilly air, the glimmer of the stars and the mysteries of the night. ***Feliz Navidad.***

As I drove towards our home, I saw a car suddenly shut off its lights in front of Trish's house. Glaring at the vehicle I oozed pass it. Though the dimness of night I guessed that the car had a cherry color. Working my memory harder, I believe the car sort of resembled the spanking brand new Mustang Trish's parents had given her as a wedding present.

Two years ago Trish had met a man, married him, and moved to Cleveland, his hometown.

As I slid from the Camry I heard footsteps. I listened, and the shoes clicking a happy dance up to the driveway, sounded familiar. Squinting, I tried to recognize the unique stride generated by the advancing silhouette.

Was it my first love? Was it—?

"Hey Kayin! Sweetie!" On Christmas Eve, from my past, in the darkness, a sensuously endearing accent greeted me.

"Trish!" I zoomed in and spotted her adorable dimples. In two long quick strides I was in her face. With tingling amazement we gawked into each other's eyes. And for the first time since our youthful play at sex encounter, I moved closer to my teen-age fantasy lover, and with no fear or hesitation, I started caressing Trish's voluptuous buttery body.

Trish had dyed her rich deep black hair. She was now a honey blonde and had bunched her long tresses into a bun. Arm in arm and giddy, we danced an African American jig as we promenaded out of the wintry air and into the affectionate heat of my home.

Trish's house key didn't fit and her cell phone needed charging. When she'd moved her parents had changed the locks. Two days earlier her father had told me that he and his wife would be out of town for the holidays. He'd ask me keep an eye on the place.

I helped Trish remove her auburn suede coat and was amazed and turned-on by the way her body's curves emerged in plain navy blue fatigues. Even an ordinary exercise uniform had emphasized how amazingly attractive she was.

The old jerk-off memories sprung back into Black Dickey and his lusting hunger quickly became a gawk in my eyes. I decided to divert the intention of the gaze and gave a critique of Trish's fashion sense.

I eyed her fine-looking ass up and down and then had to mask my aroused hormones with a perplexed expression. "You're wearing pumps with that outfit?" With a worn-out expression, Trish explained, "I drove all the way here in house-shoes and when I unfastened my suitcase the pumps fell out."

Mamma and I were full of Feliz Navidads for our homecoming home-girl. We gathered around the dinning table, and Mamma popped a bottle of chilled champagne. She gave a festive toast, happy and excited, we warmly welcomed her!

An hour of strolling down memory lane and it was 2 AM, Christmas morning. After working a ten-hour nursing shift, and the annual Christmas Eve ritual, sleep had infected Mamma's body. "I'm going to bed." Mamma said, yawning as she stumbled out of her chair to her feet. Her eyelids were heavy.

"You're staying here until your parents return." Mamma stared into the married young woman's eyes and made the southern hospitable elder's demand.

"Kayin change your linens! She's sleeping in your bed. You sleep in the living-room on the couch." Mamma pointed at me and ordered.

I fetched Trish's luggage from the Mustang. While Trish brushed her teeth and showered, I placed fresh linens on my bed.

Lying on the couch and almost comfortable under the covers, my eyes were slinking into sleep when I began sniffing. It was a sensual sexy scent and it aroused Black Dickey.

"Hey. Come talk to me. My life is ruined!" The hall light around the corner feebly illumined the living room. I peered from my pillow into a shadow, but Black Dickey clearly saw images that perked him. Trish stood mid-waist to my gaze and he followed a streak of water that was dripping down Trish's forehead. Unrestrained by the bun, her golden curls glowed from the glimmer of the hall's light. She was draped in a velvet nylon see-through gown and it drooped over the floor. Panty-less and bra-less, he was gazing upon a dream! Since puberty he'd imagined her naked.

It was fuzzy gazing through the fine material but instinctively he strained and could definitely see her mystical upside down triangle. Patches of her dark vaginal hair were staring down at him.

Veering above her pointed pouched out navel, Black Dickey now wide-awake arrived on her fertile round tits. The stimulation stirred a petit mal seizure in him. Quickly snapping out of the trance I finally witness the innocent appeal in the wounded eyes of my friend.

"Come lay with me…sniff-sniff…and hold me." Teary-eyed Trish reached for my hand, gesturing for me to follow her to the bedroom. In my room as children we'd played at love making, this was a different and bigger bed, and everything about us, was bigger.

I slid behind Trish in the bed. Black Dickey squashed into her spongy hips and she cozily placed my arms around her, securely and firmly pressing them against her breast.

As I got good and comfortable and sexually ready, Trish began sniffing out soft cries. This was an unusual and an unnatural position for Black Dickey to be in. I had to calmly constantly talk to my psychopathic Neanderthal urges. To ease Black Dickey's eagerness, to automatically hump, I had to remind myself that I was there to console Trish. I was her therapist. I was there to be a friend to her and a friend exclusively!

Trish twisted around and faced me. Suddenly an edgy quiver attacked Trish's body and she cried like a baby.

"Kayin that nigger's beating on me!" Huge drops of tears over-whelmed her eyes and cries mixed with a twisted sadness mauled her face.

"God damn him!" I had a sudden glimpse of her husband and if I could choke a mental picture of the bony runt he would be dead.

We embraced and Trish wept into my shoulder.

"I can't go back to a man like that!" She declared, and tears flooded her eyes again and she made a hurt aching holler and the awful pain caused her face to contort again.

I began to caress my friend's body with caring gentle strokes until she fell asleep in my arms. Black Dickey limped into catnaps until finally he wilted into a snooze.

Chapter Seven

I woke up Christmas morning with an angel in my arms.

White light frizzles, a making of a mustache had grown on my childhood fairytale princess, but I could still see the spryness of a five-year-old on her face. I watched Trish's body inhale and exhale and noticed a light snore wobble her nose. Thrashed all over her head, Trish's golden hair appeared like a crown that was tilted on the queen. The all night cozy closeness of our bodies and our present embrace had awakened Black Dickey. He yanked into the squishiness of her hips, eagerly desiring to salute this beautiful royal leader majestically!

I eased out of our entanglement, slid from the bed, tiptoed into the bathroom, gripped Black Dickey and gave him the pleasures he'd been denied all night in the moral world.

Water offers me a different release. Spraying the warm tingling liquid on my skin makes me breathe easier and better. I can actually feel the cells in my body replenishing. My muscles relax and my thoughts are freed.

Early morning, bubbly, bright and naked, as I dried off I had an inspiration. My hard working loving Mamma was asleep in one room and Trish was in my bed, the memories of the first loves of my life mellowed me into a generous *Feliz Navidad mood.*

Usually I'm not the chef in the family. I'm an only son raised by a single mother and the grandson of a farm girl who was raised in southern traditional cooking. I was *Mamma's little helper,* a country boy at heart and I had spent a ton of time out in the sun growing every eatable vegetable imaginable. Fresh from the garden into Mamma's kitchen, I grew up breaking lettuce, picking bugs and worms off greens and removing the stems. Mamma had me shucking corn, pealing potatoes, shelling peas, washing pinto beans until the water wasn't brown and then transferring them into more water until they swelled. I was taught how to broil, boil, bake, fry, and prepare an assortment of casseroles, stews, and soups. I've gutted a pig, caught and cleaned fish, wringed a chicken's neck and de-feathered the bird. I've even fed and milked cows, but I've never had the heart to slaughter the big friendly-eyed animals. In our house it was Mamma who did the daily duties of cooking. On Christmas Day Mamma and Trish will awaken to the aroma of a twelve pound stuffed turkey, and sniffing the tangy fragrance of nutmeg. I'd learned how to nestle this sacred ingredient into made-from-scratch pumpkin, sweet potato, and pecan pies.

The pies were done, black-eyed peas, collard greens and the yams were simmering, and the big bird had almost finished baking. One by one the two drowsy women in the house stumbled into the kitchen.

A smirk mixed with pride and surprise managed to appear in Mamma's sleepy gaze. Mamma strutted to the counter and dipped her finger into the sweet potato pie.

"Woo! That's good stuff! Yum! Yum! Yum!" Mamma gave me a wink and a big grin that said, "That's my boy!" Then she began to do what I knew she would, she proceeded inspecting and taking over her kitchen. Opening the oven she plunked a fork in the turkey and the chef began sniffing all the pots and pans on the stove.

Nuzzled with her hands tucked inside her Christmas red silk robe, Trish sauntered into the kitchen. Her eyes were sleepy and she leaned her head to one side. She looked like a grumpy little child. From sleeping on it, Trish's long silky uncombed golden-hair had been squashed. It was lopsided and swayed in the same direction her head was slanted. If I didn't recognize the moods of my grown-up cover girl the imbalance of her head would appear that the weight of her mane had influenced the bend in her neck. Similar to the way birds are alerted when danger is near and the group disburses and flies away, or when the seasons change and the flock cruises south for the winter; I knew my childhood sweetheart's head tilt was due to her sensitive moody nature.

Drawn to the flavors, Trish shuffled her furry house-shoes over to a vessel on the stove where Mamma awaited holding the top. Mamma dipped a wooden spoon inside the pot of black-eyed peas and stuck it under Trish's nose. Trish sniffed the aromas and Mamma began to spoon-feed her like she was a baby.

"UMM! UMM! UMM! This flavor umm-umm...savors in segments...throughout my entire mouth. UMM yes, this is good!" The food seemed to perk her signature impish smile. She flounced her hair to the other side and her eyes shot wide open. The pin-up girl assumed another fickle photogenic pose.

"I should've married you!" Trish said in a lively flirt as she tossed her tresses backwards. I diagnosed the flirt, as innocent and assumed lobbing her locks was the disgust she passionately felt in the partner she'd chosen. I also knew her teasing remark was a for sure sign she knew I still lusted for her.

"Leave my son alone." Shaking her head and cutting her eyes at our guest's naughtiness, good-naturedly Mamma shoved her shoulder against Trish's.

I believe the reason our family didn't have a Christmas tree that year—in fact we hadn't even bothered decorating at all—was because of my arrest. Mamma and I had been reasonably happy regardless of the penalties of living as second-class citizens in Oklahoma City. But this time the consequences of my circumstance had agitated a host of melancholy feelings and they were affecting our household.

The naked winter trees out in our backyard peeped through the living-room window at Mamma, while she gave me a video camera for my Christmas present. In that space, usually our Christmas tree offered us privacy for this tender moment. I hugged and kissed Mamma when I offered her the Christmas treat I'd bought.

Set on 350 degrees for four hours the twelve-pound turkey was done and eatable. I turned the temperature down to 200 degrees and allowed the bird to saturate in its own juices. On Christmas Day I wanted every bite of the bird to slice like butter. I wanted the flavor to savor and hang around on their tongues, sort of like the love I had for them.

Overnight Trish's cell phone recharged and she called her parents in Houston. They were celebrating the holidays with her grandparents. I found a football bowl game on TV. At halftime I tuned out the gala festivities long enough to pay attention to the commotion in Mamma's bedroom. The ladies were giggling like teen-agers, probably remembering old stories, and likely laughing at some of my misadventures.

My fly girl assumed her final pose for the evening. Trish was born authentically exquisite from head to toe. Clothes were costumes she used to hide her exotic mysteries. From the hallway she entered the living room and our holiday masquerade show had begun. Fluffed and parted in the middle Trish's long golden locks pranced and framed her beautiful face. Her hair highlighted the impish alluring attributes of her dimples. The childlike devil-may-care pixie had her unique skin care signature, a natural moisturizer that gave her mellow-yellow creamy complexion a glow. The elegance of a purple long-sleeve cashmere tunic turtleneck emphasized the smooth precision of the queen's royal forty-inch breast. Her short black cotton Fiji wrap skirt fitted teasingly inches above her knee high Franco Sarto Barco black leather stretch boots and the accessorized three inch heels placed her on a pedestal that teasingly showcased her sex appeal.

Aunt Betty baked the best tasting apple pies a human body could stand! She strutted nonchalantly through the front door in a pair of snow-white slacks and I quietly heard her Christmas red zip-neck fleece pullover singing 'Jingle Bells'. The outfit articulated her trim magnetic physique. Whiffs of her delicious goodies streamed five feet in front of her.

No make-up, country and ordinary, Mamma wore fashions that gave dignity to her no non-sense persona; her clothes were expressions of the prestigious symbols of her life. A poppy floral pin-tuck dress with shoulder pads and soft pleats gave Mamma a conventionally graceful neck to ankle profile.

Second classed in the perceptions of many white Oklahomans, Mamma, Aunt Betty, Trish, and I gathered around the festive table I'd prepared.

Most of my life I've learned bible verses. At four years of age "Jesus wept" were the sentiments I use for biblical prose and the poetic phrase became my mealtime blessings. On my tenth birthday Mamma demanded that I originate a reason to thank God. Bashfully, with my eyes shut and head bowed, every appreciation had fifteen-second intermissions. I managed to bless the cake and candle, the air and the sunshine, and of course Mamma. At the end I thanked the Creator for giving us life.

"That was a fine blessing son! You should always say and do what you know." Nodding, she continued. "As the young man of this house, this'll be your responsibility for all our meals from now on."

Mamma bit into a piece of cake and gave me an adamant smile. Since that time that's the way meals in our home have been.

Inspired by the Christmas season and the individual qualities of the people before me, the prose I used for our blessings were the unique gifts each had added to my life. We held hands and there was an empty chair for Danny.

Thanksgiving, Christmas, and New Years Day—these were holidays where African American second class households stuff themselves just like there relatives, white Americans.

After dinner we all had evening plans. I escorted Trish across the front yard.

"Hold up Kayin." We stopped at the edge. Trish groped her coat pocket.

"Good thing Daddy hid some keys in the back yard." She popped out a set of keys, and wrestled another trinket out. The package was tiny and cutely decorated, she handed it to me. Green jingle bell designs were in a sea of red and a blue ribbon was tied like shoelaces around the neatly wrapped Christmas gift.

"Feliz Navidad, this is for my handsome homey!" Chilled fog and a Spanish accent steamed from Trish's luscious crimson lips. Tiptoeing on her three-inch heels, hugging my shoulders she pulled my lips down on hers.

Trish was skipping off in Christmas' frostiness and was half way across the street; and she'd left me horny and perplexed. I ripped the gift open. It was a bottle of Viagra pills.

"The next time we do it I want to make sure you're hard and ready!" Trish yelled with her back to me but I could feel her naughty gaze penetrating my soul.

In less than an hour the prairie town's winds gust were up to eighty-five miles an hour. The little Camry fought through the surges. Christmas was one of the less lit days of the year and the light had disappeared by the time I arrived at Loretta's house at 5:30. Loretta and I had plans to exchange gifts and see a movie.

I gave Loretta her Christmas gift. It was a present for a busy up and coming professional woman. That's what I thought of when I shopped for her. A *Gateway* computer and it was last year's model. I had added more speed and memory to the used lab-top. Polished it until it sparkled. I stuck the computer inside a leather carrying case, wrapped and tied a red ribbon around it. As she observed the awkwardly figured bundle, I watched Loretta slip slowly into anxiousness.

"Ah…just what I needed!" She planted a soft kiss on my welcoming big smiling lips.

My charming Christmas gift form Loretta was a digital XM Satellite radio. I hooked the system up to the Camry and plowed through the winds en route to the theater.

Because Trish had kept Black Dickey awake last night, I dozed off into a snore several times during the movie. Each catnap cost me a nudge and some hard stares from Loretta.

Powerful air-streams shoved Loretta grandmother's three bedroomed framed home into a settling shudder. The almost tornadic winds roared against Loretta's bedroom window. Maybe it was our fear and the sound of the bluster that caused us to clutch together tighter. Cozily, Black Dickey wiggled with Loretta's half rhythms and as he twisted deeper into her storm shelter we both experienced a bunch of new and wild ecstasies. When Black Dickey would propelled his head upward, he repeatedly ascertained the joy of his Christmas present and Loretta's clitoris was the gift that kept on giving. Nature's powerful gust had the two erotic instruments perpetually embracing, kissing, and dancing to Opera, some Old Negro Spirituals, some Ragtime, some Be-pop, some Jazz and blues, and some old time rock n roll and soul. They skipped over hip-hop and Loretta's clit and Black Dickey hit their stride with William Tell's Overture of The Lone Ranger. The robust surges had Black Dickey bumping Loretta's clitoris like he was riding Silver and Loretta's flimsy backbone bucked as if her G-spot was being punched with spurs. Finally the pleasure monster invaded the bed. *Hi-ho Silver!* Climaxing simultaneously into orgasmic seizures our bodies abruptly resemble two out of rhythm drunks attacking each other. Feliz Navidad!

On the eve of the New Year, a breezy spring heat of seventy-five degrees blew through the naked winter trees and scattered dead leaves up and down streets and over yard after yard. Mamma and I ate black-eyed peas at Loretta's grandmother's house. In the company to the two religious monarchs, no alcoholic beverages were served.

"It's best to stay off the streets and away from all those fools." With a corncob stuck between her thumbs and index fingers, Mamma shook her head, agreeing with the wisdom of Mrs. Graham.

"Did anyone see the exquisite, almost mansion-like, homes middle class blacks own in Atlanta?" Everybody ceased chopping down and waited on more good news or an explanation for my sweetheart's revelation.

"There was a segment featured on '60 Minutes' a couple of weeks ago." Loretta began to initiate a soft personal eye contact with her listeners. "Educated, hard working, middle class African Americans were living in spacious brick homes down there." Her optimism was met with our shared doubtful glares. Loretta lowered her head, forked up a taste of cinnamon coated yams. Secretively, she eyed up at me giving me a go-along-with-me gaze.

Seconds passed and finally Mamma emphatically said, "After almost five hundred years in this country it's about time we got something decent." This time it was the elder Mrs. Graham doing the agreeing by nodding.

"How would you like to live in Atlanta after graduation Kayin?" The idea of moving away brought loss into the gaze of our guardians. My naive lover's question transported us away from the New Year's celebration. Big eyed, the women gawked in silence and awaited my answer. Although I had never officially proposed marriage to Loretta we all understood matrimony was more than likely in our future, but that ritual would be secondary and take place after our main cap and gown ceremonies.

"I'm sure that as soon as a black person graduates college they can't afford the cribs illustrated on 60 Minutes. Even though that TV show wants the world to believe we've come that far, I don't believe America gives gifts to us like that." The conscious spirit of a collective history of African American grief appeared on the two women's aged frowns, slowly lowering and shaking their heads, they were agreeing with me. They eased back to the festive dinner while my lover injected a jagged stare in my direction.

Loretta's sharp gaze caused my heart to skip a beat and that irregular rhythm made me think. As we began to break bread, loom and doom had hung in the air over my upcoming trial. Changing gray skies into blue, Loretta had tried to passionately insert inspiration into all of us. Probably not realistic but she was the most optimistic. She had suggested that we had a future. Black Dickey sank between my legs. He began feeling the sting and meaning Loretta's prudent gesture held. He probably wasn't getting any loving on New Year's night.

After dinner I drove Mamma home and quickly doubled back to Loretta's place. As I approached the porch Black Dickey squirmed like a dog with his tail tucked between its legs. I knocked, hoping to be exonerated and see if we could get past my innocent disagreeable gesture. I loved her and she needed to know that. I needed her comfort and support. And Black Dickey and I needed a serving of her black special peas for good luck!

Surprisingly after only a little begging by midnight I was given permission to invade Loretta's bed.

Soon the fireworks and gun blasts of all the black gangster cowboys, the hillbilly white boys, and the decent gun totin' citizens of the red state in prairie-town U.S.A. were muffled. Black Dickey's head was tucked inside Loretta's soundproof castle of ecstasy; celebrating, he brought the New Year in with his own version of a bang.

***

School didn't start again until mid January. In the meantime, I worked more hours at Wal-Mart. The anxiety of living and not knowing what was going to happen with my impending trial lived with me during the downtime. Violently, I wanted to hit or take a swing at something or somebody, to ease the fear, tension, and frustration. Instead of hurting someone or tearing something up I decided to use my bare hands to build Mamma a gift. *"Home Depot"* supplied the lumber and starting from scratch, I began to assemble new cabinets for the kitchen. The Internet was a source of instruction plus I had the assistance of a technical book from the library.

Understanding architectural drawings, using a saw and hammering all used to be awkward tasks for me. Growing up I busted fingers, drove nails in crooked and mistakenly with a saw I invented innovative mathematical angles. I learned carpentry skills by the seat of my pants. Every time I screwed up, in those painful moments, that's when I really missed my dad. "It was the money!" I was eight years of age when I overheard Mamma confiding in Mrs. Green. "Most of the time we argued about not having enough money."

Then, at twelve years of age, Mamma unburdened her heart to me.

"Your father was angry the way white folks treated him here in Oklahoma City. He wanted to escape to the West Coast." Memories of what a departed father felt and craved were the only consoling comforts I had of him while I was budding into my own life.

On January 6, I was in the sound insulation of our garage and in the middle of striking the hammer, I barely heard the phone ringing. It was my attorney, Mrs. Lora Mae.

"I need to meet with you and your mother tomorrow!" Instead of her usual confident assuredness there was an uncertain urgency in the chubby woman's flat southern tone.

"Is everything ok?" I tried not to mimic her insecurity but I'm sure she felt my uneasiness.

I heard office clatter in the background and I felt Lora Mae shelter the phone with her palm. I heard her whispering to someone.

"Uh no, everything's fine. We need to plan your case...that's all."

Maybe she was busy and everything was ok. But I couldn't shake the lingering feeling of doom and it stayed with me into the afternoon. I cut uneven boards and the hammer hit my hand more than my aim struck the nails. I didn't worry Mamma with the weight I felt from the call, I only shared with her what Lora Mae had told me.

Mamma's day shift and her overtime didn't agree with Lora Mae's office hours. I was a grown man and this was my case. I decided to meet with Mrs. Williams alone.

It was overcast, blustery and cold that night. I stood outside on the porch and stared into a dreary blue half moon. The strong winds were pushing strands of gray clouds across the sky. But it appeared as if the mysterious darkness that surrounded the moon was causing the streaming gray matter's flow. Closing my eyes, I ventured into a more intimate darkness. I began imagining and visualizing the golden-brown dead grass that was across every yard in our neighborhood. As I held my head up towards the heavens tears streamed from both corners of my eyes. Reflection and an instant clarification defined my weepy dreariness. I realized I was unleashing dread. I pictured and felt the heartbreaking emotion racing and screaming around the astrophysical universe.

The next day I drove downtown to my attorney's office. Walking toward Lora Mae's building the top of my body curiously twisted and gazed over the traffic, down the street and up to the jailed windows of the police station. Shivers of fear crawled through my overcoat and overwhelmed the breezy chills my body was feeling; it was panic causing me to shudder.

"McGregor" "Williams" & "Shannon" Law Office was painted on the window of the entrance to the office door. I must've been in shock on my first visit. I only remembered seeing Suite 105 with *"Williams"* imprinted on the glass.

The receptionist had her ginger blonde head tilted; she was busy typing on the computer. Gazing down on her, I could see black roots underneath the exterior color. She elevated her face and I felt her instincts involuntary do a double take. From behind the desk, hesitantly, she gawked at me from my shoes right up to the top of my six four frame. I was sure she'd seen black clients in her office before. I was also sure the opposite sex of a species could automatically feel a physical attraction. Even though it was un-cool, inappropriate behavior for a white woman in Oklahoma to have those sensations for a black man, I knew she was checking me out. I'd never seen a direct, overt flirt from a white woman. I had to rely on my own animal intuition. I'd seen this unusual animalistic, involuntary reaction before and I'd witnessed white women fret and embarrassingly retreat and douse water on their fiery biological natures.

The receptionist was in her late twenties and her reaction ignited the curiosity of Black Dickey and he began speculating. What color were her vaginal hairs and how pleasurable he'd feel sliding inside her. But he and I knew, in Oklahoma, that opportunity would never happen.

"I'm Kayin Jackson. I'm here for my two-thirty appointment with Counselor Williams." There was nothing sexual with her gawk this time. Even though there are many of us who speak as I do, a lot of southern white folks seemed amazed by a black man that used correct English. After her brief awkwardness once again she composed herself and offered me a seat.

"*Newsweek*," "*Sports Illustrated*," "*PC World*," and then I was the one culturally inebriated. On a glass coffee table in a downtown Oklahoma City office, scattered among a pile of reading materials, I spotted a copy of *Oprah's* magazine. Wow! Oprah could get into places that we homeys were not allowed.

Wearing a red bow tie with a white shirt, a short, slender Peabody looking white man with a receding hairline stepped from the hall that lead to the intimate offices. He looked around and gaped underneath his thick glasses until he saw my face.

"K-a-a-n Jackson." I was the only one sitting in the waiting area.

"That's Ky-ye-en." I said. I'm always slightly disturbed by the way most southern whites mispronounce my name.

"Miss" Lora Mae will see you now." Was Lora Mae's down-home southern sweet-tempered charisma just an act or was it her way of being marketable? She'd shaken hands with Mamma and me and had requested we refer to her as Lora Mae. I stood and towered over the Peabody look alike. I tilted and gazed into the eyes of this puny white man. He fidgeted. He didn't say Mrs.; he'd said "*Miss*". I began figuring, this was his southern way to say, '*nigger*', *show some respect to a white woman*. I thanked him with a nod and aggressively stepped around him.

When I entered, Lora Mae had her head down. She was busy searching through all the messily scattered papers on her desk. Without gazing up and formally acknowledging my presence, she tipped her head motioning for me to have a seat.

After sitting for a few seconds…"Do you know Robert Johnson and uh…Jarvis Conrad?" She spoke rising her head and faced me. Jarvis, I recognized was one of the passengers arrested with me and I assumed Buddy's real name was Robert.

"Are they the two guys that were sent to jail with me?"

"Yes!" Emphatically Lora Mae retorted.

"No I don't know them. Like I told you earlier, I met them the morning we were stopped by the police."

"Are you sure?" She gawked intensely at me. It was as if she was attempting to see into my soul. This white woman, I assumed had limited contact with black folk and was trying to use whatever perceptional abilities she'd developed with her other black clients and was trying to see if my reactions could give her a hint, if I was lying.

"No. I told you I met them that morning." Briefly lowering her head, indicating she was not convinced but moving on.

"Well." She scratched her nose. "They're bad guys on probation with previous drug convictions. Did you know that?" She gave me another dead gawk.

"Look. Lora Mae, I don't know them. They don't know me!" I said defiantly. Dead silence became the other person in the room.

"They both made bond." Downheartedly, gingerly raising her left eyebrow the professional white woman professed. "The district attorney's office wants to try all of you in one case. I've argued for a separate trial. I believe the judge is going to go along with the DA. Those guys have violated probation, mistakenly they were released and I don't believe they'll show up for court."

In that report and in Lora Mae's frail tone I was sensing all of my optimism about her, trusting she had an all embracing loving relationship with the DA's office, that she was part of the inner circle of white people who had power over people's future, that perception dissipated. Black Dickey became as feeble as the gradual slope that was taking over Lora Mae's posture. Pathetically her body said she was having reservations about my case.

"So what does that mean? I snapped. My whole body became an angry muscle and that force made the fat on Lora Mae's jaws jiggle.

"Crack cocaine is a mandatory sentencing offense. It'll be hard to work a deal." Lora Mae's assessment was getting bleaker. My case was beginning to look as lifeless as a Native American's heartbeat was at 'Wounded Knee.''

Banging on the cluttered papers on the white lawyer's desk I cried out. "I'm innocent! I don't do drugs and I didn't put any drugs in my car. There's got to be another way out of this mess!"

The physical disgust I expressed made this white woman's whole body quiver. My anger had frightened the heavyset white woman. Assessing, as I gazed into her frightened cat eyes, our first private adventure into the essence of our black and white relationship was making me afraid of this moment and she was obviously scared shitless.

"Where...uh...where's your mother?" Or I'm calling the police—that's what I felt Mrs. Williams wanted to add when she asked for Mamma. Behind her gold-rimed glasses, Lora Mae's feline eyes were terrified. Now she was cautiously watching me closely and had slightly recoiled backwards in the black leather chair. I had my overcoat tucked under my arm and I was wearing a gray wool suit, decently dressed as a businessman. But in her white Oklahoma eyes, I was an angry black man and she was a white woman and we were secluded.

I exhaled and I fought and resisted but I knew I needed to ease this white woman's fear.

"My mother's working today." The guardedly carefully chosen words came forward in a calm tone.

Leaving the reception area I didn't bother to notice if the receptionist was gawking at me sexually and when I left the building with my head down I wouldn't permit my eyes to dare peep in the direction of the police station.

Chapter Eight

"Eke-ah…! Woo…whoa…woo!" Loretta begrudgingly released the pleasurable moans. Trudging against her vaginal walls Black Dickey slid half way inside her landing the middle of him inside her creamy slush. The sensual melodies of *Luther* were in the background. Loretta positioned her knees even with her head and Black Dickey rolled slower and then twisted in deeper.

"Woo-whoa-woo!" He bumped against her clit and this time the moan came as a blissful cry. Loretta's backbone was arching and with the power packed shrills oozing out of each of our rhythm thrusts my spine curled and started reacting with her smooth flexes. We were flimsy like two cats. Instinctively her hips spread wide opened and automatically when her hips wiggled this was an intimate signal to Black Dickey, she was telling him she was ready for some bang-bang substantial penetration.

"Eke-ah-Woo-whoa-woo!"" The whine this time was more from the tempo changes our bodies were making. We were relaxing into each other and becoming one with her was always exhilarating.

Moments later and the animal in us came completely alive and we became the passions of our desires!

My tongue licked Loretta's ear and I whispered, "Ah Eke-ah…!" My body flipped into spasms and Black Dickey shook loose and filled the plastic glove with orgasmic juice. Sweaty and sticky, Black Dickey gasped his final breath. He had performed hard blue-collar labor, worked the twat that he loved, and was pleased with his work. He beamed with self-esteem. If there was a TV set, a cold beer, or a couch available, he was collapsing, and watching the game.

I rested on top of Loretta and exhaled in the sounds of our settling heartbeats. Since no game was on and my Christian principled lover didn't stockpile beer, Black Dickey felt completely safe stewing in the warmth of her juices. As he snuggled against her vagina's all encompassing embrace I heard him whisper. *"I don't want to move."* After the depressing appointment with Lora Mae, hiding and sinking into Loretta's affections were the only saving graces for that day.

All the overtime I was able to accumulate at Wal-Mart ceased after the first month of the New Year; the stringent, stingy giant cut me back to no more than thirty-eight hours a week, two hours short of receiving any real benefits. Since I was only part-time the company had me on duty three weekends out of the month.

Before work, I spent half the time interpreting and constructing the architectural design for the cabinets and the other half I was in agony over my other case. Building Mamma's cupboards was becoming more of a lesson in endurance than a labor of love. One day, as I hammered, I drifted in and out of the here and now. I saw the white officer aiming the shotgun at my head. Slamming the hammer down on my pinky brought me back to reality. Later, as I was sawing, a tape played over and over in my head. I was debating if I'd used bad judgment by allowing two unknown black guys into my car. A splinter slid up another finger and snapped me out of the guilt driven emotional disturbance. Finally I was seduced by smell and the foul squalor of the jail overpowered the labor of love feeling. I was done for the day.

Was I responsible for this whole damn mess? Was I using the cabinetmaking gift for Mamma to somehow unconsciously punish myself for even having to face jurisprudence?

I was frustrated with my lack of ability to break through the skin barriers that kept me from effectively communicating with white folks in Oklahoma. Our typical conversations began with the changes in the weather and that lead to lot of nothingness and that lasted for a few more awkward seconds. I wish I'd had a model to follow but I didn't know of any blacks in Oklahoma City that had first-class relationships with whites. I'd never been inside a white person's home and I didn't know any black person that had.

School started on Monday and for the next few weeks I was in and out of a funk. As I sat in the classrooms I saw professors lecture in slow motion. I was suspicious of the wisdom they offered. Were they brainwashing me? At times I found myself stuck in a daze. I was trying to analyze, figure out how different the world was for the white students. Some days I would pick one out of the bunch of blondes, brunettes, and redheads and make an effort to pierce through their hair and understand how prejudice worked in their brains? Did they have a neurobiological sticky substance transferred in their DNA? And did this gene make it necessary for them to place their needs ahead of mine? Underneath their different hair colors, how many of them saw me as a nigger just like the cop had. Identifying, understanding, and trying to recognize and realize the real relationship that I had with my fellow white collegians became more important than what any teacher was saying.

I was already paranoid of cops but now every time I drove the streets of Oklahoma City, if I spotted a squad car, I automatically began to probe the officer's physic. How many blacks had they arrested and humiliated, beaten and maimed, or even killed? Driving the roads themselves became a guide to deeper explorations. The troopers with this evil DNA, how potent were the genes generations ago and how dreadful had they treated my ancestors? Fearful evaluations of white people in Oklahoma City would creep into my awakening thoughts like the night's darkness bleeds into a sunny day's light.

By the beginning of March, on a fine bright day, I was serenaded into a mellow consciousness by an early spring robin. Perched on the ground underneath my window, the bird appeared mesmerized by a stunning budding red tulip. Enchanted, the spring bird began performing a ballad with a poised cadence that washed away my sins and glorified the flower's birth.

After eating breakfast, I bathed and as I shaved Lora Mae called again with the sordid details of the trail. This time she explained my dire situation in an even bleaker tone. She had tried to get the case thrown out because the police had performed an improper search but the officers said we were stopped because of suspicious behavior and the drugs were in plain sight.

"If only it was cocaine." Worn out and exasperated the white woman prayed hopelessly for a different world. *And, if only I was white I completed her thought.* Cocaine was a more potent and a more expensive version of crack therefore it was a white man's drug with lesser penalties, negotiable punishments.

Lora Mae's last effort had been to see if she could bargain for a guilty plea. If the district attorney would consider me a first time offender then a conviction would mean probation instead of prison. I wheezed at the disturbing conciliatory second prize! I had done nothing wrong. And Mamma had slaved and lived a life of sacrifice in order for her only son to see better days. How would she feel? She was my shero! I couldn't shame her dreams by being a convicted felon.

But the prosecutor denied offering me that measly subsequent pacification. Consultations between Lora Mae and the DAs office had halted. The court date for the four black, hip-hop, crack drug dealers was set in two weeks.

Fear paralyzed me. I was losing hope of ever living and experiencing my dreams. Panicky I decided to ditch school and work and just sit back and analyze my life. But while I was scrutinizing I got lost. I began to submerge into a bottomless pit of despair.

With the shade drawn in my room I hunched down in an old antique rocker. The chair had belonged to my grandmother. Like a merry-go-round, I swayed back and forth living in horror and speculation of an unknown future.

"Kelly" made fun of "Regis," on "The View" Barbara Walters tried to hide her political views," and on "All My Children" and "One Life To Live" the cast members dedicated their lives to living through dramatic dilemmas. The crisis that I was facing wasn't personified in any of the scripts on daytime television. The ladies didn't discuss my life on The View; Regis lived on Park Avenue and his dreams carried him on a one way ticket to Notre Dame; and on the soaps no white person, nor was there a black character facing jail-time because of his or her complexion.

Oklahoma was third in the nation in sending African Americans to prison. My father wanted to escape the state for a more humane life. Did living in this town mean living with this great disconnect with whites? Was a black person shooting dice and was it only a matter of time before the dice rolled snake eyes and they crapped out? And what if that black person lost their freedom, or ended up shot dead by the police? I asked questions I felt my father had already asked and answered.

For the next twelve days, ditching school and work, after Loretta had fed Black Dickey's appetites, I retreated to my bedroom and sloped in Grandmother's rocker. Instead of studying and pre-paring for examinations I was being educated and entertained by slowly swinging into a rhythm of misery.

Tossing and turning, a day before my trial, I awoke before dawn, restless. I sprang out of bed and jumped into my sweats. It had been a while since I'd jogged but instinctively that morning my body was compelled to move. A silver quarter moon, fading into the western horizon, greeted me. A light southern breeze drift-ed through my manicured, miniature mustache and soaked into the contours of my skin. As my footsteps approached the end of the block, from behind a lofty oak fence, I heard the barking of the Harper's shepherd. The harsh noise jeered and momentarily threw me off rhythm and inspired me to move faster. I dashed around the corner, down several blocks until I was out of the neighborhood, away from the inhabitants of the lower middle class working fami-lies of Park Estates. I passed dark open fields and shady wooded areas, my heartbeats were pounding, and after a mile outside the neighborhood I slowed to a trot. A cardinal flew a few feet over my shoulder, squawked, as if to say "Hi," or "Good morning," or "Move out my damn way!" The wayward flying creature disappeared into the dim dawn. On my way home, the past jogged inside my sneak-ers. A childhood memory crawled in me and snuggled. Along this very roadside, a gang of us had traveled a trail and it lead to our secret creek in the woods.

Breathing heavy, peering through faint light and overgrown weeds, I spotted the entrance. Tall wild weeds had overshadowed the narrower dirt path, probably because it was less traveled by today's youngsters and nature had taken over. I cut sharply into the passageway and headed for the water.

As I jogged I began seeing myself as a child. Agile and on autopilot and without looking down I skipped over small branch-es and rocks on the trail. I was sweating and skittering, fearless of tripping over an unseen object. I knew my feet were delivering me to the old thick branch. The bough was a huge limb that had fallen across the water. A foot wide and five feet long, the branch hovered only four feet above the three feet deep clear streaming waters. And at the tender ages of eight, nine and ten fantasyland lived on that bridge. With our individual illusions and our collective adolescence's imaginations we used the stick to practice our balance—walking the tight rope we called it . We would skip and dash across; someone was always pulling or pushing and someone was always splashing in the water. For the lower middle class children of Park Estates, the forestry fun spot was economically affordable and this was our circus in the woods.

The rain and snow, weather and time had withered the old oak's color. It had been over ten years since my last visit. I was bigger and as I gazed around the world of my childhood playground, the surroundings appeared smaller and a far cry from frolicking in a wonderland.

Green moss, scrawny twigs, and other vegetation had grown on the dead log. Beneath the shallow use-to-be clear waves, the silver pebbles were dingy.

Impulsively, I had a desire to climb on top of the withered log— so I did. Carefully I eased onto the branch and then flexed my two hundred twenty pounds to see if it was steady. It was. I advanced to the middle of the log and decided to sit.

Staring at the soiled rocks brought on a nostalgic feeling. I recalled as a kid I had sat in this same spot. Sometimes, I'd be completely alone, swinging my legs and daydreaming. I started dangling my legs. Somehow, the rhythms of my legs made me desire to be a carefree child again.

Removing my sneakers and socks, barefooted I allowed the coolness of the water's mist to touch between my toes. The prickles tickled and I smiled.

Silence. I listened to dawn's winds crackling through the trees and heard leaves scatter. I thought I actually heard sounds of water particles bursting between my toes. I leaned across the old branch, closed my eyes and relaxed into nature's echoes. Black Dickey settled down, shrinking. He snuggled and sandwiched himself between my testicles for cover and a pillow.

After hushed moments of meditation a strong gust of wind made the trees rattle. A dog barked and a car horn blew and I saw the image of a judge and a jury. My heart quaked, my toes curled, and Black Dickey trembled.

To have someone judge me when I'd done nothing wrong. The wrong outcome of that verdict was intoxicatingly painful. Excruciating sadness seized me. My mouth became filled with poison spit. I coughed, and spewed the pitiful taste into the stream and watched it dissolve, contaminating the polluted pebbles. The infected suds of saliva made me think of the nasty toilet/water fountain in the jail. Feeling second classed, I wondered about when this was a white neighborhood. White children must have played and stared down into this same brook. Was the water fresher for their eyes? Had blacks defiled the pebbles? Or was this world made for black people to inherit whatever things white people left for us? With my head hanging, I moseyed back to the house.

That evening I held my head high and Black Dickey rose to the occasion. Anticipation and the act of stretching Loretta's vaginal muscles affected both of us that way.

Loretta opened the door that night and I was immediately captivated. She was barefooted. Her dark brown face was clear, no lipstick no eyeliner. I admired and was turned-on by the snugness of her outfit. The dark chocolate sheer material melted into her burnt skin. Resembling a belt, the dress had golden dandelions parading around her petite waist. As she moved the flowers appeared to come alive and sensuously dance. Black Dickey yanked when he saw the way the outfit profiled her pointed nipples! She was bra-less.

Tonight Loretta was the chef. I brought chilled Chardonnay. We'd pre-arranged this cozy night together and although dread and misery had slowly inched each step with us up to this date, the awful feelings were absent tonight. Would this be our 'Last Supper' as a couple? I believe we both felt the pressure of an unknown tomorrow and that evening we consciously made ourselves vulnerable and present for each other. We celebrated like alcoholics on their last binge before going into treatment.

I couldn't take my eyes off her. It was like I was having an out of body experience. Every move she made inspired a precious dream about her. When she sighed as she raised a pot from the oven, and when she slightly sniffed the food and grimaced with bliss, it all reminded me of her sensual moans. In my imagination I saw Loretta's unpretentious appeal for sex. The savory scent of smothered onions reminded me of *Liquid Love,* the potion I'd used to give Loretta her first orgasmic satisfaction.

She forked up a juicy steak and added it to my hefty plate of gravy, mashed potatoes, collar greens, and hot buttered cornbread.

"I bet you're going to love this." Loretta sensuously licked the tip of her tongue over her lips. The robust aroma of black southern gourmet food and a tease from her made my mouth water and Black Dickey was swelling.

Who needed eating utensils as a tool to devour the pleasures before me? I ate like a caveman, tearing into the meat with both hands then sucking the fat flavorful grease off my fingers.

And wow! I couldn't believe what happened next. I thought my horny hormones were playing games with my head. It was straight from the script of an African American X rated video. Dainty Little Loretta performed an agile plunge that was seductive and the lunge landed her exquisitely sleek hips on top of the dinning table. She lifted her skirt enough that I could see she was panty-less. Flat on her back she slithered and using a finger motion she pointed at her twat, then slowly in a sultry southern African American low sensuous tone, "Eat me!"

My eyes inflated—but not as quickly as Black Dickey did! To see the demure schoolgirl completely out of character; the sight of her aggressively demanding exotic sex, for some depraved reason this newness was making my skin ooze with an excessive eagerness for her body! Feverishly, I was hard as steel. Black Dickey was a wee bit jealous that she wasn't seeking pleasure from him first.

I gracefully slid my palms under her firm thighs, eased her dress up and exposed her twisted vaginal hairs. My appetites raged! With a moist tongue I delicately swiped the top of her opening. A rich dark chocolate was what I tasted! She had perfumed her pubic parts with *Liquid Love's Sweet Chocolate Cherry Desires*. I swiped again. Loretta squirmed. I started licking up and down her alcoves and she produced her natural vaginal juice and moaned. She worked her sturdy hips to the sucking circular rhythms of my tongue thrashes. Her quivering thighs made the table rumble. With both hands she rigidly pinned my head against her vulva. My lips were smothered and there was a heavy exchange of our fluids— my spit and her sex juice. "Woo-whoa-woo-shit Kayin!" The academic God-fearing woman squealed.

Up and down I began vigorously slapping the top of Loretta's clit. With my lips pasted to her organ her whole body started riding buck-wild on my head! "Woo-whoa-woo-shit Kayin! Whoa stop! I mean—don't stop! Woo-whoa-woo-shit—wee-sweetie! " Loretta trembled. Her hips began flopping in orgasm haven and so did the dinning table.

She was bubbling and moaning with lusty pleasures when I lifted her half-naked, chocolate aromatic flesh. Blowing on the entrance of her twat I lugged Loretta's exotic scent—along with the spattered ingredients of our dinner into the bedroom.

Loretta's unending spastic progressions had excited Black Dickey. There was a bloating in him in every one of her exasperating breaths. By the time I laid Loretta on the bed pre-cum was trickling down my leg.

While I slipped on the baby prevention protector, Loretta was easing into a comfy lovemaking position. On her back, she was arching her knees even with her shoulders and tilting her head back. This basic acrobatic position seems to open her vagina wider and I knew the gymnastic gesture provided Black Dickey easy access and faster penetration to her hottest erogenous spots. Loretta's black amphibian body was squirming on the sheets; steaming ecstasies had a hold on her. I believe she was submitting; she wanted to take me to the erotic heaven she was already living in, and quickly. And angling her head she was preparing her body for more of the kingdom that would come.

Black Dickey slipped into Loretta's yawning, creamy hole. "Ahh." Animated with ecstasy he wheezed.

"Woo!" Loretta hissed.

"Ah-hum!" Black Dickey said as he rolled in rhythm to Loretta's slippery hip wiggles.

I glared down on her smiles of joy and occasional pleasure squints and suddenly Loretta unbuttoned her huge brown eyes. This would be the first time we would stare into each other's soul hypnotically for most of a love making session.

After riding on top and at a side angle, experiencing the wonders of our robust orgasms, I heaved my exhausted frame and my lifeless penis over on the flexible mattress.

As we lay on our sides, me at her back, gazing at Loretta's earlobe on her perfect chocolate complexion, I spotted a pimple. Piercing into Loretta's big browns seems to have sharpened my senses. I noticed a flaw on her for the first time.

Later as she lay flat on her back butt-naked, in-between her tits I glared at pinch marks; obviously, her bra that fastened in the front had made the imprints. Her color was a shade lighter amid the two round firm dark tits. As we prepared for doggie style Loretta twisted on her tummy and heaved her butt upward. Arched between her coal black cheeks there was an even darker smut sandwiched in her inner hips.

Round three: Loretta was on her knees when she hoisted her vagina over Black Dickey. And for the first time I saw how the rich fullness of her threaded vaginal hair trickled up and as the fur approached her navel the brush, sputtered into baby frizzles. Easing out a gentle wheeze she gradually guided Black Dickey inside. Gazing up at her softball sized, baby-sucking mammary glands, I tugged at the twins. As Loretta slithered back and forth, humping and stroking, finding her rhythm, pleasure squints appeared on the sides of her eyes. Tenderly I pinched her sturdy nipples and then traced a circle of tiny bumps that were around her smoked-colored areolas. I eased my touches to an area that was even softer—her lactiferous. As I compressed them I began imagining, if Loretta were breast-feeding right now milk would be splashing down on me. Underneath her nipples, on top of the outward extending slope, I flexed her subcutaneous, mashing the lobules. Extremely supple, the tissue felt like Jell-O wobbling in the palm of my hands. Automatically I began to squash them like I was a farmer milking a cow. In chorus with my milking Loretta had begun bouncing long stride rhythms. Energized by her moves I gazed up and saw she'd angled her head backwards, her neck muscles were straining.

"Eke-ah ah woo-woo Kayin! An exasperated Loretta heaved the sigh and collapsed on my chest. We breathed together until our respiration paces were meek and we were almost asleep. Loretta lazily winged her leg up and over my frame allowing her dead weight to plummet sideways into the safe soft mattress. I lifted Loretta's lifeless arm and kissed a crimson vein that was in the palm of her hand. Another blood carrier appeared on the only bright part of her wrist and quickly faded into her blackness. Under the shades of her armpit I saw a red pressure point again. Lying sideways, we snuggled face to face and as our eyes closed a black mole smiled at me from the bottom of her lip.

A chill awakened me that morning and with sleepy eyes I saw we were uncovered and butt-naked. The quilt was crumpled on the carpet. For a while the heat left over from our lovemaking had sustained the warmth in our bodies. Black Dickey was rubbing against Loretta's ass and her flimsy body was curled into a bow. One of my arms was flung over her shoulder hugging her tummy and the other was smothered underneath her neck. Seconds after my observations Loretta's eyes were alert.

We got up and a strange silence flirted around us. Quietly we glared at each other and in the depths overshadowing our stare was fear. That day an intimate intense odd terror hovered over our normal routines.

Loretta had the water running when I slid in the shower. The poetry of echoes from water bursting off the floor and wall's ceramic acoustics was what I heard. I eased down and touched the back of her ankle and like a horse her foot rose. Scrubbing the bottom I tried to take snapshot memories of her ankle. The bone was tiny, the texture stout and firm. As I formed foamy suds on Loretta's vaginal fur I watched the gleaming black hairs uncurl and drift into dread-locks. All juiced and leathered her pubic hair resembled a salt 'n pepper afro and it looked like an elderly photograph of Fredrick Douglas.

The last night before and the morning of my trial I was strangely seduced by a power to learn of Loretta's flaws, and the private splendors that made her more than just an ordinary woman. And as I drove home, I remembered thinking, outside of Mamma, this was as close as I'd ever felt to another human being.

Chapter Nine

All the way from the kitchen, sizzling greasy bacon popped, and the aroma hopped out of the skillet, trotted through the dining room, across the living room and when I entered the front door it smacked me in the face!

"Have a seat son." In a blue cotton robe, Mamma's back faced me; as she flipped the pig over on the other side; she was obstructing the frying pan. I sat down at the table. In some ways I identified with the blistering strips of bacon. This was a day we could both be fried and eaten. While Mamma scooped the bacon from the skillet, I gazed at the gray strands in the back of her short perm, and thought, her worries for my life were in those new and fresh wandering threads.

Before getting dressed for my engagement, I quickly completed the project I had begun at the beginning of the year. I hung Mamma's new cabinets on the kitchen wall. I'd painted them charmingly cherry—Mamma's complexion.

Usually only one cup of Java suited me for an entire day. Unusually I sipped on a second steam of the coffee with cream while I suited up nice and neat.

"Save your money and buy quality material that will last." Mamma's sage advice was in the back of my head as I observed my ensemble. Five sport coats and two complete suits waited in the wings. Was I ready for: sexy, cute Oleg Cassini's canary yellow silk; romantic-horny Belvest's chocolate cashmere; funny-flamboyant Arnold Brant's orange khaki; serious-business Ralph Lauren Donegal's gray tweed; or a merrymaking-partying Orvis Signature's windowpane burgundy lambs wool? None fit my mood or the occasion. I couldn't dress flashy for the white sober traditional crowd I was trying to impress. In the back of the closet, an angelic-conservative Arnold Brandt's Mediterranean blue silk wool outfit began to flirt with my affections. The ocean color telepathically told me what I needed and assured me that it would be perfect for these unusual circumstances. *"You haven't done anything wrong and this is how you should be seen."* The marine blue material whispered the idiom like a passionate lover.

I wore blue and Mamma had on a classically conventional cotton white blouse under a gray wool blazer and matching skirt. The spring day was sixty-five degrees and there was a gay freedom in the blustering air. I let my window down on the car's passenger side to absorb the prairie's air. I wanted the breeze to relieve the tension I was feeling.

The courthouse was an extension of the jail. Half of the structure embodied old red bricks and the new portion was made of soft auburn stones. The tiles in the hall reflected the part you were in; mirror-shine vs. a dingy tarnish.

White men and women were fully clad in their predictable business costumes. They clutched their fine leather brief cases as they walked and talked, rushed and discussed, and as they stood in the halls and conferred. These were professionals, folks that I admired and was in-training to become.

When Mamma and I got off the elevator we saw Lora Mae pacing in front the courtroom door. Before we could walk 20 paces to meet her she'd glanced at her watch seven times. Underneath her round glasses I could see her eyes had grown big on her face and her eyeballs were trembling. The meat on her chubby jaws jiggled. She inhaled, stared at Mamma and me and exhaled.

"Your cousin won't be here today. He made some sort of a shady deal with the district attorney's office." Like our previous encounter the therapist-lawyer studied our faces for a reaction.

She watched my temples bulge with fear and anger contorted my face. I had love for Danny but my ass was on the line. He was possibly the only one that could clear me. How was it possible for a man without a paid lawyer, who couldn't make bail was able to pull off a deal? Black Dickey winced. He wished himself to become a belt so that he could whip Danny's ass!

"What kind of deal?" Mamma blurted the question to the panicky professional.

A trickle of snot seeped from Lora Mae's nose. She sniffed then removed a hankie from her brief case and wiped.

"The district attorney's office wouldn't say officially but I'm sure he gave up a drug dealer."

"And what did he get in return?" Mamma cried in a sharp tense tone and the lawyer's nose twitched.

"He's been released and all charges were dropped." Mamma has never tried to hide her anger away from white people and she didn't conceal her rage from Lora Mae. Her whole face puffed-up with emotion and Lora Mae's reaction was to turn and pace in a circle.

"We still have time to plead guilty. Kayin could do one year in lock up in the county and three years probation. That's the best deal they'll probably offer." She inhaled and immediately critically studied our faces.

"I'm not guilty of any damn crime!" In explosive anger I shouted. Individuals of a group near us quickly spread into a pack of white people down the hall, and soon it seemed as if everybody in the building was gawking in our direction. Lora Mae's eyes tweaked. I'd frightened her again and apparently all the white folks at the courthouse.

In front of the crowd of white on-lookers, Mamma scratched her fingernails into the white lady's expensive black suit and yanked her into her body. With her teeth clenched Mamma whispered into Lora Mae's ear, "Lady, you take care of my son!" Being the Christian woman Mamma was, "***bitch***" was silent in her threat.

The courtroom had towering monumental lights and as we entered they began to impose an incredible shrinking feeling on me. The furnishings were exquisitely carved in the French classical manner—the adjudicator's bench, the lawyers tables and chairs, the pews where the jury sat, even the judge's mallet was stained in a lustrous rich maple. For a young guy that began life living in a house with rats chewing inside the walls, jurisprudence's over-hyped setting was extremely intimidating.

The gray haired, white woman, judge had prickly piercing features. Oklahoma's harsh sunshine had engraved wrinkles and made her appear older than what I thought she was. During the proceedings from her lofty pedestal, she would often cut her eyes unsympathetically down on me. And behind her, draped over the entire wall, were four massive headshots—photographs of judges of the past. They all had their own unique solemn frown of distinction. And I assumed these men were on the bench during Jim Crow. And there they were pasted proud, unapologetically. They were honored as the history of justice in Oklahoma City. I wondered how many black families had they hurt, killed, and treated like second classed citizens because of the unjust segregated laws? Intently gazing on them I began studying their faces, and under the influence of suspiciousness I began overtly seeing evil and hypocrisy, egotism and cynicism in their souls. Had any of them intimately ever known any black folk? And that is the question that has haunted me my whole life—the lack of camaraderie between blacks and whites in Oklahoma.

The prosecutor wore thick glasses. He was young, wiry with greasy-hair, a clean-cut white fellow. When he talked to the jury he made hand gestures in my direction, and made a few glances over at me—but never did he ever look directly into my eyes.

Before the proceedings even began, the whole exhibition had already demoralized me. From the authority of the judge's hammer down to the spit shine varnished floors, □an overwhelming pitiful shame had me in flight to somewhere, any place that I could crawl in and hide. Why was I feeling so damn unworthy? I couldn't answer that question.

To start the show, up front on center stage, Lora Mae and I were seated together at a table. There was a carved, dark chocolate pew behind us where Mom and Loretta sat. Spottily filling of the courtroom were people with their own up-coming cases and their worried families.

Diagonally to the left of us was a knee high decorative wooden gate, the entrance to the people who would judge me—the jury's box. My peers, so they say. None of these folks looked like me. The sunshine, the Oklahoma winds and the rainy weather was the total depth of the things we had in common. Instead of a nurturing relationship with white people, nature was our only bond.

With a mule's face she had unusually large lips for a white woman. No matter who was on the stand testifying her eyes would dart down on her silver-plated timepiece.

There was too much make-up on the short auburn haired chubby white woman. She had stretched the buttons to their limits just to fasten up her silk blouse. I hoped it was true that plump folk were friendly.

She sneezed, she coughed, and she blew snot out of her long sharp nose and constantly wiped it with a hankie. The hefty fifty-ish bleach-blond white woman would disrupt testimony and the lawyer's arguments by these perpetual interruptions.

Strawberry hair and a freckle face were behind the academic glasses worn by the white woman in her early forties. Her itchy eyes kept her squinting and her obsessive-compulsive nature caused her to constantly clean her eyewear.

A purple strip ran through her blond hair. She was about my age. Her luscious lips made Black Dickey horny. Her southern big blue eyes would never consider giving him any. Pale was the only emotion inserted on this American beauty, a southern white rocker-raised on blue grass, I thought. She was the hip hop generations counter-part. What did we have in common for her to care about my well being? And, here she was, judging me.

Only one of the two officers that had humiliated me out in the pouring rain showed up to testify, and he was the one that had aimed the shotgun at my head. When I spotted him, a new concentrated version of hate and an unknown fear attacked my psyche.

There he was, on the witness stand, and this time instead of pointing a shotgun at my head and spewing out offensive language, the white cop masterly lied, presenting his new reality of the crime. He insinuated to his audience that as a black man in Oklahoma I had no integrity.

"We had the suspicious vehicle under surveillance at the Villa apartments on Douglas Boulevard and Northeast 16th street." Dressed moderately in a black suit, the good-old-boy police officer pointed me out to the jury.

"The defendant parked, got out of the vehicle, proceeded to walk to a stairway and that lead him to a known drug dealer's apartment. In approximately fifteen minutes the defendant returned with three other black men." "Why is he lying?" whispering angrily, I nudged Lora Mae. "I never got out of the car. And the police cruiser was ahead of us, hiding at an abandoned service station." "Sh-sh-sh!" Lora Mae sternly quieted me. Gritting my teeth I rolled my eyes at my paid protector, thinking, she's suppose to be my inside-of-the-system white person, why isn't she stopping these lies? If this is the way justice works, the polite courtesy of courtroom decorum stunk.

"I believe the drug pick-up, the transfer, happened there. We pursued the defendant and stopped them on 8th and Martin Luther King. My partner and I removed the suspects from the vehicle. I asked the defendant if it was alright to search the vehicle and he approved." With good old boy southern charm the dishonest cop barbed his head in my direction. His description of the incident and stereotypical depiction of blacks as drug dealers was stolen right out of a bad Hollywood script. And his Okie audience—the jury— was on the edge of their seats by the drama, and I imagined them intensely smacking popcorn! This John Wayne, serve and protect, officer was like a brother, an uncle or cousin, someone the jurors knew and trusted. Black Dickey stewed. He was helpless. There was nothing he could do about white folk's perceptions in this city.

When the prosecutor held up the large plastic bag full of drugs the little fifty something redheaded freckled white woman juror snarled her leaky nose. There were slight eye blinks of disgust on some of the juror's stone faces and simultaneously, automatically they all stared at me. Even though they didn't make a sound I could hear loud rumblings. The muffled noise made Black Dickey squirm.

Lora Mae's cross didn't budge the confidence of the white peace officer. What time the cops began to scrutinize our behavior, weather I entered inside a drug dealer's home, and if I gave permission for the search seemed to be immaterial and missing in action in her questions. Anyway I began to assume, like Lora Mae probably had already concluded, a white peace officer's word against a suspected notorious nigger drug dealer would only amplify a belief already believed by the jury. I couldn't compete with the beliefs they already held.

The dean of students at the university, Professor Glean, a white man testified on my behalf. "This young man has good morals and has quality academic standards."

Reverend O. L. Wilson praised the volunteer work I'd done in the community. "I've known this young man his whole life. His mother is a Christian woman and she raised him with God's hands!" Loosening and freeing his large body out of the grip of the tight fit of the chair, the dark skin man became animated; after all he was a southern black preacher.

He spoke to the jurors like he was telling the story of Jesus to innocent children. His sermon begged for his listeners to believe an unadulterated picture that he painted of me; at times, the preacher man had me believing I was the Son of God.

"He's obedient to his mother, the church, and his community! Never ever heard anyone ever say the devil was ever in this young man. This young man loves the Lord!"

Calmly I spoke with an eloquent soft politeness and desperately tried to hide any trace of African culture. I wanted the jurors to see me as one of them. Dressed down in the cool sapphire suit I presented intellect, no Ebonics and no soul to the white folk. With deep affectionate southern sincerity, *have-mercy-on-my-soul* was pumped through my heart in the answers I delivered to my lawyer's inquisition.

Casually Laura Mae strolled over to the jurors, faced them and relaxed her hands on the marble gate. She raised her left hand pointed it at me and twisted her head in the same direction.

"Some of you have sons and daughters...a neighbor or cousin that's hard working! Hard working and attending school." Back and forth her neck moved from me to a stare directed privately at each juror. A sneeze interrupted Laura Mae but her eyes stayed steady on them and me. "...Striving to make a better life for himself...A young man that's trying to contribute to his community. Well that's who this young man Kayin Jackson is."

"Your honor will you instruct Lora Mae to ask her client a question?" In a southern good-old-boy manner the prosecutor rose and unprofessionally used my attorney's first name while addressing the judge for help.

Lora Mae pranced up to me profiling her professional swagger. She allowed me the opportunity to explain my background as a scholarship college student, the contributions I'd made as a tutor, my work experience, and the details of the crime in which I was being charged.

Laura Mae was noticeably shaken when the prosecutor refused to question me. So was I.

The entire trial—testimonials from all lasted seventy-four minutes. Both sides rested.

Down the street in Bricktown, I treated Mamma and Loretta to a crab dinner. Loretta and I were seated on one side of the booth and Mamma was opposite us. I tried to suppress the fear that tormented me. Somehow my panicky suffering submerged into Black Dickey and found life. Nervousness and distress had made him horny. Unable to have privacy in front of Mamma's busy eyes, I found my fingers under the table sneaking and caressing Loretta's ass.

"Eke-ah!" Loretta's unexpected unrestricted erotic echo was an immediate annoyance for Mamma's Christian standards. The moral disciplinarian pursed her lips together and gave me a dead gawk that chastised my poor table manners. But Loretta's semi suppressed exotic outburst had excited my neurosis and Black Dickey was growing. He wanted to do Loretta's slinky little professional ass doggie-style right on the table. The essence of my sudden intense sexual energy had originated from suppressed pain. I was an animal in excruciating agony!

"Can I help y'all?" The ice coffee blond, young, spunky white waitress said, as she appeared at our table with pen and pad. She postured gleefully with an old southern big plastic smile.

As we gazed at each other around the table a treacherous succinct silent rage emerged as our first answer. Then Mamma wisely concisely gave sound to our collective feelings.

"You can give me a guarantee that the changes y'all made on Deep Duce are real. Are African Americans finally getting their civil rights? Y'all done changed the name to Bricktown. These are cosmetic modifications. And I see you standing here serving me, but can you promise me my son's life will be better than the one I've suffered through? Can you do that?" Banging both hands on the table she gawked at the confused and frightened youthful white woman. The white woman began to tremble, her eyes jumped and her hand unsteadily made scribbles on the pad. I thought she was having a heart attack, or maybe she was preparing to run, tear ass and get the hell away from us!

"We'll have three servings of Alaskan king crab legs and the soup of the day." Calmly I ordered. I gazed at the fear in the white woman's eyes then quickly gathered our menus and silently apologetically offered them to her. Still shaking the waitress quickly seized the menus and as soon as she had them in her grasp she high tailed her ass out of our sight. Our harmonized rupture of laugher stalked the waitress' disappearing footsteps. I sort of understood some of the reasons why historically blacks have had to tell jokes and be merry during hard times.

"Old Deep Duce is what this section of town use to be called. It was those train tracks where they unloaded jobs and Oklahoma City entered into the industrial age." Mamma pointed towards the restaurant's window and underneath an over-path we all stared at some abandoned rail cars on the railroad tracks. "On this side of that railroad crossing blacks were condemned to live in isolation—secluded like a virus."

"The first 200 blacks arrived in Oklahoma City in the first land-run." While Mamma sipped her soup, I offered my tidbit of information to the story.

"They were treated like they had leprosy. And those sisters and brothers struggled with less…nothing that you children could possibly imagine. God don't like immorality." Mamma shook her soup-spoon at us.

"Since their parents and some of them had built state and plantation houses during slavery, from scratch these hungry discarded craftsmen built the original structure for this building. They had eminent masonry techniques. The new designers of this café didn't destroy the foundations they only remodeled certain parts." Mamma declared as she chewed crab and sipped on a glass of tomato juice.

"Even before statehood we were segregated from entering most of the stores in downtown Oklahoma City and Old Deep Duce became our uptown. There were black owned grocery stores and after statehood we had our own movie theatre. Since we couldn't socialize with the rest of society we had to build our own settings

for formal ceremonial and gatherings like weddings and gradua-
tions. In the 20's 30's, and 40's, on *The Soup Kitchen Circuit*, Charlie
Christian, Count Basie, and Louis Armstrong played the blues on
Old Deep Duce". There was satisfaction and a God given pride
when she said, "We struggled, suffered, but endured and we're still
struggling, suffering and enduring, and making out with what we
have!" The pain, humility and humanity, the history of Oklahoma's
black citizens was seducing her.

Nibbling on the vegetables in the broth I listened to Mamma
tell more secrets of how we overcame some of the worst horrors
of hell. I began worrying about my own future. I hoped to God by
sharing our illustrious history that this wasn't her way of preparing
me for white justice. How would I ever cope if the jury decided
against me? I chewed hard on the crab.

"Years later as blacks moved east of here, advanced into
more modern facilities, and like any abandoned area, the sacred
rituals of deep duce became the lifestyles of the downtrodden,
pimps, hustlers, gamblers, bootleggers, and of course the ladies of
the night. Gangster drug dealers and broke-ass hobos, gun battles
and knife fights, and broken cheap wine bottles, grotesque sex
and corn liquor was sold in back alleys. Black lust and black bodies are ground into the dust under this modern fashionable establishment's foundation." Mamma twisted her jaws. I couldn't tell if
it was an old angst she chewed on or was the clench for a new
frustration—my current situation.

Mamma held up a teacup and made a toast.

"More than a hundred years since 1907, statehood, here we
sit in the same legroom as whites, should we deny the past pains
they've caused and quietly pretend to enjoy their refined disguised
deviant manners?" Our glasses jointly made a defiant clack to
Mamma's toast.

Underneath the boldness of the toast, jitters shot through the
blood in my veins the same way one hundred proof grain alcohol
would probably quench an alcoholic's thirst. **Paying dues!** *"If your
skin is black in this society somewhere somehow a black person
will sooner of later end of paying for their color, and in a costly
way. Except this reality or go mad"*—the **watershed moment said.**

I was wiping breadcrumbs off my lips when Lora Mae phoned my cell.

"The jury is back." Doom and gloom and expect the worst that's what I heard Lora Mae's non-verbal expressions say.

Fear rushed through me and delivered a statement: **These white folk had convened for less than forty-five minutes on a decision that would affect the rest of my life.**

When I shared the news with Mamma and Loretta, all of our eyes met and twitched.

We finished our dinner and not one word was spoken. On our short ride to the courthouse, dread was the driver.

Behind our private desk, facing the judge, Lora Mae and I stood like we were facing a firing squad. I cut my eyes and stared at the jury. We had just left a landmark institutional location in the city, and over a hundred years ago whites began to make laws to separate blacks from the rest of the world—never had I felt the results of that great divide until this moment.

These people who were judging me, were they English, Irish, Czech, Jews, Germans, Italians, or Polish? Were they of mixed origins? Maybe all of them were a little bit of each.

Searching each of their eyes I felt the hundred years of separation. They didn't know me and I didn't know them.

"**G…..u…..i…..l…..t…..y.**" In slow motion I heard the jury foreman read the verdict to the judge and my heart pounded. Shock had mangled the other words herald at me from the judge.

Like a lost child I peeped around for Mamma. The potency in the head that she'd always held high had slightly tilted, her eyes blinked and her superwoman's face trembled. Loretta was slouched in her seat and her sweet chocolate girly eyes had the appearance of a beaten whore.

"Kayin Jackson I sentenced you to **s…..i…..x…..years in the state penitentiary!**" A quiver was all the protest I could muster when the judge destroyed my life. The jury didn't even see my blue suit all they saw was my black skin. **_Incomprehensive demoralization_** is the feeling I had in this watershed revelation.

"**Defendant is remanded into custody!**" The pointed-nosed white woman slammed the gavel down like a contestant banging a sludge hammer trying to ring the bell and win a prize at the state fair. The prosecution, jury and judge flexed their jurisprudence muscles and had won. We were done. The game was over. The guards appeared out of thin air to collect their prize. Lora Mae stepped to the side. One held out the handcuffs and the other one stood behind me.

Soon I'll wake up out of this lurid dream. This is the delusion I clung to, the denial that entertained me while I was being escorted through the back passageways of the hall of justice. The people we past frowned at me with spiteful eyes. And for weeks the power of believing I would suddenly wake up slowly diminished but the folks running the system would continue their hideous stares.

Repeatedly shifting my eyes left then to the right, I was paranoid in a killer's den. And underneath the fear I was more disgusted with the putrid system that had placed me among the evil.

My case was tried in the state's court instead of the federal system. Both institutions embrace the mandatory six years for crack possession, even for first time offenders. *"White folks get busted for the real cocaine and get to go to the fancy federal lockups. They get to play on tennis courts in tiny white shorts. Black people have to jump into the orange overalls and work as slaves in dungeons."* I'd heard this way of thinking from blacks all my life.

I was handed a baggy oversized orange jumpsuit and even for my six foot four frame there was enough room for two of me in there. My two escorts placed me into the city's holding tank. Another stone box, fifteen by fifteen feet. It housed thirty men. Some short timers, others were awaiting bail, but those like me, we were anticipating transport to county then to one of the state's prisons. My orange appearance separated me from those who wore the misdemeanor blues or were dressed in street clothes. I could feel fear emanating from most of the men without uniforms.

Grooved into the granite were gang signs and phone numbers with illicit messages like *"For some good head call Sandy at 555-8282.* A host of graphic sexual positions were creatively and even entertainingly etched. Ironically they were side by side with biblical verses.

Nauseating piss fumes ate up the air. Sniffing musk from unshaven rusty ass inmates and looking at drunks with dried up vomit in their beards; for a moment the rats that gnawed in the walls when I was a child became a comforting thought.

I felt sorry for one white man who was sentenced to ninety days because he couldn't or didn't pay some over-due speeding tickets. He had no one he could call and he had four dogs locked up in his house without food. He'd already been there for thirty-seven days. Uncertainties, defeat, helplessness and a beaten disgrace lived on his face. Over and over he would tell his sad story to anyone who'd listen.

Chapter Ten

"Joseph Rodgers!" The jailer yelled as he approached our cell. A jittery old white man stumbled to his feet. Behind his trembling frame I believe I detected a smile when he passed by and I assumed his happiness was because he was being released and was looking forward to getting another drink.

I was back inside the city's jail again, and again this time, as the first time, I never completely closed my eyes. As they walked up and down the halls, the guards' cumbersome keys clanged with each step. And through the stone walls I could hear arguments, fistfights, and vicious death threats. Day and night heavy steel doors slammed. I did have brief moments when I rested my eyes, but all those squabbles, seeing prisoners come to blows, the fear of being gutted if I snoozed, was reason to stay alert.

My heart ached for relief; for an image of something in the world that imitated sanity and for me that meant a visit from the angels in my life, Mamma and Loretta.

Soft canary yellow was the shine of Loretta's outfit on her first visit. The bright tint gave her auburn eyes the sparkling qualities of a baby chick. Good! She'd pulled herself together. Soaking through the glass window was the jasmine tang of Christian Dior; the sweet fragrance fired my imagination. I wanted to cuddle and squeeze her. I thought that maybe if I could absorb some of her stern professional grit, somehow I'd stand a better chance of surviving in this violent mad world around me.

Mamma wore a dark plum pantsuit. I don't recall a word that was said that day but their gift was optimism and decency and those spiritual morals reminded me of what I was missing. After Loretta left, I had a first-class hard-on. Mamma's presence echoed and was steeped in the philosophy she'd preached all my life, the idea that I was a precious soul.

On a cloudy Wednesday afternoon, two weeks after my arrival at municipal lock up, I was cuffed, my ankles were placed in shackles and I was chained together with two other inmates. We boarded an old van and were driven two blocks down the street to the county jail. My back ached and my legs cramped like I was an old man. The pains were the consequences of sitting and lying on concrete. And even in shackles a brief step into the outdoors of freedom gave my body a get-up-and-go and inspired goose bumps to trot up my spine.

There was another pleasure form the transfer. Earlier that day a new inmate, an older strapping bull Cajun looking brother was housed in my home. When he arrived I was standing in my usual spot, in the back staring out the window, so he helped himself to my bunk. Every prisoner is issued private bedding, a pillow and blanket. He tossed my bedding on the floor. Before he got totally comfortable I politely, decently, informed him he was using my bed. Big mistake! Civility was a weakness in prison culture. He just laid there and stared up at me with one mean eye and mumbled something vicious. I took the high road and snuggled elsewhere.

Maybe I was projecting my self-conscious fears on them. But burglars, larcenist, forgers, rapist, embezzlers, they all appeared to possess shifty hard beady eyes. And when I found out who the murders were their eyes suddenly became deviant and cold. Naively I moved around in a cloak of fear and those two personas gave crooks reasons to believe they could take advantage of me.

Just from riding two blocks and placed into another building I was processed all over again. Butt naked I was told to spread my cheeks while a burly white man looked up my asshole.

Like the city jail, the county jail had a big turnover in the population. Bailouts were common for the city. And as far as the county, inmates were constantly transferred to prisons or they were completing their time for lesser crimes.

Prisoners in the city lock-up had pre-warned me about the lice infested linen in the county cells. It was early spring and to escape the odorous prison stench the guards would keep the windows propped open for fresh air. In the mornings spanking new air would blow a freezing chill on us. I was avoiding the lice and didn't use any covers. I curled my body into a ball to keep from freezing. I had heard that it was scientifically impossible for lice to infest a mattress; that information was wrong. The bloodsuckers bit my ass all over the frost.

A jailhouse lawyer is a title you could hang on every other inmate. A convict use to only have to do half of his time before the politicians got on the tough-on-crime-campaign. Now an inmate has to do eighty percent. I was given this insight by these legal incarcerated minds. I was pleased when Lora Mae legitimized the condemned counsel's advice and disappointed that the percentage of time I'd have to do had increased. I was pissed I had to hear the information form the prisoners before being informed by my paid legal representative.

Instead of a crowded tank like the city jail, the county's cells were smaller and even though there were six bunks, because of the transfer system, I usually shared a cubicle with only four other inmates.

My new roommates JJ Birdsong, Thomas Breedlove, Chris Hendrix, and Billy Johnson were there most of the time. Billy was a smooth chocolate old-head in his late forties. He was short, stoutly built, with a short receding afro. He'd spent most of his adult life in the prison's higher education system. Muggings, assaults, grand thefts, and manslaughter, were parts of his resume. He was Oklahoma southern bred, hipped-slick and cool, a harder older version of what my cousin Danny could become. Billy had a gift for gab, a silky conversationalist with street credentials. For Billy's current troubles he'd been picked up for a probation violation—hanging out with convicted felons. This old harden criminal was to become my first professor on prisoner culture.

At first I figured the reason the middle-aged gangster took me under his wing was because there was a possibility that our families had originated from the same African tribe, and we were mystically reunited. And then I thought perhaps for all Billy's bad boy behavior, like Danny, he could've been raised by an addict or a whore and was exposed to the street life early. Maybe he was really a good guy at heart with bad habits. Later, I assumed that possibly this was just one animal sensing fear in another and I'd stimulated his nurturing instincts. Whatever his motivation was, why he initiated our symbiotic relationship, I stopped wondering. The brother decided to trust me with vital chapters of his bible on prison survival and I was grateful.

On my second evening, as I gazed out the jail's window with a hopeless stare, as I watched freedom down on the streets, my bleak gawk was tormented. I observed white free citizens with the wind in their faces strolling up and down the sidewalks and like the soles of the shoes they wore they paraded like liberty had been sewn into the souls of their feet at birth. This was indeed their country!

Billy strutted up to my back. The sleeves on Billy's orange jumpsuit were rolled up exposing his massive biceps. His short stout physique and his long arms gave him gorilla-like features.

"Staring in that black hole you're double punishing yourself young-blood!" Billy rested his hand on my shoulder. "Especially, since you don't even belong in here." With the wisdom of a psychoanalyst, someway somehow the husky baritone man knew my plight. I twisted my head sideways and glared at him. Why was he able to know what he knew? Was it my shy quiet moral ways that informed him? As we ogled each other his dark chocolate eyeballs reminded me of scenes straight out of some mystical movies. *An old African woman stirring a pot stewing healing medicines and reciting poetic Voodoo verses. Or, in the distorted version of Voodoo, she's poking a needle in a doll and casting spells.* Could this brother actually read tea leaves? His gaze turned hard and I began to believe he possessed some sort of subversive profound knowledge, ideas that only he knew, and somehow just sensing Billy owned these secrets frighten me. How could he see what an all white jury couldn't see? Did I really feel and see all that in Billy's eyes or did Billy just have ordinary hood perceptions? Any black person from our neighborhood would know a nerd from a gang-banging-drug dealer.

Why didn't the white judge and jury see this soft gentle cultural moral side of me? Is it necessary or worth fighting for a white intimacy that's extremely elusive and resistant? These questions initiated a host of new worries inside my brain that bounced in every direction for an answer. Finally Black Dickey interrupted my mental masturbation. Poking my shorts frantically he wanted to be heard! *"Probably the same reason white women won't show me their peacock feathers!"*

In the county's system, a prisoner has access to books, cards, dominoes and even a set of chess with all the black and white players. Time goes faster if you can find someone to play these games with. Billy Johnson had multiple talents he was a real jack-of-all-trades. I suspected that he'd secretly grieved because he was denied many opportunities to master his gifts. I was one of the best players on my high school chess team and Billy kicked my ass easily and continuously.

"Checkmate motherfucker! Hahahahaha...!" He would slam the plastic chess piece on the board culturally the way a black person bangs a domino down. The sound of his hammering was matched by his bloating laughter. His big wide grin would expose all the gold in his mouth and they almost matched the bullion in Fort Knox.

A week after our initial informal meeting at the window, in the shadows of darkness, Billy knelt and huddled down on my bunk.

"Look young-blood; don't trust nobody in here or where ever you go when they transfer you out. Most of these motherfuckers are selfish evil bastards." His eyes were big like that of an old wrinkled brow hound dog and his intentions just as honest.

"Where ever you get transported to strap magazines and news-papers around your waist. It will keep you from getting gutted." And with these bits of insights Billy treaded softly back to his bed.

We would have several of these summits. I found out that the penitentiary's grapevine could be faster than a cell phone. "We heard about that nigger snatching your bed hours before you arrived. Don't back down from anybody even if it means taking an ass kicking. The white man has stuck us in here like wild dogs. By placing all the untreated explosive bad assesses together he expects some major fireworks. He doesn't care. Whitey wants to strip a nigger down to an animal level and only the strong survive. You got to let a nigger know your life's important." Billy would teach his philosophy class.

I looked forward to Saturday's even more than when I was a small child waking up early to pay tribute to my favorite cartoons, *Lilo and Stitch, and The Proud Family*. Visiting hours were from 11 AM until 4 PM and every Saturday my dear Mamma would show up with the love of my life, Loretta. They placed money in my account, commissary they called it; money for snacks, reading materials, and soap to kill lice. I cherished every intangible smile of hope that was on their faces but when they left as the walls of hell caved around me, optimism was elusive.

In the county I finally got fatigued and dozed in intervals. In the snoozes sometimes I'd drift back in time, back to my old high school days. Those were good times and I saw smiles on the faces of friends and then the dream always took a detour and became a nightmare. Close-up wounded features emerged from acquaintances that had been beaten up by cops and mistreated through the justice system. Some of them were bad boys and everyone expected them to be locked up or killed. Then there were classmates like Julius Roberts, he was a regular black student. There was no curfew in the city but late one night Julius was caught walking home alone and the police pulverized him. Julius was listed under suspicion for something and was never charged for anything. He spent two weeks licking his wounds in jail. Already a fragile sensitive brother, he withdrew even further from general exchanges at school. Julius ended up dropping out in his junior year. I saw him from time to time strolling along streets wearing old clothes and begging for money. This once normal brother is now lost in a schizoid daze.

In another wink sequence, Mamma was preaching a resounding sermon on morals. "Civilized folks don't fight..." Her lecture awakened me. Shaking my head I tried to come to terms with the meaning of the dream. I gazed around at my surroundings. The cage I was living in, the iniquities that lived inside my roommates, the filth of lice that lived with us, and I knew I couldn't survive four years without breaking a commandment, nor could I live in this world by Mamma's sacred ethical standards.

The outdoors racket would dwindle when sundown came and I'd lie on my bunk and often I'd hear obscure car horns. To pass time I'd try to identify the vehicle. When my roommates succumbed to sleep I tuned into the different variations of their deep breathing patterns. JJ was probably in his early thirties he was my height but skinny. All his wind breezed right through him. Chris was a few years older than I was and a few inches shorter. He was a stubby brother. His wheezes sounded like his air was congested with blubber. Thomas was probably my age. We were the same height and weight. He was dark and I was a yellow Negro. And like me he was paranoid. I noticed he closed his eyes but I never ever heard him sleeping. Billy used all the muscles in his short solid physique. The gorilla man eased a smooth stream of air from his system.

In one catnap I remember taking an adventure back to the courtroom. Everybody was frozen except the jittery eyeballs on the jurors. The bouncing round balls joined together and formed a sphere, and that transformed into a dark tunnel, and I saw myself tumbling down this vessel. It was an infinite pit.

I awakened and had a chokehold on Black Dickey. It had been over a month since Black Dickey had relieved himself or swam in Loretta's juices. Lack of privacy had suppressed his urges. We were a rowdy bunch of men living in close quarters and I'd never played with him with people in the same room. I closed my eyes and I was back in the company of jurisprudence. This time Black Dickey took aim at Loretta's appealing petite body. My form became flat as a pancake. I squirmed like a worm across the floor and slithered up Loretta's sturdy legs and paused and peeped around. Did I dare chance sexing Loretta in front of an audience? Unaffected by society's morals Black Dickey leaped on Loretta's leg and began to hump like a seething dog. Furiously his thrust busted the strands in her black spider fishnet pantyhose. I woke up and my orange jump suit was wet and stuck to my genitals.

***

"Motherfucking Gestapo Nazi bastards!" When Ricky was delivered to us, gnashing his teeth, this profane language busted from Ricky Ray Rydell's puffy chops.

Ricky Ray Rydell was my age, twenty-one. He had wild long stringy blond hair and the young man had old scars on his arms and face. His uneducated speech identified him as a southern, rough, redneck. Ricky had a light colored mustache that blended with his goatee and this uniting of hairs made Ricky's pale face look like a goat. Stumbling into our segregated cell, Ricky integrated mature scars with fresh bruises on his cheeks. His lips were busted and swollen so badly that it drooped on his chin and extended up to his nose. Obviously Ricky had suffered a police beat down. And to further aggravate the beleaguered white man, The Oklahoma City Police Department placed him in the care of four cold-blooded angry black men and me.

"The prison exchange program!" That's how Billy categorized Ricky's situation.

"They stick a peckerwood in here and we follow the script or they will trade..." He eyed Ricky and each of us. "...place one of us in a cell with some hillbilly ass white boys.

After the intense gaze he'd had with Billy, Ricky tilted his head to avoid any further eye contact and in a straight line Ricky marched to the back. He plunged himself on the bed and quickly buried his head under the dingy lice infested covers.

As we all huddled at the front of the cell, scratching the side of his head, Billy beaded his eyes on the white boy in the top corner bunk above mine. "We've got to kick his ass! Or these damn guards will march one of our black asses out of here and give some white boys the choice we need to make." Laying out the situation, Billy was like a captain on the battlefields giving an order to charge a hill or be killed if you stand still. Billy brought forth his experience of living in the justice system and the frightening reality of how the organization works.

A brick hard pastry and raw bologna between two pieces of stale white bread was usually how lunch was served. After being repulsed by the county's menu I was in the process of fasting. I could feel acid beginning to burn inside my empty belly. I had to survive. I held the sandwich up to my mouth and to resist the awful taste, closing my eyes I meditated. As I chewed the first bite, "Wham!"

Like a sonic boon a horrific blast shook our cell's foundation. My eyes popped opened to see Ricky's head flying into the steel bars, again and again, and before his body could slither to the floor all four of them were on him like a machine throwing vicious blows in rhythm. The punches pinned his limp shell against the cage. They beat Ricky mercilessly. Blood spurted in every direction. To my surprise, a white guard, who had been waiting to collect lunch trays, watched on the outside of the cell. He dodged flying blood squirts and then stood back and inspected his uniform for stains.

After stomping Ricky the four men divided his sandwich and retreated to their respective beds and ate. Ricky shuffled on the floor inch by inch to his bunk. He used my mattress as leverage to pull his lame frame up.

Lying beneath Ricky that night, I was sure I heard blood leaking inside his body. His agonizing moans crawled through my skin and cut open my heart.

Ricky's hemorrhaging, the seepage of blood reminded me of a dog I had when I was little and lived in the house with the wood rats. Pooch was his name. Early one morning I ran across the street to the store for Mamma. It was rush hour and Mamma always cautioned me to look both ways before crossing. I did but I didn't notice Pooch chasing behind me. I heard screeching car tires, a thud, and Pooch screaming in agony.

As blood dripped from his nose, Pooch hobbled on one leg and curled up on the curb. A blue Pontiac sped out of view. I tried to help Pooch, pat him gently, but he growled and showed his vicious teeth. I thought he might bite me. He was still there that evening. Nobody in the neighborhood ever talked of veterinarians and the lucky one's barley had jobs that paid human health insurance. I took him food for the next five days. Every night I dreamed how lonely Pooch must be outside hurting and waiting to die. On the six day, flies swarmed Pooch; he was dead and swollen.

On the seventh day, all the perpetrators of the crime saw that Ricky hadn't moved from his bunk. From then on, we began begging different guards for medical help. Finally on the ninth day they brought in a stretcher. They rolled Ricky out and surprisingly I never heard a whisper of an investigation that was ever conducted on his behalf, and I never saw the white man again.

***

"Sitting On The Dock Of The Bay." Early the next morning I was awakened by the sweet soulful sounds of Billy whistling the 1960's tune made famous by Otis Redding. An hour later the hard rolls and black coffees were served up as breakfast. Billy came and sat on my bunk. He dunked his roll into his coffee and bit into the wet bread.

"Ain't none of these motherfuckers your friend. Know that young-blood!" Billy hollered and I looked around scrutinizing the other inmates. They tilted their heads and ate their meals as if they didn't hear Billy.

Billy leaned his head back rolled his eyes as if a thought or an idea was lost inside his head.

"Yeah yeah! That dumb-ass white boy had done something to piss off those damn guards or the cops. They whipped his ass and then turned him over to us to make it look like we did the dirty deed...." A sudden blink in his eyes and he was in deep thought again. "Ha! Who's going believe a goddamned convict anyway? Who cares who beat the hell out of him?" Then Billy stared at me with his hound-dog face. We both knew he was talking about our reality as well. Who cares what happens to a convict; sooner or later every felon has to face this eye-opening truth.

"Man don't you know? Not until back in the 1970's when the brothers started the prison riots at Big Mac (nick-name for McAl-ester State Penitentiary), a nigger would be beaten like a slave for fighting a white man. In the 1980's, when I first did time the birth of hip-hops bad-ass gang-bangers were arriving and we upped the ante and we made busting a white man's ass cool."

When we first began talking, I had confided in him how the cops had vulgarly accosted me and finally this was his answer.

"If you think those cowboy cops are racist here in Oklahoma City you haven't seen a damn thing young-blood. These little hon-ky-tonk towns where most of the prisons are, the guards are from those ma and pa populations and Jim Crow is all they know!" If Billy was trying to scare me, it worked.

Within the hour the guard yelled out Billy's name. He sprung to his feet. Somehow he knew his county jail time was coming to an end. Billy knew secrets about the justice system. With his bedding already properly folded Billy tucked them, blanket and pillow, un-der one arm. Relieved to get out of the city and county jail systems, Billy strutted across the floor with his head held high. The veteran of prison affairs knew his life's conditions would be better than his experience in county and he welcomed prison. He grabbed my hand pulled me close and gave me a brotherly embrace. While my protector was walking through the door he turned and threw up a defiant black power fist. He left me with his last endearing gesture, "Stay alive motherfucker!"

Chapter Eleven

I was living in a dangerous dungeon and life wasn't all that bad. Late nights hearing thunder blast and Oklahoma's sweeping rain pelting the dark streets would conjure up cozy memories. I found myself hopping on a thunderbolt and suddenly I was cuddling under a warm blanket wrapped into Loretta's sensuous slippery waters. But then again it was all that bad. I was locked up and lonely and Black Dickey felt abandoned and was horny. But briefly during hazardous weather I was able to escape the concrete steel jungle.

All the regional birds had returned from their southern winter vacation. The heat of summer's season usually begins in mid May in Oklahoma. Everyday the need to see freedom carried me to the window. As always I observed traffic, pedestrians walking, and families with children. There was usually a businessman running, I assumed to meet an appointment. Downtown, a few years earlier electric streetcars had been installed to give the Cowboy City a classy San Francisco quality. It was transportation for out-of-town convention goers to dine at remodeled restaurants and to be entertained by live bands at the revamped Bricktown. White folks were hopping on board. I saw life going on without me outside the jail's window.

I usually wrote two letters a week one for Mamma and of course one to the lady that Black Dickey worshiped. Late one night I had pencil in hand and was writing Mamma. I'd never told her about the violence or the unsanitary surroundings her son was forced to live in. I was answering one of her letters. She, like everyone else in Oklahoma City's black community, knew some jailbirds. One of them had told her, "He'll be better off when he's transferred out of the county." I'd decided to deceive Mamma. I told her I was already fine.

"What you writing, man?" Intrusively JJ Birdsong had leaned the head of his six foot four frame across my pad as I sat on my bunk. It's hard to keep your hairdo together when you're locked up and his shaggy French braids were mostly roaming around in individual strands. His up-close appearance and presence caught me off guard. I jerked and then met his eyes head on.

"Oh...excuse me bro." His eyes shook and JJ quickly, nervously backed away with his hands held high.

"I didn't mean no harm." Billy had told me about certain codes of respect prisoners used. Space. That's what JJ' was apologizing for, he'd invaded my private space.

"What's up man? What am I writing?" Calmly I gazed at JJ and repeated his question.

"I'm just dropping Mamma a note."

He rubbed his nose and paced to the center of our home with one hand hanging to his side the other was partially stuck in his jump suit's back pocket. Outside a lone car horn blew and exploded into the stillness and darkness. "Yeah. I see you working that pen all the time..." His voice became as mellow as the breeze of the summer's night air. The dark skinned man licked his tongue over his razor thin mustache. JJ was a dangerous man. He was there for armed robbery and like me he was sometimes a quiet man, but his silence had a sneaky deadly quality.

"You're lucky. You know what I'm sayin'. Right now you have a family and homeys that care about you. You know what I'm sayin'." Unlike me, I sensed his upbringing and his life's experiences had been harder.

"My mom's been in an out of this system...since I was born." Sadness was streamed into the ripeness of his tone. He piddled with the stray strings that overlapped parts of his braids. "Right now she's doing time at Mabel Bassett."

He strolled across the room and then flopped on his bunk. Lying on his side, facing a stone wall, he curled his long legs up like a child. I believe JJ was turning away from me and away from the world he'd inherited. Echoing off the brick wall his parting words crammed the summer's night air with an eerie anger. It was the painful memories of the life he was born into. *"You lucky...You know what I'm sayin'?"* The verse was absorbed into the darkness and together they made a frightening tone and dread became the night's theme.

I felt empathy for JJ's situation and then I leaned back on the bed thinking as I observed the dingy stains around stool/water fountain. I deliberated on the memory of the arrest and the trial and the separation from Mamma and Loretta. I found myself missing college and my education. I glared up at the steel bars. I didn't feel lucky. I became angry, then sad and my gloom joined dread in the shadows.

***

The weariness of incarceration was beginning to show in my appearance. During that Saturday's visit with Mamma and Loretta, they laughed teasingly at the way unshaven hair had grown in patches on my face. Their fun was met with a snarl. I was glad to see them but I couldn't hold back the reality I was living in. They were free and I was locked up. My madness began to make them self-conscious. Mamma batted her eyes in a way that said it was all her fault I was behind bars. And poor Loretta's lips started trembling whenever she spoke. Her words became measured. She tried hard not to say anything that would be taken wrong. When it was time for them to leave, Mamma had regained her authoritative composure and her gaze cut through the fiberglass. She'd stopped looking at my depressed attitude and blaming herself or tiptoeing with caution.

"Son I'm leaving you a book to read. Read it!" Mamma's tonal inflections said this was an order not a request. "It's on the life of Fredrick Douglas." Even though I knew some facts about slavery and black history, studying the subject was depressing.

Hours later that day I was scrutinizing the life of "Fredrick Douglas, when—"

"Ugh...the book that you're reading..." JJ was squatting relieving his bowls. "Ugh...I use to go to the school here by that name."

Douglas High School; I'd graduated there less than three years ago and yet I was almost clueless with the historical connection my Alma Mater had with Fredrick Douglas.

JJ's scent was beginning to overpower our little cubicle. I got up from my bed, book in hand and walked to the front of the cell.

"Ugh...I was there in the mid eighties." He got up, flushed, shimmied up and adjusted his jump suit. "Huh, I didn't graduate though…I kept going to jail." He lit a cigarette, pimp walked up to the front and stood beside me and leaned on the bars. "You know slavery ain't never ended." He had a know it all smirk on his face. "We live just like slaves right here." He winked. "We ain't got no damn rights."

It was weird standing side by side with a known criminal and him using the rationale that we were slaves. I recognized a part of his argument to be true if it was applied in my case, but for him, where would a civilized society place people like him? Maybe the criminal justice system could be more therapeutic? And maybe if he'd made better choices, or if he'd come from a healthier environment he would be a decent human being. As we stood there these assumptions and conclusions invaded my thoughts.

"And another thang—" He shrugged his shoulders. "Ain't nothing but niggers, Latino's, and po' ass white folks with bad lawyers doing real time, you know what I mean?" He could have thumped his chest or even taken a bow. He was proud of his social awareness. He promenaded over to his bed, hopped on his back and propped his arms behind his head. I returned to my bed and resumed reading.

There are always moments in the darkness when it's almost silent. The ruckus of the guards jingling keys would cease, outbreaks of noises from prisoners would die and calmness would usually enter in the wee hours of dawn.

A faint shade of light off the hall bulb was enough for me to finish reading Mr. Douglas' story. I assumed it was between 2:30am and 3:30am. Brief hours of slumber during these hours were part of my escape. Snoozing for moments freed me from slipping into self-pity and a state of morbid demoralization. Those twinkles of the morning were also Black Dickey's time. I could easily slip into a fantasy world that saw me slipping into Loretta's wiggling vagina. I had mastered sneaking under the covers and with long frisky quiet moves I could sip ecstasy juices from Black Dickey's head. But this morning my other head was being romanticized by Mr. Douglas' life.

It was easier than I'd imagined; trading in my prison jump suit for the ragged slave clothes Fredrick must have worn as a boy. In either uniform, I felt trapped and abandoned by an immoral unjust society. In Mr. Douglas' britches I pictured the overseer waiting in the wings with the whip or a knife to cut off a limb or even end my life. In the orange outfit, I could easily see cutthroat convicts performing those exact deeds. Fredrick froze his butt off sleeping on dirt floors in the winter and soaking in mud puddles if a spring rainstorm had occurred. It was summer, one-hundred-degree weather and ninety-eight at night. My cotton shorts were sweaty and stinking up Black Dickey. What if I was able to get past the guards and out of this building or how would I escape off a plantation? With either situation, how far would I have to run for freedom? With only a few comparisons of his life vs. my life my skin craved to abandon both suits.

There was another basic bleak fact that Fredrick and I had in common. Our familiar condition curled around my brain like a rattlesnake. The sickening feeling that I'd lost the everyday nurturing, camaraderie of the two priceless loves in my life, Mamma and Loretta. Our umbilical cords were severed and Frederick's was cut-off from his mother in his earlier years. When the judge pronounced me guilty I felt pieces of my flesh being torn away, the intimate connection with Mamma and Loretta spewed blood. I'm sure Fredrick and his mother suffered the same confusion and horror I'm experiencing. Even after generations the harsh parodies of the puzzle of a black man's life, some pieces still fit. The sensible passions I'd had that our society had advanced were smashed. I shed a tear packed with grief and the sad bubble informed me that inside some of the white world's heart, blacks were still perceived as animals incapable of possessing real human feelings. Looking at my circumstances and surroundings everything in my environment verified this ruthless realization. A sad Black Dickey simply deflated.

Enough! Inquiries on his time versus mine; I wasn't going to survive four years by obsessing in this pathetic mode. I needed to get into the manic part of my incarceration equation. I squeezed Black Dickey until all my depressive realities were replaced with the joyous fantasies I produced by my hand.

***

Later that morning I was cruelly awakened.

"Wha-...wha-...what's that noise?" Asking that question while barley conscious, quietly I breathed in the awkward disturbances. Agitated out of my sleep, I struggled to raise my head. I peeped through swollen eyes to locate where the sounds originated.

There he was all six foot four. He was down on his knees. His head was pressed through the spaces where the steal bars separated. And Fat Asses' chest was hemmed against the bars. The inmates named the guard this humiliating insult for obvious reasons. Fat Asses' eyes were animated and his jaws waggled. Either Fat Ass was having a heart attack or he was experiencing a grand mall seizure induced by sex pleasures. It was the latter. The militant JJ was sucking the white slave master's penis.

"Woo-whoa-woo!" The over-weight white guard with the thinning hairline stared dead into my eyes and released his orgasmic exhilaration. Why should he care or be embarrassed that a condemned man was witnessing him getting his freak on? To him we were like animals in a barn and he was the farmer.

"Hush!" JJ whispered, trying to calm down his loud lover. Two long leaps from his six four frame and JJ was on his bunk. I was able to capture a glimpse of the white man's sperm straggling off JJ's lips.

I wasn't homophobic I believed in live and let live. On HBO, Showtime, and the sex videos I'd downloaded to improve my sexual performance, I'd only witnessed a man sexing a woman. Being in a room watching one man suck another man's penis was weird for my country ass. I frowned, squeezed my eyes closed and tried to puke out the sour vision.

I didn't believe JJ was gay. But he smoked and he always had money for his habit. On visiting day nobody outside was breaking down doors to show him love. I guess one does what one has to do to survive in here.

By the time the weekend came I had washed my mind clean of the smudged semen that dangled off JJ's chops. I was ready to enjoy sanity from the couple I loved the most.

Mamma had threads of new gray hair. In an ice-creamy brown corduroy panel skirt and matching jacket, Loretta emerged as tasty sweet as a macadamia chocolate pie. I don't know if it was the simple and plain clothes Loretta wore or the distinguished added color in Mamma's hair that brought out their virtuous personalities, but for me they represented normal respectable African Americans. I gazed upon them in awe.

"Hey there's my girl." The sunshine of my life and my wonderful Mamma! So who's taking care of the rest of the world while you guys are here?" They both beamed. I tried to be upbeat for the whole session. If it was possible to do grateful from behind bars I wanted them to know how much they were appreciated.

But there were quiet breaks in our conversations. This was more than the mother of a prisoner and his girlfriend experiencing uncomfortable feelings due to the nature of our bizarre surroundings. There was something else going on. And I knew I wasn't at fault. Mamma was hedging, holding back something. She had prolonged stares at Loretta. It was as if Mamma wanted to will a secret out of Loretta's head.

A cross-eye or a slight change in one's breathing, this setting breeds a sixth sense into you. I was becoming aware of these new skills, how to read an inmate before an eruption would ensue. Yet I didn't trust the new super powers on regular people. So when Loretta strayed away from Mamma's glare I didn't ask why, I just minded my business. This was another strict rule in this treacherous society. Whatever was happening I left it between the two of them to settle.

The following Wednesday the heat and humidity scoured inside the jail at one hundred ten degrees. The dogged days of August had brought the funk. I was celebrating five angst-ridden months in confinement. The afternoon transported sobering news and there was cause for a different commemoration.

"…I'm pregnant; we're having a baby…" On the fourth line, that's what I read in Loretta's letter.

WE'RE HAVING A BABY! A mass of feelings ushered themselves into my head. We'd always practiced safe sex…How could she be?…It's been five months since Loretta and I made love….Is it mine?…That bitch! Damn whore! Was I going to be a father? My baby was going to be born a bastard. I was a helpless convict.

How could I provide for it? She's a smart woman. How long had she known? Confusion and feelings of helplessness spread out in ever direction and haunted my head.

That night I got into a fistfight with JJ. There has to be a boss of a cell I guess. The manic, dangerous part of JJ's personality showed up. Since Billy had departed, JJ had begun strong-arming food from other inmates and he'd started talking crazy to them. I overlooked these little injustices since they were not aimed at me. It was Billy who'd said, "An inmate minding his business is the best secret to staying alive while you're doing time."

I was upset and writing Loretta. In a soft tone JJ asked me what I was writing. Distressed and concentrating on what I was inscribing I didn't hear him.

"Nigger! I said what you writing?" JJ yelled and was in my face. I was already wounded.

JJ swung at me, I ducked. I bobbed and waved and caught him with a left cross that landed solid and sent him reeling. I jammed him on a bunk and pinned him there with several punches to his face. Somehow JJ was able to grab my arm and we proceeded to wrestle. We fell over the stool, bumped and rolled over bunks and tussled on the floor. I kicked, punched, bit, and finally I had JJ corralled against the floor. My knee was in his chest and I was clutching his neck. JJ was gasping for air and life was leaving his body.

"I will kill you motherfucker!" I released all the suppressed payback I had against everybody and the circumstances that had planted me there. The stockpiled rage turned into muscles and that brute force was maniacally ripping JJ's head off. Had I changed into an animal in five months? Had I become one of them? A brief moment of sanity returned. I relaxed my grip. Got up and like a caged cat I swiftly circled the cell. Instincts had taken over again.

In only five months of incarceration I had observed some of the most atrocious beatings and most of the inmates assumed this was normal behavior. Had some of Mamma's home taught compassion deserted me?

That night, while napping, I hallucinated:

***

I found myself inside the living quarters of a slave owner's nineteenth century mansion, there I saw a black woman. From what I was able to observe of her partially uncovered face she had caramel skin. Inch by inch the dream slowly exposed her nude body lying motionless over some fancy ruffled sheets. And inch by inch Black Dickey was brought to life. A pain full of fatigue and ache was woven into her facial features. Somehow I was sure this lady was the mother of Fredrick Douglas.

Her white master entered the dream and with him came the darkness of night. He stood in front of a flickering kerosene lamp that set on a table by the window. His long graybeard, thin face, and his shadow off the light made his facial features appear sinister. He approached her bedside wobbling his penis in his hand. Stoically, he deliberately heaved the injured black woman's legs over the bedpost and proceeded to maliciously molest her.

***

I woke up nauseated in the dim cell. Across the room I looked for JJ. In the early morning hours he wasn't awake scheming up a plan to kill me. He was calmly snoring. I breathed a sigh of relief. *"Watch your back"*—the incarceration paranoia said.

At breakfast JJ averted his eyes from my gaze and he offered me his old hard ass roll. I waved him off declining not because I didn't want to accept his peace offering; I did want bygones to be bygones. Like I said prison food was awful. Their best gourmets were like eating from a shinny garbage can and I was only eating enough to stay alive.

Thomas patted my shoulder and his big smile said, "Job well done." While Chris averted his eyes and I believed he was now afraid of me. Billy had left an empty space for a power struggle to occur. The roomies had witnessed me kick JJ's skank ass and now I was king of the jungle. Supremacy felt strange. Growing up I'd never been a bully or someone that would intimidate other children. For the first time in my life a superior pride, the kind of power I'd seen in gang-bangers, and naturally oozing off many of Oklahoma's whites. Now this egoism was tugging at my nuts. This strange arrogance was absent of any form of female stimulation but it enlarged Black Dickey and terrified me.

There seems to be no rational reasoning to the selection process of how long an inmate spends at county before they're transferred off to prison. I was king for only two days. On Friday, without the insight Billy had, no warning was afforded to this junior king. A guard came to the cell.

"Jackson!" He hollered my name I was hand cuffed placed in the Kunta Kinte leg chains, gift wrapped and ready to be shipped to Lexington's A & R Prison.

Lexington, Oklahoma is forty-five miles south of Oklahoma City. The facility is the holding tank for all the state's inmates until they're shipped off to the prison of the state's choice.

Black Dickey reared his neck eager for the outing and was ready to escape the confined mustiness of county jail.

Oklahoma's winds blew freedom through autumn's breezes. I sucked in the air while two other inmates and I drug the shackles. Tilting my head to the heavens I waded in the bright sun's light. The sweet puffs of air gusts landed on my skin and unlocked months of claustrophobic pores.

Chapter Twelve

"The Green Lizard," was the name of the inmate's old tour bus; we left Oklahoma City riding around in it and were dumped into the state's prisons. Previous prisoners had established all the nick-names and behaviors of everything from the people you socialized with to the rules of engagement. The next generations inherited the list and now they were institutional. Our means of transportation derived its epithet because inmates long ago thought that the buses' olive paint job was hideous.

Aboard the bus, elevated above traffic, I was able to see down on and inside cars. One white lady sat in the back of a gray sedan feeding a baby that was strapped in an infant's seat. I thought of Loretta and our unborn child and tears began bubbling. I'll never see my baby that size.

We drove the scenic route down Interstate 35 and on the out-skirts of Oklahoma City we passed by flashing motel signs, all night restaurants and full service gas stations. Autumn landscapes were filled with open fields packed with rolls of bailed hay. I was enter-tained by herds of cows roaming and there was always a watering hole for them to quench their thirst. Horses huddled under golden brown shade trees and all the livestock appeared peaceful and at home out in the open spaces.

Exhausted and weary from the county jail experience my mind drifted and I began to see blurry images:

***

Wagon wheels were grinding dirt into dusty clouds. The wheels belonged to a prairie schooner and aboard there were two ex-slaves. A chocolate woman and a jet-black skinned man drove two gray-mouthed mules. The woman had a scarf tied on her head and a man wore a sweaty tattered cowboy hat. Two barefoot boys and three little girls with plated hair walked along side the wagon. Gradually the figures became clear and I was saturated with the suffering and weariness that was painted into their expressions.

***

We arrived in Lexington and I woke up. After being locked up like an animal, the forty-five minute ride was refreshing. I grew up in this red state and as an African American for those brief moments I was able to breathe in and experience the limited freedoms the state offered us.

Lexington, Oklahoma is a small storefront of a town. If Oklahoma City was larger it would be its most southern suburb. Working class rednecks drive pick-up trucks there, the same as they do everywhere else in the state. *Oklahoma is Dodge, Ford, and Chevrolet Country.*

Like I said the A and R prison is a pass through, a processing place for inmates from all over the state en route to the state's prisons. I believe they use it to keep the local jails from over-crowding.

As a fellow passenger, Freddie Washington stepped off the bus he leaned back and shouted, "Those freak inspectors stare deep up your ass-hole here.

"Why do they look so deep here?" Someone in line asked.

"Big corn-fed white boys get off on that kind of shit man!" 'Ahahaha..." Somebody in the line said and a chorus of laughter followed.

"Naw. For weapons and dope man! They don't want anybody transferring in or taking contraband to another facility. In fact this is the only prison in the state that they have real doctors and nurses that peep up your ass." A serious informative Fred said.

We were herded off into a large room, stripped naked, and one by one we were forced to bend over. With both hands we all had to grab and stretch our hips apart while white men, medical professionals wearing white coats and plastic gloves gazed deep up our individual asses. Black Dickey shrunk in shame.

The place was newer, cleaner, and it had fresher graffiti on the walls. After being processed into the system, without a ruler or any type of measuring instrument, as I lay on my bunk, with the instincts of a mathematician, I traced every square inch of the cell. This scanty exercise was a meditation that had pardoned me briefly from fear of the unknown and speeded up time. Instead of the six by nine like the cells in county these were seven by eleven.

On the second day my head was shaven and it was a tradition to give all the new arrivals the name *"skinner"*.

The prison system doesn't offer inmates the modern luxuries of instant messaging and we're not issued cell phones or private fax numbers. A convict can't inform their families when they transfer or where the transfer takes them. To the people that loved me I was lost in the system for over two weeks. Mamma and Loretta were frantic. They called everybody that would answer the phone in the state's penal system. Fearing that I had been killed and there was a cover up, they called our black state senator, Celeste Washington. She tracked me down.

By the time I got a letter from Mamma I was reading it on another bus en route to God knows where. It was just as well, 'cause Black Dickey was about to burst. There was too much activity, too many prisoners moving in and out all the time; I wasn't able to read the vagabond convict's sleeping habits; and of course the rookie that I was, I wasn't clever enough to find a subtle spot and devote time especially to him.

Under a plump luminous orange autumn moon we boarded the bus that would take us to little country prison towns statewide. For the first time during my confinement I felt semi safe when I boarded the Green Lizard. It was familiar plus my body had been conquered by six months of overdue consistent siestas. Exhausted I was like a child in the back seat of a car on a Sunday afternoon drive. As soon as I got on the bus I began falling in and out of sleep.

Barely awake, at times I caught glimpses through the glare of the buses' darkened windows of more glittering motel and restaurant signs. I was awake then I was asleep. The sparkling signs hypnotized me. In the dead of night, landscapes and images began appearing in black and white. I heard gospel music and a blues band.

Occasionally we dropped off the interstate into tiny hillbilly towns and while in REM sleep the bus driver became a narrator, a storyteller. In an impression of an old columnist and TV announcer, Walter Winchell, he said, *"We are riding on a train"*…instead of a bus…*"This is a Quinn Martin production."* I was appearing in a re-run of the Fugitive. I was Richard Kimble a white man wrongly convicted and I was en route to a destination with death. Startled by this stark reality I awakened and was black and back on a bus.

After making stops all over the state and traveling for two days I heard the *Green Lizard's* tailpipes from the diesel engine exhale and I was boldly awakened by lightening flashes and the growl of thunder that spread over a nearly dawn darkened sky.

"Kayin Jackson."

Sleep snot acted like glue on my eyes as I struggled to open them. I was lightheaded and faint, then terrified at what I saw and the thought of where I might be.

"Kayin Jackson, this is **McAlester**". *McAlester!* Fear shook me wide-awake.

McAlester! The original Big Mac! And this wasn't the Ronald MacDonald's hamburger joint. The Ham-Burglar and his boys were not living up in here. This was **McAlester State Penitentiary!** And the bad boys living in here didn't play the part of ham-burglars on TV. They were the real deal.

We'd passed through here before and let inmates off on the first day of the trip. This had to be a mistake. I peeped out the window. Adjusting my eyes to the early morning shadows I saw the same gun towers I'd seen in the bright light of day.

The guns of reality fiercely glared down on my face. A bolt of thunder struck a chained fence that was under razor sharp barbed wire. More lightening flashes revealed the aged run down buildings and it looked like a scene straight out of a horror film. Skipping and missing beats, my heart was beating erratically. I became captive of a devastating fear before even entering the gates of the great dungeon.

Big Mac was a phrase used throughout Oklahoma's black communities long before Colonel Sanders fried his first piece of chicken. Fear instead of feast, danger and death instead of an endearing smiling southern gentleman in a white suite. That was the original perception of Big Mac for black children in this prairie land.

Oh-my-God-I'm-going-to-die-here! My blood trembled. **Big Mac!** This was the legendary big badass bogie man. This was the place where grown-ups told famous fairy-tales, as a threat to most of Oklahoma's little bad-ass black children. It was a fantasy world ruled by cold-hearted prisoners with twisted lifestyles. Rape and bondage, torture, beatings and murder; that is what seized the imagination of Oklahoma's black folk when they thought of **"Big Mac!"**

The dungeon was an awesome bloodcurdling sight **and now this scary house** was now going to be my new home.

I used the dried sleep that hung from my eyes for shaded curtains to hide fear. With the steal around my ankles I was shuffled off the bus out into pouring breezy rain by two guards; one on each arm. I could feel the aurora of disfigured dead ghost gripping at my feet when we entered the antiquated red and white checkered tile building called *The Rotunda*. In the middle of it there was an iron cage. A huge fifty-year old or so fat guard sat behind a desk in the center of the iron pen.

And then there was the reception commission.

"Black ass young nigger!" Early in the morning from the upper windows, wide-awake prisoners yelled imitating degrading jeers. "I'm gonna' fuck you up the ass!" The taunts continued coming as Black Dickey slid near my butt hole.

***

Big Mac is one of the most notorious maximum-security prisons in the United States. The structure was built in 1908 by the cold hands of those who would later make it their home and that was one year after Oklahoma became a state.

In 1907 the United State's newest immigrants from England, Ireland, Italy, Germany, Poland, the Slavs and Jews joined the American good old boys in Oklahoma in building a segregated fence around African Americans based on inferiority. This barricade was against the integrity and decency of Black Americans and to this day residuals of those barriers still exist.

Most of Oklahoma's occupations and institutions were segregated even before Oklahoma became a state. Inferior education; low person on the totem pole; and even if you're an educated Negro, *'don't apply here'*, the good jobs in this state are for whites only. That's what segregation meant.

After statehood these newly arrived immigrant good fellows entered into a covenant with the good old boys and attempted to destroy the essence of The Civil Rights Act of 1868, the 14th Amendment. To ensure blacks would forever remain permanent under classed citizens, these forces decided to seize power from black males by denying them the right to vote, the 15th Amendment. Two hundred and forty years of living under a vicious slavery system, the majority of the survivors were still loyal to Lincoln's Republican Party when they arrived in the new state. And how did the good old boys of Oklahoma help these poor destitute people? They introduced a grandfather clause and in their one party system only democrats could vote. The new black citizens of the new state were excluded from casting one single vote for the first governor.

Jim Crow from the Deep South rode side-saddle with the Boomers and Sooners into the new state and for over fifty years the nasty old man instituted eighteen heart-wrenching laws that is still causing misery and destroying the lives of Black Oklahomans.

There are over thirty-five correctional facilities in Oklahoma. Blacks make up less than six-teen percent of the state's population. Four hundred and twenty nine blacks live in Big Mac. That's thirty percent of McAlester's residents. I guess we were lucky to be placed in the state's deadliest prison.

Being raised in Mamma's house, I was aware of some of these facts on a shallow level. Illuminating hard knowledge of black Oklahoma history on a concrete level and recognizing our current situation in this country and this state has always terrorized the hell out of me! Before being incarcerated, concentrating on the horrors of the past would've destroyed my *only-in-America* model. I believe I needed to be an idealist for survival. I had to stay focused on my studies and the future. This romantic light at the end of the tunnel pushed me to succeed. I had no idea how devastating a superior antebellum persona and eighteen segregation laws that spanned over half a century had been on the soul of Oklahoma's black community and the human race. I was now a direct recipient of Oklahoma's history of discrimination and inside the prison walls I began to feel a deep hate for the white people of Oklahoma.

This bona fide history awareness didn't come because I was ready and wanted it. I was enlightened through the gloom that nestled inside the walls of McAlester. Ghosts of prisoners and the early African American settlers left impressions of themselves inside the stockades and in the air of yesteryear's prairie dust. The sandstones spoke in nightmares and the winds rustled and became alive in hallucinations. After the cruelty of prison life and living day after day and finally a strong deterioration of self-esteem I was accumulated to a grimy aura around the granite barricades and seduced by a universal human desperation to survive. Since blacks were tortured, burned, hung, executed, impoverished, devalued in life, and endured hardships under Jim Crow, their spirits were restless to share their stories. I was initiated into the excruciating pain of these brave black frontier folk and was heaved into the sandstone craters of previous prisoner's revolting hate for society. And through a series of illusions, history's wounds were sprinkled into my skin.

***

White short sleeve cotton shirt with matching pastry pants and some old tattered black lace-up boots that was the fashion, or should I say the combat fatigues, worn by the band of brothers at Big Mac. War! This was the front line of a battle zone. There were unspeakable stabbings, unreported molestations and unimaginable murders that took place inside Big Mac annually. A bunch of bad-asses and overcrowding, horrific treatments by the guards and the system, and of course race relations were all equal contributors to the violence that occurred in Big Mac. The prison had already had several national headline historical riots.

Back in the day like all southern prisons, McAlester's convicts had been slaves to the farmers. They picked cotton, gathered harvest, slopped hogs, and worked as field hands as unpaid laborers for farmers and the tax paying citizens. These undignified individuals helped transport the new invention, the automobile, and the state into the twentieth century by constructing roads.

***

I was processed and my ass was inspected again.

A, B, C, D, E, F, G, H, I'm not reciting the alphabet this is the identification to Big Mac's cellblocks. And every letter of the alphabet had its own community play ground except *"H"*, that was death row.

Just as playpens are used to keep toddlers safe, prisoner's had similar facilities that supported the safety of the community.

Claustrophobia kills or makes a person wish they were dead. Being outside whether the weather is steaming hot, freezing cold, or during 140 mph gushing winds, even if buckets of water were pouring from the sky it was better being drenched than the monotonous confinement of a cell. Playing basketball or lifting weights always made it seem as if time moved a little faster and if you could release a little tension it probably saved an inmate from getting killed that day. The alphabet letters that integrated inmates were called blocks. Their ethnicity and complexions segregated them as they enter their cells.

"*I Unit*" was medium security.

"*Don't fuck up nigger,*" the thin demonic rusty-red bearded white man stipulated as he wagged his gatekeeper keys in my face. He told me I would begin serving time living in "*I Unit*". The word medium echoed a less dangerous situation for me and even though the guard hurled the offensive remark, I breathed easier.

We marched down a quiet hall that reeked of Lysol. Overpowering sanitized fumes instead of the city and county jail's piss and fecal scent was an improvement.

Instead of hate chants and threats to do me bodily harm, a melody of snores came from both sides of the corridor. When we were almost to the end of I Unit, I heard what sounded like a mattress squeaking and someone definitely moaning. The guard pulled me by the handcuffs up close to a cell where the noises were originating. Sternly he held the back of my head forcing me to peep through the square foot Plexiglas.

What I saw made me shudder. The guard had me creeping into the privacy of a two sweaty, out of breath, corn fed twenty something, huge, butt naked white men. One huge man was pinned on the back of another large white man; they were welded together like Siamese Twins. The scenery and the awkward slushy reverberations of hairy men swaying against coarse skin and a penis bouncing in and out of an asshole, the whole episode agitated the Christian morals Mamma had instilled in me. JJ wasn't gay but he was sucking the guard, Fat Ass', penis for favors. The decent folk of my black community judged homosexual life as a sin. Since I'd never seen open gay life boldly displayed, I was confused and undecided about the matter.

The guard peeped at the two lovers and twisted his nose up. "Damn freaks!" In disgust he declared his viewpoint.

The man on top peered up at me and frowned at me without breaking rhythm. The one on the bottom smiled at me and he kept moaning and swishing his hips. Neither demonstrated any signs of embarrassment.

As if showing off to his audience the top lover suspended his gyrations. In appreciation he gradually allowed his gaze to wander up and down the muscular features of the bottom man's body. It was like he was an artist scrutinizing a painting. Having an audience must have turned him on. With added energy in his eyes, he scaled over the bottom man's ass with one hand. He gripped the man's hips and bucked quickly into an orgasm.

"Ah-ah! Woo-whoa-woo! What you looking at, nigger?" Groaning, the husky blond white man on the bottom with a penis stuck up his ass addressed me. He didn't peep to see if I was still watching. I guess a sixth sense informed him I was and Oklahoma's society had already told him I was a nigger.

"They're' your neighbors. Tehehe!" The insidious laughter and comment came from the feeble lips of my escort. Jingling the large keys, he opened the next cell. As I walked through, I thought of being sealed and confined behind the heavy steel door for three and half years. And I began to imagine the weight of the iron gateway collapsing on a person and flattening them like a pretzel! The guard's eyes pointed me in the direction of a top bunk. There was a body curled under covers on the bottom bunk. The guard locked the door.

"Damn niggers and fags!" He spewed the repulsive sentiments as if my color and the homosexual behavior cultivated a vinegary vomit in his system. He shook his head and left.

It dawned on me. Separated by a stone wall I was only a few feet away from the booty action. What did musty men sex smell like? Did gay sex have a different distinct funk than boy-girl sex? In here did they use lubricants for an asshole? Or in this primordial environment did they experience intercourse in the raw by twisting a penis up a butt-hole and stirring up lingering pieces of feces; did that serve as a gel? I contemplated further on the topic of homosexuality. I wasn't homophobic. I was naïve. It would be an awkward spectacle for my country ass to be a spectator to a man and woman having sex and now I'd been exposed to doggie style man on man.

It was still early morning. Get some rest, I thought, and prepare for the dangers ahead. I climbed on the bed and in the dim room I proceeded to count the square inches. Black Dickey interrupted my calculations by easing into an erection. He asked me a question and delivered to me a vision. "Why don't we have sex with Loretta?" The image of squishing my fingers into her squashy but muscular hips and dangling my nuts against the tenderness of her inner thighs, skimming Black Dickey over her vaginal opening and feeling the mist of her juices aroused Black Dickey and his veins flexed into a stout stance. Captured in my hand he wiggled his way down into her twat. Seconds later I quietly relieved spastic liquid out of a full Black Dickey. I decided I would count the rest of the inches in my new home after I napped.

***

*I dreamed of a fairy-tale church wedding. Standing at the altar, poised, I was suited in a traditional black tux with tails. Loretta was escorted by her grandmother and as she slowly approached our gazes became locked in an enchanted trance. Her smile was consumed with joy and it sparkled through the finely dotted veil. A fragrance of roses slowly danced an aurora of romance around the ceremony and became the background to the solo soprano's love song, **"Always And Forever."** With the congregation behind us, we stood front and center as one, and breathed out our confessions of love, honor, and respect. It was a joyous celebration.*

***

The water pressure of a stool flushing woke me up. Over sanitized Clorox streamed up my nostrils and the fragrance of burnt rotted feces caused me to choke. Suffocating and straining for fresh oxygen I searched for the awful strangling scent.

The boniest old white man I'd ever seen came into view. He looked like "Freddie Cougar—the character from *Nightmare On Elm Street*. I could see the skeletal bones of a man standing in front of the commode and he was wiping his bare shell of an ass.

"Damn Jigaboo!" When he became aware of me, his dirty words were emphasized maliciously from his filthy tobacco chewing toothless chops.

He was a hairy old rusty fart and black tobacco drool was caked into his gray whiskers. If he washed or cleaned up his skin was probably shades lighter. The foul odor followed him to the bed and I got a gust full when he flung his limp bones down on the bottom bunk beneath me.

A weird suspiciousness about the old man started gnawing at my gut. I wasn't afraid of the old frail fool. I knew he couldn't hurt me. Even if he attempted to gut me in my sleep I could easily over power him. His racial taunts hadn't shocked me. I'd been exposed to southern behavior, white people yelling degrading obscenities from cars all my life. In my brief incarceration, everything I'd witnessed and what other prisoners had told me, my understanding was that in all of Oklahoma's correctional facilities the races were separated. Why was I placed in the cell with him?

***

In twelve days the answer to the old man's mystery was revealed. The old fellow was dead. Jake was his name. Convicted of murder he was given life without parole. He had spent 37 years in Big Mac's maximum security. Only two weeks before my arrival, he was moved into medium security. The guard doped him every morning and he slept all day. At night, un-intelligible chatter dogged his sleep. In nightmares he would blindly scream gargled vicious acts of a retaliatory nature. I concluded they were possibly incidents from his past transgressions. "Ouch! Niggers, please, please don't hurt me!" I-I-I didn't mean it. Please-please, I didn't mean it! No more, No more, no more, please let me go!" Listening to him was awful. In the small 8 by 10 cell, his lurid snaps soaked in a sickening feeling that crawled at my bones. What had he done to those black people? When morning's light hit sky the pain medications would taper.

Then, the first night of sleep I had there, there was silence. His shouts and hallucinations had sub-sided. When I awoke I sensed I'd been sleeping over dead flesh.

"Old man...old man!" I stood over him and yelled. The covers didn't exhale. He was 77 and lung cancer had metastasized and killed him. Other than being at a couple of funerals, he was the first person I'd come close to witnessing life leave.

Even though I'd gotten a glimpse of his frail scrawniness, I was shocked when I saw what was wrapped around it. When the two medical professionals examined him, butt naked, he was covered in tattoos. KKK insignias, skulls and bones and a golden bolt of lightening that extended from one shoulder down to his butt then upward to the other shoulder. German swastikas were all over his arms; long black viper snakes covered his bony legs. For the two weeks we were together, in the mornings, bent over in pain, he would travel to the stool and then moving like the mummy he would scoot back to bed. The prison uniform and dawn's dimness had safeguarded the deep repulsive beliefs of my elderly inmate's philosophy.

Chapter Thirteen

My throat opened wide and I swallowed a metaphorical vision of the history of the old criminal's metastasized cancer. The mystic abstraction explained how his physical condition was connected to his bigoted attitude. Hate had spread throughout the old guy's body and killed him. I witnessed brief flashes of sketchy images of the old coot's horrid life and Black Dickey shuddered. That instant, insight to the hate and violence of this old prisoner's life was the beginning of a string of nightmares that would narrate Oklahoma's racist history. Persecuted and enlightened by these dreams, I would later develop some unique eerie instincts.

I was 21 years old and the man who shared my bedroom had died. How should I feel? I was bombarded with emotions and inside these walls I couldn't show any weakness. So I privately prayed for the old fellow's soul and cursed his corpse at the same time. He was a human being and hated black people I told myself. He deserved to die alone with haunts from the people he'd persecuted.

On my first day in Big Mac I was so frightened that I felt like do-doing on myself and stinking up the place but messing on my ass wasn't the answer. Acting like a bad ass was an option to saving my ass. The hairs that sheltered Black Dickey arrogantly stood up.

After three hours of sleeping semi-peacefully, the sound of slinging keys and steel doors opening rudely snapped me back into my dangerous surroundings.

"Jackson! Get your lazy ass out here!" Standing in the open doorway the guard hollered. They were letting the medium security prisoners out for work detail.

My first morning of prison life I guarded my movements. Under an induced spell of paranoia I developed a goofy look that probably saved my ass. Wild-eyed, I appeared unstable and unapproachable, "That nigger is crazy!" That's how the other prisoners later reported my bizarre appearance.

Surprisingly, I was lead outside and as I breathed fresh country air, dreamily I gazed across 1,500 acres of flat land that was full of golden brown leaves and grass of the fall. It was a precious view. 'Working the fields' the job was labeled.

At one time this portion of the prison's land was used for farming. Cows, chickens, hogs and goats roamed outside the home of inmates. Now the prison only used small sections for growing vegetables.

I had been caged almost seven months and the freedom of being outside, absorbing the cool breezes of autumn's all-encompassing winds made the short hairs on my skin rise in exhilaration. Prisoners had threatened my life and the guards and the correctional system had diminished my abilities to think of myself as a creative soul. I pulled off one boot, freed my foot and allowed it to soak into the red soil.

As the winds of freedom blew I peered off into the big spotty cloudy blue sky and reflected: I had been on the verge of graduating with honors and now, hastily, my life was traumatized and downsized. Now I was digging dirt and raking leaves. That was my new job. As I gazed across the blue-skies and its clouds of doom, my future appeared bleak. A sudden strong breeze and the mysteriousness of the autumn season began to reveal as well as romanticize many of the autumns of my life: *There I was in black and white photographs, and I was four years old. I was running and playing, kicking and splashing the autumn leaves. I would dance my way through the public schools. Later I was in Kodak color, driving in the wind and rain and then, appearing in Technicolor and Panoramic wide screen, making love to Loretta. We were in the back seat of the Camry under an October orange moon. I froze a frame of Loretta flexing her agile naked body. This photo was saved on DVD in my memory and an image was stored on my computer brain. I zoomed in on her vaginal hair and viewed the intricate parts of her vulva.* A fight broke out ten feet from the spot I was hoeing and my imagination slipped back into reality. Right now I would've been two months into my senior year. I'd prepared hard and since my freshman year in high school I'd dreamed of graduating with a degree in engineering. Instead I was one of the gardeners at a state prison.

***

At the beginning of the workday, the day that the old man died my hoe scraped the dirt off the home of a half-inch bug, with a red head and a black body. To escape the light and me, the creature quickly ran. The insect treaded under dead leaves and down dirt-hills, fearful of the funny running creepy crawler sneaking back to bite me and in grief over my dead roommate, I chased the bug down and split it apart with the hoe. By the end of the day I planted a tear in the dirt for my racist roomy.

***

Later that month while I was outside working I saw a huge black crow. Or was the bird a scissor-tailed flycatcher? Either way the animal soared high and began dropping altitude like a plane descends for landing. The winged creature got closer, aimed its beak, and zoomed in at my head. I ducked and the bird missed me and flew off into the clouds. The flying mammal was going to use my bushy hair to build a nest. But birds only gather material to build nest for their eggs in the spring, I reasoned. Close up, I saw it was a crow with scissor tails. Had global warming caused confusion in the crows and the sissortails parent's and maybe made them to crossbreed? Or wherever the birds were, were the two different bird species the only ones available for mating? That's when my own reality hit me. I was out there thinking about the sexual habits of birds and HELL I was in prison. My nerves ran circular sprints over the panic in my blood. I was rooming with 246 convicted killers, 190 burglars, 112 rapist, 197 robbery bandits, 26 kidnappers, 140 were there for violent assault, a long list of larcenist, arsonist—common petty criminals, and people that had committed unusual crimes that I'd never even heard of. I had a total of 1451 bunk buddies. And I'm out here in the field wondering if one type of bird is capable of having an attraction for another and making love to it. Jesus Christ!

***

A month in the life of a prisoner is different from 30 days as a free man. You don't relax in here. As each day slowly ticked away, I could feel the gentleness of my psychic features evolving into and under a hard shell. Mamma had nurtured me to love, trust, and respect people even if they didn't show me the same courtesies. But the old Kayin was fading and he was vanishing fast!

At first I acted like I was one of them, unsympathetic to the good that was in the world and I purposely denied having the nurturing love of a mamma. The machismo setting reminded me of yesteryears when I was in junior high school. These prisoners were like budding teenaged boys, puffing out their chest. But I began to agree with the sick ideas of people like Joe Thompson. He wiped the sweat off his face after a basketball game and with a deadly stare he told everybody his deadly desires. "I'm going to break my bitch-ass wife's neck!" She had him arrested and charged with assault. I associated his dilemma with the people responsible for my predicament. I nodded and saw eye to eye with his illness. Two days later when Butcher Boy's eyes lit up, this was the first time I would see a revenge vision that was equivalent to what was in my heart. "I'm going to cut the heart out of the white cop that arrested me." This time I could see the two policemen that had ruined my life. In my eyes was a hundred pounds of hate and hurt and my gaze matched Butcher Boy's threat.

No doubt about it, I was changing. Moving from Oklahoma City to Lexington, to McAlester had briefly interfered with my weekly visitations with the two people in my life that had reminded me of my own humanity and I was feeling the effects.

Although their letters were late, they were still arriving and I desperately held on to each precious word. Intimately I snuggled up to these personal notes and fondled them over and over. It was a different world in here and bonded inside their loving notes I identified some sane pieces of my fading personality.

Weekend visits were special. The decent part of me got excited when I saw civility represented in the actual physical images of Mamma and Loretta. But even in their presence I had to wrestle with my altered morals.

After seven and a half months finally the baby inside Loretta's belly was beginning to shove against the contours of her slim shapely physique leaving Loretta disproportionately disfigured. Even though she was sexually unappealing to my jailbird eyes Black Dickey was still raring to bend Loretta's big belly over and do her doggie style.

Loretta had bloated up and she looked like a pregnant Tweety Bird. Her face was fat, her jaws sagged and I'm sure her feet were swollen but they were covered and nobody could picture that condition by the size of her thin legs. The orange maternity dress she wore had a rainbow of multi-colored baby pictures and they were plastered all the way down to her chocolate brown ankles. Though I was trying to be poised and natural behind the prison's Plexiglas window, still we appeared to be uncomfortable sitting across from each other.

Loretta's usual impeccable calm and reasonable persona stumbled while she chatted about plans for the baby and her solid wall of stability came crashing down on her.

"I-I-I...don't...know...how...I'm going to make it!" All the way from the bottom of her vocal cords, Loretta's weeping tears became mixed with screeching cries. With her palms she covered her sagging face. I was dumbfounded to see fear and indecision originate from this uncompromising ambitious black woman. This was the lady whose spirit had fed me her naked body and had fueled my aspirations to become a successful black man. Now here she was weepy and weak.

"I'm going to help you girl." Mamma embraced Loretta's hands and then leaned and massaged her hands lovingly through her pregnant thick rich black hair. They tilted their foreheads together.

"I'm going to help you girl." Mamma repeated her comforting mantra as she patted the back of Loretta's neckline and an avalanche of helpless unworthiness consumed me. Black Dickey felt feeble and scrawny. I watched this pitiful scene powerless! I wanted to turn into a smoke cloud and dissolve through the glass and join in on the snuggling. I wanted to melt into both of my lady's affections. I couldn't, I was in prison and I had to suck it up and suffer these painful intense emotions for almost three more years.

"Wha-wha-what...'bout school?" This declaration of an oblivious future by Loretta made her whole body cringe with fear. Her head landed in Mamma's bosom. I was fiercely bombarded with even more helplessness and my stomach was quailing.

Graduation and doing it on time was an important ideal to my lover. The girl was made up of timetables. After our last exam of the sophomore year, late that night we drove twenty-five miles up to Arcadia Lake and had a picnic. Under the stars, on the ground near the water, we celebrated by making love.

"In five years after college, I'll be a senior programmer at a fortune 500 company; taking expensive vacations to the Bahamas and Africa...Ahahaha!" Lying on my chest after our bodies had tussled, as we glowed in joy under a May moon, I believed that night she was more excited about her life's plans than the many orgasms she'd experienced. Loretta's whole life was premeditated. And at that moment watching my baby defeated and frail, with my bare hands I could have strangled all the people responsible for my mess. My cousin, his two friends, the policemen, the judge, prosecutor, and all the white jurors, I wanted to kill them all!

On the way back to lock up, I schemed on ways to over power the guard. I would trip him and while he was on the floor I'd use the cuffs to choke him to death. I could grab the keys, exchange clothes with him and hitchhike back to Oklahoma City and be by my pregnant girlfriend's side. But then the cops would come and arrest me the next day. I conceived more angry delusions but in the end, none of them worked. The authorities would always know where to find me.

I lay on my bunk and was choked by a childhood promise I had made. I didn't blame my father for dying but his absence had left a huge hole in my life. I grieved for his presence daily. And it was a child's pledge that was haunting me. I swore I would always be there to chase away life's fears for my children. That was the oath I'd taken and as I developed into manhood I'd exhaled this mantra as easily as I breathed. Now incarceration had immobilized me. Even though I knew it wasn't my fault I was here, I would join a long line of dead-beat black men and my child will become part of the alarming statistics of black children being raised without a father's love and protection.

I'm sure many of those absent African American fathers were in circumstances beyond their control and wished life could be different. I'm not going to be there for my baby's birth. Can't comfort the child's mother during her pregnancy and I have nothing to offer my family financially. A restless Black Dickey sulked and acknowledged how impotent he was. Loretta's dream of graduating on time had died and that night as I lay on my cot I sobbed in agony.

***

Five weeks before Loretta's due date, she collapsed at school and was rushed to the hospital by ambulance. The doctors found she was suffering from vaginal bleeding; blood was soaked in her urine. A x-ray revealed a cyst was bleeding from one of her ovaries. An emergency laparotomy was successfully performed without disturbing our baby. As a precaution she was placed on bed-rest until the baby was due. Since Loretta's elderly grandmother was incapable of properly caring for her, Mamma packed a suitcase and spent the nights sleeping in Loretta's extra bedroom. She had to wake up early and cook Loretta's breakfast before heading off to work. By way of the expressway the hospital was ten minutes away. On her lunch break Mamma was able to zoom by and care for Loretta.

On November 3rd the skies dropped an early chill that settled on the heartland. In Big Mac when it gets cold the field hands are upgraded to house servants or janitors. Later I would be promoted to the laundry room. If an inmate had previous training in a trade, like plumbing, he would spend his time unstopping stools or replacing drainpipes. Training and education was no longer offered to the state's most illiterate members. In the years that I was incarcerated the temperature was the same outdoors as it was inside the prison walls. The ventilation system was broke. Your nuts froze in the winter and you'd sweat your ass off in the summer. On this November 3rd there was also something else falling from the heavens; a baby boy slid out of Loretta's vaginal canal.

My son had lived four days before Mamma, on her weekend visit, informed me I was a daddy.

"His head is round like yours and he has your flat nose." The message lit up in Mamma's eyes and her big smile was pure joy. She had on a bright ginger dress with sprinkles of dark brown leaves.

Those soft seasonal colors emphasized her grandmotherly affection for her grandson. No matter how miserable I was, Mamma's elation and her news reached into my past and lifted a memory that reminded me actually how to feel a smile.

The happy emotion dug through the phony perception of a made-up happy I'd always tried to assume whenever Mamma and Loretta came to the prison. Smile managed to slip past the inadequacies I felt being a father that was locked up. Somehow the sensation sneaked by the awkwardness of finding a dead roommate and the fistfight I had with JJ. It slithered its enjoyment through the other confrontation I had with the muscled corn fed homosexual, one of my next-door neighbors. I'm 6 feet, four inches and the husky gay man towered over me.

"Nigger I'm gonna get me some of that chocolate ass!" The sour feminized-coated southern accent leaped from the pink-faced white man named Joey. He stood in a fighter's stance in front of my funky water fountain-stool. If someone wanted to kill you or kick your ass here, the system makes if easy for that to happen. When the inmates are out working the cell doors are left opened. It was only my second day at Big Mac, I was tired and sweaty when I entered my room. Scattered all over the floor was my hope-line, the precious letters from my two ladies. Joey had ransacked my home. The stress of prison works on you when you don't have time to think about becoming an animal you just become one. Rage jumped on me and ran through my bones like the viciousness the absence of heroin affects an addict and I snapped!

"Come on motherfucker!" I screamed, threw up my fist and stepped towards the intruder. I faked a right; he flinched and threw up his left arm to block the punch. My left hand was transformed into Thor's hammer. I used it to repeatedly deliver uppercuts under Joey's chin and nose. Squeezed inside my bare knuckles were the faces of the white cops that placed me here. Separation from the comforts of Loretta's affectionate lovemaking had been hard on Black Dickey and he added his anguish in the punches.

"Umph!" As Joey grunted, I heard bone and cartilage splatter. Split in the middle, blood gushed out of Joey's nose and he tumbled backwards on the stool. Joey squatted in a silly position; he looked like he was sitting there having a bowel movement. At the time I didn't realize the impact of the power my punches had on my status in this violent segregated world. I had performed and passed two prison admirable initiations. First I'd shown valor and kicked some ass and second I'd beat a white man's ass.

The glee danced around the sorrow I felt for a fellow inmate. "Do your own time young-blood." The prophetic verse was whispered to me out on the prison grounds from a quiet veteran of the system and I believed he was an innocent man. Joe Johnson had already done twenty years of a life sentence. Together we raked leaves and tended to the harvest. He raised his rake and plunked his fork into patches of debris and that was when I first heard his sad song. The color of a chocolate Baby Ruth, this short chubby forty something inmate had no shifty con game in his eyes. Raised in the small town of Hugo, Oklahoma, and when you looked at Joe, you were looking at a black roly-poly country cowboy. His big lips carried a smile as big as the south and he had a hang down frown that was full of all the white southern cruelty. Convicted of raping a white woman twenty years earlier, he'd finally gotten a lawyer to take his case and to use new technology, DNA testing. This was going to be his magic get-out-of-jail ticket. When he learned that the DA's office in Hugo had lost his file and all the physical evidence involved in the case, the black cowboy sadly cried. "All that scrawny white girl said was that I looked like the black man that did her and that was enough for the white jury to put me in here for life." He lowered his head down and continued raking as he hummed an old Negro Spiritual.

The charismatic, endearing beam appeased the danger I felt from a threat that black inmates made because I had humanely befriended a physically challenged young white man; a definite no-no! Not because of his limitations, they rejected his color.

My new roommate spoke like his tongue was stuck to the roof of his mouth. The language he managed to form sounded twisted and forced out.

"I'm...Bob-by. Are...you...my...new...friend?" With a dumbfounded gaze Bobby took Frankenstein stiff staggering steps towards me, he had his hand extended and was ready to embrace my hand in friendship.

I shook my head. His unattractive features startled me and I'd never seen a white person approach me with such open tenderness. I was baffled. Mongoloid—Downs' Syndrome, I diagnosed him from my psychology class. In the public schools I'd attended in Oklahoma City there were Blacks, Asians, and Latinos who were mainstreamed or fit into the special education classes. I'd never been up close to Caucasians with the condition. Now, there I was, around a white man probably a few years older than I with a mind of a child. His huge round eyes were like those of a lost puppy and they were reaching out, emotionally attaching a bead with my shocked gaze. Confused, involuntarily, I took two discretionary steps away, not because of his physical repulsiveness. I'd never experienced, seen, or felt the pure innocence of a white man and disbelief shoved me backwards. A blameless dummy was living in a world full of propaganda, superiority and hate. He unabashedly pursued camaraderie, pushing right through my awkwardness he stepped into my private space. He embraced my hand. Clumsily he began shaking my arm up and down with an idiot's strong exuberance. I was taken aback at the freaky white man's gesture of undressing my prison mask and offering his humanity. An edgy pause in my eyes received him with apathy.

Every inmate had a distressing story. Some that would make you boohoo till the cows came home. Bobby's would just make you cry and say shame on society. On his 18th birthday, his homeboys had introduced him to the town's prostitute as a joke. All the teenagers were drinking and celebrating whatever they perceived as having a good time. As things sometimes do with young people and people under the influence, they got way out of hand. The middle aged white whore ended up with a broken arm, cracked skull, was gang raped and robbed. Bobby was the only one police found at the scene. He had no money for a lawyer and a family that didn't care about his life. He was convicted and sentenced to 15 years.

My son's birth gave me hope and the joy burst through the heartaches of prison life and brought bubbles from my eyes to accompany the smile.

Chapter Fourteen

When my head dissolved into my pillow that night, I welcomed sleep. Although locked up, I was a daddy. I was hardly at ease with the two realities, wasn't even close to loving those certainties but I stopped wrestling with them for one night. I was awestruck with the idea that I was a new daddy and I was comfortable with the thought that I would do the best that I could to make him into a man.

Although we practiced safe sex, I hoped that Loretta was full of my oxytosin. From my layman's understanding oxytosin is a hormone that's released by men and women during orgasm. We had plenty of those! The power in the substance is supposed to magically bond people together. The fact that we'd produced a baby together meant some of the union potion had escaped the rubber and was in her. The scientific fact that my oxytosin could live inside her for up to six years calmed me. And having a son overrode my insecurities of losing Loretta while I was incarcerated. I had indeed dick whipped Loretta's little chocolate ass! Those were the memories I had of our incredible sex life, plus our oxytosin bond fed my beliefs that she would always be there for me.

It was a night of ease; maybe that's why Oklahoma's Black history lessons began seeping through the sandstones of the prison walls. In one of my psychology courses I'd learned meditation was better when the mind was quiet. One is able to access the unconsciousness, blow through the confusion of consciousness and quickly arrive at answers. But this was different. I hadn't asked any questions but I'd never been a black father before either. Maybe I was whisked into this Black fifth dimension because I had responsibilities now and I needed preparation from the past for my son to have a better future. Then again maybe the deprivation of prison life had induced a psychosis and I was going nuts.

***

An *"Indian Summer."* That's the term white folks had labeled hot temperatures that seeped into the fall. That year we had one and I was again outside raking leaves.

Joe scooted his rake next to where Bobby and I were working. Holding his head down, he whispered like he was spilling top pentagon secret messages. "The brothers are watching you with the white boy."

"I'm showing Bobby how to work that's all." Joe didn't say weather he believed me or not, he rolled his eyes at Bobby and me and moseyed on. Con's can spot a con. The old sixth sense of the other inmates probably could see I had developed a real love for Bobby.

With newspapers and magazines tucked around my waist, I cagily lived. I didn't want a shank up my ass for being a Boy Scout. Bobby and I were cozy and cool for a little while longer. Three months later Bobby was killed. JJ Birdsong, the unhappy brother that I had lit into back in county, had made his way to Big Mac. JJ was still angry and lost and was still sucking penises. Through the prison grapevine he was known to have performed foliation on two guards for their silence. In the shower he'd gutted Bobby while they observed. Was this pay back for the ass kicking I'd given him or was JJ demonstrating the only power he had over a white man—prison justice. No one was ever charged for Bobby's murder. Cowboy Joe Johnson from Hugo, Oklahoma became my new roommate.

In the midst of murderers, thieves, and con artist the exploration into blackness began with a blinking light. While I lay as comfortable as one could get in a prison bed, asleep or almost asleep and nearly dreaming, the lights began flashing. In a more or less siesta state I was transported into a beam of disco lights that blinked in multi-colors. Red, orange, yellow, and a dark blue before the scene faded to black. A spark of brilliance and the pattern would begin again. Flashing black and white photographs became undistinguishable moving pictures. Slowly coming into focus I saw an army of red ants climbing from the desert dirt and swarming over an uncircumcised Black man's penis. A blink of the lights and the ants were replaced by the buzzing of those nasty green headed flies. They were feasting on a plate of genitals. The flies were swapped for a frying pan and I saw the penis simmering in grease. Symbols—and that was the end of the first session. Observing something akin to him roasting was obviously enough for Black Dickey. The experience kept him hid between my nuts for days.

The next sign was an even stranger adventure. I was asleep but all of my senses told me I was wide-awake. Scorching my nostrils, I was filled with a unique stench. Was it the filth of my old dead roommate? In an almost midnight dark cell I sat up in bed. Suddenly and mysteriously, from the hall, a tiny cone shaped light uncovered an open crack in the cell's steel door. I leapt to the floor, kneeled and inspected the bottom bed for the scent that was polluting my snout. The dead man's corpse was gone and so was Hugo Joe. On my knees I followed the spark of light to the barley-opened door. A shimmer of light spiraled into a thin line down the hall over the aged prison floors. A large ceiling light was at the end of the hall and gazing down the passage, I saw that on both sides all the cell doors were wide open. I crept and peeped into the homosexual's den. It was empty. On down the hall, one door to the next, I saw no one was at home. Had they all escaped and left me here all alone?

In the blink of an eye, I was transferred outside in the jet-dark prison field and the only light was a bright full blue November moon. The wind was whishing and the swirling spine-chilling cold tones blended in with the darkness.

"Swak! Swak!" All of a sudden I heard a wretched noise and it jumped inside my heart. I squinted into the dim moon's light and identified the distant noise; it was a band of buzzards. With their wings spanned, a pack of the creatures circled the moon. For a moment I was jealous watching them celebrating their freedom.

The scent came back overriding my envious bird watching adventure. The odor was as strong as a four-day-old dead rat. It started strangling the black air. I choked and tried to run and escape the funk but my feet began sinking into the earth. The dirt became as soft as marshmallows. I tripped and fell on my knees and hands and the putrid smell intensified.

From glimmers of the moon's glow, I could barely see broken bits of human intestines surrounding me. I started to feel squiggly maggots nipping at my nuts. The swarming parasites curled circles around Black Dickey.

Struggling, I was able to rise up and now each step I took, I slowly sank but I was gradually moving across the field. Finally I collapsed face down and like bees swarm on honey, flies covered me. My prison clothes disappeared. The stinky slimy odors of death fitted me into its suit.

I awoke in a schizoid frenzy. I ripped at my skin for sticky stinky stains. Along with the fantasy, the leeches had disappeared. In the shower remembering the bewitching episode, my body's cover twitched. I scrubbed the top layer of my hide until I drew blood.

As I swabbed my room, I thought of the burning black penises in a skillet, the interlude outside, why was I trespassing on the insides of human corpses? I wondered if these occurrences would dominate my nighttime of prison life. Had the hostile days of prison life generated a snap in my unconsciousness? The daylight hours of added aggression was hardly the therapy I needed as a solution for my sleep problems.

As a result of viewing a penis being sautéed, I would stare with suspicion at what little scraps of meat that were served at the prison. The fantasies of sexing Loretta would cease for a while. During that time Black Dickey lost his power, dried-up and wrinkled. My rod looked like an organ that belonged to a ninety-year-old man.

Three days before Thanksgiving two inmates were stabbed. One of them died. And just like on the outside, the holidays delivered the gifts of family intimacy and a large dose of depression if those memories of the kinfolk were dreadful or missing.

Sometimes the monotony of washing and separating thousands of matching prison uniforms permitted half seconds for me to wander into memories of Mamma, Aunt Betty, Danny and I. On one particular occasion we were all loading into our Ford station wagon. I was five and we were headed down to Grandmother's house to share our Thanksgiving. Grandmother lived forty-five miles away in Langston, Oklahoma.

"The town Langston and the University were all black before Oklahoma was a state." Half way to Grandmother's house, Mamma would stare at my naive curiosity and reiterate these sentiments every time we were on highway 33. I always smiled and thought

Mamma was teasing. How could a town exist before a state was created? I hadn't been exposed to American history, the migration into the west; and for a long time I wondered why the school and the town were all black?

Laying a log on the burning flames in Grandmother's fireplace, I would become mesmerized by the blue and golden blaze, the sizzling of wood cooking, and then a sudden pop and crackle. The noise would cause me to jump and break the spell. Outside Grandmother's cabin, Danny and I would play and explore the woods and soon we would always get lost among the countless trees. The aroma of pecan, pumpkin, sweet potato and apple pies always lured us home. The tasty ancestral recipes were lined up and cooled in Grandma's kitchen window. The flavors dipped into the mist of autumn's fragrance and always rescued us from the forest.

I was folding some fat prisoner's pants when I heard someone mysteriously whispering. *"Edward McCabe, Edward McCabe, Edward McCabe...Edward McCabe."* In the daydream, in the woods, the breezes vibrated these words. Someone was changing my real life memory. Who was *Edward McCabe?* The glimpse of the good old days was gone and what remained was the scent of prison-soaped laundry and the methodical sound of the churning washing machines.

In early December after recuperating from giving life to our baby, Loretta made an appearance at the prison with Mamma by her side. The dark autumn stripes on her cotton blouse hid some of her leftover dumpiness. The exuberant new mother proudly shared the baby pictures. He did sort of resemble me. I smiled at the little guy.

I had written Loretta and Mamma of the decision I'd made. *"My child was never to see his father behind bars."* I didn't believe it was a good idea to expose a child of a black man living in prison as a normal lifestyle. Plus I didn't know how I would respond to the rage of him being so close and not being able to hold him. And the idea of him leaving without me would tear me apart.

Even though Loretta was conservatively sheltered in autumn stripes, I could see her breast had a juicier plumpness. Especially when she animatedly demonstrated how she used a pump to pro-

pel milk from her breast. Black Dickey enlarged when she dramatized the suctioning.

"The machine has 8 adjustable suction settings and 4 regulat-
ing cycle speeds." Waving her arms, using her hands to express the
different cycle swiftness Loretta flinched, batted her big browns as
if the machine was hooked up to her tits. "And I tried all the settings
and the speeds! " Loretta bashfully said and all Black Dickey could
see it was him thrusting inside her and that he was the cause of her
flesh flopping and not her new toy machine.

"And it comes with a backpack, a battery pack and an AC
adapter." With that bit of information I sensed Loretta had dealt
successfully postponing the completion of her education. She was
ok with the time-out to have our baby.

"If you're breast feeding why would you need that machine?"
I had to ask since I wasn't part of her new life with my son.

"Oh Honey, sometimes I swell with milk, leak, and wet my
clothes and it feels and looks awful…" With a baby's sad and helpless face Loretta explained. Still I wondered what women did before they had breast pumps.

"…And when I go back to school in January, I need the luxury
of knowing I don't have to worry about how my body is functioning." Loretta the planner, she's always been a step ahead of life's
challenges. Maybe she'd even forgiven me for getting her pregnant and impeding on her initial graduation plans.

I counted each pace walking back to my cell. Melancholia
added extra weight to my prison boot. What was in my future?
What did I have to look forward to in January but survival? And, if
I lived through prison life, what sort of life could I have or expect. I
would be an ex-con. Maybe my son and his mother's life would be
easier if I wasn't in the family photo. This downhearted weight was
causing my feet to ache. The cell door was a welcome sight.

***

*It was early twentieth century and the flames off the hot sun
reminded me of the Sooner State in July. A vegetable patch comes
into focus; the rows are manicured. At the perimeter, a gust of wind
scatters her blond hair and mysteriously I already know she's a first
generation white woman from Old England. She stares in admira-*

tion, not at the beauty of her bountiful harvest but at a half-naked shirt-less black man in the middle of the field. The sun's bask has stained her pink face but still she squints into the sunbeams and her lust devours her in fantasy. The sweat drips off the black man's well-defined muscles. She lifts her long pasty skirt and settles on the tailgate of a pickup. The black man is a sharecropper. He slightly leans while he works the hoe. The bloomers she wears are too hot for the season and it inhibits her fingers from directly massaging her wild desires. Obsessed by passion, in a rush, she yanks the underwear down kicks the material off and digs into her vagina while she straddles on the tailgate. Soon she's enthralled in orgasmic pleasure; her legs kick frenziedly and she bumps her head on the bed of the vehicle. Lying limp and sweaty under the hot sun, the lady settles down and recaptures her composure and status. Quietly, she casually steps into her abandoned underwear, pats off her dress and stridently walks up a concrete path that leads to the land owner's two story framed mansion.

***

Nightmares and illusions would accompany me into the darkness for the rest of my incarceration. Confusion and psychotic arguments with other inmates were already part of my daytime routine.

***

I'm crawling in a round cement tunnel. The hole is narrow and dark. There's only enough room to move if I slide on one elbow at a time. When I rest, I breathe heavy, my body swells and for a while I'm stuck. I taper off inhaling and shrink. I begin to trudge the journey into the shady cave again.

I'm numb. I'm no longer inside the tunnel. I'm inside a coffin. Somehow I know I'm part of the U.S. mail. With a severe jolt to my back, I become aware that I'm traveling on a stagecoach. Unknown and unseen, I feel the wheels plodding up rocky hills and often the ground is unleveled. There's a pool of water at the bottom of the box from yesterday's heavy downpours. I sip the water. The next day the extreme heat dries up the water. The knowledge of slavery recently ending seeps into the illusion but still I had an urgency to escape the Deep South. Moving from town to town

without getting arrested isn't easy. In Mississippi, like most south-
ern states there are codes that have been passed to keep black
people docile and working as field hands in order to maintain the
plantations and the southern way of life. Inside the wooden box
I'm terrified of the life I'm fleeing. If a black person didn't have a
job he could be arrested as a vagrant. This became a southern law
immediately after slavery ended. As a black man, I didn't want to
travel from town to town and risk an arrest and end up performing
slave labor on a redneck's farm. The box was the safest way out
for me. The postal people were not careful with this package and
my body is bruised and Black Dickey is raw. I wish I was stuck in the
tunnel dream again.

***

It's the roaring twenties in the new Oil State. Auburn haired
Alina eats polish sausages and barley remembers her grandpar-
ents were from Poland. She doesn't celebrate Christmas by eating
wigailia and she is unfamiliar with the Easter blessing oplatek. She's
no longer interested in dancing the polka, she wants to learn how
to honky tonk with the native cowboys. Endogamy hadn't perme-
ated Alina's desires in a lover like it did her parents and grandpar-
ents. They had lived in Polish communities that were steeped in
Polish traditions and separate from the America she desired for her
life. She had fantasies of English, Irish, and German boys; people
she'd met in the neighborhood and at the public schools, people
she'd been exposed to. Watching some of these stout guys instinc-
tively moisturizes her vagina. She had affections for them all her
life. Alina simply wanted to be liberated: she wants to integrate her
Poland into her America. Since she's been told that a black man
is more like to a chimpanzee rather than human, the idea of him
as a lover would be bizarre. Alina doesn't bother herself with idle
introspection; she doesn't try to understand the psychological and
sociological dynamics of society. It's easy for her to convince her-
self to except the hate and believe the dominant group's propa-
ganda about black people. She has desires for a crime free neigh-
borhood and a decent education for her children. These wishes
would always supersede any logical concerns she may have had
for blacks and whites integrating. Women were given the vote in

Oklahoma in 1926—if and when she decides to use this power it wouldn't digress from the standards and morals of the society in which she seeks acceptance. If asked how and why she arrived at her societal-political choices she would quickly tell you her grandparents didn't participate in chattel slavery. This tidbit of insight allows her the freedom to seek her own white picket fence and her own emancipation into America's apple pie. Strangely I was aware of the names of Alina's grandparents and the history of their heartaches and desires. Aurek and Basha arrived in McAlester in 1877. Aurek got work at The Osage Coal and Mining Company. A few years earlier coal had been discovered on Indian Territory and the black gold attracted the white business folk. Aurek was near the bottom of the labor pool just ahead of Blacks and Mexicans. No matter how hard he worked, for his generation, his ethnicity wouldn't advance in the financial professional hierarchy of the coal pit. They were modest folk and they began life on the plains living in the mining community. The company owned the house his family lived in and all the stores where they purchased goods.

"All of them were never against us", but most of them were unaware of the affects of slavery. I wanted to consider that most of them weren't aware there was a lobotomy performed on us. For generations the system of slavery dislodged Africans from the oldest philosophies on the planet and the cornerstones of their survival—their religious and philosophical belief systems. It would be hard for me to acknowledge that civilized people would knowingly approve of Jim Crow. I'd like to assume if shame and misery, ostracism and religious persecution, and poverty and the bigotry that drove Alina's grandparents out of Poland, if suffering, excruciating feelings could live in the DNA, from one generation to another, then certainly Alina's attitude towards Blacks might be different. Somehow I knew this particular adventure into dreamland wasn't about the few Poles who did protest but the many that apathetically didn't. Alina was **free, white and twenty-one** and would pursue her American dream. She married an English American and their children would mix with the Irish. Their offspring would blend in with French and German Americans.

***

The holidays had passed and I was going to be shocked by a wintry surprise, a harsh coldness that only unsheltered cold-blooded animals from the North Pole should experience. Like I said, earlier there was no reliable central heating or air conditioning in Big Mac. The winter's chill would freeze through the thin layer of skin that covered and was suppose to protect my bones. As I lay under the thin state provided blanket, my breathing was slowed and measured. I listened to my heartbeats as the chambers transferred warm blood out. I trembled at the crossroads when the cold blood flashed in. I visualized the icebox that must be outside. At night I could see frostiness across the prison field in the darkness. As I sought sleep, Black Dickey squirmed. He nudged himself against the inner walls of my thighs and prayed for holy heat. The slithering friction between my compressed thighs reminded him of embarking into the opening of Loretta's luscious affectionate vagina.

For the rest of my winters, when darkness came, I began negotiating and some nights I traded the frosty delirious tremors for a frightening escape into the historical nightmares.

Chapter Fifteen

I've seen scenery of the old south's cotton fields on the Discovery and History channels. Even when I saw the landscapes in movies it was difficult to relate those cotton balls to my life. Grandmother had black and white photographs of her and my great grandmother, great uncles, and aunts toiling in the sunshine on Oklahoma's fiber-rich fields. "We pickin' cotton and pullin' bolls." The sentimental elderly woman would mimic her mother as she explained the pictures. And now the memory of her yesteryears of old Oklahoma and the even older south was cast in a vision and talking to me.

***

"Pick me!" I heard someone with the heavy baritone vocal cords of James Earl Jones. Asleep, I was suddenly awakened in a hallucination and a sparkling light brought in the dawn. The Jones vocal cords appeared to echo out of a cotton plant that was close by. Close by where? I couldn't see my body in the meadow. The dream had escorted only my eyes on the journey. Up one row, down another, I gazed atop the cotton wild flowers and my eyes were sent spiraling down a stalk to where it entered the dark red dirt. Underground earthworms squiggled and I saw the roots of cotton plants as they strung seeds. Suddenly I was back peeping on top of the cotton plant. I saw gleaming dewdrops, and prowling on a limb a Polise wasp hid beneath one of the plant's green leaves. Somehow I knew the bee was hunting for a caterpillar to eat.

In a twinkle I witnessed two months growth of a new kernel of cotton eating sunshine and rain and changing into flower buds. Another flicker, another three weeks of nourishment and the blossoms opened. Like chameleons are sensitive to their environment's color, the flower's modifier was age. In three days the creamy whites turned into mellow yellows. I felt Black Dickey aroused when they bloomed into pretty pinks. He was sad when the flower withered, died and floated to the ground. Left on the vine and inside the bolls I spotted some miniature football shaped green cottonseeds.

Similar to the purpose of ovaries, after they mix with semen and construct embryos, the bolls have asexual seeds. They turn brown, ripen, and expand. And just like a baby sliding out of a birth canal the seeds split the boll and burst upon life's scene as fuzzy white cotton. The fluffy strands looked like tasty gooey carnival cotton candy.

"Over here boy!" Even though I was invisible to myself, apparently someone in the fantasy was able to see me. My eyes searched around for the sound. Finally I spotted some tiny gray bugs crawling on a nearby cotton plant.

"Those are boll weevils boy." Suddenly the sun's rays sent straight lines that beamed and exposed the origins of the Jones' vocal cords.

"Those little beak headed bastards are going to eat my ass up if you don't hurry and tend to me."

The plant's deadly situation made me think on my own reality. Was I finally free? Where were the guards? Was I really outside the prison walls? Black Dickey interrupted, automatically offering his two cents about his fantasy. He'd almost exploded when the green covering unfolded in the cotton's creation process. Somehow he'd managed to associate the opening of the plant to sex. He saw himself pleasuring Loretta and the unfolding was her slender muscular legs flexing the ecstasies of an orgasm. The brown bulb became an exotic pair of chocolate nylon bikini panties but none of it was real and he knew it.

"Hahahaha...my dear young man there are neither gates nor guards halting your vivid imagination." He'd heard my thoughts. The cotton ball wobbled and I began to get a glimpse of his personality. He reminded me of my old black over-weight high school teacher. *Mr. Wise* was the legendary name the student body had given Mr. Willie Williamson. He always offered wee stories full of wisdom in his daily lectures.

Shrewdly the cotton plant's eyebrows rose. "I'm the symbol of black slavery and white superiority!—". He said and paused. During our momentary stare and silence, I sensed he wanted me to hear more of his story and the meaning of his pronouncement.

Since he was a mind reader, I remained quiet but graciously he allowed me to see underneath his white cotton veneer. As the boll weevils vanished I saw distinct features of Mr. Wises' smutty flat nose and his short grayish afro.

"Before they invented indoor toilets all sorts of folks would hide behind those trees." He pointed with a stem that acted like an arm for him. I stared in that direction; shrubs and a towering forestry full of green oaks appeared. "People would squat and release feces or piss behind those bushes right down into the dirt. The rains would come, the winds would blow and all that nasty stuff would one time or another be swept away. But some of the ingredients would end up mixing in with me." The old fellow sniffed up and down and all over himself. I assumed he was sniffing for stinky residue.

"And then y'all make clothes out of this scum that's in me!" He said, as he tilted his head back, his belly out and did a hearty James Earl Jones laugh. "Ahahahaha!"

"I'm going to lay some old soil stories on you young man—" He paused again. This time he waited like he was waiting for my approval to begin or was the gap part of his theatrics as a story-teller?

"Mother Africa's piss was the first taste I had of the bitter water! Yum-yum!" I didn't know what shocked me most, him saying Mother Africa, or the way he smacked his lips as if he actually enjoyed the taste of pee.

"Yeah. Natives are the descendants of Africans. In fact all folks are." This I knew but at this time I wasn't aware that actual Africans were on Oklahoma's soil. A warm wind carrying camaraderie pleasures emptied into me and for a moment all the insecurities I had of a world based on the skin color vanished. Briefly I felt peace. This harmony squeezed my life's universe together and I was emotionally connected to every thing that was human.

"Many-many…many moons ago, caravans full of African explores floated off Africa's western shores over the Atlantic and natural currents landed them on the continents of South, Central, and North America." Night and day and night and Black Dickey thought surely those adventurous sailors got horny. Black Dickey began to envision the vast Atlantic's water dashing on a topsy-tur-vy ship and the hips of naked black women flexing on the edge of the vessel. The ladies butts were in rhythm with the waves, splashing and they were grooving with the tempo of their lovers. Splattering water and semen dripped out of a bunch of vaginas, trickling down their dark stout legs. The sticky substance swayed like a river that streams awkwardly off mountaintops. Coagulating, the sex juice formed trails that dipped into the shadows of the great Atlantic Ocean.

"In the last few hundred years, even though the Natives were most of the humans inhabiting Oklahoma, a group of white folks sold the land to other whites. France swapped the land to other new occupiers of The United States. And neither were the landlords. Oh the U.S. government paid the Natives a small sum and then they swindled them out of the rest. This was 1803 and the bargain was part of the Louisiana Purchase. In 1824 the Caddo, Wichita, Quapaw, Osage, Kiowa, Apache and Comanche tribes kept an eye on the Irish and English Americans when they began to build several forts across the territory." The jolly belly of the bulb jiggled and James Earl began whistling the first verse of the tune *America The Beautiful*.

There was a sudden grimace swelled to the cotton man's face and the puffiness made it appear like he had swallowed his whistle. Then grief began to dominate his features. The pain made lines on his forehead. He quoted the first part of Taps and hummed like a harmonica. *"Day is done, gone the sun...."*

"In the 1830s, more than four thousand Native's perished on the trip...*The Trail Of Tears.*" The cotton man began the second verse. *"Fading light, dims the sight...*

"A white miner found gold in the Georgia Mountains and the great Cherokee Nation had to pony-up and mosey on down the road to Oklahoma. *Um-hmm!*" The frown on the cotton man and the um-hmm explained how absurd and selfish it was for white folks to take care of their desires first and the hell with the generations of Cherokee's that christened Georgia as their homeland.

"More white folks were moving into the best fertile farming land in the country the southeast. Other Natives in that section also had to pack up their belongings and move to Oklahoma. The Chickasaws, Choctaws, Creeks, and Seminoles stepped in the long line with The Cherokee. All gathered their possessions and with hardly any food, supplies or medicines, the chiefs, braves, squaws, and children had to walk more than a thousand miles in freezing winter temperatures." I heard babies crying and saw images of feet swollen with blisters and dead women lying face down in the snow. Buzzards pecked their bloody carcasses. Black Dickey flinched as if it was his skin the feathered scavengers were biting. It was my first winter living in an Oklahoma prison cell, I didn't need any more scenery to know what a beastly chill felt like.

"They were known as the Civilized Tribes. 'cause some were indoctrinated into the European culture. Countless had become Christianized and had built churches. And programmed into their new American customs, many owned and enslaved black people. Black folk walked across the country de-humanized by red people and they both were repulsive to the white race." I scowled at the Creek blood I had in me and shamefully tried to repel this bit of immorality from pumping out of my heart.

"Now, let me tell you about the sex distribution in Oklahoma.

"On some level the English and Irish were already screwing each other's women before they sailed over on the boat and they certainly were doing it during colonial times. Before the pre-land rush days occurred in Oklahoma, they began knocking boots with Native American ladies for free land…uh…well maybe some were in love." By his stutter and merry smirk it was a hint that the *'In love'* declaration was a joke. "It was customary for the tribal chiefs to offer land to a son-in-law. But the American way is, it's better to fall in love with someone that's got something, right?…" With widened eyes he paused to intuitively know my response. I guess I agreed, 'cause James Earl continued. "And the white folks specialized in Cherokee women. Unlike white chattel slavery, under Creek and the Seminole law it wasn't a death sentence if some of the brothers enjoyed the pleasures of the native's family's jewels—the women." He winked and smiled.

I began to see images of white folk having sex on beds and on their knees down in the dirt. Native women with their buckskins had their skirts lifted and black men's hip's humped between their thighs, and emotions of orgasms were smeared across their red faces. And I squinted at blurry images of Native women having orgies with white men in the light of day, and on hills and behind naked trees and bushes, while nature's wild animals watched. I saw wood fires flaming in the dark and black passions burning inside tepees.

"The English and the Irish either loved sex or they loved the land...or both." He finished whistling the second verse of Taps, *"Fall the night."*

A dream stole the next sequences out of the hands of the cotton story-telling man. I was whisked right into the 17th century. Don't know how I knew what century I was in but I did.

***

Scampering, tripping on the unleveled land, with the agility of a cat, the scanty clad black man was back on his feet scuttling. I saw glimpses of him entering a county through the backwoods and leaving a county the same way. State after state hound dogs viciously chased his scent. He hid in the forest, slept naked under leaves, while poisonous snakes, bugs and tarantulas wiggled on him like he was part of the shrubbery. Moonlight and under the stars was when he traveled. Terror lived in his feet releasing endorphins that guided his every step past the bounty slave hunters and the patrols. His path wasn't to the North but into Indian Territory. When he arrived in The Native's Land he married a Kiowa squaw and became a valuable member of the tribe...

***

The next slides resembled scenes from an old time movie with antiquated visual affects. The camera silently transported me into a dark dense fog. I'm already anticipating I'll end up at Dracula's castle. The sound is turned on and I began to hear creepy whistling winds. Wind blusters scattered the haze and a better camera light is installed and it illuminates a trail of wagon tracks. The camera zoomed up to the top of a weather-beaten wooden signpost— "Arcadia Cemetery". Wind gushes flapped the sign and the barbwire that's holding it up makes rickety noises. Below the sign was a tin billboard. Inscribed on it, in a nutshell, it said that the cemetery was segregated until 1966. Dead black bodies were on the left and the white carcasses were on the right side of the dirt road. The light flashed to the left:

***

Moses Gray	Maggie Lou Gray	Elizabeth Gray
Jan 3 1721—	Mar 29 1756—	Jun 15 1772—
Jan 21 1788	Dec 8 1821	Aug 12 1854

***

Intuitively I became aware that a number of blacks had escaped slavery and had landed in Native Territory but they weren't apart of any tribe. Descendants of the African explorers were already there and I wondered if the escaped slaves knew them. Then another thought occurred; all these people had declared their independence before the colonies had proclaimed their independence from England.

Since the Gray's were side by side I assumed they were probably husband, wife and daughter.

Then a spotlight shinned on the stones of three dead children:

Jean Roberts	Joshua Roberts	Daniel Roberts
Feb 9 1804—	Dec 19 1802—	Jun 13 1801—
Sept 18 1810	Sept 18 1810	Sept. 18 1810

I was hoping a disease that a primitive medical community couldn't control had caused their deaths. A house fire...or...or maybe white folks had decided to kill the children like they would choose to slay a squirrel or a rabbit! With sorrowful teardrops, Black Dickey wet my underwear. But, wait a minute, there probably weren't that many whites in the territory.

***

"Uh-uh. The distribution of the women! Stay with me boy!" The cotton fellow cut his distinguished eyes at me and I knew he'd entered my alternate illusion.

"Bugs and maggots were able to crawl on the white woman's dead vulva before the white folks would allow a black man's dirt to rub across her pussy!" His critical assessment made me shutter.

"Uh-uh. Back to the distribution of the ladies! The misses were off limits to the black penis. If your eyes even met a white woman's, young man you were subject to a lashing or you'd be tarred and feathered, or hung. Sometimes they would sever your genitals if you didn't show white women the proper respect." The cotton man demonstrated the Uncle Tom's simpleton's tone; he began shuffling and he made his eyes appear huge. "Always tilt your head when addressing a white woman. Address her as ma'am, or miss even if she's a child." I saw clear glimpses of a black man and a popping whip cutting open his skin. His blood dripped down his back and suddenly the cotton man gave me a sly wink and the slave's agony was emptied into my veins. AHHHH-SHIT!

OH SHIT! OH SHIT! OH SHIT! I was crammed with more than this man's pain from a whipping. Humiliation, torment, terror, rage, shame, sadness, hopelessness, grief, distrust, hate, despair, these raw emotions exploded all at the same time through the center of my heart!

"And this was only a fleeting second of feeling this slave's insides." I exhaled and only the natural horror of being a black man in the twenty-first century remained.

"That's how the sex distribution was." His judicious stare told me that the professor was satisfied that I was paying attention to his lessons. Even though I knew I was living in the remnants of slavery and Jim Crow I finally had a concrete understanding why all through public school white girls in Oklahoma City didn't see me as sexy. They'd been brained washed. I knew that some were prejudice and I assumed it was solely a matter of preferences for others. Even though the ideas were planted inside their ancestor's heads, the programming was still affecting all of their sexual instincts. A piece of Black Dickey's esteem was relieved and he breathed a of sigh relief; there was nothing wrong with him.

"Hey! Hey! Hey! Don't try to do a summation on white folk when you have only a tiny part of the story." With an irritated posture Mr. Wise warned.

Even I know slave owners didn't circumcise their slaves and most mob hangings and castrations were done in the United States before the 1960's. Without notice I was swept into another vision. There I was viewing pictures that illustrated images of dissected, uncircumcised dark penises'.

"If one peals an apple or an orange, if the same action is applied to removing the foreskin of a penis, is it pealed or stripped?" Appearing before me was the crown or head of a penis. It had jagged edges that were ripped to the shaft exposing raw foreskin.

A botched circumcision—ouch! Or had a black man committed a crime by stepping out of his place.

The scientific inscription for the penis' pee-hole is the urethral opening and I witness a procedure where the penis was slit down the middle by a butcher knife. Flies took me on a journey of the anatomy of a black man who had been castrated. A cluster of them ate at the penis' blood supplier, the Cavernous Artery. Black Dickey dripped a tear. He knew without this oxygenated juice there would be no more erection for the brother. The Corpus Spongiosum, the erectile tissue that covers the pee-hole was filleted, cut up like a fish. The two chambers that string the length of the penis the Corpora Cavernosa, the spongy tissues were slashed like a wiener being prepared for a hotdog bun. Black Dickey squirmed at the sight of the Cavernous Nerve Bundle. This sensitive arousal center was smashed. The scrotum was cut in half exposing the two testicles. The testicles were cracked and you could see the semiferous tubules; the organ that generates sperm. Black Dickey fainted! Maybe because he didn't want to see any more gruesome red bloody tissues of his kin and for the rest of the tour, I was only shown black and white photoflashes. But these images of the decapitation and the flies escorting me through the dissection of a black man's penis would probably be etched into Black Dickey's psyche forever.

"Hey young man, I'm over here!" There was the baritone man again and I heard something swishing. It sounded like someone pissing. The fuzzy whiteface cotton man was big smiling. Some of his green limbs had turned into mocha arms and hands. Protruding beneath his belly was a dark chocolate penis. Piss rustled the tops of the other vegetation.

"Mine is working just fine.

Now back to the story. How ironic was it that in 1850, and a few years later in '57, the supposedly and assumed to be the wisest white folks on the planet, The Supreme Court, locked down the rights of blacks? They passed The Fugitive Slave Law and The Dread Scott decision, while the eastern shores were being flooded with river rats, and the downtrodden European immigrants in quest for their own liberty. The United States' laws ripped the throats of the Southern slaves. Escape, hope, freedom up North was no longer an inspiration or an option. Northern free blacks were harassed and some were even stripped away from families and drug down south into slavery."...Stripped away from their families! This news aggravated the rage I already had for my pathetic predicament.

"The potato crop failed in Ireland, 350,000 starved, and many of the survivors got on the boat. A failed revolution and a destructive economy in Germany, many of the Jews got on the boat. Political refugees fled France after they had their own disastrous revolution and many of them got on the boat. Later in the 1870's, overcrowding, low wages and high taxes in Italy—many of Little Italy's best got on the boat." The cotton man hummed and pounded on the dirt and made drumbeats to Neil Diamonds **We're Coming To America.**

"Before the Italians took the boat ride toward liberation to the good old U.S.A..." With a sneer he raised his hands, and made quotations, *There was a Civil War.*

Like Mr. Wise the teacher, often the cotton man would take a break from his serious history lessons and get personally involved with his student.

"Uh...uh, let me ask you a question Kayin?" The cotton man's hesitancy was that of a guy getting ready to ask a trick question.

"Yes." Giving him permission to lead me to whatever point he was going to make.

"And I bet God didn't make enough love to spread around the world and the poets of the ages haven't imagined the poems too express how deeply you feel for this woman in your life?" His eyes tore into me; he'd posed the question with the elegance of an English Shakespearean actor. Slicing through my prison machismo defenses he revealed an emotional truth. I loved Loretta like the heartache Romeo felt for Juliet and the cotton man recognized that.

And in un-Shakespearean English I replied. "Uh-yeah." The cotton man slowly nodded.

"Ding-ding-dong! In 1863 Lincoln rang the bell issuing his Emancipation Proclamation and the jingle was heard throughout the south. Ding-ding-dong! This echo vibrated an orgasmic jubilation in the slaves. In 1865 congress passed the 13th Amendment and black folks were hypothetically going to finally lavish in that swe-e-e-t—swe-e-e-t jubilee christened as freedom!" He said this with an alluring sarcasm and suddenly I was barraged by visuals of those days. I saw black folk bare-foot dancing, high stepping and giggling in brogans prancing up and down the fields and shouting to the masters to take that damn cotton and shove it! For a moment I wished I 'd seen some hip hop baggy pants teen-agers giving them the finger, cussing, and sticking Uzi's and A-K 47's in THE MAN'S face.

Dressed in a creamy white tux the fiber man became a balladeer.

No more auction block for me
No more, no more
No more auction block for me
Many thousand gone
No more peck of corn for me…
No more drivers' lash for me…
No more pint of salt for me…
No more hundred lash for me…
No more mistresses' call for me…

Chapter Sixteen

"**Section 1.** *All persons born or naturalized in the United States, and subject to the jurisdiction thereof, are citizens of the United States and of the State wherein they reside.*" The baritone of James Earl Jones resounded. He beamed with the eminence of a black preacher reciting the word of God. He had the roar of a politician declaring his populist policies and was gritty like a patriot affirming his or her God given rights to live and do what he or she was willing to die for. *"No State shall make or enforce any law which shall abridge the privileges or immunities of citizens of the United States; nor shall any State deprive any person of life, liberty, or property, without due process of law; nor deny to any person within its jurisdiction the equal protection of the laws.* Now that's section 1 of the 14th Amendment, signed by Congress in 1868. The Civil Rights Law that was suppose to lift a black individual higher that a pig, or a goat, and raise their status from three fifths of a person to a whole human being." With his features animated he exhaled and absurdity and consternation gripped his face. "This is the American dream, a promise that has never been fulfilled to African Americans."

"Damn silly humans needed a law to enlighten them, to demonstrate care, respect and affection for every human being." Mr. Wise shut his big brown eyes and shook his round fuzzy gray head in disgust.

"On April 9, 1865 the Civil War ended. Five days later Lincoln was killed. On December 6, 1865 Lincoln's Emancipation Proclamation, the 13th Amendment, was ratified and that same month the Ku Klux Klan was officially born." The cotton-field darkened, lightening streaks danced across the sky and an explosion of thunder shook the ground. I heard the shrill of a bullet soaring and I saw blood pouring from the back of a bearded white man. The next frame the man is dead. Appearing in black and white I saw bloody photographs of black children with severed legs and a few of their bodies were chopped off at the torso. A clip of a dislodged black man's head with the eyeballs jotted and clear fluid dripped from his sockets. All lay in a cloud of dust as horse's hooves kicked and thuds resonated from galloping steeds. Wild white men concealing their vampire eyes under ghost garments are mounted on the stallions. The horsemen scurried off to hunt other niggers. In another scene, as far as my eyes could see, there was a trail stacked with black dead bodies. There were no gaps between the corpses. And I noticed I'm shown this scene immediately after the Civil War and after black folks had danced the jubilee jig.

"Andrew Johnson a southern sympathizer cried, 'Poor white folk done lost their slaves,' boo-hoo!" Sarcasm moved his motions as James Earl lifted a white handkerchief and blew his nose. "After Lincoln's assignation, Johnson became president and he decided to restore power to his antebellum friends. And they immediately initiated sanctions against blacks and restored privileges for whites. Restore! I guess life was equal for a split second in America but if you blinked you missed it." Huge white lips appeared on the dark face of Mr. Wise and he whistled *I Wish I Was In Dixie* and jams to the music.

"And before whites had a chance to get use to blacks as equals, slave codes and regulations extended their antebellum social superiority behavior. They were actually borrowed laws from free northern states. During slavery, these statues were used to control blacks from having equality in the north. In the summer of 1868 the ink was still wet from the ratification of the 14th Amendment and these unnatural policies devoured the good spirit of change. The 14th Amendment had little effect on the attitudes of whites or the conditions of blacks. The Supreme Court's 1896 Plessey vs. Ferguson Decision legalized venomous anti-social ways of life against African American's Civil Rights and the Jim Crow Laws were born.

The cotton man started staggering, his eyes rolled around and he tumbled into a tree and fell. The fumes of liquor attacked the air.

"Some white folks are like alcoholics and once you're an alcoholic you're always an alcoholic. There is no such thing as making an alcoholic into a successful drinker. In denial, an alcoholic will substitute one drug for another one but is still an addict. They can get strung out on stimulants, crack-cocaine, barbiturates, and psychedelics. You can treat a heroin addict by placing the addict on morphine or methadone and even when the addict is completely drug free, doctors will tell them that the drug was only a symptom. A sober untreated alcoholic still has obsessive-compulsive tendencies, weak coping skills, and destructive behavior. The best cure is abstinence and a spiritual life can make them into healthy moral humans." The cotton man stuck his hands in his pockets and kicked the ground.

Instantly snapping out of his frustration, in a white southern twang the cotton man was back offering advice. "Code number one. Stay away from the pure sanctity of the white female! If you want to legally exercise your God given instincts use them on a nigger wench."

"Niggers were born to pick cotton and to work under a white man. If you want a different occupation, I suggest you get a court order signed by a southern judge. And if you're not working I'll have your black ass arrested for the new vagrancy law and the sheriff will find a white person's farm for you to work on to pay off your outstanding fine for not having a job. Thinking about leaving town you better have a note signed by your *daddy white boss*! Good luck with that. If we catch you roaming in a town without that sacred letter, you will be jailed. Nigger I want you living on the outskirts of every southern town and on rental property. We're not going to sell or allow you to own nothing." Mired in contempt the cotton man delivered his white southern speech and gazed at me with a redneck's stupid smile.

And I began to reflect. The way a robot has sensors, whenever I drove out of a black neighborhood and entered a white section of Oklahoma City, I could always feel Black Dickey bracing himself. An unusual nervousness and an unnatural agitation would always crawl on top of my skin. I suddenly realized those codes have been transferred through history and were riding as a passenger with me all through the white side of Oklahoma City. This was my box. The same carton used in the dream on the stagecoach—except I'm only traveling inside of a town, not from town to town. But I better have my license, insurance, and registration papers. A nigger never knows when he'll be stopped and arrested for driving while black. In college, every time I finished a test, I had doubts and wasn't sure if I'd be graded under the same scrutiny as whites. Through the white professor's eyes am I viewed as less than? I was transporting paranoia. I wondered what Maslow would say about my development or of a society that perpetuates these conditions?

"What was the country going to do with a bunch of broke ass uneducated niggers? Laboring in the fields, cooking and cleaning, making the master's clothes, nursemaids to white children, building the masters homes and the state houses free of charge. It wasn't like these sisters and brothers didn't have skills. For those days and times they had excellent resumes." With his palms up and with a stupid look the cotton man once again, slowly rolled his big eyes.

"Generations of sweat for more than two hundred and fifty years. You would think they deserved severance pay wouldn't you?" Tongue in cheek, he presented a question he knew we both knew the answer to.

"But the congress delivered a resounding **No**, defeating the **Forty Acres and A Mule bill,** 126 to 37. These same white folk punished the Natives of Oklahoma for their ownership of slaves. The Indians had to supply their ex-slaves with forty to hundred and sixty acres. Do as I say but not as I do." I knew the government was wrong for not giving us something to survive on.

"Not only were most of the newly freed folk illiterate they were victims suffering from many abuses: Rape, child molestation, brutal beatings, combat fatigue, extreme esteem issues, and all the other mental illnesses known to mankind. On top of all that they were sent out into the wilderness without their rich African culture and religion.

"The government should've given the ex-slaves who were national heroes at least some land. Instead the Negro was left penniless and homeless. Kicked to the curb!" James Earl swung his leg high and his jaws swelled. The cotton man balled his fist, animated he emphatically condemned the United States government's resolution.

The scene changes in the dream. I see the cotton man standing on the bay and instinctively I recognize the Mississippi waters. Swimming under a dusty rising heat haze the air melts into an orange summer's sunset. The cotton man uses the soulful vocals of Paul Roberson and serenades me to the tune *Ol' Man River.*

***

Some time during the daytime and between bedtime and nightmares my hair begins to dread. Two years into my sentence, less combing or grooming and my wool naturally styled itself. It automatically tightened into knots. Although race relations are horrible in here and there are malicious beatings and killings among blacks and whites, there is yet an unspoken brotherhood, an intimacy that exists with all prisoners. Sometimes black and white inmates' laugh together, some times heart-felt stories are shared. Time passes slowly and you can absorb another person's culture. In these sensitive exchanges a person can get lost and there's an altering of your personality. Their tales can become apart of your own way of life. Two Rastafarians, who were of the Jamaican tribes that never were slaves, were now my neighbors? Breathing an aura of strength, these brothers paraded the prison grounds as if they were kings. They easily resisted the influences of the other inmate's bad behaviors and the prison's induced soul sicknesses. I wanted what they had and I wished my history wasn't what it had been—that of slaves.

***

"Here ye, here ye! Step right up folks!" This time the cotton man had on a white top hat and a stripped shirt. He was decked out as a carnival ringleader or was this costumed cotton fellow an auctioneer?

"I'm the republican candidate for president, Rutherford B. Hayes. Here's the deal. The deal of a lifetime! For four states and twenty electoral votes I'll remove the federal troops out of the south, end reconstruction, and keep all the southern white women safe from the nigger rapist by stripping them of their constitutional rights. The privileges we theoretically just gave them only eleven years ago! Need a rope?" He tipped his hat and twirled a rope into a lasso. "That's the agreement that was made by the new republican president to the democrats of congress in 1877." And that was the last memory I had of the hallucination that night.

The next morning while I washed my ass under the ice-cold shower, I closed my eyes and quivered. The cool wetness was equivalent to the outside weather. Behind my eyelids, I began to see barren trees and brown leaves scattered over dead golden grass in a pasture that spread long and wide until the earth met the sky on all sides. Suddenly the retched noise of *Al Jolson's "Mammy"* began to tweak through the spigot. Behind my eyes, snowflakes fell and I saw the flurries melting. Springtime came with the rains and the grass changed into green. Strange fruit was growing from the trees. The limbs were producing black bodies. Necks stretched one to two inches like rubber bands. Diagnosis: they were hung. As far as my eyes ventured and from every tree I could see naked black male corpses dangling. They suffered from the dislocation of the spine with a snapped two-inch gap, and that formed the transverse severance of the spinal cord. The hanging death had caused damages to the central nervous system; I was witnessing the affects. There were urine stains on the victim's legs and their last bowel movements were stuck in their asses. A few droplets were on springs green grass. And all the brother's genitals were manipulated.

The shower experience began to take on a similar journey I'd had as a child at our state's fair. I was riding in a cart inside the scary house. As I traveled into the darkness, whenever the cart bumped into an object a skeleton lit up. The flesh on the hung bodies began flashing on and off the bones like a Jack O' Lantern. And I could see a close up of each dead face.

That night James Earl explained aspects of the visions in the shower.

"Some of the newer immigrants, now American citizens, the English, Irish, Italians, Jews, French and Polish, would join in on the nations traditions. This fresh sea of white faces ate hotdogs, participated in picnics and learned to enjoy their favorite pass-time—and without due process of a trial they lynched niggers."

Then the cotton man used Vincent Price's accent to dramatize the horror:

"Mostly under the guise of protecting the white woman's purity, forty-nine blacks were known to have been lynched in 1882. Fifty-three in 1883—fifty-one in 1884—seventy-four in 1885—seventy-two in 1885—seventy-six in 1886—seventy in 1887—sixty-nine in 1888—ninety-four in 1889—eighty-five black in 1890—one hundred thirteen in 1891—one hundred sixty-one 1892. God damn, it was getting to be almost every other day, pick-a-nigger and string one up!" The man of strands threw up his hands the way a black preacher does when they're feeling The Holy Ghost but his grazed wet eyeballs suggested he was experiencing what living in hell was like.

"The sun was touching the sky straight north, little white children ran through wild flowers and played in a pasture, butterflies glided above tables full of hot delicious cuisine or was the day rainy? Did it snow? Were the winds blustering? Did kids slide on the ice? Did the little ones chase autumn leaves or were they soaking under lightening skies? The guardians of the young, drunk on adrenaline powered by hatred would turn into a mob. With child in hand, each of them would struggle through the crowd just to have a hand in hoisting a black body up on a rope. For killing a black person, and to be photographed and part of a post card; a valued treasure they could send relatives; these white folks were celebrated as national heroes. The deed would become part of their contributions, stories they shared around quaint family fireplaces. Maybe killing a black man to them was the same as a father going hunting with his son, and they were only passing on their heritage.

"One hundred eighteen in 1893—one hundred thirty-four in 1894—one hundred thirteen back in 1895—seventy-eight in 1896; one hundred twenty-three back in 1897—one hundred one in 1898—eighty-five in 1899, and to celebrate the turn of the new century those white folks strung up a whopping one hundred and sixty in 1900." Through the magic of my illusion the cotton man transformed again. My eyes tweaked and I saw him wearing a red, white, and blue, All-American hat for the occasion. I heard whistles blowing and saw fireworks explode into a midnight sky.

"One hundred five in 1901—eighty-five in 1902—eighty-five in 1903—seventy-six in 1904—fifty-seven in 1905—sixty-two back in 1906—eighty-four in 1907—eighty-nine in 1908—eighty-nine in 1909—sixty-seven in 1910—sixty in 1911—sixty-one in 1912—fifty-one in 1913—fifty-one in 1914—fifty-six in 1915—fifty in 1916—thirty-six in

1917—sixty in 1918 seventy-six in 1919—fifty-three in 1920—fifty-nine in 1921—fifty-one in 1922—twenty-nine in 1923—sixteen in 1924—seventeen in 1925…"

The cotton man's statistics faded under a chorus of begs and pleas and agonizing screams that almost busted a hole in my eardrums. Even while awake, for years I've been haunted by flies swarming and eating rot off mutilated black carcasses.

Devastated by what I'd seen and heard I was compassionately serenaded by the cotton man. He changed into the precious jazz voice, Lady Day—Billie Holiday. With her signature flowers, and they appeared to grow out of her peek-a-boo hairstyle, and through her song "*Strange Fruit*" we commiserated together.

"Enough of this torture, these images alone should make a black man impotent whenever he veers within a mile of a white woman!" Exasperated the cotton man produced a handkerchief and wiped sweat off his forehead. "All the executions were not only black men, some sassy sisters swung on the noose too!" The cotton man's tone was mocking and condescending and even though he was patronizing, the situation insinuated a black woman was killed for getting uppity with a white person, this was frightening.

A brief image was blinked into my third eye and I saw miles of African American women stark naked hanging on flimsy limbs. Who were these women that America had murdered? And an awesome hurt spilled into my heart. Were some of them my relatives? Probably and possibly they were a friend's great, great grandmother, aunt, uncle or cousin. Maybe one or even some of them were part of Loretta's family tree. Maybe that's the reason I only saw a glimpse of the depravity. To see someone, a recognizable mother's love hanging on an old oak would've been too hard on my senses to contemplate. Black Dickey began to weep pee.

***

I'd already seen the cotton man transform himself. One night he appeared and he had dark sunshades on. He was leaning like Stevie Wonder and was parked at a black piano bench. I zoomed in to see his fingers scaling the baby grand, slowly he proceeded to play in the rhythmic styles of Stevie; and began crooning, *Sometimes I Feel Like A Motherless Child*.

Inside this dream I felt myself cuddling in Mamma's arms and heard her whispering a lullaby. I drifted in and out of the hallucination all night.

Another night and I was dreaming again. I saw the cotton man as a white man wearing a ten-gallon white cowboy hat. His big proud smile assured me he was the good guy, or was he? I watched him become Gordon MacRae! He whipped a rope into mid-air and lassoed it into a perfect circle.

"Yeeow! Ayipioeeay!

"Brand new state!

Brand new state, gonna treat you great!

Gonna give you barley, carrots and pertaters,

Pasture fer the cattle,

Spinach and termayters!

Flowers on the prairie where the June bugs zoom,

Plen'y of air and plen'y of room,

Plen'y of room to swing a rope!

Plen'y of heart and plen'y of hope.

Oklahoma, where the wind comes sweepin' down the plain

And the wavin' wheat can sure smell sweet

When the wind comes right behind the rain.

Oklahoma,

Ev'ry night my honey lamb and I

Sit alone and talk and watch a hawk

Makin' lazy circles in the sky.

We know we belong to the land

And the land we belong to is grand!

And when we say

Yeeow! Ayipioeeay!

We're only sayin'

You're doin' fine,

Oklahoma!

Oklahoma O.K.

Oklahoma, where the wind comes sweepin' down the plain

And the wavin' wheat can sure smell sweet

When the wind comes right behind the rain.

Oklahoma,

Ev'ry night my honey lamb and I

Sit alone and talk and watch a hawk
Makin' lazy circles in the sky.
We know we belong to the land
And the land we belong to is grand!
And when we say
Yeeow! Ayipioeeay!
We're only sayin'
You're doin' fine,
Oklahoma!
Oklahoma O.K."

"Yeeow! Ayipioeeay!" The roly-poly man spun and bowed and on one knee he breathed heavy and waited on applause from an invisible audience.

"They claimed it was because of the natives support of the south, and so after the Civil War the United States flat out took the western part of Oklahoma. To keep us away from them and make it safe for white folks, Lincoln and other congressmen had considered turning that part of the territory into a Negro colony. But Lincoln was dead, white folks had already discovered coal in McAlester and in other parts in that region. East Coast white folks needed beef and the easiest connection was the Kansas railroads. A lot of cattle lived in Texas. Big business now had a reason to build a railroad that ran right through Native Territory—Oklahoma. Yeah!" Dressed in an eighteenth century business suit he ducked and weaved his head left and right, the cotton man rubbed his hands together and he became a greedy scheming businessman.

Remember those brand new English, Irish, Italians, Germans Jews, Russians, and Polish people, the latest U.S. citizens?" I nodded.

"Since they had already sailed across the Atlantic, most came into the New York ports and it was crowded there. Haha! It's always been crowded in the Big Apple." This information tickled the cotton man. "Traveling on a train or in a wagon to become owners of no money down deals or free land after they'd fearlessly sailed the great Atlantic, this cross country trip was probably boring to most of them. But the excitement of being apart of the American Dream must have thrilled them to no end! These new frontiersmen even encouraged relatives to make the boat trip to America. You also had a bunch of po' ass white folks and saddle tramps whose families had been in the states for generations and were still penniless. To some of them Oklahoma would finally become their family's American Dream. To them it would become their Never-Never Land.

Chapter Seventeen

Dapper and cool as James "JT" Taylor, the lead singer of *Kool And the Gang*—he boogied to the music of their hit song "*Celebration*".

"Images of a life structured on independence and without the white man's thumb stuck up their asses had lived in the Africans' spirits for generations in America. To those black folks who made the trip, Oklahoma would be their paradise on earth. More than two thousand Freedmen, former slaves, black cowboys, carpenters and builders, and even black bandits were at the starting gun for the first land run in 1889. They walked in tattered brogans and upon blistered bare feet as far as Florida and New York. Wagon trains formed in Virginia, The Carolinas, Alabama, Texas, and Mississippi; all over the country black folks were loading up their modest possessions and heading towards their pieces of heaven.

You would think that traveling across country, entering into an unknown wilderness, that food, disease, snakes, wild animals, outlaws, even weather conditions, or perhaps a collapse in transportation would be at the top of the list of things for these brave black people to fear—but no. The KKK, sheriffs, the local officials in every little southern town was a threat to stop every revolution a wagon wheel made and each inch a foot scuffled. The new vagrancy laws gave them the power to put their meal tickets in jail and work on a plantation for free." This time I saw the pictures of history through the cotton man's eyes. In small southern towns, husbands and wives were drug from wagons and stripped naked and whipped. After stealing their meager possessions, along with their children, they were jailed. I saw white men raping many of the women and little girls. Many families were separated and sent to work free on different plantations and never reached paradise.

This sad pictorial by the cotton man of the black families' agonizing experiences to the old west spurred a shameful memory. Located at grandmother's home in Langston, a rusty old wagon wheel stood at the entrance beside the mailbox. In my junior year in high school our class took a trip to Washington D.C. In the process of exploring the Northeast, we boarded a bus to New York and Philadelphia. I was fascinated and frightened by the skyscrapers and I shrunk among the masses. I felt even smaller when we came across a few hip-hop young people. When they found out where our group was from, they were downright insulting. "They still got cowboys down there?" "Welcome to America! Hahaha!" "You ever do it with a goat?" "Do they have cars there, or do you guys still ride horses? Hahaha!" Yes. Thank you. No. Yes and yes. And by the way I did grow up riding horses. My grandmother had six on her farm. They lived in a red barn at night and during rough weather but mostly they ran wild in the pasture and ate off the land. She had two pinto ponies, a spirited appaloosa, and three saddle breeds. The young black people of New York City made me feel embarrassed about my upbringing and the state I'd grown up in.

Also inside that dream I imagined how romantic it must've been to have sex under the moonlight in a covered wagon. The image of caressing a squashy female inside a cozy covered wagon aroused Black Dickey and made him swell. I heard owls hooting, coyotes and wolves howling, and I felt the coziness of the thick deep darkness. The stars began dotting the skies with light and that twinkling scenery transformed the wilderness into an enchanting wonderland. I sniffed air that wasn't consumed with toxic waste. A mysterious pure form of oxygen rushed up my nostrils and sprinted sprightly throughout my veins. I got a buzz high off its exhilarating freshness.

"Yo-yo! Young man pay attention." The cotton man rolled out the teacher Mr. Wise to scold me for daydreaming.

"Unless you were a Sooner—folks who jumped the gun, sneaking into the territory before the start of the official 1889 land run—then you were able to steal Native land legally. Ain't that a bitch... the white man and his laws!" Disgusted the cotton man continued.

"If any good can arise out of a wrong, one could say that God generously gave strips of Oklahoma to the beleaguered ex-slaves. You could even say He did what the U.S. government didn't do. He delivered them out of Egypt and right into the wilderness of Native territory. But just like the Israelites had to survive in the wilderness,

Blacks had to survive racism and disease, land-grabbers and gun battles with Indians. And as bullets blazed and as the infectious disease of racism was passed on to future generations, black folk were busy building dugouts and tent cities. They transformed them into farmhouses and that grew into more than fifty black towns.

Imagine ex-slaves electing mayors and town councils, building neighborhoods and raising families, owning banks and grocery stores. Imagine African American farmers growing their own fruits and vegetables and then sending the produce off to market. Imagine Blacks teaching their young in schools, preaching to the congregations and teaching them about the black experience in churches. Imagine brothers making the devil's brew pot liquor and corn whiskey and the freedom to dance and celebrate in juke joints on Saturday night!" The cotton man performed a slow-drag as if he was hearing music and was gyrating rhythms into a woman.

"No curfew laws, able to go and come as they pleased! Ah-yeah." Relief and gratitude was smeared across his face and joy consumed the storyteller's eyes. "And in these all black towns this was one of the first times in America's southern history young black men weren't disgraced by the color of their skin. With dignity they could pursue and freely court a black woman in Oklahoma. And sexing nourished, corn fed, big muscle legged, country colored girls was never better!" Ecstasies were in James Earl's gaze and he was big smiling again. "Booker T. Washington visited Boley, Oklahoma in 1906 and declared the city the best home ever for Negroes to live. Perhaps Mr. Washington's remarks were swayed by one of those powerful legged country gals." The cotton man winked and belly-laughed again.

***

Even though I was sleeping, the nightmares were depriving me of real rest. As I tossed and turned, one night scarcely audible and dying into the background was the cotton man's history lessons. Making their way to the forefront were visuals of barren meadows of olden days absent of people. Tumble weeds, trees, rivers, and dust swirled up into the big sky leaving behind miles of stunning captivating picturesque views of the wild animal kingdom.

I heard a barrage of animal tones that sung in harmony. I flipped on my cot falling deeper into sleep and the background melodies from the creatures met me there. Beating into my brain were baritone agonizing hollers, high pitched sopranos screaming cries of loss, unrequited dreams, and restless needs. Slowly, I began to see the faces of the background harmonizers, and they were all African American males.

Soon after that nightmare, an out of focus glimmer of a man with a ghostly emerald glow made his appearance. For several nights, every entrance into the darkness, the hazy image added a precise fragment of his soul. First I saw a scruffy afro, then an inch of grubby facial hair. The charcoal color of his huge lips featured a red spot on his jaw. Finally I saw his long slender frame radiating. As I ogled upon his energy field, I felt a raspy scraping into and on my psyche. It was as if the phantom was etching a memory of him into me. The next morning I was at the end of the unit's hallway moping and I tinkled a bit of wee-wee in my prison pants when I spotted the specter's glow and his full protracted lean body in the doorway.

Hurt was engraved in beady bits of misery into his transparent persona. I had seen this ache mired in features of elderly black men before. The sagging angst almost made dimples on their faces. These black men had condensed their life's tragedies and somehow transformed them into dignified qualities.

"These gentle men were denied liberties, the possibilities of becoming whole and the opportunities to enrich the lives of their families. They refused to neither kill nor steal nor be buried in resentment and they wouldn't allow the white masses to measure and label their lives as failures. Instead of these bitter blows of defeat crushing them, they sucked out the sour taste and turned this acidity of abuse into sweet moral victories." The specter had used the engraving he'd etched into my soul to communicate and he gave me a clear defining understanding of the lives of those sacred men.

While I rested that night, the image spoke and this time I saw the words coming directly out his mouth. His tone was strong and full of rich flavor.

"I'm Jim and I was what you young folks call today a *horse whisperer.*" Right before my eyes in slow motion I saw the old geezer change into a young lean muscular man. He was still smutty looking.

"Horse trainer was the job the white master gave me after he'd seen how tender I was with animals. I could always get most creatures to do almost anything. My father had taught me how to stroke them gently, gaze into their eyes, and cozy myself into the tiny openings of their souls. I saw him work his magic. His knack for easily accessing this peculiar charm originated from my African tribal roots. My father was snatched out of Nigeria as a boy and brought to this country, and when the master saw how he was able to make friends with critters he had Pa carry out all the animal training duties. That was his job before master decided to sell him. He traded Pa just like the animals Pa was caring for. I was a young pup when Pa was sold away from the family. For years I worked in freezing winters and under hot suns supplying ancient charms on the horses, and on...Tehehe—" As if ashamed he covered his mouth and laughed. "...and I worked that old ancient charisma on the master's misses too; I was doing her while I was planning my escape.

Master would take me on horse buying and trading trips to nearby Tennessee farms. He depended on my judgment. He and the misses didn't know anything about horses and neither of 'em had any farming abilities. Only know-how he had was ordering and beating Negroes and slinging his rod into little slave girls and making them bleed and cry. He was my age and he owned land, Negroes, and animals because of a birthright, and the fact that he was white.

Anyway, Master got to where he was too lazy to go on our expeditions. He had me doing all his traveling and biding. Course he never gave me any money. Those arrangements were done over the telegraph. On many of those trips, I'd usually get my beanie wet with a slave girl. And quiet as it was kept on those same business trips, I was one of them niggers in the haystack. I was double dealing, doing it with some of the other white master's misses, cousins, and nieces.

In the spring of 1858 I was well into the second year traveling alone and trading. I was also mapping out an escape route. The Fugitive Slave Law narrowed my choices to far West or Indian Territory. Wherever I was heading, I'd decided to leave when the weather was warm and arrive wherever in warm weather. Didn't want to be looking for a place to live or build a home while I was freezing my ass off.

In the middle of April the master sent me to fetch a team of horse's two counties away. The night before I left, I hammered my master's wife like a mad man. It was my final wham-bam thank you ma'am and good-bye. See ya!

The next day, oh yeah—I did my job. I rode over and picked out the breeds, telegraphed Master, suggested what he should bid and yeah, secretly, my colored friends prepared manumission papers for me. That evening I snuck in the barn and I aggressively got my stick wet on a cute Tennessee slave woman. When we finished, like a Tennessee Gentleman, I tipped my hat to the lady. I took the master's livestock and from my slave lover's master, I seized two pistols, three rifles, ammunition, food, and a bunch of horses that were not part of the deal. I rode off into the sunset and I tipped my hat to the southern way of life. And as I journeyed up on a hill, I stared into the twilight and I sort of guessed at what my age was. I was close to twenty-five. Moseying over and down the hill I realize I was saying good bye to the only way of life I'd ever known.

I had legal papers that said I was free, but traveling with a herd of horses, a colored man had to be careful going across counties and into different states. Plus after I didn't show up, my master and my slave lover's master had placed hefty bounties on their stolen stock, and dead or alive on me. Traveling at night with fifty-four horses, I had to handle them with expert precision. I grazed them in the dark and we waded across lakes and rivers under the moonlight. I had to keep them quiet while we hid in the woods during sunlight. The big fellows are skittish of stepping on snakes. I had to make sure the herd stayed calm and didn't stampede when one of them spotted one of those slithering poisonous worms.

At the beginning of the harvest I arrived in Native territory. There were plenty of catfish to fry. Orchards were filled with wild nuts, pecans, nigger toes, and rows of juicy fruit trees. That's how

I survived. To stay alive I had to kill bandit renegade Indians. The lost natives tried to steel my herd and murder me. In the middle of Indian Territory I finally met a welcoming Creek tribe. Neither of us knew the others language but I figured out a way to swap some horses for a squaw wife. The Creek Chief Opothleyahola was a gentle and generous man. He threw in two hundred acres as a wedding present.

"God damn it! I damn nearly pooped on myself. Amazed while I was in a daze, inch by inch I allowed my eyes to linger on the bountiful splendor of the prairie's scenery. The cream drop spots on the pretty lacebark pines; ten foot crabapples withered in pale pink; vibrant shades of the season's yellows, oranges, reds, and purples appeared on the maples and oaks. This charitable chief gave this colored man the first item he'd ever owned—and it was a bonanza!" The slender dark man slapped his knee and big smiled.

"The chief was big-hearted but he was also a fake. And I don't mean fake in a bad way. Later I learned that Opothleyahola recognize colored English, he'd heard the noise a long time before I ever showed up doing my dance."

The long legged fellow performed a soft-shoe finale and then within my dream the specter addressed me.

"Kayin, you're an educated man. There must be a law in the astral world that says spirits have to communicate to the living on their level, you think?" It was rhetorical; he didn't expect an answer.

"With that said, listen up! When the wise red man spotted me trotting into his habitat with the horses, he'd already figured out I had stolen the herd from a white man. That act alone made me his friend. Opothleyahola admired my style.

As I got to know the chief, he welcomed me inside his community. His village was huge. The tee-pees and farmhouses were scattered and they extended for miles. Like the good neighbor Opothleyahola was, I was allowed to roam as I pleased off into Creek territory. Only exposed to one lifestyle all my life, and God knows that slavery was the wrong model, I explored The Creek reality. I was culturally shocked to witness Creek women sitting Indian style as they cuddled and rocked little kinky headed babies in their laps. Some of the tots had their tiny puckers on the women's red nipples. Little wool-headed straight legged children ran and played with full bloods throughout the village. I found grown black men my age and older and half-grown men and women mixed with black and red blood, and even elder sisters and brothers of a dark ruby shade.

In time I was able to get to know some of the brother's, red and black. We fished and hunted together. The Negro Creeks and I swapped slave stories that were full of miseries, but we also made fun of our ex-white masters, asinine wretched amusings that's only understood by the Negro culture. Most of the blacks had made the horrid trip from Florida, and some were still slaves, but even those were allowed to pop a piece of native ass. This was an eye-popping noticeable difference from white slavery. Even up north a freed nigger could get slaughtered for as much as a wink at a white honey. The Creek slaves worked for their owner in the day and most had free time in the evenings with their families. And un-like white owned slaves, hope lived in there lives, they knew in time there was a possibility of being released from bondage.

"I had other skills. I was more than a horse charmer. Since I was a boy, my Pa and the senior slaves said we exported our farm-ing and planting talent from Africa to America's soil. Some of the Black Creeks were born into the tribe, some accrued through a trade from whites, and some escaped from plantations. Most of the agricultural estates that the runaways were from only special-ized in growing cotton or one or two types of vegetables. Since my horse-trading job took me to many farms I learned how to plant pinto beans, greens, sweet potatoes, cabbage, melons, tomatoes, squash, and every other eatable vegetable from other slaves. And because of my natural heritage, born with a green thumb, any sort of seed I placed in the ground and with nature adding a little rain and sunshine, with The Almighty's blessings, we could make any vegetable grow!

Chopping trees down, clearing the land for a field of crops is backbreaking slave chores. Finding wild kernels to plant would be a miracle, God's work. But we did. The Creek farmers dealt with the army and other white farmers, and I did business with the na-tives. And once you have one seed it's yours forever.

In those days most brothers didn't believe you were a man if you licked a woman's private spot to get her to squeal. Satisfying your lover by using your pole, that was one of the ways a brother achieved manhood. But I believe a woman is like a wild stallion, you have to know how to gently, patiently please them before you ride them." The horse trainer grinned affectionately at the wisdom he believed that was contained in this motto.

"I was an adventurer, I used tongue, lips, all the trappings an experienced explorer would apply when discovering unexplored terrain. My tongue traveled up and down, sideways, flicked every nook and cranny inside Taima's sacred place. Taima, that's my wife's name. When we were making love I would scream her Native name's essence, *Crash Of Thunder*." He whipped out his long tongue. He was able to curl it under his chin and he thrilled me with this circus trick. "I'd suck and puck on the lips of her sanctified spot, push the lips away and glide through the opening. Maw on her innards and watch my woman shriek! Ooh-wee! My joint would seriously swell watching her lust for more." As he revealed his enthralling lovemaking experiences his lusty desires were inflated in his features.

"The misses and I, our first home was a dugout. Lack of comfortable space limited the amount of sex we had and that cramped my style. Baby girl promised me that if I built a house I could swim in her pool of delights more often. Neither of us were strangers to hard work but with more loving as an incentive, I busted my ass building that home. Tamia's vision as a woman and homemaker drove her. In our first year together we built a three-roomed framed house. Of course Crash Of Thunder rewarded me after the first room was built. I was a free man and I wanted sex daily. Since she was also free we always spent a lot of time negotiating.

We had two fireplaces and one was in the bedroom. Listening to the rain tingle against the cabin's roof made it cozy and romantic. As we made love, the orange blaze off the flames would make huge shadows out of our motions. I tried to move with the rhythms of the raindrops into baby-girl's precious spots. Hard, fast, medium, and when the water dripped I performed slow and deep and long circular twisting motions!" Joy was pasted on the old man's shameless grin.

Chapter Eighteen

Off and on during my prison term, I was bothered in the darkness by this long lean fellow.

"Leaving slavery, I had selfishly left many friends behind. Regret stuck in my back like a butcher knife and how they were still suffering gnawed at my soul. I had nightmares. I saw my friends in the images of helpless lambs being torn to shreds, slaughtered by a vicious pack of wolves.

When the war broke out I was ready and willing to act as a scout for the Buffalo soldiers and fight for the brothers and sisters I had deserted. Imagine an ex-slave getting paid to help free his people." He wiped his forehead with a dingy handkerchief and his broad smile was liberating.

"I first met the band of brothers, the buffalo soldiers in the spring of '61, while they were patrolling my land for Grey Coats. I supplied the soldiers with fresh mounts and gave them a tour of the backwoods. I felt peculiar when the commanding officer offered me a fee. I wasn't used to getting paid for my services. I had a wife and a baby on the way, responsibility. So graciously, I accepted the money. In fact on many occasions for several days the troops ended up living in tent cities on my land. My wife baked and cooked for them. Of course I took care of the horses, and for their thirst and cleanliness we offered them the use of the lake. Every time they passed through, we got paid!" With a rewarding smirk, he used an African American cultural gesture. He used one hand and smoothly pealed off invisible money to the other hand.

"Our governmental services turned out to be a real money-maker! I had taught my wife how to make home-brew and I always kept plenty of fermented pot liquor for myself. And Kayin, you know a bunch of brothers tasting spirits are going to need to wet their bones!" I nodded, not knowing if semi-intoxicated or drunk men meant they had to have sex or needed sex. "I'm a God fearing man and I believe everybody's got to work out their own morality with the big man. Kayin, don't even start to believe that I'm what folks call today, a pimp. Those Negroes were horny, they had some gifts to swap and I knew some Native ladies. I got them together and they all had big fun! Every time the soldier boys traveled through, I ended up charging the U.S. government for room, board, and entertainment.

"In the summer of '61, the Johnnie Rebs rumbled across our land. Our place was forty-five miles north of the center of the territory and soon there were always confederates on patrol around our little house on the prairie. I was already aware that my neighboring native brothers, four of the Five Civilized Tribes had been forced to fight with the confederate, but only a piss portion of the Creek stayed for the battles. Rather than sacrifice any of his braves and their families for the war, my friend Chief Opothleyahola and most of his tribe high-tailed it to Kansas. They clashed with the rebs all the way.

"I tried not to blame some of the natives for going along at gunpoint with the confederates. Although some of the tribes had slaves, I don't believe they understood how devastated Negroes were under the strong fist of the white man's slavery system. The Cherokees had adopted more of the southern white's cruel ways and were harsher on the slaves. Maybe because they had more white half-breads and maybe that meant they were more influenced by the white man's culture. From what I could tell the Creek and Seminoles were more humane to the Africans and I believe black men hit that cherry hole more often with squaws. Let me repeat a slave owned by a white man, that brother would never reach a position where the white man would offer him a white woman with his blessings. 'It would be considered 'a sin against God.' I've heard southern white folks declare these sentiments with burning passions, as if only God himself could've anointed them with this truth. To them it would be like a hen getting humped by a wild bore. In their view, that's how unnatural sex was for a colored man and a white woman. White folks believed we were two different species. I don't know how they justified sexing and mangling four and five year old colored girls. I've seen them beat the children's daddies in the youngster presence then turn around and use those same bloody hands to hold his daughters down and drip sex juice into their tiny holes. Dried fluids from his thang would later find its way into the child's mamma. And then they have the nerve to call us lowlifes." Disgust and disbelief exploded in this sensitive man's scowl.

"You know just like in your day, the U.S government owes China and Japan billions of dollars, they started owing Natives for land way back in the day. All those forts they built in the eighteen twenties were emptied, and most of the soldiers were sent east to fight and they left an unpaid bill. And that's how the rebels were able to easily rush in and take command of the Natives.

"I foolishly hoped the dressed in blue bugle white boys, the fort builders, would not act like their southern counterparts. But when they came on the scene they began willfully busting the squaw's buckskin skirts. While I toiled in the fields all day Tamia was busy tending to the farm chores and for a while we lived in fear. What would happen if the confederate, or U.S. Calvary, or a renegade native, or even a runaway black man would wander across a female alone in the woods? The mere thought of them harming my honey was making me insane.

"So in the spring of '62, Baby Girl and I made the decision. We abandoned our little cottage and went on the road. We became spies for the U.S. government. My daughter—now a toddler, Tamia, and I lived in the wooded Indian territory for the remainder of the war.

"Crash Of Thunder became my traveling love buddy. When I was slaving for the man, and he stopped going on the horse trading trips, I rode all-alone. Never rode with a female all day and then later rode her all night." He gave me a mischievous wink and his emerald glow sparkled.

"Crash Of Thunder was a lean girl, six-teen, maybe seven-teen years old when we hooked up. Bow legged, she had sturdy hips and her back was as nimble as a bending knee. Back in Oklahoma's early days everywhere you looked, the sky was blacker and glitter in the stars sparkled brighter, even the air had a dark creamy sweet taste. And grabbing her powerful hips, having her bow legs curl around me and her limber back arching like a rubber into my love strides, this was pure heaven. We'd cuddle and romp up a ruckus in the woods. She would whisper soft ekes and ahs into my ears and her ecstasy cries would be drowned out by crickets and owl hoots. The wilderness and the war became a blessing. I'd never had loving with a woman willing to give it to me almost whenever I wanted to get it. I was reborn every time I exploded into my baby's lovingly hugging pleasures. The only thing that slowed me from doing my daily and nightly duties was a dim-witted accident. We had camped down by the Arkansas River, I was pumping Crash Of Thunder hard one night and my pecker flopped out and skidded on a twig. I caught a splinter in the bad boy. Ooh-wee that shit hurt!" With pain swishing over his face he leaned and grabbed his balls. "I was glad I carried a stash of pot liquor in my saddle-bags. Infection, gain-green, blue-balls, all sorts of conditions could have happen to my piece. Instead, every morning baby-girl bathed my dipper in alcohol and she would kiss him good night with her sweet lips.

"Right after July 3, 1863 we would learn that General George G. Meade had kicked the hell out of General Robert E. Lee at Gettysburg. The largest battle and defeat of the rebels up north, and the folks up there thought the war was dwindling to an end, but we knew the fighting wasn't finished down here.

"One of the Creeks forced into a gray coat was Crash Of Thunder's oldest brother Akando. There were many Natives that acted as soldiers for the south but were spies for the north.

"Akando didn't surprise us when he rode into our camp. He'd reported to us before. But he usually brought us information in the dark. That's when he was able to sneak away and not be missed. But it was broad daylight and when Taima and I spotted Akando approaching, we assumed his visit signaled he'd become a deserter. We didn't know that the secrets he carried would lead to the downfall of the confederate's control in Native territory and end the Civil War."

***

The vegetation was altering into golden brown and dying, the seasons were changing again. Blood and guts are what the eyes notice when dissecting a freshly killed frog or a cat in a biology class. For two and a half years here in prison I had seen men cut each other up like pigs. And at night during those years I had delusions of dead people who told blood and gut stories.

Mamma was like time on a clock. Faithfully she made her weekly rounds. I saw Loretta less often; our time together became monthly and I was seeing the love and devotion we once shared and cherished fading in her frail eyes.

***

The frontiersman would always pick up the dream where he'd stopped.

"The Texas Road had been carved into the dirt by the United States government as a stagecoach transportation route to supply the use-to-be union forts. The road traveled from Texas, along the borders of Arkansas and Indian Territory, up to and between the Kansas and the Missouri boundaries. The dirt road was constructed way before the Civil War, before the railroads, and wayway before the highways and interstates. Since the confederates had taken over Native territory, the Texas Road was used to supply southern soldiers, rifles, artillery, ammunition, food and goods to Fort Cobb, Fort Arbuckle and Fort Washita in Indian Territory, and over into Arkansas, Fort Smith.

"According to our family scout, the confederates were planning an ambush. The conspirator's only depot station was on the Texas Road at Honey Springs—now I hear they call the town Muskogee. Six thousand gray-coats secretly gathered at the road station and awaited the arrival of supplies, ammunition and three thousand more men from Fort Smith. On July 17th they were going to bushwhack a handful of union soldiers at Fort Gibson, twenty miles southwest. This was why my brother-in-law had risked his life, deserting the confederates, and came to our camp in broad daylight.

"The Arkansas River runs through Hot Springs. Akando, my daughter, Crash Of Thunder, and I rode along the river, creeping and bypassing the gray-coat's encampment. We journeyed twenty miles southwest to Fort Gibson and alerted the commanding officer of the surprise attack. Without sleep or rest the commander ordered a group of us to ride hard and fast into the dark for reinforcements at Fort Scott. It was a long 175 miles journey up north. None of us wanted to be at the fort if the attack occurred a day earlier, so we agreed to leave. Later we would all laugh at the notion of staying and waiting to be bushwhacked. There was talk of leaving Baby Girl and our child at Fort Gibson, but Akando and I didn't trust a bunch of testosterone fighting men to act honorable when it comes to a woman's prized valuables. On June 24th we left Fort Scott with back up, and that included 200 supply wagons. There was no need to sneak when we were packing a shit load of artillery. On July 2nd we rode by the confederate's encampment at Honey Springs. They fired on us and we fired back. The 200 wagons took their sweet time rolling on the old creaky bridge that crossed the Arkansas River and we moseyed on up the road to Fort Gibson for further instructions.

Now, there were nearly 3,000 of us blue coats and we were up against 6,000 gray-coats. The Buffalo Soldiers were with us; we had more than enough angry brothers ready for the fight. I was satisfied with the odds. Instead of a confederate ambush, in the dark we tiptoed down the banks of the Arkansas River and the union forces began their own surprise assault.

On July 17th we attacked the confederates in a left-right formation. In the center of that structure were the Buffalo Soldiers. There were gun battles and hand-to-hand combat brawls and guess what, we tore those southern white boy's asses up!" He jumped in jubilee and tight-fisted he delivered some roundhouse punches.

"This was one of the first times in U.S. history that blacks were legally able to deliver vengeance against the oppressive slave system. Now I'm not a violent man, don't believe in harming another living soul, but the rage I let loose that day was raw and took some old aches out of my bones. Our wrath of destruction on those white boys was like the devil was let loose from hell! The fires of redemption were in us and we smoked their asses to smithereens! Lord, have mercy on all of our souls." His eyes softened, closed, and he bowed his head.

"Never did see hide nor hair of the 3,000 rebel back ups. The Honey Springs victory proved to be the Gettysburg of the Trans-Mississippi west. The south was wounded and limped and lingered on like an injured dog for almost two more years.

"It was mid summer, scorching hot, and Baby-girl and I had had enough fighting. It was time for us to ride off into the sunset.

"Crickets chirped in the brush, and under warm moonlights Tamia and I covered our naked bodies with the stars. A layer of the horror of my enslavement had been cleansed and some of the guilt and shame for abandoning friends was washed away. I felt like a new man. I believe my rod grew an inch longer, two inches thicker, and I knew it got stiffer. On the prairie fields my wife's crimson flesh became transparent as a cloud and it was my doorway to heaven. I dissolved chocolate orgasmic ecstasies into her airy soft tissues all the way back to our cabin.

***

"Back at home, Baby Girl and I were like two wild dogs stuck in an orgasmic bond. But our passions were suddenly doused with cold water by the United Stated government. I know the chubby cotton man has already informed you how they took the Native's Land. The two hundred acres I'd sweated to produce rows of vegetables, the land that our little house on the prairie stood was in the middle of the territory and was part of the infamous **Unassigned Lands**—and this was personal. The government took half the state. Punishment the big boy bully U.S. government dished out against the Natives who were often forced to go along with the confederates, thus, siding against the union. That's the legislation congress passed. Now, let me give you my view and more details on how they took the land.

"In the 1870's, the big cattle ranches in Texas wanted the **Unassigned Lands** for grazing, the even richer railroad folk wanted to lay tracks through the terrain, and connect Texas to Kansas. By linking the states together, they could easily deliver the Texas livestock. No need to pay the trail hands and cowboys for labor on long cattle drives, and there was always the risk of losing precious cattle along the way.

"The east was swelling with new foreigners daily, and those red-neck Boomers from Kansas and Missouri were hollering for free homesteads. Guess who wins when white folks want what the Natives or anybody else owns? I guess you've got a taste of when the government and society dismisses your needs." The frontiersman tapped his finger on the place where my heart had been attacked. "Ranchers were allotted fields to feed their herds, workers laid rails, and finally, they took the whole damn state for pennies an acre. And they still haven't paid that bill.

"I know you've heard Negroes crying and singing the *white privilege* song before. This situation directly affected my livelihood and I'm here to tell you, there ain't nothing worse than when the white man comes to get what's yours!" In a different way I understood. The white folk's system had stolen my freedom and education, and the love of Black Dickey's life and the endearing daily affections of a mother.

"After the Civil War and before the first land run of 1889 the Buffalo Solders stuck around Native Territory. Courtesy of the brothers of the union army, I was able to add six Springfield rifles and plenty of ammunition to my collection. The fire power kept away the desperate land grabbers during the land runs."

***

At first I was fearful of entering the darkness. I don't know exactly when listening to the tall dark stranger's historical stories transformed into soothing lullabies, but that's what happened. His courageous tales of surviving as a black man through slavery and pre Civil Rights America became my escape route from the daily fear and insanity of prison life. At bedtime I began summoning sleep in order to seek comfort in this black man's strange world. Somehow I knew that some of this sage's sagas were keys to my own life. His features of a young man faded, the guttural speech of an elder began to speak. Shinny bald, withered and wrinkled, he sloped, his bright glow became dim, but the old frontiersman was still black as tar.

***

Other images invaded the shadows of night and one particular black man uttered his story.

***

I was on the first land-run. I rode in a wagon pulled by Old Susie, my mule. The old girl ran us clean all the way to what's now known as Oklahoma City. My stake was 160 acres or more on the northwest side. In the beginning, I lived alone in a dug-out. In five years I had built a home, cleared brush, plowed and planted crops.

It got lonely out on the plains. Horny and desperate for a female's touch, I needed to plant some other seeds, but into a woman. My neighbors were all white and God knows none of those pink women were in a hurry to bust a nut with me. So I took off to Kansas in search of a wife. I thought having land and a farm would make it easy to attract and catch a fine black woman, but I was wrong. It took me almost a year to find a woman willing to leave her family, invest and believe that Colored people had a future in The American Dream. When we came back to my farm a white man had the sheriff run me off. He said we were trespassing on his property. I could barley read. I had to teach myself what words I did understand, but I knew I had filed the right deed papers. Well the Misses and I, we moved on. And this sort of land grabbing happened to a lot of us Coloreds. The freedman, folks that were part Native and had been here generations, these people had just been allotted land, even they were swindled out of their property. If the white man wants what you have the law is going to be on his side."

He faded away.

***

"Hey-hey-hey Kayin!" My main illusion, the cotton man, was back on the scene. He stood out in the field and tilted on a stalk like a person would lean against a tree. James Earl nonchalantly puffed on a corncob pipe.

"There are a lot of sad stories of a black man's life out on the prairie fields. White folks brought their antebellum rituals right into the virgin winds of Oklahoma. It was a struggle for a black man to maintain a hard penis." The cotton man's allegorical remark *"hard penis"* had nothing to do with sex and then again it had everything to do with getting screwed.

"The 'Badlands', Native Territory was also a hideout for bad asses; a home for bank robbers, and murderers. That's what the region was known as before the land runs. Oklahoma didn't stop being lawless just because it became a state, although some of the crimes committed were viewed as acceptable Christian Caucasian behavior, these transgressions were insidious, inhumane and against God's true nature.

"Little kinky-headed colored boys were in need of education the same as little white pony-tail freckle face white girls. The first brick wasn't laid before the good old boys in the mostly white towns decided to create lily-white school boards. And they passed laws segregating black boys from white girls. Forget about the 14th Amendment, the black folk's civil rights bill of 1868. *No State shall make or enforce any law, which shall abridge the privileges or immunities of citizens of the United States; nor shall any State deprive any person of life, liberty, or property, without due process of law; nor deny to any person within its jurisdiction the equal protection of the laws.* Segregation was planted amongst the prairie weeds before the landmark Supreme Court segregation decision, Plessey vs. Ferguson in 1896 and way before statehood in 1907. Right after white folks squatted on the new territory they had a bowel movement, and out popped Jim Crow." The cotton man was back narrating his *True-Crime Story* with an attitude.

Chapter Nineteen

"The foreign folk that just hopped off the boat, stepped ahead of colored folk and right into white schools. White people had better jobs and therefore made more money. The Italians, Jews, Germans, Russians, Poles, everybody was able to integrate, and was offered the opportunities to pursue and enjoy old school English, and Irish mainstream women as lovers." I was half awake, but still sleeping, when declarations I'd heard many times from the black community while I was growing up and now they were confirmed by the cotton man.

"One year after Oklahoma became a state, in 1908, if a black man and a white woman acted on any instinctual attractions, and made love and tried to make that magnetic force a legal binding agreement; after already executing a shameful disgraceful deed in the society that mattered—if they married, they both could be put in prison." James Earl used Vincent Price's accent again and that made this bit of history even scarier.

***

One night I walked out of my body and joined the dream.
***

I was in Oklahoma and the year was 1957. I saw myself as a spirit—a naked spirit. It must have been hot because I could see sweat bubbles dribbling down my chest. Moisture rolled off my navel and made a circle around a rock-hard Black Dickey and melted into my nuts. I was standing in a room that was crystal white. I saw my hands above my head and positioned like I was crucified. There is no blood on the white wall or my hands. On the other side of the room there was a pasty decorative oak dresser connected to an hourglass mirror. The two pieces dissolved into the snowy scenery. Fresh red roses soaked in a vase, this gives the room an elegant décor and a queen sized bed ads a flair of romance to the vision. Lounging on the bed I spot the reason for my hard rod. An Italian woman is half dressed, trim and young. She has dark hair and her skin has olive shadows. No panties are under a black slinky half-slip. Her pear-shaped tits are naked. They appeared to be size B and were proportionately an ideal fit for her petite structure. Black Dickey springs with excitement at the titillating view. The Italian lady senses and hears Black Dickey's animated vibrations. She rises up on her elbows, looks around for my cosmic ambiance. An emerald rosary necklace dangles between her breasts. I appear in the mirror and she meets the lust in my eyes. Her eyes trace the moisture as it flows down my body and when she spots a throbbing Black Dickey she twists her nose in contempt and disgust.

***

A velvety silk pair of panties with a matching wire-free bra was sprawled over a summertime white quilt adorned with roses, lilacs and wheat; the two views had beautiful butter borders. The delicate lingerie fit snugly against the body of a beautiful Irish blond. She uses two fingers and eases them both beneath the silk panties. She masturbates under the hood of her vagina and smiles at Milton Berle on the black and white RCA television. While Uncle Miltie is in drag, flashes of Black Dickey and the rest of my nudity appear in color across the screen. The blond snatches her fingers out of her hole! Aggravated, she aggressively jumps to her feet and flicks the TV off. My reflection obviously frightened her, or I must assume she'd rather dream of making love to Uncle Miltie in drag than stare at a naked nigger.

***

Black Dickey drips pre-cum. The naked ass of a shapely French woman is bent over while she performs toe touches, and watches Jack Lalane on TV. Her hands reach her feet and the pretty lady strains to hold the position. I peep from her rear, her vagina opens and I see the hood and both sides of the inner and outer labia are greased in sweat. Black Dickey salivates more pre-cum. The French lady's sixth sense feels my presence. She peeps between her legs. Black Dickey is an inch away from her ass. The French woman faints.

***

"Ahahahaha!" James Earl's hearty laugh snapped me out of the phantom phase.

"You're a peeping tom! Stalking naked white women, huh?" Was he ashamed of me? Was having a sexual dream immoral?

"Back then if a white man knew that a black man was thinking of fornicating with a white woman, if the white society could some way know a black man's thoughts, they would make a law and lock your ass up or kill you." James Earl said, shaking his head.

"In the late 1890's, in the prairie-land, still referred to as Indian Territory, most blacks in the all-black paradise towns were illiterate but so were most Americans. In spite of their ignorance these black people were dancing and enjoying their new freedoms. From sun-up 'til sundown they whacked down maples and redbuds, dug up dirt and grew crops. They built homes and schools and grocery stores and made their own clothes. They would sweat picking cotton in the fields, and they rejoiced and sung gospel songs like *Wade in the Water, The Gospel Train, and Swing Low Sweet Chariot.* In Oklahoma's larger segregated cities, the centers of power, most blacks had menial jobs. The rich white elite were busy appealing to the instincts of those uneducated and racist white folk, advising them that it would be a good thing to protect their white heritage, namely their white women, so they passed segregation laws." He yawned as if by him telling the story in my dream was messing with his sleep, or he thought every black male on the planet had already heard this tired tale.

"An upbeat cadence of ragtime was tapped in colored prairie juke joints, while white honky tonks are introduced to Scott Joplin's sluggish adaptation. I think I like bubbly better." He did a split and scooted to his feet. "Keep up with me boy, I'm about to shuck and jive." The cotton man scuffed up the dirt and then performed a soft-shoe tap. By gradually grinding his hip he did a slow drag, strutting right into a tango. He stood straight and skipped into clogging. In his finale he kicked up dust and jitterbugged up and down the cotton fields singing.

"Hello my baby, hello my honey, hello my ragtime, summertime gal..."

***

I was still smiling in my sleep, enjoying the jolly entertainment delivered by the cotton man, when he bought me back into a reality of the nastiness of history, again.

"1890: Education [Statute]

Every three years, an election for school electors is to be held to vote for or against separate schools for white and colored children." The cotton man had forewarned me of such a law, and now he was actually saying and displaying the words in black and white.

"Only a year after these brave black people had traveled way across country, fleeing the antebellum south for a freer better America, they found out they were stepping into the same old shit. Again, they were cut-off, separated from the rest of the world." I began to have visions of sad, shamefaced crushed Black folk, who were shut out from participating in crafting a law that would leave them receiving less money for education. Second-hand, hand-me-down school books and in one room shacks; schools that hid on dirt roads in the woods off and far away from the white intellectual society. Black Dickey's academic competitive stature shrunk. "Like I said earlier, the soon to be 'sooner' territory was ahead of its time. They instituted segregation six years before the Supreme Court's Plessey vs. Ferguson in 1896." Quiet chants echoed inside Black Dickey's head, 'stay away from having sex with white women...'

"Little country colored children, in the gay 1890's, chased butterflies and hummingbirds over fields full of daffodils, and wildflowers, while in 1897 influential white men planned their future and their children's future by introducing another education law:"

A separate district will be established for colored children wherever there are at least eight black children. Unlawful for any white child to attend a school when there are too many black children (or vice versa)." Quiet chants echoed inside Black Dickey's head, 'stay away from developing some affection for white women...and vice versa for them.'

***

"The year Oklahoma became a state, in 1907 *The Education law was written into Oklahoma's Constitution.*

Separate schools for white and colored children to be provided by the legislature. The new immigrants, English, Irish, Polish, Jews, French, and even the Natives, Chinese, and Japanese, if your skin isn't black come on in and make love to our women and pursue the American Dream. Niggers you'll have to build your own school for higher education, and so the Negroes built Langston University. And graduating from that school will only qualify and allow you niggers to become teachers of other niggers. If you want to be a scientist, engineer, nurse, dentist, doctor, lawyer, or go into a profession requiring postgraduate education, then leave the state of Oklahoma. And don't come back here, we're not hiring niggers for those jobs." The cotton man explained. And reading between the lines an already emasculated Black Dickey heard loud chants echoing inside his head, *'Nigger we'll make it so you'll never ever be good enough for a white woman to be attracted to you.'*

***

"**1907: Voting rights law**
Indigent persons housed in a poorhouse at public expense excluded from voting. Exception made for Federal, Confederate, and Spanish American veterans. Po' ass niggers, don't even try exercising your civil liberties.

***

The first voting rights law was for the po'est of po' black folk. That same year of statehood, Oklahoma made another law to make sure that just the po' black folk stayed po'.
1907: Voting rights law
Required electors to read and write any section of the state Constitution. Exempted those who were enfranchised on January 1, 1866, and lineal descendants of such persons. Declared unconstitutional in 1915; however, provision for literacy was upheld. And the literacy ruling wouldn't be rectified until 1937; eleven years after women of the state were given the right to vote." Negroes, we're going to strip you from having any say so on how this state's institutions are built—that means how money is spent and how laws are passed." Chants echoed inside Black Dickey's head. *'No power and no white woman will want you.'*

"A person could lose his or her life if they taught a slave to read, and most poor whites couldn't read either. If the Negro wished to exercise his 15th Amendment right, we expect the ex-slaves and their sons to be sophisticated. They were the only Oklahomans taking literacy test." The cotton man said in a dismissive way. Dejection, shame and fury, these raw emotions wrapped themselves around Black Dickey's sensitive head. Hard chants echoed inside his head, *'You stupid fool you're not smart enough to be with a white woman.'*

***

"Another education law and this one had meat on it, a monetary penalty."

1908: Education [Statute]
Public schools within Oklahoma are to be operated under a plan of separation between the white and colored races. Penalty: Teachers could be fined between $10 and $50 for violating the law, and their certificate cancelled for one year. Corporations that operated schools that did not comply with the law were guilty of a misdemeanor and could be fined between $100 and $500. White students who attended a colored school could be fined between $5 and $20 daily. A teacher has always been punished for choosing to work in Oklahoma. The state has always been among the poorest states for them to earn a living. It must have been insulting to actually, legally, restrict and ridicule educators." Absurdity was the cotton mans tone. Quiet chants echoed inside Black Dickey's head, *'white women stay away from having an emotional connection with black boys...'*

***

"1908: Railroads law
'All railroad and streetcar companies to provide separate coaches for white and black passengers, "equal in all points of comfort and convenience." Penalty: Railway companies that violate the law fined $100 to $1,000. Passengers who fail to comply can be charged with a misdemeanor punishable by a fine from $5 to $25'. Conductors could be fined $50 to $500 for failing to enforce the law. Back of the bus nigger 'cause you ain't as good

as us and we don't want you too close 'cause you stink." Chants echoed inside Black Dickey's head, '*You're a different species and we don't want our women close to you...*'

***

"While Negroes from New Orleans came to Oklahoma and stomped to recollections of Buddy Bolden's B-flat jazz improvisations, Oklahoma's first legislature and first governor were busy signing the:

1908: miscegenation law (Also known as 'senate bill number one')

Unlawful for a person of African descent to marry any person not of African descent. Penalty: Felony punishable by a fine of up to $500 and imprisonment from one to five years in the penitentiary. There it was, sanctioned; the fear that dominated the ideology of white America. White women don't have sex with a black man or we'll lock you up and kick your ass by destroying your self-respect; we'll treat you like a nigger. We might even kill you! Black men, we'll castrate you, lock your black ass up, and murdering you is definitely on the table!" Chants echoed inside Black Dickey's head, '*stay away from sexing a white woman...*'

***

"***The miscegenation decree would be the law of prairie-land for the next fifty-one years. In 1967, three years after the new 1964 Civil Rights Law, the Supreme Court's Loving Vs Virginia decision would overturn all the miscegenation laws. But the damage had been done; Oklahoma's America racial sexual personality was neatly permanently ingrained in the psyche of its citizens. Or was it?.***

***

Pay telephones were being installed all over Oklahoma and in 1915 the state passed a Public accommodations law. **The decree required telephone companies to maintain separate booths for white and colored patrons.** Some businesses had only one phone; if you're colored you certainly couldn't touch something a white person might use." Don't infect anything a white person might use with your nasty nigger germs. Oh my God! I thought about *Maslow* and his *hierarchy of needs*, and these segregated rules of white society. Extricating only one of its members from using the same telephone, I wondered what he'd think.

***

"The 1921 miscegenation degree:
Prohibited marriage between Indians and Negroes. Citizenship and land allotment issued by the Dawes Commission drove a wedge between Blacks, the Seminoles and Creeks. The most divisive strain was the sword the white man gave the Cherokee. There were more whites with Cherokee blood, and if you were of mixed blood then of course the white ingredients to the mixture were more valuable than the Black blood. In fact Indians were forced to adapt into white culture and to abandon their own. Children were removed from their tribal home and shipped off to boarding schools. Their traditional long hair was chopped off. And I guess some lucky or unlucky ones were allowed to attend public white schools. And by 1920 whites had already swindled the majority of the Native's land and the acres they had given the Black Indians. Since natives barely understood English and blacks could barely read the language, the land was easily confiscated from both parties. Chants echoed inside Black Dickey's head, *'stay away from anything that resembles a white woman, you're the least of the humans on the planet...'*

***

"In 1921 The Education Statute was energized with a specific stiff punishment.
'Misdemeanor for a teacher to teach white and colored children in the same school. Penalty: Cancellation of teaching certificate without renewal for one year. Chants echoed inside Black Dickey's head, 'they're making sure a white woman never develops or has any affection for me...'

***

"1921: Public accommodations Statute
Required maintenance of separate accommodations for colored persons in public libraries in cities with a Negro population of 1,000 or more. A black person couldn't even read beside a white

person in the same building. In Oklahoma City there was one library for blacks on the northeast side where Negroes lived. The rest of the annals of learning, on the southeast, southwest, and northwest, belonged to the best people." Chants echoed inside Black Dickey's head, *'You'll never get a chance to have a casual conversation with a white woman so forget about y'all having sex...'*

***

"Louis Armstrong burst on the entertainment scene in 1914 and music's lyrical phrasing has never been the same." Bubbly lips, charcoal shine, the cotton man appeared as old Satchmo.

"Come on and hear...come on and hear...Alexander's ragtime band..."

So in 1925 Oklahoma City's all white city council issued an entertainment ordinance

1925: Entertainment City Ordinance

Black bands were prohibited from marching with white bands in Oklahoma City parades. Also, white Golden Gloves boxers were prohibited from sparring against black boxers." Quiet chants echoed inside Black Dickey's head, 'stay away from having sex with white women...And don't even think about kicking a white man's ass.'

***

"Those on the edge of life, poor blacks that were barely surviving had already felt the results of the 1929 stock crash years before the collapse. A lot of black folk were packing their bags and heading north for a more humane life.

"In the nineteen thirties in Oklahoma, the feet was the Colored folks' main source of transportation. Those that could afford to ride a horse rode or were passengers on the back of a wagon, while white people were busy buying cars.

***

" In 1937 Oklahoma passed the **Public Carriers Decree:** *Public carriers to be segregated.* Don't hop in a cab, a coach, on a train, not even a bus, and expect to sit next to a white person." Quiet chants echoed inside Black Dickey's head, '*stay away from sexing a white woman...*'

***

"At the picture-show, in the 1940's, white folks were gawking at and hearing Gene Autry play the guitar, and they yodeled in the back ground to *She's Somebody's Old Fashioned Sweetheart.*

The war was over in the mid forties and the government rewarded the returning white veterans by offering FHA/VA low interest home loans, and only a few black soldiers in Oklahoma ever received these gifts. Instead public housing was invented for the coloreds and po' white folks; of course they were housed in separate facilities.

After blacks had fault and bled in another world war, in 1949 the good old boys in Oklahoma got together and decided to institute **The Health Care Law: Called for a consolidated Negro institution to care for blind, deaf, and orphans.** Although they're unable to see, or hear, the white blind, deaf children are too good to mix with niggers with the same difficulties. Quiet chants echoed inside Black Dickey's head, '*stay away from the blind and physically challenged white women...*'

***

"The wise leaders in the state legislature and the governor in 1954 passed the **Public Accommodations Decree: Separate restrooms in mines required.** Even underground a black person couldn't shit in the same space as a white man. I guess they were trying to prevent interracial homosexuality." And voices echoed, *stay away from the white penis!*

***

The 50's whooshed in Chuck Berry and Americans were doo-wopping and rocking and rolling to this *Brown Eyed handsome Man.* With a processed hairdo and snuggling a guitar, there was the cotton man again, hunkering down. He scooted across the field and belted out *Brown Eyed handsome Man.*

***

In response to Brown's 1954 victory over Board of Education, in1955 Oklahoma's lawmakers re-mandated the Miscegenation decree of 1908 with a more frightening appeal.

1955 Miscegenation Statute

Marriage of anyone of African descent to one who is white prohibited. Penalty: Up to $500 and one to five years' imprisonment.... The same year Emmett Till was bludgeoned to death for his fourteen year old boyish flirt at a Mississippi white woman, in Oklahoma the lawmakers also said, we don't care what Brown said, we agree with what happened with Emmett, and we'd like to yell! '*Nigger stay away from flirting with a white woman!*'

***

The last Jim Crow Law in Oklahoma was passed in 1957.

Adoption Statute:

Adoption petitions must state race of petitioner and child. If you're black get back, you're not raising any child that's not black." Quiet chants echoed inside Black Dickey's head, '*stay away from developing an emotional attachment with white children...*'

***

"With all these denigrating laws, white professionals: doctors, journalist, teachers, psychologist, and religious Christian leaders joined the politicians and perpetrated this inferior Jim Crow caricature. Jim Crow was an antebellum mistral show character. A white person dressed as a smutty faced clown with huge painted on red lips. On stage he danced a jingle. Hollywood gave the part to *Step 'N Fetch It.* And the idea that all blacks were retarded, lazy, and with minds like children, this perception was perpetuated on the big screen around the world. Now I ask you, Kayin, what self respecting white woman would want to jeopardize her life and screw somebody like him." I didn't think he wanted an answer so I remained quiet.

"With more than four hundred years of brain washing that defined who was more human, the spiritual nature of the human race has been wounded." The cotton man had finished for the evening. All of the roadblocks in the lives of black folk and the history of the twentieth century slept with me that night. I awoke and thought how could people be self-actualized in Maslow's hierarchy theory today?

Chapter Twenty

After a delusional night of fantasizing a hell of a story, I woke up the next morning horny but I couldn't get a hard on:

***

She's the third generation in the new state. Her name was Laura and her family lived on Robinson Street in one of the first mansions build in Oklahoma City. Like most cities, Oklahoma City's housing development began where the jobs were located, downtown and in the nearby areas. Robinson runs north and south and straight through downtown. North was usually associated with the more affluent white folks. Laura lived north of downtown. Like most wealthy folks in the new state, they enjoyed eating delicious meals and a good number of these rich folk hired the best cooks—colored women. "Domestics" they were called.

Laura's mother hired one of those black women to cook for her family. Sometimes this domestic lady would bring her son to work, he was Laura's age. As a little girl she'd learned to play the white classically cultural children's game doctor/nurse. One day she introduced the game to "Sammy", the domestic's son. While she had yet to know all the ins and outs of the supremacy game, she did know that since his mother worked for her mother she could make all the decisions. Her first choice was the role of the doctor. In the back yard she had Sammy lay on the picnic table for an examination. "Stick your tongue out and say ah." Laura ordered Sammy. A curious little girl she shined a flashlight in this ears, laid her ear against Sammy's chest, then she unbutton his pants and pulled them down. She had seen a penis before but never a black one. She was shocked to see the young boy's penis sticking straight out and stiff. Sammy had an involuntary hard on. Later Laura learned what happens to an older teenage relative when she allows a black penis to invade her private parts; a black teenaged boy impregnated Darlene, Laura's cousin. Being good Christians— against illegally aborting a human life—Darlene's mother sends her to visit relatives, where Darlene gives birth to a black baby, and the family places the child up for adoption. Laura matures and she remembers her fascination with little Sammy's penis. All grown-up, Laura marries, has three children, and adopts all the attitudes of her racist society.

Laura had natural female desires. With a penis penetrating her she'd never had that scrumptious ecstasy explosion with her husband or with any other white man. Frenetic with pent-up desires she learns how to finger herself into an orgasm. But Laura has a secret. Laura is a housewife and her husband works as a legislator, during the weekdays Laura sneaks over to the eastside and cruises for black lovers. Her first black lover was a young man she'd hired to do yard work. After a season of afternoon delights, he left town. That's when Laura began to journey to the colored side of town. Sammy's penis was charcoal and Laura preferred young stout smutty cocks. Sometimes when the clock was ticking and she hadn't hooked up with a perfect jet-black man, and she had to get back across town, she would snatch up any colored man. She'd hire him to make love to her. Her compulsive desires required the housewife to have at least two or three escapades with black men a week. To prevent the mistake made by her cousin, she always wore a diaphragm and would carefully, while perspiring with desires between her legs, place a prophylactic over her lover's penis for added protection. After each sinful sexual act she never took the time too relax in her lover's arms or beg for comfort. Her ritual was to regress back to her white Christian morals, the laws of the land. Laura would become bitterly ashamed and rudely dismiss her black lover. "Get the hell off me nigger and get out my God-damn car!" Laura would race home and scrub her body raw, especially her vulva. She'd douche the inside of her vagina with vinegar and even used an antiseptic. Spic and span clean of any hint of a sexual odor, or a nigger's contamination, Laura would feel snow white on the outside again. To cover her inner guilt for her bad behavior she was ruthless against any civil rights for blacks. She and her husband supported all the Jim Crow segregation laws. Laura became president of the "Lady Southern Belles", a restricted white's only social elite group. On weekends her extended family would burn crosses late into the night skies; they wore white cloaks, and held sermons of hate, and her gang called their activities, 'saving the purity of the white race'.

Most of the black community was aware of Laura's secret life. At barbeques, black men laughed at her and compared notes on the 'little white-hot ass nymph. In kitchens, black women gossiped and feared for their husband's and their son's lives and they warned them to stay clear of the dangerous hussy. One afternoon an unsuspecting black teenager who was unfamiliar with her antics was flattered by her sexual flirtations, and oozed over the opportunity to have sex with the sultry seductive white woman. The boy had a huge 10-inch long instrument and it was thick. Laura struggled tugging the tight rubber completely over and on his sexual apparatus. Finally, she covered most of his penis. The 6 foot 4 boy, instinctually driven and curiously excited about having sex with his first white woman, he became impatient with his lust. He jammed all ten inches in her and exploded in fast hard rhythms. Laura screamed in pain and pleasure. When he removed his wet penis the rubber stayed inside, stuck to her vaginal walls. Still laying on her back in the car seat, she became frantic at the idea of his juices living inside her. Acrimonious words were shouted along with her regular sermon. "Get the hell out of here nigger!" She slapped his penis—as if she was slapping the face of a man. She raised her legs and savagely kicked the boy out of the car. She hurriedly opened the glove compartment, retrieved a box of white plastic antibacterial gloves and a box of sanitary napkins. With two fingers inside a sterile glove she removed the rubber with the sticky orgasmic juice, and then stuffed napkins up her vagina to absorb any excess semen. Laura tossed the gloves out the window and sped off into the sunset. Some venereal diseases are silent in women, so it was over a year and several other black lovers, when on a routine doctor's visit she was diagnosed. Laura had the clap. She knew her husband had extra-marital affairs around the office and elsewhere, and since she hadn't observed him complaining whenever he pissed, and didn't notice his penis throbbing in pain, the loving couple never had the clap discussion. In Laura's mid fifties she developed a case of Alzheimer's, and non-stop she spilled out the secrets of her sexual escapades with black males to her husband, family members, and anyone who would listen.

One Thanksgiving the family was sitting around eating a festive boasted turkey with lifelong friends present. Suddenly, Laura's eyes become animated, and in detail she describes how the big black ten-inch penis entered her tight lily-white vagina. Laura reached underneath her dress and began to finger herself. "Stick that big black hard cock deep into me! Woo-whoa-woo! Deeper! Deeper! Woo-whoa-woo!" In an aggressive animated spectacular way, Laura tossed her skirt up, droped her underwear, started humping the chair and had an orgasm. "Woo-whoa-woo shit!" Laura's husband was astonished, angry and ashamed of her inappropriate behavior, just as much as he was sad and disgusted with her pitiful condition. And before Christmas Day he institutionalized Laura into a nursing home.

***

One Night I was barely in R.E.M sleep, and the cotton man scared the crap out of me with a heartbreaking tale—a story that's part of the sooner state's dark history.

***

"If Japan's atrocities at Pearl Harbor prompted President Roosevelt to selectively choose the word 'infamy' to describe how bad the bloodbath was, then there must be a worthy adjective for the black community and the rest of the world to offer the victims of Greenwood—the once thriving black community in Tulsa. In 1921 the neighborhood was bombed by the State and National Guard, black families—women and children—were gunned down, gutted, and burned in flames." James Earl said in a sullen tone. Tears full of hurt dangled on his cotton eyelids. I braced myself for the tragic the cotton man must be feeling and the story he was about to tell. Like a batter approaching the base in the World Series, with two outs in the bottom of the ninth, no one on base, the score is tied; fear or maybe it was habit, I had to cuddle my nuts for security before I got into my batting stance. That's what I did, I cradled Black Dickey's sac and prepared for the origins of the cotton man's misery.

"The slang, 'remember the Alamo', is forever infused into the American psyche. The boogieman or boogie-woman as this case applies, the name Sarah Page should live in infamy—whenever a white woman arouses a black man, and the world should re-member Sarah Page. Seventeen-year-old Sarah was an orphan, an elevator operator and white, and she was quite aware of the power she possessed by merely hinting rape, if that man had black skin. On May 30th, 1921 Sarah flexed her vaginal muscles, her white-female-supremacy, and literally squashed blood and sweated tears from—at that time—the most successful black community in America's history.

"The National Guard flew airplanes, dropping incendiary de-vices—and some folks believe the fiery explosives were nitroglyc-erin shells—right down on Tulsa's Black Wall Street. The Tulsa police, the State and National Guard joined 15,000 crazed whites and they used machine guns, killing 300 and maybe as many as 3,000 black children, women and men. They looted and burned 1,500 homes, 600 black businesses, 21 black churches, 21 black restaurants, 30 black stores, and two black movie theatres.

"In 1908, a year after statehood, oil was discovered in Tulsa. In those days this black gold strike was equivalent to the rich gushers in today's Saudi Arabia.

"Every part of the country, white losers, drifters, dreamers, hill-billies and mountain boys, businessmen, engineers, roughnecks, and plain white folk, raced to the get-rich Oil Empire. Boomtown! And by 1921 Tulsa had 400 oil and gas companies. And almost overnight 90,000 white folks had moved to the untamed city. Al-most overnight neighborhoods were constructed. Million dol-lar mansions were built for the millionaires. The middle class had paved streets, inside plumbing, all the latest inventions, washing machines, and vacuum cleaners. White folks were on easy street. They sat at ease and relaxed in the day's comforts, while enjoying sweet-sweet music on their new phonographs.

"Leaving dead-end penniless sharecropper lives and the harsh antebellum rules of Mississippi, Georgia, Alabama, Tennessee, the deep south and all over America, blacks blazed above mountains, plowed through woods, waded down rivers and poured into Tulsa, looking for a little more of the 13th, 14th, and 15th Amendments, their promises of the American Dream. They had survived slavery, a situ-ation a thousand times more degrading and abusive than Farrah

Fawcett's burning bed, scathingly worse than a battered wife's nastiest nightmare.

At the turn of the twentieth century, generations of slave runaways were already in Tulsa. Ancient Africans had settled in South American, and migrated to Mexico, from there they'd entered this country by way of Louisiana. Up from Louisiana many traveled on and lived among the Natives in Tulsa. They had survived by munching on deer, buffalo, fish, vegetables, nuts, and nigger toes for years. Other blacks that occupied the area were descendants of Indian slavery, and some of them had actually stepped all the way from Florida and Georgia and had personally endured the Trail Of Tears with the Creeks, Cherokees, Seminoles, and the Choctaws.

Whites used some of the new industrial technologies and built taller buildings. They constructed airplanes and conceptualized ways to make better and faster automobiles but any theory or brainpower applied to conceive a sensitive social consciousness for blacks was still in the Neanderthal stages.

Even before oil was discovered, before statehood, Tulsa introduced southern separation from Blacks into the social structure. There were 6 pm curfews for coloreds, and vile signs in sections of the city like, 'don't let me spot your black ass after dark'. And of course, unconstitutional segregated neighborhoods. When the boom occurred blacks were banned from working and making big money at any of the city's majestic oil industries. 'Don't even come in and spend your hard earned cash in my white store', this had to be one of stupidest business decisions ever made.

"So blacks labored tirelessly building there own city within a city. The resilient and crafty black folk constructed restaurants, clothing and appliance stores, entertaining pool halls and theatres, schools, recreation and religious centers. They were folks under siege, yet there existed a southern camaraderie, and everybody knew everybody society and this fellowship brought a homey prosperous spirit into the black community.

Tulsa had 15 black doctors, obviously they did not attend medical school in Oklahoma. Neither did several black lawyers and many other professionals. One black lawyer challenged the constitutionality of the Tulsa's Jim Crow system all the way to the Supreme Court. And a black newspaper owner often editorialized on how bad racism was in the city. The numerous business own-ers and professionals drove fancy cars and lived in spacious man-sions, and a few managed to move across the tracks into the white neighborhoods. But the majority of Tulsa's 10,000 blacks were ser-vice workers: laborers, porters, dishwashers, and domestics. Wells were used as their water supply and women soaked the family's clothes outside in steel tubs and scrubbed them on washboards. From the sky, the black neighborhood backyards looked a lot like old-fashioned rows of cotton in a field. Wooden clothespins were snapped to wet clothing securing them to a line of thick wire that stretched between two poles. Three or four rows of these poles were assembled in every backyard. And, as the clothes fluttered in the strong southern breezes, they dried under the sun.

"Tulsa's oil boom was similar to gold fever in California and Col-orado, selling a woman's body and crime came with the explosion. Gambling, gangsters and drugs and bootlegged whiskey, and did you know society's lowest of the living, the original southern black pimps, and the white whores were some of the few enjoying pro-gressive upscale intimate interracial relationships? For the first time in southern history you saw the arrival of the first black pimps, and they were sampling and selling white women. If a brother could spend a little change he could have sex with a white woman." The cotton man said salaciously. He singed his thumb across his index finger, like he was counting dollar bills, but it seemed to me he was slipping on the facts.

"Didn't you say in 1908 the state had outlawed a black man and white woman from…" "Who said anything about marriage? We're talking twisting into the pink without any legal papers!" The cotton man finished my question, correcting my misunderstand-ing. "Now uh prostitution was illegal, so was bootleg whiskey. The entire state was a completely dry state until the 1950's. Gambling was banned but the average Joe still did it, and there were a host of other gangster activities, like police payoffs and a racist mayor that worked for the Klan.

"Can you imagine what a black man with cowboy and pimp tendencies would look like?" His eyes rolled and he produced an image of a charcoal black man whittling a toothpick in the corner of his huge lips. He was underneath a sporty white cowboy hat that had a colorful Indian feather protruding from the back. "To be a black pimp in that frightening era of white superiority, you had to be a bold bad ass hombre with killer, deadly, passionate lover techniques. Cool and cold-blooded the brother had to have stones that would scare the shit out of most white boys. The most important quality—if a pimp has qualities—" With elevated eyes the cotton man smirked. "—He had to have the ability to deprogram a white girl from centuries of a supremacy ideology. The cool pimp had to be a miracle worker; he had to place her under his spell. Hahaha—he had to be smooth and innovative. I guess you could say pimps were revolutionary bad ass brothers that were way-way ahead of their time!" Laughing heartily he grabbed his belly again.

Restraining himself he reflected. "Hmm some of their descendants are probably those hip hop Negroes with the Fort Knox smiles styling in the big pink Cadillacs." He leered at me to see if I caught the similarities—I did.

"Now can you imagine the seething that must have happened in a white man's heart? Seeing a brother parading around town with white women slopped all over him, breaking all the social rules. Even if the white women were outcast whores, the brother had to have nuts made of stone. The fact that no white person has ever been prosecuted for the immoral lynch killings, hanging a black man being considered legal had to be in the back of the notorious pimp's heads." The vengeful eyes of a white man in 1921 spilled a bucket of hate into my bloodstream, and the fear of his ruthlessness shriveled the shit inside my intestines.

"Nine months previous to Sarah Page's rape cries, the corrupt white Tulsa police department had delivered an eighteen year old white boy, Roy Belton, into the hands of a white mob for the murder and robbery of cab driver Homer Nida. Roy was driven in Homer's cab by some of the mob members out of town to the location where he had allegedly killed Homer. Roy was lynched with apparently police officers applauding the vigilantism. A 'Righteous Protest,' were the headlines of the local newspaper, The Tulsa World. It was 1920 and Oklahoma was still the Wild Wild West. That same week, a gang of thug cowboys had lynched a young black boy in

Oklahoma City. Infant societies they were, Tulsa had joined a long list of Oklahoma towns that had lynched a man."

And suddenly appearing out of an orderly pattern, murdered and naked and hanging from trees, the black faces I saw were intimate and personal. They were down home Oklahoma black sisters & brothers. And as each one of them was executed, slowly, I witnessed their tortured expressions.

***

Woodward, March 3 1891; Henry Argo December 21, 1892 John Cudjo; Chickasha, May 31, 1930 Father Bailey; Oklahoma City, July 16, 1907 Edward Berry, Shawnee, August 6, 1915 William Campbell, Pond Creek, May 25, 1901; Peter Carter, Purcell, August 24, 1911 Henry Conly, Holdenville, June 16, 1917 Cora, Guthrie, Wewoka, November 4, 1913 Benjamin Dickerson, Noble, January 27, 1914 Carl Dudley, Lawton, April 9, 1916 John Foreman, Nowata, September 29, 1916 Sanders Franklin, Paul's Valley, August 14, 1913 James Garden, Muskogee, December 24, 1907 Peter Johnson, Edmond, October 1, 1898 L. Magill, Madill, June 29, 1918 Oscar Martin, Idabel, April 3, 1916, B. S. Morris, Watonga, September 16, 1896 Laura Nelson and Son, Okemah, May 25, 1911 Powell, Nowata, September 29, 1916 Henry Ralston, Paul's Valley, August 14, 1913 Marie Scott, Wagoner County, March 31, 1914, Sylvester Shennien, Wilburton, June 26, 1909; Dennis Simmons, Anadarko, June 13, 1913, Edward Suddeth, Corneta, October 22, 1911; Samuel Turner, Muldrow, January 1, 1912; Bud Walker, Mannford Creek, December 6, 1911; Dr. E. B. Ward, Norman, May 9, 1915; George Washington, Wagoner, September 4, 1915; Crockett Williams, Eufaula, August 7, 1914; James Williams, Colbert, March 31, 1907; In Ki Wish, specific; locality unknown, September 16, 1894; Unknown Negro, Unknown Negro, Lincoln, September 26, 1894; Unknown Negro, Chickasha, July 2, 1906; Unknown Negro, Choctsaw Nation, May 23, 1906; Unknown Negro, Mannford, November 15, 1910; Unknown Negro, Durant, August 18, 1911; Unknown Negro, Wagoner County, January 2, 1913.

***

(Eighty years later the saga of the Wild Wild West continues. Per capita, in 2001 Oklahoma would become the legal execution

capital of the free world. That year the state would legally murder Wanda Jean Allen, a mentally retarded black woman.)

***

"Pouring salt on the sore of an already racially divided city, the upstart Tulsa Tribune newspaper had run a series of articles attacking an ineffectual corrupt police department. The headlines suggested an uprising by the citizens against the criminal element of the police department. Ten days before the riot, The Tribune ran an editorial on the epidemic of prostitution. A former judge quoted, 'Black men are at the root of the problem. We've got to kick out the Negro pimps if we want to stop this epidemic.' Another featured a white man supposedly representing morality, a person of the cloth, the Reverend Harold G. Cooke. He traveled with an undercover detective to so-called shady hotels and rooming houses and saw black men and white women participating in what he declared as 'disgusting behavior.' 'They were singing and dancing together.' Can you imagine what Jesus would do if he saw this repulsive behavior?" The cotton man snickered, sarcastically rolling his eyes. "In another dubious situation he reported observing black porters routinely trading money for sex with young white women to depraved black customers. Like any other preacher delivering a Sunday sermon, he exaggerated how hot the smoldering brimstones were, and high the temperatures in hell can rise. Reverend Harold acted like there was a black porter pimp on every coroner in Tulsa selling the sexual passions of white women. He lied and condemned the intimacy of any black male, white female relationship. For the average white honky-tonk reader of that article in 1921, the reverend had stirred the red evil of the vampire in their eyes.

In 1921, seventeen-year-old Sarah Page had a job no black person in America was qualified for in Tulsa; she was an elevator operator in the Drexel building. To its credit the Drexel building was the only facility downtown that allowed black shoeshine boys to enter and empty their pee-holes. Nineteen-year-old Dick Rowland was also an orphan. By the age of five Dick, along with his two sisters, were sleeping and eating scraps off the streets in Vinita, Oklahoma. Soon grocery storefront owner Damie Ford adopted Dick.

A year later they moved to Tulsa. Dick went on to play high school football at Booker T. Washington and after getting a job shinning shoes he dropped out.

Tulsa's black community would go on to say that Sarah and Dick had to have known each other before May 30th and this wasn't the first time he'd pissed her off. Dick had surely ridden on Sarah's elevator many times. And according to his adopted mother this wasn't the first time nineteen-year-old Dick had literally rode seventeen-year-old Sarah. She said Dick and Sarah were lovers.

When police questioned Sarah, she claimed attempted rape. Dick said he tripped and accidentally touched Sarah. Damie said her son and Sarah had a lovers quarrel, but a nearby merchant had witnessed a black man arguing with a white woman. And before the day was over the story was that a black man had molested a white girl, and the rage of the Dick and Sarah episode spread like wildfire throughout the white community.

On June 31, police arrested a bewildered Dick at his adopted mother's home. The sun fell and a sea of 15,000 white enraged cowboys and honky tonk red-faced white women emerged with darkness on Dick's new home—the jail. They were toting sticks, carrying pistols, and waving shotguns.

Were first and second generations among the gang? Were the new Americans part of the White Sea, or was the crowd just the usual good old boys and gals? Who knows? We do know that those new Americans were able to get oil jobs and attend integrated schools, and the 13th and 14th Amendment rights should've been provided to all Americas' citizens.

Right across the tracks from downtown the ex slaves and their descendants got wind of the lynch mob. Twenty-five Word War I African American veterans decided to make a visit to the jail. Brandishing pistols and riffles the black men parted the sea of white and had a meeting with the sheriff. After receiving assurance from the sheriff that young Dick was secure in his jail the black vets headed back across the tracks to Greenwood.

'Across the proverbial railroad tracks', beginning in the 1900's that's how most decent sized southern cities had been unconstitutionally constructed; separating blacks from better living condi-

tions, job opportunities, and black men from having an intimate relationship with white women.

"Those uppity niggers have got some nerve, strutting into town and telling us how to handle our business!" In response to the band of brothers, the cotton man mimicked the reactions of the mob in an old southern Okie twang.

"Not used to taking orders form black men, and certainly foreign to their nature was a gang of black men flaunting firearms in the old masters' direction. Whew! **Supremacy** must have boiled in their blood!" He emphasized supremacy with a wicked wink.

"As the hours passed in the new uncivilized prairie town a shade of hate was echoing into the dark skies. Later seventy-five black vets rode downtown. Again these men stopped at the courthouse, and again offered to protect the prisoner. Officials refused, again. En-route to their vehicles, plowing through the vicious swarming vigilantes, one white man ordered a brother to give him his gun. The brother refused. They struggled. The gun went off. And the passions of the 1921 Tulsa riot were let loose.

Whirling clubs, rifles, shotguns, and revolvers the groups exchanged firepower. Dead blacks and whites lay bleeding on the city's streets. In front of the courthouse, the police, supposedly protectors of all its citizens' rights, broke into a hardware shop. They stole guns and ammunition, arming most of the whites. They joined the vigilantes and the two gangs teamed up and chased the blacks down avenues, alleys, and back-roads, around buildings and eventually back to the tracks.

To protect the women and children in Greenwood, the ex black military men made a stand on top and inside of empty box cars at the railroad tracks." It was as if I was seeing scenes from an old black and white western movie. Instead of High Noon or the OK Coral it was midnight under the stars, and bullets were flying from both sides of the tracks. Adding to the high drama, on another track, another train whistled up full of passengers. Ducking buckshot black and white travelers had to quickly choose which side to hop towards.

The picture faded to black, and whispering in the dark a black male survivor relived the horror:

"We were kicking the shit out those crackers, the Tulsa police department, and the state guard, before the National Guard
joined the fight. The military units used our tax dollars, and they
started dropping explosives out of airplanes that destroyed most
of our homes, and possibly a third of the black people, and almost everything in sight. After the nitroglycerine blasted the neighborhood, the police and the mob went on a rampage. Machine
gun bullets ripped into helpless babies and women. The murderers broke artifacts, robbed homes and even stole money off dead
bodies. The larcenist burned the whole damn neighborhood to
ashes." The man's face lit up under a lonely candle in the night
and I saw the man's tears glow.

"Actually a few hundred blacks held off the mob, the entire
Tulsa police department, and the Oklahoma State Guard until
dawn." The cotton man offered clarity to the battle.

Then an elderly black woman spoke.

"They wanted our land and we wouldn't sell.

My dear neighbors had been married forever and older than
dirt and they were blasted in the back of their heads with shotguns.
The home where they'd lived and raised children was smoked to
smithereens.

While I was tearing ass, getting on down the street, I saw a sister jump from a two story window to escape her burning home. A
white man walked over and shot her on the ground and dragged
her by the feet back into the fire. Oh-my-God! I prayed for him.

Black women half-naked, in nightgowns, some wearing only
panties and braless, tightly held the hands of terrified crying toddlers; as they scampered bullets would smatter their backs, asses,
heads, and the agitated white mob would stampede right over
their wounded and lifeless bodies. Like a big party parade on a
Saturday night, white men Yip-peed-it-up, and black men and
women were strung to and drug by cars up and down the streets
of downtown Tulsa.

My grandmother had told stories of some good Samaritans.
They were whites that had sheltered, fed, and protected runaways
in the under ground railroad, and we found some of their descen-
dant in Tulsa. Out of the 10,000 blacks that lived in Tulsa before the
massacre, 300 to 3,000 were dead; 6,000 were rounded up and ar-

rested; 500 fled the city, and 500 of us were rescued into the homes of those Good Samaritans."

***

The cotton man interrupted.
"In 2000, the final report of The Oklahoma Commission To Study The Tulsa state riot of 1921 concluded it was a conspiracy by the Ku Klux Klan and the white business owners. In some cases, the business owners were the Klansmen and they wanted the land.

***

"The day after, not a cloud was in the industrious boom-town prairie skies. Billows of gray-black smolder rose as substitutes and resembled thunderous matter." The cotton man offered the parody and I saw the scenery.

"Some of the blacks arrested were forced to dig graves and push charred and the bloody remains of their cherished husbands, wives, daughters, and sons down into unmarked gravesites. It was a massacre." His big eyes were choked with horror. Wretched tears dripped down into his white beard.

"No white person was ever charged for murdering, looting or burning. In fact immediately after the riot the grand jury's report said the initial twenty-five black vets that offered the sheriff help in protecting prisoner Dick Rowland were responsible for irritating the white crowd, therefore initiating the disturbance. The twenty-five brothers were blamed for the riot. The insurance companies didn't cover riots. Although the police department participated in the burnings and killings, the city of Tulsa wasn't held responsible. Without state or federal assistance, the remaining blacks froze for several winters, and survived hundred degree summers, and under tornadic conditions they lived in tent cities until they were able to scrimp and save and rebuild. A few days after the devastation, Sarah changed her story to a bump instead of attempted rape. Immediately Sarah skipped town and Young Dick was released."

Weather my eyes were open or shut, for weeks I saw mangled burnt phantom children, and I heard them screaming. Haunted day and night by these spirits' miseries, I became infuriated with a vicious vengeance against all white people. But tiny natural impulse wisdoms, or instinctual needs of Black Dickey were the saving graces of the nasty hate that consumed me. He had already lusted on the probability that there had probably been 37,000 white women, in Tulsa of possible good will.

Chapter Twenty-one

Some days in prison were better than the nighttime night-mares, but every minute there was a nightmare.

***

"That white woman had the nerve to say she thought we were friends." The image of a bony black woman appeared to me one night. "She was asking me about this and that, about...colored folks business, and then she had the audacity to say she thought we were friends. I looked her up and down and finished cleaning her house." She twisted her face in a way only capable by an aggravated black woman. "That Norman Rockwell picture she had hanging on the wall was nothing like the America I'd known. This white woman was half my age, calls me Olivia, and I have to address her as Miss Jane. They have this big ass brick house and her husband hustles enough on one job...and they've got plenty! I toil around here cleaning up after her nasty lazy ass, and my husband has two gigs and we live in a three-room shack...barely making ends meet. And she thought we were friends." The dark lady dusted and stared into the photograph on the wall and her shoulders shuddered. She appeared to be in complete disbelief at the white woman's assumptions and the phony picture of America. The quick blur of the dream vanished before revealing what the year was.

***

Philosophers and psychologist will tell you that humans are creatures of habit. If we continue to do the same silly things repeatedly, no matter how insane the behavior, we learn to love that dim-witted conduct. I had been confined behind bars living in danger for almost three and a half years and I hated every moment. The system refers to them as repeat offenders. I had seen several guys go and come right back and none of them ever told me they couldn't wait to get back and see me. There must be something terribly wrong out there that brings these poor souls back into this hell.

As scary as some of the lurid dreams and hallucinations were, the visuals of history had somehow acted as a protector. When I froze in the winter, the nightmares of freight were like warm blankets. At least they made the nights tolerable. And when I would sweat feverishly in the summers, I was initiated into the historical drama of real black pain. A shank up my back or a beat-down wasn't nearly as bad as the badge blacks have had to wear. I was not alone. This awareness made me feel secure with my own circumstances.

I had been a good boy for almost forty-two months; a couple of unreported scuffles, and once upon a time inside of me there'd lived a tender heart. Now it was under piles of disgust, anger, fear, and hate. Gone were bits of baby-fat and a schoolboy's idealism. Isometrics, intensive weight lifting, had made my 6' 4" frame into firm pure muscles. Along with my opposing physical features, I had accumulated a grocery list that detested almost everything in the white moral world of the Oklahoma that I knew. I'd bagged the items into the presentation of a nasty snarl.

I tried to rationalize: prisoners and life in prison wasn't totally responsible for the snarl I wore. What cemented the sneer was the absence of my endearing lover, Loretta. I was suffering and obsessing from the torture most inmates sooner or later undergo. Was my lady lying under the candlelight at night giving my loving to somebody else? Had some other penis squeezed between her outer labia, gyrated on her inner labia, banged her hood and sparked ecstasies into my baby's clit? I finally concluded, if I weren't locked up the idea of innocent little Loretta cheating wouldn't be merry-go-rounding me into madness. Incarceration was responsible for all my problems.

Loretta had hustled and graduated mid-term. With baby and all, she was still near the top of the class. A year ago her grandmother died, she was raising our two-year-old son and for a year and a half she'd been working her ass off as a programmer for a company that gave the state its electrical juice. Loretta swore to me that her life's responsibilities were the reasons that she'd sporadically visited. Black Dickey didn't believe her.

Anyway I used the snarl to distance myself from prisoner wanna-bees. "Don't mess with that cock strong nigger, he's crazy!" The growl had imitated insanity when I first arrived at Big Mac, but this time the sentiments were real.

It was October 17, that was the day I had decided to start the countdown. Six months, or one hundred eighty days and I'd be a free man. I awakened and the lost feeling *happy* was found again. The new bliss hadn't removed the snarl. Happy was now the unusual emotion among many awful feelings.

But that was in the morning. In the afternoon, I was warm and cozy with the hope happy had given and wasn't prepared for the news that would shatter the foundation of my life.

Mamma had a heart attack and died.

The grief ripped into my slight optimism. It was as if Black Dickey had a hard on and was spliced in half with a butcher knife. I'd rather spend the rest of my life in prison, if I could get those weekend visits with Mamma. Now, my freedom and future meant nothing. Memories of all the moments of my life with Mamma clung to my flesh and cried.

On a stormy, pissy, rainy Saturday, in honor of the state's compassion for inmates, my right to be at the funeral of an immediate family member's funeral was respected. Drably I drug my distraught soul along and was escorted by two deputies for one hundred sixty-five miles over the countryside, a three-hour drive up to Langston, Oklahoma.

Water dashed out of the black skies in the middle of the afternoon and gusty winds splattered the streams in all directions.

The wet weather swooshed underneath the mortuary and withered the customarily historical fashionable sturdy hats on the heads of the black women that attended. Umbrellas blew open and exposed the spokes. Dark dresses blew up and exposed the white, yellow, black, brown, pink, red, silk and cotton slips. The valiant women of Mamma's church had driven forty-five miles from Oklahoma City and gathered around her coffin. All held their heads high. On the dim day, the skies lit up and thunder roared and the preacher's voice sounded like God from heaven was offering Mamma's eulogy. Rain and tears soaked the mascara and rouge down the made-up eyes and faces of the women in the group, as they solemnly sung the old Negro Spiritual, *Precious Lord, take my hand*.

In a straight line, the black commiserates waddled in the mud and upon saturated grass through the thrashing rain with their heads lowered to Mamma's final resting-place. Handcuffed and an officer on each side, I stood with bowed head and a soggy expression at Mamma's coffin. I listened to each approaching soaked footstep. Since I was a small child I could identify the step beats of all of Mamma's friends. Each rose in body and spirit, one by one, and my eyes met the shuffle. Teary they offered heart-felt condolences that cracked a hole full of sentimental emotions into my hard prison shell.

There was a sudden huge gust of wind and rain and I had to wince to see the last emerging footsteps. Black Dickey recognized the curvy physique before Aunt Betty raised her head. I hadn't seen her in three and a half years. Her lean body was fuller figured and she was more attractive. Her big eyes wept with loss and she lunged and bear hugged me.

When she released me her son Danny and my girlfriend Loretta immediately popped into my head. Where were they? Were they together, screwing? Naw, her whole soul detested him. She saw Danny as a low-life. Hmm? Maybe opposites attract, I began fearing the worst possible scenario. Maybe in the back of every woman's psyche, they longed for a badass Neanderthal, some hard raw loving! Naw, no way, this wasn't happening with my sweet disciplined-minded Loretta. I chose a few other demented scripts to briefly sink under my skin for their absence. But Mamma had been a mother to Danny when his own mamma was on crack. The selfish bastard! And Loretta, she couldn't break into her busy schedule and show Mamma some respect. The lying ungrateful bitch! In this downpour, she's probably all cozy, giving her body to somebody right now. Mamma had treated her like a daughter and this is her payback. Bitch! Hurt and anger gave me permission to allow these filthy emotional responses. Another breeze came and suddenly the clouds darkened, and I believe Mamma was telling me to remember, this was her day.

I was standing in the mud next to the coffin and an overwhelming hurt filled with humiliating regrets started destabilizing my body and I began weeping like a baby. Mamma's casket was lowered into the hole and my knees gave way. Mamma, I should haves and if I could haves…guilt and grief crushed me. As I knelt there was a downpour and tears splashed on my face, and the onslaught of water was more internal than external.

After a minute the guards jerked me up and tried pulling me away but my foot got stuck in a mud-hole. I wiggled the sludge loose and only by chance I glanced at a weird angle at the near-by headstones.

***

Taima "Crash Of Thunder" Beard   James Beard
Born 1842   Born 1833
Died 1925   Died 1937

***

Crash Of Thunder! The name shook the emotional dysfunctional hell out of me. Beard was my great Grandma's maiden name. If she was…then was he? Was James the same Jim in my hallucinations? I searched for great grandma's grave and four stones down, there she was.

***

Janie (Beard) White
Born 1861
Died 1962

***

As we retreated to the police cruiser, the rain swished against the faded headstones, and in blurs I was able to distinguish that we were passing more Beard gravestones.

"Damn boohooing gospel singing black ass bitches!" The fish faced white officer released those pitiful words out of his carp shaped mouth. He mangled his face and blasted me a nasty stare. He opened the vehicle's back door and shoved me inside like I was a dirty rag doll. He hopped in the front, wiped the water off his face with a towel and tossed the cloth to his buddy.

"It's the middle of the week, nigger wenches ought to be cleaning toilets!" He and his partner giggled a laugh that had been handed down through the ages; way back from the Deep South. Grown out of generations the malicious degrading jeers had developed into a character. For making the excruciating retched racket, multitudes of black men have probably had to smother their emotions, grit their teeth, and restrain themselves form choking the shit out of them.

As we drove past the cemetery gate I turned and read an old rusty metal sign that was nailed between two deteriorating poles:

Beard Cemetery
Donated in 1897 by James and Tamia Beard
Burial Home
For The Colored People Of Langston, Oklahoma

***

"I've walked or rode a horse traveling every inch of these backroads son." And there he was—with his long legs crossed, lounging on the other side of me, in the back seat of a state owned vehicle. It was the old frontiersman, horse thief, run-away war hero. He was as I last saw him, an old man. Captivated, I observed his smooth black skin. A few crows feet under and on the outside of his eyes and they symbolized the hard life he'd lived, and his character. His jaws were slightly sunken, his beard and eyebrows were gray. He wore faded blue overalls, and was still black as tar. Was he my great-great grandfather? The phantom puffed on a hand-made corncob pipe. I peeped up front to see if my escorts were aware they had another passenger. No, both stared ahead, the driver was nervously navigating through the window washing the weather was freely giving. Neither saw this imagined image nor did they smell his smoke.

"Kayin, the white man sold my maw when I was close to about twelve years old. When I would go on trips with Master, and even when I later traveled alone to different counties, my eyes never stopped searching, I never quit asking questions. In life I never saw her again." His weary eyes longed for a love that had long ago disappeared, and the two beads harmonized a dreary wretchedness with my eyes.

He puffed on the pipe and created a cloud and when the smoke cleared old James was a young Jim. The deputy that drove squinted around the dashing rain to read road signs as we approached the interstate.

"I met Eddie McCabe, a lean yellow educated fellow three miles southeast of here, near the Cimarron River, and that was during the first land-run in 1889. Old Eddie was bright eyed and he believed he had brilliant ideas." The old man smiled on the memory, the camaraderie he'd had with a man he once knew, and it seemed like some of Eddie McCabe's ideas had tickled him.

Eddie McCabe. Eddie McCabe. Hmm that's the name that was interjected into my daydream while I was washing the funky prison uniforms. I was remembering being in the woods at Grandmother's house. So who was this Eddie McCabe that had entered my playground?

"Eddie loved black people and he had dreams for them." He thumped his pipe. "He fiercely fought for their right to be free. These battered dismal folk; ex-slaves, their sons and daughters deserved a better way of living. Separate and away from the vicious system white's had created. A separatist, Eddie was Elijah Mohammad way before the Black Muslims were born in America. At that time he knew a black man couldn't live side by side with white folk and receive justice and equality.

On the day of the run black folks were springing up tents everywhere. Soon Colored folks were raising livestock, planting and growing their own foods, building schools and churches, taking care of their children, making laws for themselves. And on some summer evenings, after sweating all day working the fields, those backwoods winds would gently come in sprinkling cool breezes and a black person could feel safe enough to fall asleep under a shade tree.

"I know the cotton man has already told you that Lincoln preferred to separate whites and colonize Oklahoma as all black. That was also one of Eddie's ambitious ideas but for different reasons. Lincoln wanted to protect whites from blacks and Eddie wanted to protect blacks from whites. And, as we know, that plan never happened for either man." The pioneer man hung his head as if he felt the weight of his friend's and all of black America's defeated vision.

Then suddenly the old fellow appeared to dust defeat off and his head popped up. "But more than fifty colored towns in the new territory ain't bad for a dream. There were, at one time, joyous pieces of Africa in America right here in Oklahoma!" He seemed pleased and self-assured and satisfied by his friend's dreams.

"On Saturday nights, colored folks danced in Eddie's dream! Negroes were able to hoop and holler and cut up as they pleased! They shucked and jived in juke joints and were often romanced intimately by solo piano players as smoke rode on top of corn whiskey fumes. Charlie Christian, Count Basie and Louis Armstrong all made their rounds on *The Chitterling Circuits* to the black towns." Inside of his appreciative glow he showed me miles of glorified emancipated black faces. "Their souls were let loose and sometimes you could see shadows of their dead slave daddies and mammas jazzing in their feet.

Bright smiling faces on black children entered into the world without seeing a cruel white person for years. Little black boys and girls bare-footed waded in the back wooded creeks and freely explored, and played. They lived in tin roof farmhouses surrounded by sheep, cows, pigs, chickens, and orchards full of apples, peaches, pears, pecans, and walnuts. We had fields full of juicy watermelons, onions, potatoes, peas, beans, golden corn and those stalks unfolded like eagles spreading their wings.

Of course we had violence against women. Some folks say this sickness was inherited, a by-product passed on from the cruel culture of slavery. Usually the preacher would speak to the fellow. If that didn't help the lady's relatives or the congregation would take care of his trifling ass. But mostly as far as my eyes could see black love flourished freely on the prairie fields.

Folks walked or rode horses or in buckboards pulled by mules to get to wherever they were headed. In the evening time colored people would sit on the porch and wave when they saw you passing by. We all knew each other." I saw this vision adorned in tiny smoke clouds from his pipe.

"Eddie had been a government official in Kansas, he knew how to do business with white folks. John Mercer Langston, Eddie said this man from Virginia was the first colored person elected to congress. He thought the legacy of a town should have dignity and a promise for future generations. Of course I thought Beard had certain nobility." The old trailblazer smirked teasingly. But I thought why not Beard, Oklahoma. The old frontiersman had lived a life I was proud of. "Eddie was a talker and he knew how to get his way with black folks too. Tehehe!" In his expression I saw his friend and him negotiating, this time he shook his head and smiled graciously. He'd conceded to his friend's wishes.

"In the land that promised plenty for all, in Eddie's dream he wanted colored folks to have the same opportunities that white folks had. We both donated twenty acres and the new community of Langston was born.

Life was harder back then, Kayin. The only race of people that needed an Amendment to receive rights was us. And they took those away. We didn't have the freedom to pursue higher education that would mean mixing with whites and in Oklahoma, that was a no-no, son." This wilderness man who'd journeyed west and conquered this harsh world for a moment appeared defeated.

Resiliently he was back again. "So the broke and uneducated ex slaves and their sons and daughters had bake sales, auctions, picnics, and we got a matching government land grant. The colored craftsmen constructed a school to educate our own." Wow! Those folks had heart. **The Colored Agricultural and Normal University**, that was the first name us country colored back-woods folk came up with. Tehehe!" The gray on his eyebrows jumped when he laughed.

"Back then we had more colored women like your God fearing mamma. In fact to get the school off on the right foot we began having classes in a Presbyterian Church. In those days God blessed more colored women with a gracious sacrificing soul like your Maw's!" His eyes became soft and his tone was full of gratitude.

I stared into the autumn rains and felt the wind flurries vibrate the vehicle. Wet leaves were tossed and scattered across our path as we passed Langston University. Students scurrying to classes were under umbrellas and skipping through water pools.

His eyes got big while he admired his donation to a dream. "Trees, bushes and all these buildings; looks like the campus has spread to more than four hundred acres. It's grown into a magnificent campus!"

Mamma had told me that before the late 1960's, the graduates of Langston had educated most of the black children in the state.

There has always been a part of me that believed that our ancestors hadn't done enough for our freedoms. It shouldn't have taken
them this long to make such small steps. But this coming together
by the African American communities had begun with bake sales,
and the pieces of our history were beginning to fit.

We drove to the service road that would usher us to the freeway. The officer expertly maneuvered uphill through rushing, down-
hill floodwater. Halfway up, a mini-mart service station was on the
right side of the road.

"Goddamn it nigger! We're risking our lives on this goddamn
excursion and now the state says we have to feed your black ass!"
Forty-two months of prison cuisine and the possibility of chow from
the outside made saliva carve a river under my tongue, overflowing slobber through my teeth. The thick skin suit I'd gotten used to
from the guard's harsh rhetoric, I slipped it on.

"Of course the depression hit most colored towns, and Oklahoma's colored farmer's way before the stock market crashed in
twenty-nine." The frontiersman puffed lazy smoke circles out of his
mouth." In the early 1930's the stock market had crashed, the railroad companies stopped sending trains through black towns, and
that was the only way most of us got our crops to the markets.
We were broke and couldn't feed our families, and here come
those dirty dust storms. And those bad times inspired a white man,
John Steinbeck, to write *The Grapes Of Wrath*. Some of us weren't
aware that annually the way we'd planted crops, our unscientific
approach to growing agriculture, helped create conditions that
caused grainy dust clouds to blend in around us disguised as air.
The best ingredients of our lands had taken flight, killed the soil,
and was choking the shit out of all of us. Black and white came
together and agreed with that was the final nail in the coffin, it
was time to give up and a bunch of us moved on. A tiny minority
of us stayed." I saw dust peddles buzzing in front of the old farmer's
weary eyes.

"Here!" The officer opened the car door on my side, and like
tossing a bone to a dog, he flung the paper sack into my lap. He
adjusted the handcuffs from my back and placed them in front.
On the three-hour ride to the funeral, torn up with grief, I'd been
oblivious to the pulverizing ache the steel had indented into my

back. I only became aware of my discomfort when the cop re-positioned the braces.

My taste buds had forgotten how delicious cooked ham tasted with simple lettuce-tomato and cheese. I chewed every bite a hundred times savoring the flavors.

The closer we got to the prison, the worse the storm got. Ball busting thunder shook the car. I could hear fear grip our expert driver's hands. As he waded through water, over hills and around curves, several times the frightened shitless policeman nearly hydroplaned us to hell.

"Your Mamma gave you more than most people, black or white. You got a decent foundation." The old man puffed another smoke cloud, and as the smoke disappeared so did the spirit I'd come to know as my great-great grandfather. Both were gone.

Soon my outing was over. The cop drove through the prison gates and my body would circulate the venom of grief in a tiny cell. I would exhale the torture of the incarcerated life for one hundred seventy-five more sluggish days. And, even worse than that, I was haunted by a son's life I'd never seen.

Chapter Twenty-two

On March 18, two days before the spring's solstice, the summer birds were still further south and the winter's deep freeze still had a grip on the season. The skies were gray and the trees were bare, and I had survived prison. I was given my civilian clothes. The money I'd earned, for four years of hard labor was the sum total of $165.00. This nest egg was also my life's savings.

Before prison I had heard of halfway houses, job training programs, and psychological counselors, places and professionals that would assist in the inmate's adjustment back into society. That was all fantasy bullshit. Since the state's budget for psychological assistance for prisoners was a low priority for the state's legislators, why was I under the illusion I'd receive special assistance when I was released? Oh but they did splurge a little money on halfway houses, only for a lucky few ex-cons, not me. I was given the phone number and address to a parole officer and was told to contact her within two weeks. Since I was convicted on drugs, a weekly impromptu urine test at $20 a pop was ordered for my probation.

If you're broke hit the road Jack, walking. If you have enough money for a bus ticket, grab a seat on the bench and wait. Daily a bus travels to all points south and north. If you were blessed to still have a friend, a family member, if someone still cared about your life, they would be there to drive you off to a new life. Aunt Betty was waiting in Mamma's Subaru.

I despised the spunky way she hopped around and opened Mamma's car door for me and then I had to put up with Aunt Betty's constant cheery chatter for the entire ride to the city.

When we were fifty miles away from the prison the air began to taste sweeter. In a zombie-state, frequently I stared out the window and followed lone wintry weather sparrows as they flew over distant hills and disappeared into the cold gray skies. The winged animals' flight patterns began to represent a paradox for my life without Mamma. I was free and without Mamma, and that meant, I was free to wander off into the world and fade away.

I should have been used to Aunt Betty's babble. After Mamma's death she appointed herself as my only tie to the outside world, as if I had other choices. Betty was there every Saturday afternoon to console my grieved robotic personality. On her first visit, she informed me that Mamma had deeded the house to me but there was still an unpaid mortgage balance, and it would take nearly three years to pay off. She had decided to move in and continue settling the debt, that way when I got out I wouldn't get hit with a foreclosure notice. "I'm going to keep the white folks from stealing your mamma's shit!" Betty said, and even in my zombie consciousness I agreed she was right. Later the little ex-whore confirmed my suspicions that the only other intimate love of my life left, was long gone, and was giving her precious body to somebody else; and oh yeah, she was married. I didn't have any free spots to tuck that awful pain. I was already aching with loss, now Black Dickey had to cuddle up with rejection.

The huge oak tree in the middle of our front yard didn't appear to have aged four years, but the branches were still baron; stripped from the ripeness of the approaching spring season. The bony limbs looked as lost and as desolate as I felt inside. Because of my unique relationship with nature, animals, and the seasons, I realized I was projecting the loss I felt into what was natural for the scenery. I couldn't help obsessing in this extrapolative mode. Just like jail had carved a life of cruel experiences into me, scenery, creatures and cyclic yearly changes also continued defining who I was.

The attributes of the genes from my grandmother were split between her two daughters. Some were more dominant in one daughter than the other. They say Mamma had a natural gentleness for animals. Whereas sober, Aunt Betty had inherited her culinary skills. Don't get me wrong; my mamma could burn up some good delicious meals! But Aunt Betty was born with chef skills. She was an artist, and could mix and burn some gourmet dishes that would leave a person's mouth savoring the tasty flavors hours after they'd eaten!

Waiting on the range for my homecoming was a scrumptious entrée of Aunt Betty's tenderly juicy-slice-with-a-butter-knife roast beef. Her secret spices were handed down through generations.

But when Aunt Betty added her own specialty mix, she created a new distinct traditional taste; homegrown vegetables, carrots, onions, green peas, and corn, Aunt Betty smothered those natural nutrients and, to-die-for flavors, in the same pan she baked the roast. Yummy! Brown sugar blended splendidly with tangy nutmeg on sweet potatoes and I savored every delicious bite. Her home-made cornbread was burnt on the edges giving the bread a rich gritty greasy crunchiness. Aunt Betty's fat-back mustard greens and her soupy black-eyed peas made me feel connected to a kinship that was full of culture, generations of black life that I could only imagine but not understand.

My body had forgotten how the steady flow of warmth out of central heat could calm the nerves and assist the digestive juices. The soft carpet acted like a chiropractor's hands against the soles of my bare-feet. I paused on every cushioned step and squeezed the tender threads into my veins. Black Dickey stretched, yawned and eased into a nap.

Our bathroom was quaint. An oval mirrored vanity with four oak drawers, a stool, and bath and shower. Taking a bath became an intimate encounter. I no longer had to step on a mildewed cement floor and share a spacious all boys' facility. And in prison if the nozzles were functioning, most of the time the spigots only dripped. And if I got lucky I was hosed with lukewarm instead of a freezing cold sprinkling. I didn't have to be cautious anymore. No corner of the eye second looks for a shank in the back or for someone aiming on jamming his rod up my ass.

Aunt Betty's chocolate delicate scented soap had a tasty smell, and a gentle moisturizing feel that made me want to eat the bar and make love to myself. As I lathered, I sunk into the female mellowness of my Aunt's exotic wonderland of suds. Her private play field was full of ultra rich mint chocolate chip ice creamy aromas, and I wished if the passions in the dissolving popping bubbles could cleanse four years of infested prison funk. I soaked in the tub for more than four hours.

As I cracked the door to my bedroom, I spotted my Dell computer in the back corner near the window. Slowly I gazed over the creamy oak desk and spotted its accessories, a video camera and combo printer/copier/fax machine. I'd bought all the devices brand new, two years before I was incarcerated. And now in the cyberspace world they were probably dinosaurs.

I entered the room and was overwhelmed with lemon freshness. Mamma had left her cleaning calling card. Slowly I moseyed into the room and tried to absorb the innocent memories of growing up in the space, I wanted this energy force to aggressively recapture that soul. But the rage of the caged experiences said no. Naive pre-prison instincts told me to hurry and power up the Dell to see if the machine still worked. I desired badly to know if I still had all my saved files. Quickly, as the inspiration came, the need exited. I didn't give a damn about a life I had once lived.

I was out of prison, and there should be enthusiasm behind that thought and reality. And I was inside of a safe soundly bolted home, and out of habit I locked my bedroom door.

I switched on the light and was surprised by a new six foot Panama bed. As I appreciated what I thought was Mamma's last gift, miniature pieces of bliss entered my body. The bed's headboard had a tropical style with a wicker finish and decorative necks and ball finials. It was trimmed in elegant bamboo. Four mushy throw pillows colored in pink fresh flowers laid atop a butter cream Egyptian cotton blanket. I lifted the blanket and wanted to eat the strawberry sheets. The rough prison linen had scratched permanent abrasion into my skin. As I lay on the mattress it melted into the shape of my shell. I clung to the pink fancy pillows and thanked Mamma for the homecoming gift. And as I fell asleep I felt my body shedding tears of joy, and then abruptly, patches of loneliness came crashing in.

I woke up and the awesome aroma of country sausage provoked me to immediately get up. The house was silent and that meant Aunt Betty had already gone to work. She'd left me a warm plate of eggs, sausages and pancakes in the microwave.

Aunt Betty had been a busy little whore for the last four years. She'd transformed her life into a respectable lady. Aunt Betty had gotten her Bachelor's degree in nursing. She now worked at the same hospital where Mamma helped saved lives, St. Anthony's. Two nights a week the ex-whore took care of an old rich couple that lived in the most prestigious neighborhood in Oklahoma, The Nichols Hill's. Outside of attending A.A. meetings, she'd joined

Mamma's church and converted her religious and spiritual values into political action and was a card-carrying member of the NAACP. Imagine an ex crack-head now legally dispensing some of the same addictive substances she used and use to sell illegally. And probably giving medical services to some of same white and black men she'd sold her body to.

The freedom to eat civilian food brought out the animal in me. For at least the first three days I didn't use any utensils. After I had devoured breakfast I would flip the TV on in the living room and would relax on the couch. Even though a part of me knew Loretta was out of my life, as I watched *The Today Show, Little House On The prairie, Regis & Kelly, Judge Joe Brown, Judge Mathis, Judge Judy, All My Children, One Life To Live, Divorce Court, Sport Center, and Oprah*, I would daydream of a life with my sweetheart and our son.

When the shades were pulled down and Aunt Betty came home, I moved my TV viewing into the privacy of my bedroom. For two days in-between HBO movies, soap operas and the law shows, I ate breakfast out of the microwave, lunch was leftovers out of the refrigerator, and at night Aunt Betty would prepare a sumptuous supper. I didn't answer the phone, look out the windows, open the front and back doors, nor did I take a trip to the back yard. I didn't know if the old oak and the pecan trees or my basketball goal was still back there, and I didn't care.

I did take care of Black Dickey. Semi-nude sexy white women leaned over to pick up objects and partially exposed their juicy tits on the soaps. The pink, black, and brown ladies had buck wild sex on cable. After four years of secretly jerking off, right there in the privacy of my six-foot Panama cradle, I openly boldly choked Black Dickey with energetic thrusts and he blew up!

On day four I awakened and began my regular rituals. I headed for the kitchen to retrieve the breakfast that awaited me in the microwave, and surprise, surprise, surprise! There was Aunt Betty sitting at the kitchen table sipping coffee.

"Good morning." Aunt Betty said, as she winked, batted her eyes, smiled, sipped and swallowed coffee. If I didn't know my aunt's history as an ex prostitute I may have thought the fluttered under-eyed gleam was her sly way of flirting with me, but I knew better. Some old gestures are hard to break.

"Your breakfast is on the stove. Have a seat and eat with me." Holding her cup in a saucer she sipped and pointed with her head at the chair across the small round honey-pine table. It was after 7 a.m. and Aunt Betty still had a robe on and curlers in her hair. She must be off today, I reasoned.

I was preparing my plate when Betty suddenly rose and dashed by me. The upper cabinets and a countertop separated the stove from the back door, which lead to the garage, and Aunt Betty sprung it opened.

"Look! There's your Toyota!" She flicked on the light and her charming beam searched to see if revelations of joys were in my eyes.

"Oh wow!" With a forced smile I politely said and tried to be surprised for my aunt's sake. My car brought back memories but not the thrills she expected. She's been good to me every since Mamma passed. Truth was, seeing the Camry was like remembering the day I was arrested. I had a glimpse of the cop with the shotgun pointed at my head. The vehicle struck another chord. It was the day I lost Mamma and Loretta, my career; the day when my life was ruined. Staring at the Camry gutted up bad memories of a life that was gone forever.

"It's insured and tagged. Rose was starting up the car daily before"...Aunt Betty was saying as her eyes met mine, and we understood the silence. "I've been turning the motor on once a week. Firing those pistons is supposed to somehow circulate fluid and maintain the transmission." Aunt Betty was offering hope to a person that just didn't care if any parts on the car worked or if I ever drove the vehicle again.

Aunt Betty closed the door and we both strolled to the table and sat. Since I wanted to appear civilized I grabbed a fork to eat the western omelet, and a knife to spread butter over my pancakes and chop them up.

It was a large bamboo African bag and it was beside her leg under the table. As we sat, awkwardly Aunt Betty leaned and gathered her purse. She began piddling through it. Whatever she was searching for she located it and held onto it, and gazed up at me before she lifted it out.

"Your driver's license has probably expired, right?" Betty asked, as she continued to shield whatever she was hiding, until I responded.

"Uh-yeah." They had expired over a year ago, and it was one more thing added on the pile of had-to-dos of my when-I-get-around-to-it list. Since Mamma was gone I'd dumped the whole I-had-to-do file; I didn't want to do anything.

Aunt Betty finally lifted a brochure from the bamboo bag. She laid the booklet in the center of the table so I could read the name, *Oklahoma Department of Transportation*.

"I'm off at the hospital on Tuesday. I could take you for the test then." Aunt Betty said, as she finished off her coffee. She sprung up with the saucer and empty cup in one hand and dashed to the dishwasher.

"Throw some clothes on, I need you to help me with some shit today. This old white couple I'm nursing at night, they're giving away some appliances and furniture to Goodwill. I need you to help set that shit out on the curb for pick up." Although Aunt Betty was a Christian she still expressed herself in street language.

As Aunt Betty sashayed out of the kitchen I mulled over her request. She hadn't asked me if I would, she'd demanded I do as she says. This was an old fashion way an older black person would tell someone younger and expected them to do whatever. It was a respect request. As I finished breakfast, I wondered what the ex-whore's bedside manor was like.

My aunt had told me details about the famous white couple while I was in prison, but then everything was fuzzy. Suddenly, I had a glimpse of the duo my aunt was referring to. As long as I could remember there'd always been local commercials featuring the good old boys of Brown's furniture store. When I was little, at least ten to sixteen times a day, the whole Brown family and their friends and relatives were featured strumming guitars, square dancing; they all partied and sung country and western jingles in red state Oklahoma. The furniture store was stapled in the minds of Oklahoman's as solid as the *'Boomer-Sooner'* tune was glued to the hearts of fans of the Oklahoma Sooner football team.

I opened my closet door and admired through plastic coverings my collection of suits. Mamma had preserved the compilation. Even the creases in my Levis were intact. (I was wrong. Aunt Betty had maintained the dust-free zone. She'd hand pressed everything, and she was the one responsible for adding the sweet-sour citrus scent for my room.)

Instead of a thirty-two inch waist, my six four frame had firmed down to a tight thirty. I've never been a hip-hop brother that would expose half of his draws to the world; the baggy look, showing your ass, wasn't in Mamma's dress code. I threw on a beige Hilfiger sweater and tightened the thirty-two loose jeans with a belt. It was still frosty cold outside so I zipped my body up in a navy MontBell Neige downs Jacket. I guess I was doing as I was told.

As I entered Mamma's Subaru, from across the street I spotted Mr. McGregor, Trisha's father. He was snuggled all up in an overcoat, gloves, and had his black brim pulled down. He raised a friendly hand and waved. Since I was eight years old I would shiver every time I saw him. He didn't know I was the first one to sex his little girl, and I liked keeping that a hush-hush secret.

On our way out of the neighborhood, Aunt Betty drove past Loretta's home. There was a for-sale sign in the yard. Aunt Betty must have noticed the flood of miserable memories in my eyes when I gazed at the property.

"Little girl got married to a lawyer some eight months ago, I told you that didn't I?" "Yeah." My reply, begrudgingly streamed out and the fact that he was a lawyer stayed inside me steaming.

"They have a handsome home up in Edmond." Ah-shit! I wanted to believe that my sweetheart was giving my love away to a looser, but knowing Loretta, the girl keeps her eyes on the financial prize. The female that had introduced me to passionate sex was now living large and had moved on to the type of neighborhood she'd dreamed of since she was a little girl.

"Life goes on." Aunt Betty said consoling me, and her brow wrinkled up carrying a caring emotion. She seemed to be expressing genuine compassion for my situation. But! 'Life goes on'—I'm supposed to get over losing the only lover that I've ever had and move on? What kind of reassuring bedside manor was this silly whore feeding me?

It was almost eight-thirty and I wanted to think about something else. If Aunt Betty's little task took too long, I was going to miss Regis and Kelly and probably both Judges Brown and Mathis.

We entered the Nichols Hills neighborhood and all year round it seemed as if this wealthy section of the city maintained green manicured lawns. Hovering above the high sandstone and granite brick railings, the small Subaru became morphed by meandering tree limbs. A lot of the money had migrated directly from the city's earliest pioneering downtown estate houses. In this cow town, this neighborhood is considered as the Beverly Hills of Oklahoma City.

"Day or night, in this part of town black folks use to get stopped, or arrested getting this close to rich white people." I heard Mamma say.

Aunt Betty inserted a combination, the gates parted, and she pulled around a twelve-foot antebellum fence and turned into a winding cobbled driveway. It escorted us through a wintry forestry for half a block. Cracks between the barren trees and I got glimpses of some sidewalks that traveled around a lake. At the edge of the jungle, there was a children's playground, a swing set, monkey bars, and a sea-saw. It was as big as the park in our neighborhood.

I'd seen the Brown's moving diesel vans on commercials and on the streets of Oklahoma City my whole life, and there one was, parked in front of the owner's mansion.

We stepped out of the car on top of a sandstone curb and proceeded to walk up ten stairs made of Colorado River rock. Aunt Betty leaned on the sandstone rails for support. At the top, slowly gazing around with bucked eyes I took in all the abundance of the Brown's magnificent estate.

A bluestone patio edged in granite was outside the main entrance. The mahogany French doors fascinated me. They had twelve reflective lead glass panels on the interior and thick insulated glass on the exterior. Savannah Gray brick was the color of the two-story enterprise. A decorative round mahogany window was at the apex. Six panels of mahogany double casement windows appeared to extend around the structure. The roof had sections arched in pristine purple.

Aunt Betty rang the silent doorbell and we waited at least a minute before Aunt Betty started snooping through her purse. I heard keys jingling.

"It's cold out here! I called that old man and told him I was on my way, and now he's taking his goddamn sweet time answering the door. Hell I have keys!" My impatient and freezing aunt said. I don't know why, but I became nervous and ashamed for us. This was going to be my first entrance into a white man's house. And this was an affluent white man's establishment. A few days ago I was locked up and my aunt was still an ex- prostitute. Besides that we were black. Were we worthy of stepping into this society and if Aunt Betty used those keys would it be ok for this white man to shoot us for crossing into his kingdom without an invitation?

No sooner had Aunt Betty popped the keys from her purse we heard someone behind the door. A cute white girl about my age peeped behind a cracked door. She spotted Aunt Betty and beamed a hi-I-know-you-friendly-smile and shoved the door opened. Flurries of her long wet red copper spritz hair hung over her eyes. She flicked her head and the stray tresses flopped back into her dew. She had a better view of her visitors. I watched sweat profusely roll off her face. Instinctively and immediately Black Dickey's lust said hello while Aunt Betty did the formal introductions. Cherry was her name, and automatically he sized Cherry's firm construction to be about five foot five inches and passionately measured her for a fit with my six foot four frame. Cherry's hefty meat-balled size tits were smothered under a lime seamless sports bra. Her wetness highlighted her nipples. Breast dimensions, about thirty-two. Four years of sex depravation caused me to impulsively gawk down on the two goodies. 'Welcome to freedom!' I thought I heard her tits whisper.

"I'm sorry for the delay, I was upstairs working out." She apologized and I was sure this white female averted her eyes with a friendly flirt up and down my physique. Since I'd never confirmed that a white girl had ever responded to me with lusty eyes, I didn't trust my prison-suppressed instincts.

Cherry escorted us through the family's marbled entrance, and our heels clicked as we tap-danced over the glazed crimson hardwood floor. In the foyer an Egyptian rug gave my shoes a magical feel. The three of us took flight up a spiral autumn-brown cedar staircase, and this jailbird felt regal when I gazed over my shoulder down on the Brown's royal toys. Thousands of dollars of luxurious artistic possessions lined the dining area.

Chapter Twenty-three

For a moment I stood atop the stairs captivated by all the Brown's riches. Odd as it was, my ability to identify expensive quality furniture and antiques wasn't cultivated exclusively at the university. I grew up in the Internet age. Goggle search engines, online dictionaries, and Mamma had bought me a set of encyclopedias. She'd enriched my childhood with old-fashioned picture book games and made sure I had access to a world of class and culture.

The living room's borders had a fine New England Rustic carved panel. In the back area there was a colonial oak step bookcase, and a cabinet that had sliding glass doors. A vast Portuguese round pedestal table sat in the center and a dozen immaculate goan canned chairs surrounded it. I could easily see the Brown's relaxing and entertaining other wealthy folk. A marble classical snow-white French Louis XV fireplace and an English walnut Louis XV piano were on opposite sides of the room. The angle from atop the stairs altered my view of other valuables. And I was trailing Cherry and Black Dickey wanted to concentrate more on our escort's riches, her sturdy little hips. Her buns twitched as she femininely pranced and the creamy white silk short-shorts she wore made an overlapping wrinkle. The creases revealed the lining in Cherry's bikini underpants. Fixated, I noticed on her upward thigh twirl, every time Cherry moved forward, a portion of her hip was exposed. Four years of pent-up lust and Black Dickey fantasized grabbing our guide and molesting her from back end.

Upstairs as we walked past an open door, curious, I peeped inside and saw rows of spiraling black leather theatre seats. It was a private movie theatre. I guess the Brown's didn't show regular DVD's; they had a big screen motion picture platform. We passed several closed doors and finally Cherry marched us into a room spacious enough to set my whole house and back yard inside. It was an inside gymnasium. Exercise bikes lined the far wall. A boxing ring was in the middle and was orderly surrounded by rowing machines, weight lifting benches and racks of Olympic weight plates, work out mats and several home gyms.

A white man, squatty and dumpy, old and bald on top, with ten to twelve gray strands on the sides of his head was lying on a bench. He gritted his teeth while he pumped barbells. When he spotted us he stopped and sat up. Out of breath, wet with sweat, he wobbled to his feet. He embraced Aunt Betty and she planted a kiss on top of his head. She introduced us, and instinctively he gawked up at me the way white people do when they see a large black man.

"You're a big guy Kayin." Mr. George Brown Junior said, as he looked me up and down again. His father was the founder of Brown's home furnishings and now his late eighty or early ninety some thing son had inherited millions if not billions. I shook his hand and forced a smile.

"I've got to shower and get ready for work grandfather. I'll leave our guest in your amiable hands." Cherry told the old man and us. She then turned and faced me and hid her expression away from her grandfather's eyes. Cherry curtly averted her eyes down and intentionally she let me know she was tracing my body. When she arrived at Black Dickey she stopped and flicked her eyes up and locked into my eyes and winked. Her candid sexy glowering flirt, was it real? Cherry quickly twisted around and pranced off. The sudden snapped motion caused her drying red copper spritzed hair to wiggle with an attitude. The little bitch was teasing me, I thought. Even though I wished all the women on the planet were attracted to me, I sure didn't believe any white woman in Oklahoma was. In my twenty-four years that sort of shit had never happened. Was this white girl actually flirting with Black Dickey? Naw, after today I'll never see her again, she's just a little tease, I reasoned.

Mr. Brown motioned with his eyes towards a cane that was propped against the wall and Aunt Betty retrieved the stick.

"I'll show you all the merchandise I'm giving away. A big buck like you shouldn't have any problem with these bits and pieces." He gave me a friendly poke in my tummy with his cane and grinned.

Across the hall from the Brown's private gym, one of the doors I'd assumed was a closed door turned out to be an elevator entrance.

"You go with Mr. Brown Kayin; I'm going to check on Mrs. Brown." Aunt Betty said and took off down to the end of the hall, she turned the corner and disappeared. Damn! How big was this castle?

The old man told a short story about when he was a young man on our quick trip down. I smiled and he thought I was listening. I didn't hear a word he said. What could a young black ex-con have in common with this filthy rich old white coot? Those comparisons occupied me while he was talking. I'd never been in a white person's home and I was sure not too many black people had ridden in Mr. Brown's private elevator. This old fart was speaking to me like we've been neighbors for years. His nature was gracious and the contrast of our lives confused and angered me. He was white, privileged, rich, and never in his old life had he experience the deprivation I'd seen in only twenty-four years. How could we possibly have anything in common?

The kitchen area was as long as our entire house was wide. Cherry oak glass cabinets, a center island, stainless steel appliances, granite countertops, and a pantry that lead to somewhere; I wasn't able to see where, we were only passing through. The kitchen and dining room windows were the size of doors; through the curtains I saw an extravagant swimming pool area and a backyard patio that was far reaching.

The old fellow limped on his cane around the enclosed swimming pool. We past six twelve foot, majestically decorative stone fountains. They looked like they were stolen from Julius Caesar's kingdom. I was gawking on the expedition while the old man was constantly talking, telling more stories. After we entered a five foot steel black gate, Mr. Brown swiftly hobbled across a trail that was made of Colorado Colored bricks. This passage took us to two laminated cherry oak bridges. As we crossed the wooded suspension bridge, the old fart tugged the braided rope rail and thudded his cane against the planks, and I felt the creek waters surge under our feet. Gazing back from the banks I saw spring's tiny green plants budding in the black mud. Beyond the crossing there were twin two-story log cabins, complete with wood carved banisters and refined Hollywood hillbilly porches. The naked winter trees in the background gave the houses a cozy, rough frontier appearance. Both structures had two back-to-back triangle windows that met at the upstairs apex. Two six sectioned double hung windows were below. The personalized carved banisters on the porches offered the illusion of real old western authenticity. The scenery made me travel back to those pioneer days of Daniel Boone, Abraham Lincoln...and slavery.

"Kayin I want you to empty all the furniture out of this cabin...." We stood in-between the two cabins and he pointed to the lodge on the left. "...and move the stuff to the van that's parked out front. There's the moving equipment." Mr. Brown motioned to the porch and I saw a dolly, some hand trucks, and a strap. He then gave me a sturdy handshake, stared into my gaze, like we were two businessmen completing a deal. I watched the old wealthy bastard hobble back to the big house as I reflected. He could've told me this shit upstairs. This conceited motherfucker wants this stuff packed into one of the Brown vans, why not one of Goodwill's, since that's where Aunt Betty said the shit's going to end up.

Once I was inside the cabin my attitude towards the old fellow mellowed. Four years of surviving in a tiny room was absorbed by the freedom of staring into an old fashioned fireplace. Bemused, I wandered into and through the living room and kitchen. Again, I found myself gawking and appreciating the finely engraved furnishings.

In my head I bounced around, arranging a loading packing pattern for the two downstairs bedrooms. Long-stepping up the stairs up to the loft I found another bedroom. Just one of the Brown's log home's furnishings doubled the amount of stuff in our entire home. I walked back outside and scrutinized how I would utilize a damn dolly, some shitty hand trucks, and a strap that would probably break a mule's back, this was all this old man gave me to work with...damn!

While I whistled and labored, my thoughts no longer lingered on the old man and our differences. I didn't have a chance to regret missing my daytime TV shows, nor did I give Black Dickey graphic doggie-styling banging pleasures with Cherry's fine firm ass. Haunts of my prison experience captured my dreams: Stabbings, killings, death, and the constant fear of these incidents happening to me. I replayed the actual events like I was watching a scary movie.

Within an hour of the motion picture I had hauled four beds, a pine dining room table and chairs, four brown leather bar stools, a Barcelona table and chairs, two chestnut drawers, a black leather office chair, a computer desk, a Japanese corner cabinet, refrigerator, electric range, washer, dryer, across the bridge. I had stacked the furniture and appliances neatly and efficiently inside the Brown's storage van. When I finished, I thought, if Aunt Betty hurried we could get home in time for Black Dickey to salivate at the exquisite skimpy fashions worn by the women on *All My Children*.

I located a vacuum and a broom in the closet and swept and dusted, and tidied, and left the log house. I entered the same glass patio door Mr. Brown and I had exited. A milk chocolate fat black woman wearing a red polka dot apron rushed from the kitchen area and rolled her huge brown eyes and then she gave me a nasty snarled. *"Don't you know how to knock Nigger?"* It was silent but it was insinuated in her expression. *"And nigger don't you know these are my white folks"* was suggested in the way she aggressively positioned her hands on her hips and strutted off.

***

I was in my bedroom watching TV when I thought I heard Cousin Danny's inflection resonating from the living room. For the past forty-eight months I'd spent countless hours obsessing on ways to kill him. I'd never stopped wanting to murder them all; his two hip-hop buddies, the arresting cops, the whole damn white jury that found me guilty. I wanted to snap the skinny prosecuting attorney's back! And the judge hammering her gavel, completing the racially insensitive demoralizing process, I dreamt of jamming that sledgehammer up her ass and watching blood flow. If there were no therapy programs for the extremely bad asses that are being released out of Oklahoma's prisons daily, I knew there was no psychological assistance set aside to help me. And since Mamma died, depression lived unconsciously and consciously along side vengeance and both had carved their own personality into my soul. Knowing Danny was close revived that vicious part of me.

"Kayin! Kayin!" There he was banging on my bedroom door. Should I attempt to take his life now or sneak up on him and let the perpetrator of his death be unknown to the world? I damn sure didn't want to be inside of a cell again.

"Kayin! Kayin! Nonchalantly I drug my ass out of the recliner and flipped off the TV and opened the door.

Danny's eyes were glazed. Had he been drinking? Underneath a bebop cap his unshaven face was slightly swollen and the nylon burgundy sweater he had on swallowed his use-to-be stout physique; his appearance was puny and ragged. I was always two inches taller than my cousin but never better built; now I was both. With an outstretched smile and opened arms my cousin welcomed me.

"Hey man!" As he grabbed me I noticed he still had cock strong hands. He pulled me into his chest. "Damn it's good to have you home man." He sobbed. His cuddle was gentle like a woman's, and for a moment I didn't know if I wanted to have sex with him or kill him. The longer our hug endured, his blood surged into mine, and even though I resisted I began to assimilate the flow of his life force into my own. That hug heaved compassionate memories of us together. I'd used our life experiences to feel love for many of my fellow inmates that had crack-head parents. They were similar to Danny. I knew he hadn't gotten enough love as a child. I managed to squeeze an ounce of affection out for my cousin. We both exhaled from the embrace and the next breath eased out a puff that was packed with four years of suppressed rage. That surge of hate was too great; I broke loose and plowed two quick powerful combinations into Danny's face. The potent punches sent my cousin flying across the Panama bed. Lying on his back Danny shook his head, as if he was fighting, trying to keep from losing consciousness.

"Ah-hell!" Danny cried out. He stared at me and our eyes locked.

"Come on! Kick the crap out of me! Come on I deserve an ass kicking and then some." Danny yelled. He threw up his hands, like he was surrendering; he was going to let me beat the shit out of him.

"Man I'm sorry I didn't visit...didn't even come by when you were in county! Man you know most brothers are paranoid going behind those walls. You never know if they're going to keep your black ass or not...you know what I mean, man?

Breathing hard, I was energized with the prison experience and the years of contempt I'd felt for him, I gritted my teeth. I wanted to kick and pound and pulverize my cousin into a bloody mess.

"Come on Kayin! Kick my ass on this new bed I bought for you!" Teary eyed, like a child, my cousin was begging to be punished.

We both cleaved to the hypnotic gaze. Misery, sorrow, regrets and pity made their appearance out of the shadows of Danny's soul, and my gawk at him began to weaken.

Danny released his gawk and I exhaled. He sprung from the bed and quickly pimp-walked pass me off into the hall; abruptly stooping he leaned over the decorative pot of African Violets. He snatched and jubilantly held up quart bottles containing Courvoisier and Hennessy.

"Celebration time! Come on!" Danny did a bump and grind boogie and winked. "I know you're not a drinking man, after where you've been...believe me this is the time to get funky!" Freeze fizz drizzled on the exterior of both jugs. Danny popped the tops, handed me the Hennessy. We treated the quart jugs like they were toasting glasses; we clicked the containers together. Danny kissed the top of the Courvoisier and gestured for me to follow. I did, and we both guzzled a swig.

We wolfed down several mouthfuls, got tipsy and the liquid courage gave us permission to take a walk down memory lane. Sipping on Hennessy was breaking down four years of walls built on layers of suspicion of everybody and everything. I was drugged into an open relaxation of old déjà vu.

"I don't know how you wandered off into six feet of water and began sinking? I had seen you paddle across four feet all day long." Danny hopped out of my computer chair and began mocking an eight-year-old version of me drowning. His intoxicated eyes popped wide opened, he puffed his jaws and wildly flung his arms, imitating my desire to swim and stay alive and the water's influence trying to drown, killing me. Danny could always run faster, jump higher, and he learned how to swim earlier. He'd always performed most physical activities better than I had. I fault through Hennessey's paralyzing affects and grabbled up a question. Why was he bringing up this episode out of our life, why now? Is this his way of apologizing? If he hadn't saved my life back then, I wouldn't be here now. Was that Danny's thinking? Whatever it was, this would probably be the best and last concession I'd get from him. I stopped wrestling with sensibilities and allowed the alcohol to do its job.

Danny reached his inebriated hands down and patted his Levi pockets; he was searching for something. His exaggerated motions seem to surprise him when he found a cell phone in his back pocket.

He speed dialed.

"Hey. Come on over now." Like I said earlier, I'd always admired and envied Danny's suave low volume conversations on the phone.

Even though the Hennessey was doing its job, after spending time locked up, I was conscious of time. Ten minutes later the doorbell rang.

"I'll get it." Danny slurred and stumbled to his feet.

Seconds later Danny returned. He dramatically shrugged off his bebop cap and took a bow in front of my opened bedroom door.

"Here you go my brother, welcome home!"

Five feet maybe three inches and she had short bleached snow-white hair. She wore a silk crimson camisole and a pierced naval ring dangled above her black nylon mini-skirt. She was a thin girl and her limbs looked artificially attached to her ninety-pound body. No white woman had ever been inside my bedroom and for that reason alone I imagined her as the fairytale character 'Little Bo-Peep.' But even under the influence, my prison instincts told me the twenty something-white woman's cocky street smart persona was neither lost nor meek.

In a stupor I rose. Danny was in between Bo-Peep and me; he nodded at both of us and smiled with a devious gaze. "Shelia this is my cousin Kayin."

Suddenly Danny's cell rang and he answered. I was half-loaded but my ex-con instincts noticed Shelia inventorying her surroundings. The tough little white girl tweaked and appeared vulnerable when she spotted the half-emptied whiskey jugs on the floor.

"Brother Man I got to hop on this gig. I'm an entrepreneur—I own a janitorial service. Cleaning filthy shit behind the white man's nasty ass; ain't that a bitch!" Disgusted Danny flashed his old conniving grin.

Soon as he said that the doorbell rang again. "That's my ride." Danny winked at us; walking almost sober he left and closed my bedroom door behind him. His introduction for Shelia and I had been short and sweet.

Tipsy, I sat down. And the momentary lost little lamb transformed into diva Shelia. She slid down one side of her top, exposing one sexy delicious tit to my starved instincts. As if she was hoisting up a tree, Shelia moved her little short ass in a snail's pace from the floor up my legs. Sensually gazing up at my eyes she kissed my zipper, and then sat her tiny ass on Black Dickey. Hugging my shoulders she scooted her vulva across his easily and already stimulated plumpness. I gripped her ass with both hands and pinned her to him. Shelia began to spin a slow rhythm, and like a magician pulling a rabbit out of a hat, she swiveled a flexible hand down between us, expertly unzipping my pants. She began softly stroking Black Dickey. Up close and super-ceding the vulgar scent of booze on my lips, Shelia smelled like a lady who had taken a little whore's bath, and then sprayed sweet perfume on to cover up fresh hot musty sex deeds. Black Dickey, unlike me, blocked the odor, and immediately melted into her hand caresses and bloated even bigger.

The sensuous little lady shimmied her tiny physique all over my six four frame. Either it was her professionalism or her animal instincts, but Shelia was sensing I was hot and bothered and ready to burst. As she sat on my lap Shelia elastically wiggled her face down to Black Dickey's house, and with her tongue she effortlessly boosted him out of my pants. I shrugged my pants down to my knees and watched Shelia use her lips to masterfully insert a rubber on Black Dickey. Loretta had struggled with both hands with the same simple procedure.

Shelia hopped off me and performed a freaky belly dance strip tease. She teased and enticed while she detached every stitch that covered her pink little bare ass. Half drunk I drooled, this was the first time I'd seen a naked white woman that wasn't in a magazine, on TV, video, or at the theater.

With graceful captivating elegance Shelia extended both hands seductively out to me. I grabbed them and we promenaded to the six-foot Panama bed. Butt-naked Shelia curtseyed, inviting me to lie down first. I slipped off my shirt and wobbled out of my trousers and boxers. I fell backwards on the bed, and Black Dickey resembled a flagpole standing on the moon. Shelia leapt on the bed, landing on her knees. She spread my legs, leaned her head down and licked her chops on Black Dickey like he was her Last Supper. Wow!

Charmingly Shelia had initiated and orchestrated our little lover's feast. To be done up and down by a stranger, someone other than Loretta, it was odd for Black Dickey and me. Some of Shelia's tongue licks reminded Black Dickey of Loretta and our last love session. But Shelia was a professional lover and it showed.

I never wanted to ejaculate or maybe I felt it was indecent to drop my load into a plastic bad and have maybe some of the juices leaking into Loretta's mouth. Shelia had my hips wiggling in rhythmic frenzies. I squeezed the back of her snow-white head while her tongue and lips slurped powerful sensation on and through Black Dickey. Full of her voltage, I felt I could hold back no longer. With the power she produced in my penis I thought I could easily burst through the condom and propel ecstasy juice clean down to her larynx.

But Black Dickey was addicted to the slippery seduction of the hole that's where he preferred to burst loose. I raised the hungry girl's slobbery face off Black Dickey. And at that moment I knew how babies felt when they were in mid-stream sucking on a milk tit and the mother would pull their lips off. It was the in-between-ness that I saw in the whore's deserted eyes.

I elevated Shelia's bare ass up on top of me. Without gazing down she arched her back and guided a wet safely wrapped Black Dickey into her vagina. Black Dickey eased inside her and absorbed the oozing pleasures nourished by the stretching veins in her vaginal walls.

Shelia began shimmying her hips in a fast pace rhythm, her pleasurable ahs and ekes sounded fake. I believe her whorish profession had taught her this was a quick way to make a John shoot his wad. I wasn't feeling her swift-moving vagina. There was no return or erotic feedback, a turn off for Black Dickey. If I was still a virgin or not an experienced lover, I believe Shelia's quick motions would've worked. Loretta's twat had perfected Black Dickey's sensitivities to vaginal and clitoral changes. Maybe she'd spoiled him. He needed to feel the muscle chokehold of a clit and the flushing of an orgasmic vagina to deliver him to ecstasy. I held a tight grip on Shelia's ass with the palms of my hands and stopped Shelia's rapid squirms. Pressing firmly on her butt cheeks I repeated slowly hoisted upward, Black Dickey was sensitively searching for the top and the back of her vaginal hood. I performed a series of impressionable long lingering uphill circular rhythm thrust to activate her hidden clit. Finally an eke in her breathing and a twitch in her thigh and gradually Shelia's body became part of my beat.

Introducing her own body rhythms Shelia gyrated with a slight bounce while she scooted her vagina back and forth across Black Dickey. The strokes were as if her clit was licking Black Dickey and he was a delicious lollipop to her.

Soon Black Dickey could sense Shelia's clit swell and he felt the friction from her vaginal walls slowly hemming him in. Her rhythms became more instinctual with a funky flair and the tones of her ahs were pronouncedly distinct, louder, and real. Slowly I rose to my feet and Shelia began erotically jumping up and down and rolling all over Black Dickey.

Chapter Twenty-four

"Y-e-e-h…b-a-b-y! F-u-c-k me! Fuck that pussy!" On the edge of an animal's orgasm Shelia frantically trembled out incredibly vulgar remarks. She clutched my hips with both hands and positioned Black Dickey securely against her clit, and her whole body erupted in spasms.

Eating up Black Dickey Shelia wildly shouted, **"OH SHIT BABY!"** And as her hips shimmied on top of Black Dickey, and while I was still in a drunken stupor, I saw flash visions of seventeen-year-old ***Sarah Page***. Floating above Sarah was the image of a black woman burning in flames. Glimpses of Sarah and the black burning woman was all I saw, then they immediately disappeared.

After a moment of Shelia's petite physique jerking with seizures she collapsed. She cuddled her face on my chest. Briefly she was cooing like a newborn baby. As she softly oozed hisses she delicately dropped wet kisses on top of my chest.

Shelia lifted her head and regained sort of a sense of her street sensibilities, or was she being endearing, when she coolly informed me that Danny had paid for the whole night. I hoped she was at least happy to be here. Her body said yes but the hustle in the business minded little whore never did say.

When we repeated offering up the soul of our bodies to each other, feeling the endearing sensations, this time it was Black Dickey gripping her cheeks. With every circular rhythm he was haunted by four years of missing a vaginal-hole and the emotional closeness that embracing a human body offers. And I aggressively tried to grab for the gusto that well being godly feeling, the sensational sensations that's only passed from another human's skin. Black Dickey plunged his pent-up craving desires into the depths of Shelia's passionate, affectionate hole. When I hit ten on the scale of ecstasy, I let loose a pre-historic scream. "Y-E-E-O-O-H!" After I blew up, this time I was the one that was acting like a child. I cooed soft breaths over her breast. Then, like a man-child, I fell asleep.

I was awakened by a loud ringing telephone. My alcohol-convoluted wits blitzed me into thinking I was back in prison. I thought I was hearing the systems emergency lock-down alarm. I sniffed sex fumes before opening my eyes. Endearingly, the little whore was butt naked lying under my armpit.

"The color today is 'blue'; we need a urine sample before 5 pm...." That was one of the many messages left on the machine. It was a good thing that I'd decided to listen to the outside noise today. Shelia and I had slept past the Today Show, The View, Judge Joe Brown, and it was 12:15 pm. Judge Mathis and All My Children had been on for fifteen minutes.

I peeked through the front door curtains searching for Mamma's Subaru. Damn! The car wasn't in the driveway. Aunt Betty had driven the vehicle to work. I panicked. I needed a ride to the clinic downtown.

Damn it! This damn was the power of guilt. Guilt worked its way through my alcoholic fog. Suddenly, I was embarrassed at the thought of Aunt Betty being in the house, while I was in my room having sex...and with a paid whore! Even though Aunt Betty was an ex-prostitute I'd always shown her respect.

"Three eggs over easy, four strips of bacon, two pieces of toast, one stack of pancakes, and I like my coffee *black*", Shelia winked and emoted a freakish sensuality when she said *black*. "Make me breakfast, I'll give you a ride downtown." I didn't know what time the bus ran and Shelia made an offer I couldn't refuse.

When I looked for Mamma's car in the driveway I hadn't spotted Shelia's spanking new beige Camero parked on the street in front of the house.

Flooring the gas pedal Shelia took off. We dashed up, down, and around corners as if she was racing in the Indianapolis 500. Slightly petrified of the fast ride, I clung to my seat. As I watched her maneuver, an **ah-ha** emotional reality rushed to the front of my brain. *God damnit if I was driving like a bat out of hell my black ass wouldn't have made a block without the cops popping my ass with a ticket or popping my ass with a bullet. I saw the shotgun in my face again.*

I was surprised this white woman knew the back-roads of the black side of the city. Shelia strategically moved through seven miles of traffic and we were downtown in less than seven minutes.

She pulled to the curb in front of the urine-sampling clinic. When she left her motor running and flipped me a business card I was taken a-back. This prostitute was offering me her digits, and…

"Uh—would you mind waiting and dropping me off at home." I was used to a ride being a round trip.

Shelia gazed at her watch as if she already had some place else to be. "Naw. Can't do. I said I'd drop you off." She was angry or annoyed with my question or her situation, Shelia's features became sharp and silently her street gestures said, *"get the hell out of my car!"*

As soon as my feet hit the pavement, my drifting one-night lover sped off in the Camero. I stared into the intermittent sun sparkles in the gray skies, snuggled my bare hands deep into my beige camel overcoat pockets and watched my one night bootie buddy disappear into traffic.

Not familiar with the procedure of pissing in a cup, I was self-conscious to tell the fine golden brown receptionist with the perfectly trimmed short afro that I was an ex con, and my mission was to deposit pee. I was as fidgety as a child sitting in class with his legs crossed, desperate to piss but afraid and ashamed to ask for permission from a mean teacher. As I approached *Miss Brown Sugar*, she didn't even bother to look up behind the circular enclosed counter. Sister girl popped a tiny plastic container on the desk, and in a monotone expression she explained the procedure. I guess she'd repeated the same memo to everybody all day everyday. I guess her job must be down right dull. I first had to pay the fee to leave my pee. After doing my business, without leaking a drop, I purposely bobbled the cup full of urine on the counter. It was just a maneuver to connect with girlfriend's pretty egg-shaped chocolate eyes.

The whole experience was demeaning. I hustled my half-ashamed ass out the door with my tail between my legs. Hunkering down I lifted my overcoat's collar up around my neck and prepared to meet the cold early spring.

Four years of deprivation in prison, now I was free, scuffing the sidewalks through downtown Oklahoma City's swirling chilly winds. As I walked the fresh breeze blew a different awareness over my soul. I detected the twang of an old car's cold motor turning over. I saw business professionals rushing into buildings while the traffic buzzed. Hard faces were on people and as we passed each other I noticed we all seemed to exhale and exchange the same frosty smoke. On the edge of town I witnessed a harsh scenic background. Lost eyes were on the scruffy clothed homeless. Black, White, Latino, Native American, and Asian; despair was colorblind. On their backs inside duffel bags I saw them shuffle and carry their life's possessions. I finally found my bus stop. I cuddled under a naked tree and waited forty-five minutes on a bus.

Freezing, waiting on transportation that ran every hour and then riding on plastic seats that carved into my ass, I began to get a sense of what it must've been like to ride on a backboard wagon a hundred years ago. Traveling old fashion wasn't the way to go, especially since I had a car wasting away in the garage.

Eight P.M., in the cozy warmth of home I studied the state's driver's manual. The doorbell rang.

"Hi sweetie, I brought pizza and two movies!" Underneath a plum scarf Shelia appeared reserved. She was dressed like the girl next door that was dropping over to borrow a cup of sugar. She'd bathed, oiled herself up in lavender and a taste of lilac aroma accentuated the air. Wearing a white furry collar on a coffee cream suede coat, the nomad pint sized Shelia naively smiled up at me.

I hadn't called her and invited her over, but I certainly wasn't going to kick her out of my bed—if she decided to go there.

Before we watched the DVD's, while Shelia was hanging her coat in my bedroom closet, she noticed I had a chest set box on the top shelf. The little harlot had the audacity to challenge me to a game. Since we were in my boudoir, Black Dickey was already aroused and was ready to physically tussle with Shelia's little ass. I felt my testosterone levels shoot sky high when Shelia dared to compete with me in some mental gymnastics. This would be fantastic foreplay, I thought.

Instead of me beating on my chest from start to quick finishes, the little street whore easily dominated my conventionally trained educated ass in three games. I'd already suffered defeat at the hands of an illiterate multi-convicted criminal and now a young street whore was whipping my ass. Like my own injustice, I wondered what society had done to these obviously intelligent humans that kept them from being who they should really be. Once again, I thought about Maslow's hierarchy.

Losing to Shelia humbled me, and beating my ass appeared to elevate Shelia's hormones. Completely satisfied with her abilities to take me down a notch, she giggled real pleasurable laughter.

Shelia comfortably paraded her naked ass around my bedroom teasing me; her dance reminded me of a boxer that had just won the heavyweight championship.

She clicked on my TV and popped in a video. And similar to a snake unwinding, Shelia propped and curled her limber petite physique comfortably on my lap. With Black Dickey hard and perspiring with desires, we ended up postponing feeding his sexual appetites. We relaxed in the recliner and got hypnotized by the two DVD movies and fell asleep.

In the middle of night's darkness I awakened. Maybe the reason was Black Dickey got nervous 'cause he missed the feel of Shelia's bare ass on his head. Before I could rise and search the house for Black Dickey's dinner, I heard the flicker of a cigarette lighter. A yellow-purple flame shimmered near the window. The scent of jasmine moved towards me along with the wavering fire.

"Kayin wake up." The soft whisper of Shelia's voice exposed her as the tiny torch carrier and the gentle nudge of her fingers near Black Dickey lit his fire.

Glimmers in the candlelight surrounded by the jasmine aroma and Shelia's sixth sense, she was able to locate and embraced my palms. Once again she initiated intercourse. "Let's do the nasty before daylight comes." A mysterious sexy seduction invaded the darkness."

Underneath the miniature sputtering candle, and Al Green's merciful nature, I rose and reached for my lover's bare ass. I was shocked and Black Dickey was disappointed. The little white slut had put clothes on. After sitting on my lap butt naked all evening, Shelia had some sick fetish, the whore wanted to be seductively undressed—like a real woman, I suppose.

Deliberately, slowly and gently I slipped Shelia's frame out of the cheetah baby-doll blouse, and then freed her tits out of the grasp of the flowery seamless no strap nylon bra. Effortlessly, I unzipped and tugged her ass and legs and toes out of the obstructing purple Zen Capri pants. Caressing the crack in her ass, I flexed my fingers into the silk black T-back thong and twisted the fabric off.

For some reason I was curious. I wanted to see if there was a difference between a black vagina and a white one. The nervous twinkling of the candle's light forced me into a more focused concentration on the details of Shelia's pubic hairs. Unlike Loretta's tweeted mane, Shelia's hairs were flat and flimsy and straight. A few wayward strands slithered wildly down the sides of her outer labia and extended all the way to her ass-hole. Loretta's complexion was mid-night black and it made sense that Shelia's outer labium was lighter. As I continued peering through the flickers off the dim candlelight, this was also true with the rest of Shelia's inner vaginal apparatus. The insides of her labia were constructed identical to Loretta's and both junctions of their hoods resembled a wrinkled noodle of a turkey, of course Shelia's was brighter.

A subconscious photogenic memory had developed inside Black Dickey and he now had an awareness of where Shelia's clit was. Possessing concrete instinctual sensitivity made it easier to tease her nerve endings. Circular rhythms, all the way in thrusts, some jabs nearly in and almost out of her hole, and anytime Black Dickey was ready for her to spasm he knew how to drive hard direct strokes straight to Shelia's spiritual erotic center. I evoked divinity because that morning Shelia expressed our love making in religious tones. Dramatically, she acted like a black woman filled with the Holy Ghost on Sunday morning. Blessed with multiple orgasms, she shouted, "OH GOD! OH GOD! OH GOD!"

A few weeks into our weekly Friday night rendezvous', and after me celebrating a birthday, I found out Shelia was a year older than I was, twenty-six. One night after a vigorous sex session a tiny crack in her guarded armor opened. She was spent and said so. Breathing hard, weak and venerable she fell and rested against my chest.

"You are the only person that's ever made me come!"

Later in our relationship, after a similar spastic episode, Shelia was pathetically exuberantly exhausted. During pillow talk I asked her what her white roots were, and the street girl in her sharply replied.

"I don't know and I don't care!" End of conversation. I realized some white folks had probably gotten comfortably integrated with other ethnic white cultures and to them the mixture didn't matter anymore.

***

Rap-tap-tap. "Hey Kayin get up! There are people here to see you."

I was half-awake when I heard Aunt Betty knock and yell at my door. I opened one eye and saw Shelia snoozing cozy under my armpit. Our early morning rendezvous was fragmented, but I remember peeping at the digital alarm clock, it was 5:15am when I blew out the candle and that ended our sunrise love summit.

"I'll be out in a minute Aunt Betty." I hollered through the door. Aunt Betty's annoying interruption reminded me of Mamma's wake up calls from old school days gone by.

Sleep mucus cluttered my eyes as I gazed towards the blinking clock on my computer desk. It was 9: A.M., Saturday. I had been locked up for four years; Mamma, Loretta, and Aunt Betty; they had been my only visitors. I've been out six days, who could possibly want to see me?

Uneasy I rubbed sleep out of my eyes, stumbled to my feet, tied on my robe, emerged to the hall entrance, and peeped around the coroner. In the far north side of the living room was the dinning table, and there was Aunt Betty. With her back toward me she talked and waved her arms as if her limbs were extensions of the tones of her voice, and they were singing to a captive audience. She moved to the side of the table, and big as shit was Mamma's preacher the Reverend O. L. Wilson. He sat around the table with three teenagers.

Reverend Wilson was a huge man, 6'4" the same as my height. I'm 210 pounds; he was at least 280 pounds. He approached me with a grizzly friendly all-man smile. This chocolate man was in his early sixties. He had sizeable lips and perfect gorilla ready-to-eat-you big teeth. The good reverend's handshake mauled my hand, and his hearty bear hug caused me to exhale and slightly cough.

"Good to have you back with us son. It was a wet and sad day when we buried your mother, son." He plunked himself toe to toe and six inches away from my eyeballs. The big preacher man's steady gaze penetrated a bundle of good will into my soul that was also intimidating—I blinked. "It's good to be back sir."

He positioned his hand on my shoulder and steered me towards the dinning area. He introduced me to the teenagers. Ricky, James, and Charles, they stood and extended handshakes across the oak table.

"Sister Rose made me promise I would get you back on track… and back to giving back to the community."

I gawked at the man of God, and then one by one I stared into each of the teenagers' eyes and glumly swallowed what the Reverend had said. What was he asking me to do? *Giving back to the community!* Did the big portly bastard say that? Goddamn man, I just got the hell out of prison…and where the hell was the community when I was locked up? Damn! Anyway, what could I possibly offer? Share stories of people getting stabbed, murdered, and molested up their asses? Or should I demonstrate how to perform secret, noiseless jerk-offs!

"These young men could be brilliant if they were tutored in math by the right person." Hell I'd studied and sacrificed my whole damn life and what did that do for me? I was amazed that this man of God would come to me, of all people, and make this request.

"This society hasn't gotten any easier for black children since you were tutored. Our children still need to work twice as hard." As the preacher man delivered his small sermon, the part that irritated me the most was, he was here to carry out a promise he'd made to my mother. I was suspicious of that motivation. He made the whole situation appear like Mamma made the appeal to him on her deathbed.

But whenever I hear Mamma's name my body is shrilled by disobedient sensitive bumps. Four years of cryptic prison confrontations, Mamma's death, and the loss of Loretta's love chopped the warm fuzzies off before they rose up and settled on my neck. Much had been taken from me and I wasn't in the giving business anymore.

I believe the man of God recognized the rising opposition to his proposal in my body language. The reverend even threw in a togetherness-brotherly wink in his salesmanship when he brought up my past. I had been tutored but what good had come of that. As he spewed his black rhetoric, 'us against them'; I think he saw that even his race loyalty remark hadn't budged my resistance.

"Coffee Kayin?" Aunt Betty asked. She gave me the same slanted sly eyes I'd seen on Mamma when she was covertly manipulating and insisting I do something that she wanted, and I was resisting. Aunt Betty sat a cup of the brew that breathed smoke on the table in front of me. The preacher man pulled out a chair, and reluctantly, I eased into it. Patting me on the back, the good reverend gracefully ushered me up closer under the table.

Ricky, a cold black creamy lanky senior, was studying calculus. James was stubby and chubby and was bronze tanned; he was taking trigonometry. Charles, the youngest, was creo-colored. He had a *Ben Wallace* afro and was cramming for a quarterly Algebra II exam. The reverend was right, they were bright guys and acquainted with the formulas, all they needed was tweaking on when and how to apply which mathematical rule. I guess I was doing what Mamma would've wanted; I was in the tutoring business again.

Betty warmed leftovers up for the reverend. Talking loud and laughing heartily, the two carried their old fashioned holy testimonials into the kitchen.

Mesmerized by the teens' curiosity, I rediscovered lost memories and was submerged into an old life, the world of numbers and angles. I was having mathematical brain orgasms. For those precious moments I forgot about Mamma's death, prison life, losing Loretta, and the guilt of neglecting a son I'd never seen.

We were a half-hour into our session when Shelia, all nestled in her suede coat, emerged from the same hall, the entrance that leads to my bedroom. I'd also forgotten that Black Dickey had a butt naked lover lying on his pillow.

The kitchen noise ceased and the noiseless spell was placed on us around the dinning table, it was as if God sent down the silence and the black folk were struck with culture shock. Bucked eyes gawked on the little white whore.

Dazed by the crowd's gapes, Shelia became the delicate deer of our headlights.

Suspicious questions and nosy judgments were echoed in loud hushes. Reverend Stokes was eating a rib, lettuce, and tomato sandwich. He froze and the meat and vegetables dangle off his huge lips. If prison had taught me one thing, I'd learned how to ignore bad situations when they happen. After inventorying the state of affairs, and while Shelia was in her own ethnic distress I said my salutations.

"Good bye Shelia." I decided my white whore wasn't anybody's business.

"I'll see you later Kayin." Shelia said. She opened the door, instantly disappearing.

The reverend and the students never asked me who or what she was to me. They never saw her at the house again either. Of course Shelia still spent Friday nights with me. I told her about my tutoring schedule and she said, "I'll leave an hour earlier." The young men did ask several questions regarding prison life, and I told them all about the historical nightmares and how I survived the deadly dungeon.

That brief enlightening session with those teenagers ignited my soul, inspiring a dream that was trapped in grief and almost destroyed by the agonies of prison life. I had a three-year-old son and I needed to find a way to love him before he became another black statistic.

Chapter Twenty-five

Tuesday morning Aunt Betty chauffeured me to the department of motor vehicles. *Starting all over like I was an adolescent,* this idea rode with me on the ride and I picked up other insecure hitchhikers on the way. *I was a convicted felon and had lost the right to vote, The 15th Amendment.* When wind gushes began rocking the car, I thought I heard Mamma whisper. *"Tons of black and white people have died for you to inherit that right son."* Spooked by the reality of that message I began to feel inadequate as a citizen of the United States, The 14th Amendment, and as a human being. *"And two tons of black and white folks suffered mercilessly for you to feel that you were somebody."* Mamma's spirit was whipping me. Then, It whisked over me like a charismatic omniscient lover fulfilling promises and magically intervened on my emotional beat-down. And this message swam to my core, *"My son shed his blood and died in order for you to feel his glory."*

At 8:10, sunrise, the DMV was already congested with sixteen year olds displaying MP3 players and chatting and text messaging on the latest cell phones. Four years of unproductive idle hours in prison had prepared me to wait without complaining and wait without any form of entertainment. Aunt Betty and I sat with the youngsters while they quietly partied to Billboard's and MTV's top twenty.

There were five separate lines. The driver applicants shifted from one line to the other. The rows dwindle the nearer an aspiring license operator got to the last line. The disqualifying process: have no outstanding warrants or pending disciplinary against your license: have three pieces of ID; pass the computerized written examination; and at the final step was the driving test. Impatiently, some of the teens left before their names were called to get into the second stage.

Aunt Betty and I chatted while I stared at the instructions on the walls and observed pimples on the young faces. I gave Black Dickey permission to fantasize shedding the outfits off the slinky dressed under 21 females.

It was two hours before I took the comprehensive driver's test. I was done with it in less than ten minutes.

Aunt Betty left and brought burgers back. No food or drink was permitted on the premises was one of the rules on the wall. I stood at the entrance with the door cracked, didn't want to miss my name being called. I felt like I was still a virgin to good home-cooked or fast foods, I easily wolfed down two super-size burgers in less than half a minute.

I parallel parked, drove the speed limit, flashed on signals before I changed lanes and turned, stopped at the lights and stop signs, and for the third time in eight years the authorities photographed me. On this occasion I wasn't finger printed. I was given my second Oklahoma's driver's license.

I chauffeured Aunt Betty back home through blustery winds while tiny sunrays of hope began to surge up my spine and those miniature optimistic bits of light inquired, 'is *it possible, could I really get a new life?*'

I spent the evening in the garage changing the oil and spark plugs, replacing carburetor parts. I even installed a new distributor and set the points. I did some bodywork on my Camry's crumpled hood. At three in the morning I was backing the Camry out into the driveway. Thirty minutes later under the porch light and using a garden hose I had scrubbed off four years of grime.

The spring birds were returning and under a descending moon at 4am I was serenaded with melodies sung in diverse rhythms by the feathered flying choirs. Only a week and a day since I was freed from prison, with the windows down I cruised up I-35. One quart of slick 40 was added to the oil exchange, and I could feel the grease lubricating the motor's molecules, cleaning the corrosive engine and delivering new energy. It was the edge of springtime. Under cool windy breezes, I was free and I became drunk with the rejuvenation of smelly engine parts; airy goose bumps riveted up the back of my neck.

No sooner had I laid my head into the comforts of a down pillow and was settling into a worry and fear free sleep when the telephone rang.

"Good morning Kayin!" I recognized the sluggish southern aged Okie voice of Mr. Brown. What could that old fart want?

"Young man you did an outstanding job moving that furniture."

"Thank you." Damn! I hoped the old fart wasn't asking for another favor.

"I need a strong buck like you to work in my furniture store... hahaha!" His laugh was harsh and dry and not real. "You'd be performing practically the same task." But his offer surprised me. I wasn't looking for a job, well...not right away. I didn't spend almost three years in college busting my ass to go and work in a goddamn furniture store. I was half-foggy and the half of me that was aware had me hesitating and considering the rich man's offer. I was a convicted felon. My limited resume, real work experience, was with Wal Mart. A furniture transporter earns a decent living wage. And by the way what other good company is willing to hire an ex-con?

"Your Aunt Betty, we care for her, she's part of the family." Part of the family...I wondered what this white man meant by that affectionate remark? "She informed me of your unfortunate incarceration. I'm sorry you were locked up for something you didn't do. Son, you've had a bad time of it lately." Was this old white man for real? Aunt Betty that bitch, telling my business to this white man, she's got some nerve!

"$18.50 an hour with health and dental benefits, how about it Kayin, can you report to work tomorrow at 8 am?"

Housing, the cost of living is cheap in Oklahoma and in this country only Mississippi pays lower wages. Twenty bucks a pop for weekly piss samples and I don't know how much I'll pay for a parole officer. Mamma is gone. I'll have to start contributing more of my monies to room and board and I have a son to take care of. Plus I have prostitution expenses. After being forced to restrain Black Dickey for four years he needed steady tender loving care.

"Yes sir! I'll be there."

***

For the first time since I'd been out of prison I looked out the window. The early bird sparrows chirped and danced in the back yard. Through the flowery kitchen curtains, I watched what I thought was the season's first Red bird land on a blackjack oak limb. I sipped hot creamy coffee; Aunt Betty flipped flapjacks, and complained how she was going to have to practice tolerance with the ER's incompetent interns.

"God help me! Those stupid bastards, and the doctors, and insurance companies are collecting most of the cash from all the high rising medical cost…assholes!"

The moon dipped in the west, dawn's light was rising in the east, and as I exited the neighborhood and entered 36th Street I noticed that all the vehicles had their lights on. I flicked on the Camry's lights.

Brown's Furniture was Far West, on the outskirts of the city. I pulled into the lot and I'd forgotten that the store took up an entire city block. Not knowing where to park, I left the car in the empty customer's lot.

'The honest man's friend' that was the footnote under the Brown's Furniture sign. I remember this jingle was part of the earlier commercial campaigns. Like I said, they were the good old boys. The honest man's friend, accompanied with guitar music, the tune chimed in my head.

Through the locked glass door I spotted an off duty policeman, I assumed he was acting as security. I knocked on the door. Our eyes met and I didn't blink.

"I'm Kayin Jackson, and…"

"Yes, I know who you are." Eight inched under my eyes, the twenty-five or six year old baby-faced white policeman glared up at me. In an eye blink I watched him muster a cowardly soldier's stance in order to inform me, that he knew something frightening about me. By his challenging stance he wanted to let me know he wasn't afraid of me, but he blinked.

The fragrance of pure fresh finely stained pines, cedars, and oaks nourished the air. Passing the beanbag, desk and chair section, I caught the eye of a lively auburn haired, tall and lean forty something-white woman. She hurriedly stepped towards me.

"Are you Kayin?" She smiled friendly, extending her hand.

"Yes I am."

Exuberantly she said, "Welcome to Brown's Furniture, I'm Mrs. Rodgers! We expected you to be here last week, but Mr. Brown got backed up. He usually doesn't oversee the hiring but I understand you're a special case." She slightly winked and the crinkling under the southern woman's eye forced me to pay attention to her wrinkles. *'Special case?'* This had me wondering if her scrunched eye signified she knew details of my life, that I was a jailbird?

"Follow me please and we'll get you orientated on how we do business around here." I followed the butt of a blue long corduroy panel skirt up and down aisles, through a showroom of splendid oaks, pines and iron beds; we passed custom made dressers, elegant tables, rows of chairs, lamps and pillows, fine wicker settees, contemporary glass and ceramic vanities. It was a place of pleasures for furniture and Black Dickey got horny gazing at Mrs. Rodgers' aged yet springy firm ass.

Mrs. Rodgers leaned in the adaptable beige leather chair, and was half way through the do rules and don't regulations, when a side door opened to her office. Cherry, old man Brown's flirty little granddaughter emerged out of an even more private office. At 7:45am Cherry's features were intense and her tone was direct.

"Jeanie I need that list of French tables we're considering ordering."

Startled by her dramatic entrance I leaped to my feet and casually nodded. And Cherry was obviously surprised by my presence. Uneasily she showed me her pearly whites and I swear I saw her blink and slightly gaze down as if she was measuring Black Dickey.

Like a genie out of a bottle, Cherry appeared and instantly disappeared. Cherry snatched her cute figure around and that fast motion flipped her long red copper spritz hair. Direct and business minded the girl had attitude and that was sexy. Her stilettos made sharp rhythmic taps as she marched to her office. Her perky tits had been smoothly displayed underneath a wool caramel V-neck sweater. An awakened Black Dickey gazed at the swagger in her hips and the impressions they made underneath the matching caramel flared mini skirt.

***

Part of Cherry's job was taking inventory. She made daily trips to the warehouse where peons like me worked. Always greeting me with a grin, and slyly she continued to register horny glances at Black Dickey. I continued to give feedback to her erotic glimpses by staring and lusting at the way her hips strutted as she walked away. After work those lust reactions became persistent. They became exotic dreams. In them I was ripping Cherry's panties off and doing her doggie style. Was the little rich girl only teasing Black Dickey? Could he possibly get some of that funky stuff? If there was a possibility I needed a plan.

One evening Danny showed up after dinner. Even though I still harbored evil feelings against my cousin and I knew he'd never seduced a wealthy woman, I also knew Danny had made love to more than two women.

Night's shadows were welcoming the spring and darkness was appearing later in the evening. It was 6:30 and my cousin and I bathed in the prairie's fresh breezes as we sat around the plastic patio table in the backyard. We were gazing into the twilight of the northern skies that's when I decided to share the situation I had with Cherry.

And Danny said, "Sugar mamma hasn't figured out when and how she's going to drop them draws for you! Probably hasn't mustered the nerve yet. And she's probably never even come close to letting a black man hit it. Your black skin is probably an in vogue thing for her rich spoiled ass. Plus, people by nature are curious." The all-knowing and powerful sex expert god that lived within Danny had spoke. He stared east in the dusk as if he was seeking more wisdom.

"If that bitch is peeping at your rod she's definitely looking for a way to get screwed." Again he peered into the east, and seconds later...

"Cuz' is going to get him some rich white twat...hahahaha!" He slapped his leg whacked my hand giving me a high five and laughed.

"Be patient. Don't ask for it. Bitches like that want to control. Even though she's checking you out the stupid bitch may be completely unaware of her natural animal instincts. Doing a black man is new to her she's probably nervous and afraid. It's like a rerun of...of...of; you know the TV show with Dr. Spock?" I nodded but couldn't think of the TV program. "...She's like traveling to a place she's never been before." I understood his analogy and the concept. "Be cool. Don't even flirt back. That might scare her little silly ass off. Let her mind catch up with her horny body. You got to allow that freak to come to you. Got to let a woman like her believe she's finding her own way. Let her take her own sweet time when the panties come off." Danny nodded, he was confident with his meditative solution. "Every woman that ever wanted to give me some, they always found a way to give up that ass! It's a woman's nature to complete the mission of their little horny desires. Well unless some man messes it up, by doing some old silly ass shit." Danny glared at me and smiled. I believe he appreciated I'd confided in him and maybe that meant I'd begun to forgive him.

"I wish I had me a wealthy bitch. I would get the 'ho strung on my Jones's like an addict, and then I'd take all of her motherfucking money. Hahaha!" The stars began to twinkle, the night pulled down darkness and as Danny rose a refreshed vigor appeared and it seemed to make his swagger come alive.

***

I never did adjust to the repressive authority and restriction of prison life. Now I was a civilian. I was waking up before dawn and the solitude of solo jogging five miles was a different routine. But out there alone, every step and breath I took told me what I was already aware of—prison had adjusted a life inside me.

Lifting and moving furniture strained a different set of muscles; diverse from the tension I felt boosting crunches, curls, and power presses. My body was tight! I had control over how much pressure was applied when performing push-ups on a stone floor, or while I employed my cell walls to do isometrics. *Son, be proficient in whatever you do and the Lord will always have a job for you.* Sometimes in the midst of wheeling and loading furniture I could feel Mamma's eyes guiding my movements.

A white woman and a black man, both of them middle aged, were among the twelve sales persons Brown's Furniture Store employed. The company had ten white delivery loader-drivers, and including me, there were eight stockers. Jeanie Rodgers was controller and the C.E.O. was Cherry's father, George Brown III. Cherry was *C.E.O* in training or Jr. C.E.O. Whatever title Cherry held, behind her back the small work force made fun of her management abilities, and obviously envious of the nepotism bestowed upon the little rich girl. Even in a diminutive work force, conniving politics thrived. But like breaking a prison code could get you killed, scheming got you ahead. Early on I realized I was the strongest and my size was intimidating. For the first time in my life I used this feature as an asset.

After two weeks of busting my ass, I received my first paycheck from Brown's furniture. It was my largest payday ever. But if my life hadn't been interrupted and if I was a practicing engineer, my back wouldn't be sore everyday and I would've been living larger. Happy and ungrateful, I compromised and just felt ok.

Guilt was gnawing at my nerves like a parasite. I wasn't responsible for the cruelty that had happened to my life but I'd fathered a black child, and he had no idea how malicious life would be for him because of his complexion. At three years of age, and if he was lucky enough to develop into black manhood, my son had no clue at this time in America that his chances were one out of three of doing real prison time. In my prison nightmares, those heroic African Americans had suffered unimaginable evil. And whatever survival methods they'd used, I needed to understand their secrets and pass them on to him.

That Friday evening, the same day I'd gotten paid, I sat quietly around the dinner table with Aunt Betty. I was sure that this in-everybody's-business-woman knew the whereabouts of my son.

"Aunt Betty I want to see my son." She lifted the fork that she'd raked chicken and dumplings together and slowly cut her eyes at me.

"That's good Kayin...Yeah. That's certainly a good thing. Most folk that's been through the shit you've been through, well I don't believe anyone would blame you if you kicked that bitch's ass." Aunt Betty smacked on her food, under eyed she gawked at me. I could see her trying to see if I had bad intentions inside my head. I wanted to bust Loretta's ass but I was sure I wouldn't. Would I hurt Loretta and end up back in jail? I didn't acknowledge Aunt Betty's assumptions either way.

"Loretta's husband, what's his last name?" I'll *Google* him; maybe I'd find a phone number or an address; the under eye stare from her continued.

"Hold on." Aunt Betty was still chewing when she leaped from her chair and headed in the direction of her bedroom. Within seconds she returned.

"Here." She handed me a torn off piece of notebook paper.

"I found this among Rose's papers. I'm sure she wanted me to give it to you." Wiping her mouth with a napkin Aunt Betty sat down. Under eyed, as I read the address off the paper she vigilantly studied my reactions.

"I never will forgive myself if you go over there and act crazy boy!" My aunt warned. She's never been a person that concealed her feelings or opinions.

The weak muscles of a smile made a rare appearance on my face and another tender moment happened, when I rose I kissed my Aunt on the cheek.

"Thank you Aunt Betty."

Shelia and I made love later that night. And I don't believe I'd ever been in the middle of an orgasm and imagined life being better than busting a nut, but the joy of meeting my son enhanced the spastic bliss.

Saturday evening I heard Seminole drumbeats when I exited I-35 and entered the city of Edmond. Although I'd attended the University in the city for almost three years I'd never heard the rhythms of the Natives before. Up until the land run of 1889 this had been the Seminole's hunting grounds. And up until the late 1980's I'd heard this little college town was extremely hard on black students. A black person couldn't drive at night without being stopped by the police. Sure it was unconstitutional. The cops needed to feel in control and white people needed to feel protected; those two sensibilities alone made it ok to inconvenience and harass black folk and deny them their constitutional rights.

Like Oklahoma's all-black University, Langston, the first classes at Central were held in a church—a segregated one. *The white God didn't care to educate blacks and whites together;* a wee cynical voice whispered. Mamma always said white folks habits are hard to break. Black Dickey cringed, full of anger and sadness at the whole history of the city. Once again he sagged against my nut sack.

I could've taken the scenic route down Kelly or Eastern Avenues. Those paths would've taken a little longer. I could've—but I had an urgency to meet my son. On either of those trails there were no landmarks that said I was entering the city of Edmond. I used to hear Mamma say, "Where there used to be a forestry of blackgums, crabapple, lacebark pines, maple and smoke trees, the expansion of new housing and commerce had sealed the gap between Oklahoma City and Edmond. The little city is now considered a northern suburb of Oklahoma City."

In the almost three years that I drove to school, five days a week, outside of the university, main street, some fast food restaurants, and a few gas stations I realized I was unfamiliar with the neighborhoods in the city. Why would I be? Mostly white people lived there and I certainly didn't know any of them. Fortunately I had this realization before I left home and was able to Google for directions.

Every city has trailer trash, a middle class and affluent neighborhoods. There were no black ghettos in Edmond and I was searching for a new development area on Oak Road. After over a century of unconstitutional segregation the city had finally been persuaded to allow more upscale people that looked like me into the housing market.

9115, the number was painted on the curb. A freshly cemented driveway steered a path to the three-car garage and you could've placed all the cells that I'd lived in for the past four years in one of the vehicle's homes. A burgundy Lincoln Town Car and a dark blue SUV occupied spaces outside two of the three closed doors. I parked the Camry on the street.

The lawn was turning green and the hedges were manicured, and along the driveway a private sidewalk provided an escort to the steps to a four-foot sandstone porch. Next to Mamma's and Loretta's grandmother's homes, the little go-getter Loretta had pressed forward and had gotten into a midsize fairytale dream castle. The two-story canyon russet pristine crimson brick house had an enchanting mahogany oak door that welcomed visitors. And as far as I could see her story-land home had double casement eight sectional windows trimmed with turquoise all around it.

Before getting out of the car, I stared at the palace and imagined and sighed, if it wasn't for the police, my cousin and his buddies, the judge and district attorney, and that all white jury this could have been our family home.

A part of me traveled the path to the porch as a peasant, begging to see my son. Another piece of me walked with anger and in each step I was as an abandoned lover and a father and was demanding explanations and rights.

A short 5' 6" or so bald on the top—looked about thirty-five, extremely light, damn near white, but he was a black man, came to the door. He was conservatively dressed in a white shirt and had on thick glasses.

"Hi I'm Kayin. I'm here to see my son." Peering up at me he seemed unimpressed and indifferent that I was here. I suspected even before I introduced myself, saying what I wanted, he already knew my story.

"Wait here." He pulled the door almost shut, leaving it cracked. Moments later Loretta appeared.

"Hi Kayin." Loretta's eyes were soft and her demeanor was guarded. Awkwardly our eyes cautiously performed an off beat dance. Shyly she rolled her brown eyeballs up and down my physique and when she'd finished her lids quivered. I believe the shake was a sexual uncontrolled animal instinct. But I could be wrong.

"Come in." She wore a short sleeve silk tieback rosy blouse with a matching slinky skirt. I followed the back of her skirt sashaying and imagined her bootie smoothly tugging against a harmonizing pair of rose silky panties. Black Dickey's dog memory lusted for a reason to twist Loretta around and peep and see if Loretta's kinky curled vaginal hairs had changed. And as I tagged behind her down the hall I had an erotic neurotic urge to sniff her for the old sex scents.

At the end of the corridor, we entered the dinning room, a bright light exposed a new and different gallery of exquisite African American Art. Some paintings I'd seen others were new.

"Have a seat." I relaxed in a pine chair at the dinning table.

"I'll be right back." She exited and before I finished admiring the soft indigo tones of the decorum, Loretta returned with a toddler balanced on her side. Releasing his grip from around her waist she lifted the boy into my arms.

Finally her eyes glared deep into mine as she made the introductions. "Kayin this is your daddy." Loretta quickly left us alone.

Even though most of his features, nose, lips, and the shape of his oval head resembled Loretta's, his complexion was a blend of my lightness and Loretta's darkness. I spotted the old horse whisperer in his eyes. He cuddled in my lap and appeared to be studying my face. After a few moments Little Kayin became restless. He squirmed down my leg. And before I could catch him the three years old did a Frankenstein fast walk out of the room and scuttled around the corner.

"Mommy-mommy!" I heard his echo.

I pursued the little fellow and saw him push and enter a door. Before I reached the entrance, simmering pots and an appetizing flavor caused me to pause. I leaned and peered through the open top portion of the kitchen's shutter gates. In the middle of the room I saw Loretta decked out as a little traditional homemaker. She had a white apron strapped around her and was holding the top of a boiling pot. She pressed the tips of her cocoa lips on a wooden spoon, sipping for adequate seasoning or maybe the taste was to see if the brew was done? That 'us' dream swam through me again and said, *She could've been my wife preparing Saturday's dinner for our family.* Black Dickey wished it were him her lips were savoring.

Chapter Twenty-Six

"Would you like a bowl of beef stew?" Without turning around Loretta knew I was watching her. I desperately desired for her to use her crystal ball and see that Black Dickey wickedly wanted to serve her.

"Sure."

In the dinning room I held an active Little Kayin on my lap and feed him bites of stew out of my bowl. Loretta watched over us like a mother hen.

"He acts just like you sometimes." Her enraptured gaze told me she was intuitively fascinated the way Little Kayin and I behaved together. And her comment got me wishing my son, our similarities would spark Loretta into a conversation down memory lane about *us*, but it didn't. She did ask about my family's health history and she told me Little Kayin had suffered earaches and infections up until a year ago.

Almost an hour and a half passed and as I stood at the door, ready to leave, I was holding my son's hand; that's when I saw an old flash of Loretta's serious business attributes.

"You'll have to hire a lawyer and establish visitation rights. You, showing up here today without a warning…this was a freebee!" Loretta stared at me and her eyes had fire in them, the down to dealing color of Loretta's personality made an appearance. She's always disciplined herself in getting whatever messages, expectations, intentions, and her points of view out in the open. Except when she decided to dump my ass, give my love to somebody else, and then married that bastard. She is what she is, I reasoned. Her restrictive guidelines for seeing my son angered me. I'd been locked up for four years. This was the first time I'd seen the boy. My prison instincts told me to bust her in her face but my better nature said I should proceed with caution. Disagreements of this nature had gotten people killed or back in prison. I gazed down on Little Kayin; he'd moved over to his mother and was tugging on her apron. Neither Loretta nor I had a relationship with our fathers. I wouldn't let that happen to my son.

"Ok." I nodded, not knowing how much a lawyer would cost, nor did I know the procedure for establishing visitation, but I agreed.

"Are you working?" She asked that question with raised eyes. Her need to know was to inform me of another resolution. I nodded.

"You'll have to begin participating in the financial responsibility of your son." Damn bitch! You've got all this, at least give me a chance to get my ass on the ground. I wanted to scream this at her, but I didn't.

Little Kayin hopped on the side of her hip and I could see the little scamp had gotten addicted to clinging to his mother's waist. I was jealous. I couldn't hug his mother like that. I smacked the little fellow on the cheek and said good-bye.

Loretta's husband never joined us.

Darkness had come and from a distance I could see a trail of car lights flashing on the interstate. I took the scenic *Kelly Street* route home. The exit signs leaving the city of Edmond and entering Oklahoma City had been removed. I still heard Seminole drumbeats and I knew I was departing their territory.

***

Cindy Sherman was a forty-two year old white woman. She was a husky shorthaired brunette. Cindy had a pudgy mid-drift and it usually tugged over a tanned leather big buckled cowboy belt. Since she didn't necessarily need a restraint, the belt was a lifestyle and not a fashion statement. She always wore tight faded cowboy blue jeans. Cindy's pants were neatly tucked inside a pair of men's cowboy boots. Tossing her arms back and forth she would scoot across her office with a John Wayne swagger. "I'll violate you if you fuck up nigger." Part of her tough persona was trained by the prison system; another piece was maybe inherent. I believed Cindy was butch-gay. But the element of her character that caused me distress was that she was a racist. This slice of her behavior was probably exclusively made possible because of the quality education she'd received growing up in Oklahoma.

"Drop off twenty dollars a month, stay employed, and don't fuck up or I'll violate your black ass, nigger!" With her legs propped on her desk, arms folded, and a nasty snarl, Cindy spoke to me like I was a child, an unwanted stepchild.

***

Summer's heat was settling in on the prairie town, and as I socialized the psychological affects of institutional living into my daily life, this process was sweating me into a different and new man.

Instead of making a costly mistake and paying a lawyer $1,500 to prepare and file two legal documents: a parenting plan and one for visitation rights, I downloaded the files free off the Internet and represented myself. During the court proceedings I was ordered to pay child support and granted legal visitation rights to be a father to my son.

Sometimes my responsibility of taking care of my son would leave me owing Shelia for sex. Even more devastating than a sex debt (an on-going debate I have with Black Dickey) was the federal government's denial of an educational grant to an ex-con. Even though I didn't have a real zeal for engineering anymore, in honor of Mamma I wanted to finish school. I found out that the people that need assistance the most get the least.

Little Kayin had stopped crying when we drove away from the security of his mother's home and the little fellow had started calling me daddy. And just like horses and dogs shed their winter coats, women began to get nearly naked. Sports bras, tanks, t-tops and silk camisoles exposed the tips of brown, black, and pink little nipples. Slinky tops titillated the willing admirers and the tiny trimmings dominated the fashion world.

The lust that suppressed Black Dickey for four years grabbed a center seat and examined a colorful assortment of naked brown shoulders tangoing in switching motions. Coffee-creams, rosy-pinks and the color spectrum of completions adorned their bodies with belly button rings and gyrated tassels slightly above sexy low rider trousers and slit mini skirts. Women flaunted almost naked and almost revealed their precious vaginal hairs, teasing Black Dickey, offering him only a mere glimpse of their precious passions.

Wealthy women were unwrapping in the same styles; the materials were finer and were probably custom made *for their asses only.* What was apparent and appeared to belong to the Caucasian culture was Cherry's mating call—out on the loading dock she'd pinched my ass on two occasions.

Southern heat along with the humidity united with Cherry's exotic perfumes and baked a sensual musty aroma. I could see her steamy sensuous vapors. Her fair bare skin around her halter-tops had tanned and the lazy hazy breezy air flares under her low rider skirts exuded this spicy funk that was tasty to Black Dickey. Cherry's bashful glimpses at Black Dickey had become bold come-get-it winks. I believe she assumed that when she aggressively tweaked my ass she was expressing passion, but the pinch stung. Black Dickey didn't agree. Desiring to feel the appetite of Cherry's clitoris, Black Dickey grotesquely changed her prickly touch into a mystical turned-on.

Our crew of warehouse loaders and driver delivers could be interchangeable if a loader decided to upgrade his license. Needing a dollar and a dime raise, I was back at the department of motor vehicles. In June, I was promoted. By July 15th Little Kayin's child support payments were upgraded.

It was Wednesday and half of the week was done. It was after 9 pm, the store had closed when I pulled into the employee's parking lot. John, a short freckled face white man had complained of backaches all day. He wobbled from the truck, hobbled to his pick up and sped off. I was tired and was ready to go home too. I punched in the code and pushed the red button to open the warehouse's garage door. I had to drop off the van's keys.

I inhaled deeply and the twilight of the vacant furniture store's night security lights made cozy shadows around me. I heard light taps and it sounded like a woman's high heels. Immediately I saw the curvy silhouette approaching.

Twinkles of Cherry's features came gradually into view. Her blue eyes were as intense as the wildness was in her spritzed hair. Black Dickey spotted Cherry's right pink tit dangling out over the top of her white and orange silk camisole. The organ was round, plumped and looked as juicy as a delicious red apple. Sparks bounced off the new furniture and made oblong shadowy shapes. I squinted and saw Cherry's low riders were unbuttoned and slightly unzipped and Black Dickey zoomed into the tops of her orange nylon panties.

Cherry slowly moved toward me. Her heels began to clack instead of click and the slow snap echoes dramatized how completely alone we were in the deserted furniture store. She came within an inch of me, less than that from a sprung Black Dickey.

"Kayin I want you to fuck me!" The little rich girl's tone was alluring and razor sharp but the cursing was phony and foreign when it spurted from her rich culturally bred lips. I guess she was nervous. It was a bad imitation of a hip-hop sister and probably an even worst impersonation of white trailer trash talk.

As I stared into her quivering eyes the tension amused me. 'Star Trek'! That's the name of the TV show. Cherry was acting and I guess she was attempting to travel where she'd never been before. I was her new and strange world. Her eyes twitched with fear but bravely with both hands she reached down clumsily grabbing and squeezing a solid steal Black Dickey.

I palmed Cherry's hips and drew her unbuttoned low riders against Black Dickey and grinded into her hard. Cherry's thighs squirmed into my rhythm. I licked on her exposed tit, and in one swoop Cherry managed to slither out of her trousers and the orange silk panties.

"Eke-wee! I knew you would be this good." Leaning her head backwards the influential heiress' tone became a sultry seductive woman's cry. She leaped and clutched her hips around my waist and began humping buck wild! Her body was acting like the desperation of a wine-o sucking for another taste of alcohol out of an empty bottle.

Her powerful thrust overwhelmed and inspired Black Dickey. He searched for wiggle room, a way for me to slip in and sway my hips into Cherry's tenacious humps. A white woman was attacking him with raging desires. He was inside the state's largest furniture store, and he had the luxury of romancing, doing the nasty on his choice of some of finest built beds in the world. Holding onto the glued gnat I took stiff steps to a honey maple queen size bed and pried us apart. I laid Cherry's nearly naked body at the bed's head on top of two fluffy pillows. She snatched her top off while I stood over her and undressed.

Preparing for Black Dickey's entrance Cherry bent her legs even with her hips and laid them flat, an eagerness of lust rested on her face. Glimmers of light sparkled through dark shadows and exposed spots of Cherry's nakedness.

I crawled on top her, Black Dickey slid against her outer labia and suddenly Cherry's whole body recoiled. Terror emerged in her eyes. The two shaky pupils pointed me in the direction of her hand; it was flinging a condom. Using my elbows for props I rose. In the darkness Cherry felt the texture and size of Black Dickey and tugged on the glove.

Staring at her tiny lips I licked across them while Black Dickey nudged inside the tip of her opening and the simultaneous motions made her whole body shudder. Touching our tongues made her butt wiggle. She surged her ass upward moistening the tip of Black Dickey and I sensed her clitoris begging for friction. After doing hard prison time, waiting in a cell hour after hour, day after day, that was the reason I told myself I didn't immediately respond to the spoiled little rich girl's clitoral urgencies. I pulled Black Dickey away from her vagina. Cherry wrapped her arms around my back tight. She began thrusting her hips up as if she was a little kid jumping for a lollipop and a grown up was holding it slightly above her reach.

After watching her strenuously hump thin air for almost thirty seconds, while she grappled and squeezed her embrace around my back, I decided to slam the head of Black Dickey half way inside her. "O-o-o-wee!" She squeaked. He rubbed the slanted part of him into a rhythm against the top of her hood. Cherry's butt buckled and she aggressively squeezed Black Dickey's touch all the way through her hood straight into her sensitive clitoris. Black Dickey was shocked when he suddenly emerged with the full potency of her dynamic clit. He jerked. Our union transformed her body into a sensitive vibrating machine.

"Woo-whoa-woo-shit!" Cherry squirmed out of rhythm, I believe she'd had a mild orgasmic seizure. She quickly eased her hips back to the beat for more pleasures.

My chest rested against her juiced breast and I heard her rapid heartbeats. Suddenly she frenzy gyrated out of rhythm again. Maybe her off beat movement wasn't a mini orgasm, maybe this was the way she fucked. Cherry grabbed my hips and pulled Black Dickey deeper into her unprepared un-stretched resisting vaginal walls.

"God damn it!" Cherry hollered. Clutching her nails into my back, her vaginal juices automatically started pumping more lubrication around Black Dickey. As her hips humped her legs flattened into a wider spread. I began to move into her vagina with deep fast circular rhythms.

"Woo-whoa-woo! Fuck me!" Cherry slithered sideways across the bed. Her legs sprouted up even with her head. As the animal in us fucked in the bed, we bounced and we traveled on a wild ride. Her neurotic sexual moves took us from one side of the queen size bed to the other. At one point I stared into Cherry's crazed eyes while her head and her outstretched legs dangled over the bedside.

In and out and around I drove Black Dickey as our sweat mixed. I could hear the slush of Cherry's vaginal waters.

"Ah-ah-ah-ah-ah-ah..." Cherry strung together some ah's and they began to sound like rhythm lyrics to a hip-hop song.

Her body started floating in wavy curves. A ripple sprang from the small of her spine and swam to her stomach and then stroked the left side of her hip. Osmosis fluxed the rhythm to the other hip. The flutter sank into wiggling desires that landed between her thighs. Absorbing her whirl, I adjusted my cadence and directed her passions straight to her clitoris and we rode the tide.

"Woo-whoa-woo! Do me-e! Cherry's voice shuddered and her body became spastic. She rolled our bodies over landing on top of me without ejecting Black Dickey. Cherry began vigorously jerking her orgasmic vagina around Black Dickey in and out of rhythm spasms.

"Woo-whoa-woo! Shit! Shit! Shit! Shit! Goddamn it! Fuck me black man!" As she screamed, extreme passions were etched into her face.

Our bodies were dripping sweat as we lay side by side. We were completely satisfied with the expectations and it showed in our sexual afterglow. End of round one.

Suddenly the bed shook like an earthquake was occurring in the Bible-belt State. In the shadows of a dinette set, I thought I saw the images of a charcoal skin man stroking the forehead of a mule.

"This was my land and Mr. Brown took it." It was the black man that was on the 1889 land run. He had filed deed papers to the property on the northwest side of Oklahoma City, and some white man had taken his land. Most African Americans are only aware of the beginning of Oklahoma City's black history is on the eastside. I laid there with a wet body a limp Black Dickey and was flooded with details of his story and the prison nightmares.

After Oklahoma became a state in 1907 the whole state adopted Jim Crow segregation laws. Even though the NAACP won a decision against segregated neighborhoods in 1915, conspiracy by neighborhood associations and realty companies, the fear of the Klan, redlining by banks, loan and mortgage companies and of course the United States government, the isolation policies persisted.

Why was he appearing here, telling me his problems in the middle of some good loving? Both Black Dickey and I begged to know why now. The ghost gave me a bone-chilling stare and then vanished.

Finally after three frenzied sex sessions Cherry collapsed and she rested her clammy head on my chest. She stared into my eyes and with an exhausted smile she breathed a sigh that was rich with unbelievable gratitude. That was all the intimacy of a pillow talk we had. Twenty minutes later it was time for Black Dickey to shoot his final load. I did Cherry doggie style, bumped her little hips for the next half-hour. I'll never forget the gaze Cherry gave me when she was on her hands and knees. I was humping her ass and she was reciprocating the action, Cherry twisted her head and looked at me, worn-out and exhilarated. And then the passionate wounded animal said, "I'm totally spent."

At 3 O'clock that morning, under a full orange moon and a summer's light breezes, I escorted the spritzed haired princess to her violet-red Aston Martin convertible. I opened the door and Cherry leaped and embraced my neck.

"Get an HIV test. I want to feel your skin *touching me.*" She whispered the request in my ear. I nodded wondering was she asking me to do this because I was black or was the stipulation made because I'd been in prison?

***

Was it the affects of incarceration or was I at the age that the explosive noise caused by firecrackers sounded louder in my ears. Many African Americans in Oklahoma don't celebrate the 4th of July with the same sentiments as whites. But the day bothered me for another reason. *Independence*...I've always lived in Oklahoma and I've never truly felt and lived the life of that concept. In prison when the holiday came around I was a victim of that philosophy. I would sulk in sadness and anger and complete aloneness would engulf me. Escaping the noise on Independence Day, I turned the volume on high to my CD player. In meditation I pondered. Why were some of us freer and had more rights than others? Would life in Oklahoma's America always be that way?

Of course my test was negative and Cherry's last HIV results were six months old. Cherry informed me that she was on the pill. I assumed the wealthy fem-fatale's twat had been active since I was last there. I was sure she still had other lovers.

Without a glove Black Dickey's nerves trimmed up and down against Cherry's pink vaginal walls and his sensitivities were free at last. It was the first time he'd entered the great electrifying waters alone. Thank God Almighty he was free at last! I believed he had an indication what *Jubilee* felt like for the slaves and was probably clueless to what Dr. King's declaration meant.

Cherry and I played house after hours in the furniture store for weeks. On occasions, when Cherry's father worked late and she was longing for some loving, Cherry's credit card introduced Black Dickey to luxurious embroidered, laced, floral, tropical, and custom designed sheets. The southern hospitality of the Hilton, Marriott, Sheraton, and the remodeled old Skirvin provided the room service. Late nights I would cruise behind the wheel of her Aston

Martin on the freeways with the top down as the night air of freedom sprayed over our skins.

The log cabin behind the mansion, the one I'd removed furniture from, was where Cherry lived. Completely redecorated with the finest lumber money can buy, our episodes there became adventurous and they made my blood pump hot and cold. I was the hired hand sneaking in shadows and sliding my penis deep into a rich white woman's affections. I was giving her slobbery convulsive orgasms in a wilderness wooden shed behind the big house. Although Black Dickey was thrilled with the extravagant cuddling, the fact that our affair was a secret, sometimes left me feeling insecure, dishonest, inadequate, and ashamed. Out of the nightmares and the black and white history of America I felt like I was just her modern day *'nigger in the haystack'*.

***

Tutoring in the black community takes place all year round so does making love. I had spent a night of passion with Shelia and Saturday morning, as usual, I worked with the same three teenagers. Aunt Betty had been begging me for weeks to contribute some free time to our local NAACP and that day I did.

On a dazzlingly bright sunny afternoon I drove down Martin Luther King Avenue to Northeast 27th street, the location of our local civil rights branch.

More than fifteen percent of Oklahoma's population is African American. I thought it was odd that there were only thirty or so parking spaces in the lot. There were only three empty spaces and I assumed this was probably a full house for the members. I got out of the Camry, paused behind the opened door and casually watched four elderly black women in colorful church hats walk towards the entrance. Out of nowhere a spanking brand new baby blue Cadillac veered sharply into the tiny lot. Speeding, cutting around a corner the car swerved into the space next to me. The Cadillac might have smashed me like a pancake if I hadn't quickly leaped back inside the Camry. Sprawled over the front seat, fearfully, I watched the driver quickly maneuver the Cadillac alongside the Camry and park.

As I gained composure and was getting out of the car, I peeped and saw the blur of a female rushing towards me.

"I'm so sorry! Are you alright?" She dropped her cell phone into her Italian leather tote and the pretty olive skinned woman was by my side affectionately cuddling my arm. The fear in her eyes caused wrinkles to appear on her forehead. Her cute shaded skin glowed under the noon sun and in her hyper feverishness the strawberry streaks that highlighted her black hair were rumpled. Who was this strange pretty little white woman that had entered the black community, and without hesitating, rebuffed the morals of Oklahoma's society by touching my personal space? I doubled checked to see if we were at the home of the NAACP.

"Sure, I'm fine." I told her and I believe she mistook my surprised and curious smirk as an expression of pain and confusion.

"Let me help you, sir." She pulled our embrace closer and arm in arm we strolled towards the entrance. I was 6' "4" and she was 5'3" or so, with each step we took the soft feel of her arm alarmed Black Dickey. I peeped down behind her dainty pink flutter sleeve blouse and saw her round olive tits were hugged and tucked in neatly under the care of a nylon flowery Bali bra. Moseying down her landscape a silk pink floral print mini skirt fit snugly around her shapely hips. Back on top of the scenery the roots of her hair were black and curly and Black Dickey imagined what the middle view was like.

Abrinna Livingston was her name and she was Jewish. Since we came in together we walked to a table and sat down. Old and young black women and even the eyes of little black girls froze and followed us.

Inside the NAACP gathering we were entertained with speeches. A bronze skin man with huge lips, a receding salt and pepper hairline, when he spoke a crumple formed on his forehead and it appeared to induce hoarseness to his tone. He announced a membership drive. And a heavyset, big bosomed middle aged woman graciously gave information on an upcoming conference that taught techniques for voter's registration and grant writing. The event today would be my first date with Abrinna. The freedom organization later had a bake sale and a car washing fundraiser.

Chapter Twenty-seven

Abrinna and I were the same age, twenty-five. She grew up on Oklahoma City's northwest side and had attended the most prestigious private high school in the city—Cassidy Square. An Oklahoma University graduate, Abrinna had taught fifth grade for three years. I gathered tidbits of her life's story as we washed cars together.

Humiliation and shame was a tad of my personality I didn't want Abrinna to see, especially on our first date. I was wiping the top of a Pontiac and Abrinna was below, squatting, scrubbing the tire. Instinctually I scaled her body, again. Gawking over her panty-lines I examined her crouch. Peeping down her blouse I lusted over her tanned tits. She gazed up and caught me staring. Abrinna gave me a hostile gaze and covered up.

She surprised me by quickly getting over my intrusion. We made dinner plans for that Wednesday night at an Italian restaurant. This would be the first time I'd be eating out with a white woman. Even though we'd eaten together, Cherry and I had always tiptoed behind the scenes. And Shelia was just like me, an outcast.

The maitre d' at Olive Garden was a cute brunette and appeared to be a college student. Under eyed is how she greeted us as a couple and she pleasantly smiled. She led us into the land where the decent white folk were dinning. The diners quietly impersonated our escort with disbelieving and unaffectionate stares. And we felt those cold uncomfortable gazes. Both of us born in Oklahoma, neither expected anything less from our fellow citizens. We were seated near a window in the middle of Little Italy.

"At least they'll serve a black man here." Sarcastically, I whispered, while ushering Abrinna into her seat.

"At least we're not going to jail and we're not facing a lynch mob." Abrinna replied with a cynical smirk. Thus our bonding began; our *us against the world attitude.*

"Their Pork Filettino is um…tasty delicious!" Abrinna smacked her lips and I wanted to lick the red luster lipstick off them.

A fourteen-karat gold Star of David with diamonds this exquisite pendant dangle near Abrinna's cleavage, without me ever asking or ordering Black Dickey had already tasted his appetizer. The jewelry gave me permission to stare at the top of her personal exposed jewels. A low cut silk mock wrap sleeveless blouse, teasingly, exposed the top half of her bare breast. This time I had a question when her eyes met my private assault on her body.

"A Jewish girl, ordering and eating some pork in an Italian restaurant. Doesn't that necklace say to the world that you're kosher?"

"I'm a fan of rap music and bling-bling, and all that articulates is this I'm part of the hip-hop culture." The teacher's wit and charm seduced us to a mutual grin and we began to forget about the peeping crowd.

I ordered chicken marsala and Abrinna had a taste for plain spaghetti and meat sauce. When we looked at the wine list we both had a thirst for red Secco-Bertani Valpolicella.

"Ever had dinner with a black man before?" My question slightly disorientated Abrinna. She gawked and blinked. With her reaction she'd already answered.

"I've never been asked out by a black man before. And that's not totally their fault." She sipped the strawberry sparkling water she'd ordered, cleared her throat, and I sensed the teacher was about to give me an in-depth lesson on her life.

"I grew up Jewish in an all white neighborhood. Grade school and high school were all private, and for the most part all white. Four years of large classes at the University of Oklahoma, the percentage of blacks there is low. My environments have offered me less of an opportunity to be around African Americans. And if you haven't noticed, I'm shy. It's hard for me to meet people in general." She flashed a demure smile.

With her opening up like that I felt free to share aspects of my life. How my life was affected and enhanced by growing up in a mostly all black section of the city. I informed her how I lived and experienced life today as a black man and how I grew up in a single parent home. My interest in electronics and the recent loss of Mamma, I shared paragraph episodes of each part of my life. Of course I left out the four years of prison life.

"High school was demoralizing. Outside of remaining a virgin, I never ever received an engaging eye from a white girl!" Maybe I exaggerated the damage when the words came out. I noticed Abrinna's whole facial expression sagged. It was like she wanted to apologize for all the sorrows in my life. So far I could see there was nothing superficial about Abrinna Livingston.

A few of our fellow dinner guests had relaxed their stares and were chowing down. Abrinna twisted spaghetti on a fork and was consuming tiny bites.

"You know two of the founding members of the NAACP were Jewish?" The gullible expression I had told her this was news to me.

"In 1905 thirty-two outspoken black people first met on the Canadian side of Niagara Falls to discuss lynching and other injustices occurring against people of color in the United States. And the first name of the National Advancement of Colored People was the Niagara Movement. A year after the Niagara gathering, two members of the Jewish community, Dr. Henry Moscowitz and Mary White Ovington, a social worker, joined the crusade." Amazed and embarrassed that a white person had some knowledge of black history that I didn't, I sat across from Abrinna with my mouth wide opened. I always thought white people knew more degrading details of how they've treated blacks than what they let on. On TV the united front was always to deny or omit that any awful abuses really happened and the news commentators always rushed to share the good deeds that whites have done.

And as she spoke I began studying her eyes. They danced like they were concealing a fire of emotions. She was sensitive and I could feel she knew and had feelings for others and maybe she was even more compassionate than I was.

Detecting that I was infatuated with what she had to say as a person, my intimate interest appeared to spur Abrinna into a calm comfort. Or maybe it was the alcohol. As she expressed herself she was guzzling down glasses of wine. The affects of the spirits appeared to spur her into hastily rolling bundles of spaghetti and she was swooshing it down.

"My great-great grandfather and his two brothers rode in a covered wagon in the first land run in 1889. He opened the first grocery store in Guthrie. At that time, a lot of blacks had settled there."

"You ever think that's the reason white people relocated the capital to Oklahoma City; because of the large black population?" I don't know where that question came from, all I'd learned in a lifetime of Oklahoma history classes was that Guthrie, Oklahoma was the location of Oklahoma's first capital. Mysteriously in the middle of the night a bunch of good old boys took all the records and whatever paraphernalia that was necessary for a city to become a capital and they moved the supplies to a very white location—Oklahoma City.

"That's probably possible?" Without hesitation she didn't offer an argument that would defend the racist actions maybe made by her ancestors. Abrinna considered the possibility, and I was liking every moment with this little Jewish girl.

"My great-great grandfather sold feed and seed and he bought fruit, pecans, nuts, vegetables, beef, pork, chickens, and eggs from the black farmers. His brothers grew beards and traveled all over the state in covered wagons and sold products. Sewing materials, needle and threads, cloths to make clothes, curtains, sheets and bedspreads, and watches and rings, fruits and vegetables, dishes, pots and pans, some of everything for the pioneering family. They were like Santa Claus in the spring, summer, fall and winter to many small-town families. Lots of towns back then didn't even have a store and families that lived there depended on my great-great uncles." Glitters of excitement and pride captured Abrinna's eyes as she spoke of her family's tree.

Shivers trotted up my spine and I heard the voice of my grandmother. "A bunch of gypsy loan shark Jews is what they were! They sold everything you could dream of and a lot of it on credit. You know you pay interest on credit. Demanding money they would drop by your home at any hour and if you weren't there, they'd show up on your job. Those gypsies would hunt you down like a dog to collect. I believe my grandmother died owing on the high interest. Never could pay them off." The quivers left and grandmother was gone.

"When Oklahoma's early business owners, political community, and religious leaders were writing the states' constitution, there was a phrase that mentioned *'Jesus'*. The Jewish society protested and the phrase was removed." I could see Abrinna was happy with the stand up confrontational dealings of her forefathers. I chewed on mushrooms and garlic bread and the spirit of the old black frontiersman had my saliva glands dissolving a list of spicy questions. "Where were the Jewish, English, French, Italians, Irish, and Polish people when the state was making all those 18 segregated laws? I didn't see any of them up in arms and leading a revolt against these undemocratic immoral rulings that disenfranchised blacks and denied them civil rights." Mamma had told me Clara Luper and some black grade school students had sit-ins in the late fifties and early sixties and were arrested and spent time in jail. Thurgood Marshall and the legal team of The NAACP, along with Martin Luther King, Malcolm X, and the Civil Rights Movement, forced the government to sign the 1964 Civil Rights bill and that ended most of Jim Crow in Oklahoma and the United States. "Where were these civic minded people when blacks could only be hired as janitors and ditch-diggers, dishwashers and maids, porters and laborers, domestics and service workers, for meager salaries to feed and take care of their families?" The old fellow whispered what he wanted me to hear and then he was gone.

Abrinna was a decent young white woman and to me she'd already done more than most white folks. She was reaching out to the black community the best ways she knew how. I saw no need to hurt her by asking her about a black life she had no answers to and probably never knew existed.

That evening we continued our in-depth conversations on topics that mattered. I was experiencing a cultural exchange on race with this olive skin creature. She was the closest colored mammal to a Caucasian that I'd ever had a decent intimate dialogue with. I was cherishing our discourse.

"Abrinna, I've grown up watching Jews on TV and I've always been curious. When I heard the word Yiddish as the Jewish language and in the Bible Jewish people spoke Hebrew, what's the difference between Yiddish and Hebrew?

"Tehehe!" Abrinna charmingly giggled at my ignorance.

"Kayin my dear Yiddish is considered a bastard language. The language is formed mixing German and Slavic with Hebrew. The Ashkenazic's from Germany, Eastern France, and all over Eastern Europe grew up integrating Hebrew with their national language. Wherever Jewish people were living they would mix Hebrew with that nation's tongue. Tehehe!" She smiled at her own amusing story and reached across the table and caressed my hand. Her eyes did a slow flutter and the meek process was like she was ashamed for using the foul word bastard. Her tender touch seemed to be apologizing.

"My great grandmother married an Irish American. She hadn't grown up in the strict indoctrination of the Jewish religion like her parents. Swamped with country and western culture since childhood, she square danced and sung hillbilly songs and learned how to holler, yea-hoe and hee-haw!" Outstretching her arms impersonating a hardcore redneck, Abrinna quickly timidly glared around at the crowd. Their eyes were dead on us. She cowered and returned to her mellow decorum.

After finishing off her spaghetti, I caught her sneaking gawks at my sautéed chicken breasts. She continued dappling with her fork in an empty plate and finally she said, "Do you mind?" I nodded and the tiny figured ravenous Jewish girl snatched a large chunk off my plate. She acted like she was the one who'd spent the last four years eating prison food.

The old frontiersman's rational appeared in my head again. "The lil' gal's grandmaw was allowed to enter the white world, huh! That story was probably told to her children then they started telling the tale like it was innocent and sho' 'nough pure as snow. I didn't hear her describe how her grandmother resisted white folk when blacks were kept out of white society. Did her grandmother ever go to a black juke joint or visit the decrepit neighborhoods that blacks lived in? Seems to me, she was all about getting into white society and being accepted; while we were left alone to struggle with police brutality, poverty and injustices by that same white society she was steadily trying to get in!" My great-great grandfather had his say and was gone again.

"Even though my great grandmother married an Irish, she still educated her children in the Jewish culture." She was smacking on a strip of chicken and I could taste her lips tasting the chicken.

"As I grew up, challah, gefilte fish, bagels, Matzah ball soup, knish, blintzes, cholent, holishkes, tzimmes, kugel, and delicious Jewish apple cakes, Great grandmother taught me how to make many cultural delicacies from scratch." As she chatted about her great grandmother I had a vision of little Abrinna stirring a big bowl in the kitchen innocently glaring up at her grandmother. Abrinna came from a neighborhood where bank presidents lived. She probably lived next door to the mayor, or a member of the city council, or congress. People that divided up the town's money and made decisions for the city's future. This was the picture I was painting of her as I was sipping wine, listening to her stories.

I observed a wholeness that sparkled in her persona when she shared her handed down traditions. I sipped on more Secco-Bertani Valpolicella and I was showered with a weird melancholia. I knew the old frontiersman's was my second generation in the United States, and most slaves were stolen from West Africa, but what tribe was I from? What family customs and recipes were lost as a result of slavery?

"You ever ate any Jewish chow?"

"Bagels." I smiled awkwardly. I was wondering if all bagels were considered Jewish and if so had the ones I'd eaten been prepared in the Jewish tradition."

"Friday night, come to my home and I'll treat you to some old fashioned Jewish treasures." I nodded. The idea of being invited to a white person's house fascinated and frightened me.

Abrinna began eating off my plate and we smacked in unity. Our rap session became rhythmic. Our unique munching harmony made us an even more unusual salt 'n pepper couple, more twisted and uncivilized in the perceptions of the white on-lookers.

After we finished feasting I gazed around and the group gawk of our fellow dinner guest had died down to individual sneaky stares.

We had stuffed ourselves and I'd been on my first date with a white woman. I had been gawked at by the masses while consuming upscale civilian Italian food. After being locked in a prison cell for four years, I didn't care about anyone knowing I was out with a white woman. Substantive imparts of our lives were opened and now the tones we exchanged were delicate and playful. We hypnotically gazed at each other. We rose from the table in harmony and our arms hugged as we strolled out of the eating establishment. If ogles were on us we didn't notice.

In the back and in the shadows of the eating establishment is where Abrinna's baby blue Cadillac was parked. Holding hands like partners in a dance Abrinna assumed the lead. She squeezed my hand and we paused in front of her car. She leaned against the hood.

"I'm sorry this crazy society placed you in prison." My heart fluttered. She knew! How? And I thought...It had to be the work of nosy ass Aunt Betty. While I was freaking and feeling stupid Abrinna embraced my shoulders tilted her head up and on the tip of her toes she rose and gently brushed our lips together. We hugged our tongues together and made circles and flicked lust into each other.

An aroused Black Dickey whispered to me, "Let's dry-hump and screw her right here tonight." Behaving on his instincts, I quickly ducked past the dangling Star of David and nibbled my tongue down behind the daintily silkiness of her bra. I buried my head into her breast.

"Eke! Kayin we better stop." She said as she tugged the back of my head. Abrinna's ass was already pressed against the edges of the baby blue Cadillac's hood. Her legs had begun struggling, trying to grab a lock hold around my hips. I made passionate rings in the sensuous regions of her tits and cooed soft air on the pair. Abrinna tenderly protested as she stuck her tongue inside my ear.

I braced black Dickey into where I thought the top of her vulva was and the car's hood squeaked. Slowly, I scooted her chocolate nylon fiesta flip skirt up and Black Dickey's sensitivities pinpointed the top of her genital cleft and with intensity he gradually grinded.

"Eke! Woo-whoa-woo! Kayin we better stop." With sucking whisks, again feebly objecting, she grabbed the back of my head with both hands and tilted her head back, her body quivered. She began easing into matching my rhythms. The shocks on the Cadillac started squeaking. Conscious of the noise Abrinna muffed her moans into miniature falsetto o's. Her stilettos fell on the pavement.

I heard Abrinna's sheer beige panty hose slit in her crotch, the area that Black Dickey was mangling. Black Dickey could almost feel moisture on the outside of her labia. The feedback sensations of our syncopated rhythms revealed to him the potency of her muscular twat. With every intense hump and grind I could sense her vaginal walls desperately thirsting for more pleasures. Abrinna released my head leaned and began banging on the car's hood. Twisting and turning, her body pumped fast rhythms. With all her strength she cuffed her arms underneath my shoulder and the little naïve Jewish girl bucked on the fender into Black Dickey like a wild bronco.

"Oooooooo! Oooooooo! Oooooooo!" Her falsetto's tones raged. I sensed and diagnosed the invasion of convulsions on her body were a new experience for Abrinna, I had seen the same symptoms in Loretta.

Reviving from the seizure, lying flat on the fender with her head tilted I peered at teardrops that wouldn't fall from her bloated eyelids. Gentlemanly like, I offered her my hand and as she arose I gave her a handkerchief. Wiping her eyes, she glared down and then she looked up at me with a fragile shyness. It was as if she was aware I knew this was her first orgasm. She covered her face with both hands and scooted off the car.

***

The dusk was setting and finding Abrinna's house between Macarthur and Portland wasn't easy. When I drove the Camry up Cecil, down Glenway, as I maneuvered, sort of lost, I thought of myself as a black man entering a foreign country; it was like the end of the *Cold War* and I was entering East Germany for the very first time. This section of the Oklahoma City use to be a forbidden neighborhood for blacks. After driving in circles I stumbled on Abrinna's house.

Twenty-five years old and the Hebrew schoolteacher had inherited or made enough cash to own a home. Or she earned a fat salary to pay mortgage payments on an eight-foot canyon brown brick fence, a yard that was twice the size to ours, and steps to a cement porch to a house the color of desert vista blocks and it doubled our little home in Oz.

"Ah roses! Come on in and I'll place them in some water." Abrinna held the dozen roses to her nose and sniffed the aroma again. "Ah."

"Ah...I love the fresh scent of yellow roses." She took another whiff.

A country cottage floor lamp acted as an intimate guide. The low lighting emphasized the sparkling caramel finished shine on the cedar floors and generated shadows of mystery on the room's borders.

Abrinna wore a chocolate sexy slit skirt that offered a willing eye a side peep at her canary yellow panties. She coordinated the warm brown with a black fishnet blouse that exposed a mini bra that matched her panties. Her wardrobe was teasing Black Dickey mercilessly.

Clutching the flowers Abrinna pranced toward the fireplace and retrieved a vase that was on top of the mantel.

"They'll fit perfect in here." She nodded in agreement with her own idea and gave me an invitation to follow her.

I scooted behind her and allowed the horny Black Dickey to observe the twitching movements in her hips. I had uncontrollable urges, since they'd been repressed for four years I asked the question, had my impulses gone wild? Either way, I love to watch and wonder about the appetizing delights that a woman's ass has to offer. In the dim shadows I engaged in chasing one incredible ripple of Abrianna's ass. This emotional attachment instinctively propelled my eyes downward. Barefooted she flounced on a mat that was elaborate and probably expensive.

"Wow! What a magnificent rug." Seeing the glint of appreciation in my gawk Abrianna paused and spoke.

"A gift from my grandmother, it's a 19th century Jewish purple Beshir with Boteh design."

We continued the tour. In the next hall a Tiffany floor lamp's light glazed over the floor like a flashlight and led us through a glass door. Orderly decorated with checkered cloth napkins, the dinning table had a homey old-fashioned decorum. The eight-foot table had stainless steel spoons, knives, and forks in front of each chocolate chair. For intimacy, Abrinna had lit a cherry candle at one end. Draped neatly underneath the table was a multicolor designer rug with *'Hanukah'* inscribed in blue.

"Dinner is ready to be served, if you need to freshen up, the bathroom is down that corridor." She pointed in the direction with her head and whooshed off to the kitchen. My hands were clean but I assumed if you reject a dinner host's invitation to wash up it would be improper or they might even assume you were nasty.

Jewish art carved in wooden frames lined one side of the passageway: *The Jewish Scrolls, Prayers Ascending to Heaven, Holocaust, Rainbow Shabbat,* and the *Children Of Abraham.* The drawings on the other side shook my senses, giving me more of an appreciation of whom this Jewish girl was: *Malcolm X, Martin Luther King, Thurgood Marshall,* and some guy named *Charles Hamilton Houston.* The wall light fixtures on both sides diffused the illumination in the corridor and gave shadows to the paintings. The dim setting christened the works of art, memorialized the figures and made the people appear as saints. The Jewish girl displayed her gems of historical and religious purpose inside her royal domain and these sculptures probably magnified what was in her heart.

As I stepped on down the corridor, different from the spiritual and cultural art, was what had inspired Black Dickey to be at the Hebrew girl's home in the first place. It was a peek-a-boo portrait of Abrinna, bare-ass naked. A tasteful depiction of a nude Abrinna, the supposedly shy schoolteacher, was flamboyantly plastered on the bathroom door. My gawk was drawn to and stuck on how the artist drew her, hefty puffy swirls of curly jet-black fur smothered her vagina. The myriad of hairs was like a magnet to Black Dickey. He instantly had a hard-on and I suddenly had to piss at the same time.

I emerged from the bathroom and skipped through the hall with even cleaner hands, and an emptied Black Dickey. The artistic preview he had of Abrinna's naked body inspired him to work hard and fast for his dinner. I entered the dinning area and Abrinna met me with a hot sample of brew in a spoon.

"Ah…hot…spicy and delicious!" The soup that Abrinna spoon-fed me was simmering. I should have blown sweet little puffs to cool the soup. But Black Dickey was still fueled by passions and was busy peering at her scanty seductively dressed body and imagining if her pubic hairs resembled the painting? The worlds of curls had invaded his wits and I couldn't think straight.

Abrinna stood over me and served matzah ball soup and a crispy brown flour potato knish that was full of onions, chopped liver, and cheese.

"Oh wow! I can eat the flavor alone and get full." She bashfully smiled at the compliment, and shamefully brushed her opened slit skirt against my hip. She pounced in a chair that was at the head of the table and I sat at the corner next to her. Black Dickey salivated impatiently waiting on his desert.

No music, TV, or the restaurant's offensive evil stares were in the background. The only racket was ours. Squashing food, clinging utensils, and the swallowing of white wine; these natural actions were magnified into affectionate intimacies.

"Who is the creamy almost white man with the Caucasian hair in the painting that's hanging next to Justice Marshall—the Hamilton Houston brother?" I sucked in a sliver of liver and notice the meat was still dangling off my lip while I was speaking.

"Ah-hum. He was the dean and law-professor at Howard University, that brother was Marshall's teacher. He orchestrated most of the law suits that finally broke the back of Jim Crow." This time Abrinna was more compassionate with my ignorance; she simply tasseled her hair; I believe she was trying to downplay her brilliant knowledge of black history.

As a child I read Batman comics. I learned that Batman had wits that could detect when trouble was close and they were christened as his *bat-senses*. In prison I became skilled at how to stay alive. I observed and had to understand the motions and emotions of prisoners. If I hesitated or didn't react in time I could easily get killed. There must be a certain mixture of darkness and light in mid-summer's evenings when the sun is sinking and shadows begin to appear. On queue, with my distinguished observation, a herd of crickets launched into song. I stared through the open curtains and tuned into nature's noise. Then I heard Abrinna nibble on a potato and her air conditioner became the lead vocalist. With each bite that entered Abrinna's lips, every black drop of darkness, as the crickets harmonized background music for our love song, my prison instincts sensed I was going to get some loving tonight.

Chapter Twenty-eight

"Abrinna, you're supposed to be a little bit introverted, right?" She nodded as she raised her eyebrows and started chewing slower.

"How does an inhibited person undress for an artist to paint a portrait?" Black Dickey was becoming impatient and he wanted to move the discussion towards her naked ass.

Her eyes widened and she lowered her head. Had I embarrassed her?

"Ah…" Slowly rising she had a surprise smile. "The bathroom painting! Ah-huh…I sort of forgot that was there." Shyly she slanted her head again. Then, making eye contact with me. "I was in my birthday suit for an entire art class." She wiped her lips with a napkin and prepared to explain.

"I was a freshman. Even though it was only thirty miles away from home, I was away from home, away from mom and dad. My roommate and I thought the experience could help cure my social shyness and…" She dipped her head and appeared intimidated by what she was going to share. "…And help me love my body better." Black Dickey didn't care if she loved her body in a healthier way, he loved it already and he wanted to see all of it, the real deal!

"How close to the painting do you feel is near the authenticity of your body." With a glint in my eye I smiled at her.

"Uh…haha! I believe the student that did the one I selected to take home was the best. She even captured the scar above my navel and all my other flaws." Abrinna rose and lifted her fishnet blouse and pointed at the scar. I stood, leaned and touched the healed abrasion.

"How much of the curly hair is yours or did the artist go overboard with her creative imagination?" With a hard stare into her brown eyes I placed my hand on her knee and wobbled it.

"Ah-ha!" It was a mischievous ah-ha and she added a teasing smile. As instant as her awareness appeared in her devilish glee, abruptly she dropped her head and removed my hand. Was she insulted or embarrassed? Suddenly Abrinna snatched up her empty plate, bounced up and she scurried away.

Damn! I thought after the intense action the other night in the parking lot and the way she was seductively dressed that directness would turn her on, but the straightforward manner had pushed her away. Panicky my thoughts ran and got lost inside a confused hellhole. Damn! I couldn't figure out women.

"Kayin what do you think?" I heard her, then I saw her naked. Whoa! With outstretched arms she profiled for me. And with an alluring gaze she stroked her eyes down over her nakedness, as if the gesture was begging for my approval. Her breasts were big for her compacted physique and her full-grown nipples were standing at attention. Curly drizzles of hair made a trail down her navel, and the worlds of curls were packed around her vagina! Black Dickey popped on hard and if I hadn't sprung from my chair, I believe I would've sprained him on the seat.

Confident and not second guessing Black Dickey's instincts, I whipped him out and a copy of my other calling card. I was hoping that the raw sight of Black Dickey would get her juices flowing and the lab report would give us permission to proceed with sex.

"Here are the results of a recent A.I.D.'s test."

"Oh cool! I got mine and I'm on the pill. In her reply I believed Abrinna's was accepting what Black Dickey was ready to do. But suddenly her body shriveled and her eyes darted and she lowered her head. Embarrassingly, Abrinna shielded her breast with an arm and she covered portions of her overgrown pubic hairs with a hand. I had witnessed Loretta perform the same act before our first sexual encounter.

"And...and can you believe I've only had one partner...and that was two years ago?" Abrinna timidly eased that news out and slumped into a chair at the table. Her index finger started twirling strands of loose hair on her head. I stood over her and grabbed that hand and palmed it on Black Dickey's head. Abrinna shuddered. She gazed down on him and slowly her head rose and her eyeballs enlarged.

With her eyes on me impulsively she sprung to her feet and began unzipping my pants. I slid off my shirt, slacks, and shorts. I embraced her nakedness and Black Dickey became familiar with his new aphrodisiac, the bushiness of her worlds of curls.

I'd already decided if there was a next time if we actually made love, and if she had her labs I was going to eat her little ass out before pleasuring Black Dickey.

Abrinna rolled her tongue into my mouth. I boosted her up in my arms and marched into the living room, laying her on the 19th century Jewish purple Beshir rug. Some spirit or something compelled me to make love or baptize my body fluids with this Jewish woman on the memories held in the cloth.

Parting her legs, I blew soft whistled o's over and into her massive pubic patch and watched her body flinch. I was amazed the way her curly hairs swirled. Slithers of jet-black curly hairs flowed on both sides of Abrianna's labia. The scent of her vulva had the aroma of an exotic body mist, a delicious eatable fragrance. She had bathed and sweetened herself up for tonight, or did she always keep it tasty down there.

With the tip of my tongue I parted Abrinna's labia at the bottom. Flicking up at her hood, bit by bit, I felt her clit muscle slowly swelling, and inch by inch my tongue entered her vaginal walls. Gliding gradually upward until I felt the top of her hood I started sucking the flap. Her flesh shuddered and automatically her thighs and legs widened. Suddenly with every lick her vagina wiggled and automatically with both hands she scaled my back. And then, there was the falsetto sound again. "O-o-o-wow-shoot! Kayin what are you doing to my body? O-o-o-o!"

Abrinna's mid-section squirmed into sweet rhythmic stomach flexes that arched her backbone and those contractions flooded her hips. The grasp of her hands on my back became a firm pull behind my head. And as she made love to my face, her vaginal hole began swishing with fluids.

"O-o-o-o-o-o-o-o-shoot! O-o-o-o-o-o-o-o-o-stop! No-no-no-no-no...O-o-o-o-Kayin." Scary, that's what her turned-on tones sounded like. When I first heard Abrinna's falsetto passion pleas the noise had frightened me. I thought I was hurting her. Abrinna began to roll all over the throw rug, dragging my head along.

"O-o-o-o-o-o-wee-shoot-shoot-shoot-shoot-shoot..." Abrinna's body heaved out of rhythm and that's when I knew she was orgasmic and that's when Black Dickey started preparing to take the Jewish woman into his Promise-Land.

Rising up I watched her teary eyes widen. Her body quivered and it was like seeing an alcoholic drink that first taste of liquor to ease the shakes. Abrinna's body slowly collapsed and a moment later, exhaling, she rose and stuck her tongue through my wet lips. Satisfying sex has to be spiritual. I felt Abrinna's gratitude dissolving into my saliva.

Toasting the occasion we sipped on more white wine until we were ready for more of the breathtaking affections our evening offered.

My 6'4" frame hovered over her small physique and slowly I soaked my chest into the muscles and veins of her firm plump breasts. She bent her legs at the knees like a pretzel, arching her back. I guess this was the way some women prepared their vaginas for entrance. Even with the river of suds, Abrinna's twat was a tight squeeze for Black Dickey. Relaxing her vaginal muscles into a wider and painless opening required learning a new sweet science. Black Dickey had to twist sensitive jabs into her. I had to allow her hole to naturally swell. I had to be like a doctor delivering a baby. Black Dickey had to pay careful attention to Abrinna's exhaling oozing falsetto squeals.

Once her vaginal walls were ready to accommodate Black Dickey he squeezed slow rolling rhythms into her hole until she came. Repeating the same process, Abrinna climbed on all fours and then I doggie did her. Every position she hollered excruciatingly, erotically, and passionately. At times while we were making love on the 19th century Jewish purple Beshir rug, her feverish shrieks emulated the torture undergone by someone experiencing an actual crucifixion.

***

The summer's sun was pulling down the shades on its final days and Black Dickey was sizzling on a spiritual high. Living until adulthood, and finally finding one sexual hole to play in and then traumatically forced out of the game for four years, a resilient Black Dickey was pleased to have three foreign and unique vaginal cracks to dip into for pleasures.

Since I'd been locked up, was God now giving every black man in Oklahoma City three white women? I thought about my still all black neighborhood and that fleeting thought let me know that this reality wasn't happening in Oklahoma City with most black men. I've always been a fair looking guy, and growing up in Oklahoma, like I said earlier, I'd felt a white woman's lusting eyes on me. But those eyes were guarded, and the glares never broke the state's moral code. I knew my 6'4" framed body was firmer, had penitentiary life given me an edge, a dangerous appearance that was attracting the white ladies?

Was it moral to be sleeping with three women? Should this be an ethical dilemma for me as a black man to have sex with any white woman? Only when the sexual dates collided and I was juggling scheduling did I even pause and seriously consider the principles of sexing three women as an ethical question. The white society I had grown up in had robbed me of a life. Living in Oklahoma's America a system where the 14th Amendment existed only as a legal document, after the deed is translated through the perceptions of the white social order, the paper meant I was worth nothing, and that was a cruel joke. I wasn't sure when and how these evil forces would take my freedom again. So every time I had sex with these white women I enjoyed every exotic moment of ecstasy and treated each experience like it was my last sex and there was no tomorrow.

Shelia was my consistent Friday night lover. Even if I cancelled, which wasn't often, Shelia had a key and would come by and treat herself to popcorn, pizza, watch a movie, bathe, sleep in my bed, and sometimes she would spend the evening in my aunt's room laughing and having quiet talks. I believe my aunt was mentoring her. The street-smart whore would still charge me for the evening.

Cherry's weekly hormonal whims controlled when and where we had a sex session; secret pinches on my ass while I was moving furniture, a whisper in my ear when we passed each other at work, these were her sex signals. Cherry would switch her hips like a slut and I couldn't wait to jump on her aggressively out of rhythm clit and create some funk.

I remember one morning awakening with a regular sour breath, with added ingredients, booze and Cherry's vaginal juice.

As Cherry relaxed her sleeping head on my chest, at a distance I could smell the dried sexual sweat between her legs. When she awoke we both staggered to an upright position on the bed.

"Has your family ever known any black people?" As we were dressing out of the blue I was possessed to ask that question. I'd seen her nosy protective black maid at the mansion, but she worked for them. So this seemed like a fair question, so I was ok with the spirit world's inquiry.

Cherry rocked her head, puzzled, and I thought maybe her bewilderment was the result of a hang-over. As I gazed into her lost eyes the semi-deep cultural related question seemed like it was hurting and irritating her brain cells. Or did the query insinuate the idea she belonged to a family of racist. I watched her probe her family's history.

'Susie', all the Brown's called her by her first name. Quail Springs nursing home, that's where Cherry escorted me to meet the ninety-five year old frail dark brown skin woman. The aged lady who'd dedicated her life to caring for four generations of Brown's, and had denied herself a social and family life, and also she'd severed her connections with the black community, still had her faculties and her priorities in order. She treated Cherry like a princess and she gawked at me with suspicious eyes. The only time I'd seen that misdirected loyalty out of a black person was the gawk given to me by her successor, the Brown's cook. Cherry knew her simply as "Susie". I address the ninety-five year old black woman as Miss Susie, and my display of respect had no affect on Cherry's life-long training or Miss Susie's allegiance.

"Do you know where Miss Susie is from?"

"No."

"Do you know any of Miss Susie's relatives?"

"No." And that was the extent and the end of my social-racial conversations with the princess.

Abrinna was my priority. And it was probably her tight vaginal walls and the passionate ekes in her falsetto moans that made her special for Black dickey. But I'd like to believe it was more. Our natural cultural exchanges were real and resonated. I believed we shared a genuine affection and appreciation for each other. Abrinna was the only lover who told me that because of the myriad of orgasms her monthly cycles had changed. Any preset date with Abrinna would always override the impulsive wild rendezvous with Cherry. Cherry had to settle for quickie bombastic orgasms. And Shelia would get to rest her twat with the amenities of room and board and of course she had a free payday.

Outside of embellishing Black Dickey's feverish twinkles off the sensitive bite of Abrinna's rigid vaginal walls, and her taking time outs to recuperate her tender sore nerve endings, we partied. We danced until the clubs shut down. We had picnics out in nature's woods, chowed down on hotdogs at minor league baseball games, and got contact highs off marijuana smoke while snuggling and enjoying concerts in the park. We were always the odd couple arriving to see traveling plays.

Abrinna and I jogged and walked hand 'n hand at dusk up and down her use-to-be white-folk-only neighborhood. As the white folks did yard work, washed cars, and children played they all peeped and some even gave us hard gawks. I felt echoes of fear in their gawks attacking me in every step. I heard the language of the mean white streets of yesteryear and today. Nigger reverberated from the dust of days gone by out of little white boys that had played ball and pre-teen girls that had scorched the pavement jumping rope. In the past nigger had been the topic of family barbecues. To those southern country white folk, nigger was said as comfortably around dinner tables as taking a bite of pork was. Nigger-nigger-nigger-nigger-nigger-nigger...sometimes I heard the word louder than the sound of my footsteps! Nigger mutely eluded from our evening observers and was boldly engraved in the shadows of the history in this still mostly white neighborhood.

Assessing what we thought the inner city school children's needs were to successfully finish high school, Abrinna and I wrote and procured a $500,000 state tutoring grant through the NAACP. Since the majority of the employee recipients, the tutors, were from low-income families, our system fed money back into the black community.

***

As the crispy brown wrinkled leaves scattered in autumn's winds, I watched clusters crinkle and trail at the feet of children as they skipped and ran to catch the early morning school buses.

On those mornings, driving to work, nostalgic movie memories of Mamma began to play. Mamma appeared in the dark of autumn's dawn on the Camry's windows. The windows reflected her image as clear as a mirror. She was buttoning my coat, pulling my stocking cap over my ears, checking to see if my shoes were shined and kneeling to make sure the laces and loops were even and tied correctly. As I left for school, waved good-bye, her weary frown always tossed me a kiss.

***

Brenda Simmons was a twenty-three year old five foot eleven inch cocoa-chocolate curvy vivacious welfare mother with three children, and every male that was present at the first fall NAACP gathering took notice of this tall tasty glass of black tea.

Bursting into an orderly NAACP assembly, ripping and running Brenda's three children made a chaotic entrance and the towering bombshell hustled in behind them, hushing the commotion.

"Shush! Y'all get over there and sit down." Obediently the little devils became angels.

Immediately, after the meeting convened, Brenda's table was swarmed. The men acted like a pack of wild dogs in heat. Or were these civic fellows offering plain old southern courtesy and the brothers felt obligated to beam as they greeted a new member.

After Abrinna had visited with some of the members, I escorted her to her baby blue Cadillac. If I was a spider-man my spider senses were tingling. From a corner eye glance I noticed Brenda and her flock nestled outside the NAACP door and I believed she was intimately examining every move we made. Since I couldn't spin a magical web and my only adventures that related to any of Spiderman's paranoia were induced by the prison system, I'll label my gift 'incarceration awareness.'

I waved at Abrinna as she drove off the parking lot and as I casually walked towards the Camry I could hear a herd of hoofs coming closer. With the key in the door I peeked over my shoulder and there they were, Brenda and her bunch.

"Would you please give us a ride home, sir?" With the down-home charm of a southern black woman's naïveté, Brenda politely begged.

I was picked out of a crowd of ready and willing gentlemen that probably would've driven the full-sized buxom woman anywhere she desired, and yet, Brenda had waited like a spider in a web and I became her prey.

Sitting along with me in the front seat, Brenda's skirt skidded up towards her juicy thighs and Black Dickey saw potential in her exposed long muscular legs. Black Dickey's appetites cut short my inquiry of why me, his simple answer was, why not him?

Of course when a person's depending on their feet for transportation in one of the country's largest cities per square miles, and the next option is an inadequate bus system that doesn't maneuver through town on a timely fashion, when that individual gets an opportunity to have a personal chauffeur they'll sometimes cram in as many errands as possible. First stop was to an affordable grocery market and that wasn't on the African American's eastside. Several Blockbuster Video Stores were in areas where mostly white folks lived, but Brenda's Aunt Reba had a rental home located on the eastside. That's where Brenda spent the most time and I had begun banging my horn before the family trickled out one at a time.

It's weird how a twenty-five year old ex-con can spend an afternoon in the presence of children and offer simple things like a candy bar to a five year old girl and smile when she happy-hops. Buy a video game for a seven-year-old boy and witness the charm of bubble-eyed joy appear. And God help the brother who dates the mother of an eight-year-old man-of-the-family. The little man toted groceries into the apartment rolling his mean eyes at me.

Brenda lived in public housing on Northeast 36th and Prospect. This edition was built in the early 1970's. On the edge of my blue-collar neighborhood, the place was only a mile away from my home. The short distance was irrelevant but every black person in the city could easily observe and measure every inch of separation from the African Americans that worked pay-check-to pay-check—the property owners, and those that lived in government housing—the-have-nots.

Like the subsidized government housing units on 16th street, Aunt Betty's ex-residence, these poverty sections of the city were dangerous drug and gang war zones. And the police routinely violated the 14th Amendment, the civil liberties of these poor and often illiterate and often addicted unfortunate citizens. There were security gates for this unit, and it was cornered off like a prison, squad cars patrolled the vicinities 24-7. Working middle class African Americans in Oklahoma City usually avoided the deficient spots mostly because they didn't want to get shot or harassed by the cops. I assumed they wanted to keep the few precious freedoms they enjoyed. I entered the zone at my own risk and fear took over the steering wheel.

I stopped at the security gate and two patrol cars passed behind me. The driver of the second vehicle cruised slowly enough for me to see him giving me a vicious stare. After passing he accelerated and circled the block. The other car had already parked across the street directly at my rear. Outside of trying to scare the hell out of me, I believe he was checking and writing down my license plate.

I coasted with autumn's blustering winds as they scattered leaves, garbage and other debris from the entrance to our arrival at her unit. The aroma of barbeque and a stench of marijuana baked in the air. Exhaling the scenery, I witness the passing of liquor in brown bags and patches of young adults and teen-agers congregated on some of the steps of the individual lodgings as hip-hop music blasted. Tumbleweeds blew across lawns and half of the units were boarded and this gave the housing complex the appearance of a ghost town. One might even surmise that some of the inhabitants were preparing for a tornado.

Brenda's apartment had the congested smell of over sanitized Clorox cleanliness and it reminded of the prison environment at Big Mac. The children's achievement awards along with their crayon colored art hung on the walls of the scanty furnished dwelling.

"Thank you so much for everything. Would you like a pop?" Brenda said as she unpacked groceries. She pulled loose a single can of coke from a six pack and handed it to me.

"Thanks." I took the refreshment, checked my watch and saw it was almost 7 pm. I had a date with Abrinna in an hour. "Uh...I've got to hit the road.

"Kayin here's my number. Can I have yours?" Brenda scampered after me with a torn off piece of paper in her hand. I relaxed my hand on the doorknob and allocated the responsibility to an alert Black Dickey for his own interpretation of Brenda's engaging gift and request. Was having sex with her worth it? I had a child I didn't need a ready-made family. I made half-ass arguments while Black Dickey's powerful authority dictated I accept her number and give her mine. He said a quick prayer hoping that the sexy super sized woman would call.

After work on Monday I drove Brenda on another errand and our foreplay had begun. Mid-week two more task for the Camry, and while Brenda undressed details of her life my roving eyes caught a glimpse of the huge dark chocolate areola rings around her big nipples, and I imagined them flopping in an orgasmic frenzy.

"I hate living and raising my children in these damn apartments! I have to find somewhere to go and escape everyday," a dismayed Brenda said. She flopped into the seat and slammed the car door. Her round eyelids were full of water and the stagnant tears gave the welfare mamma a lost, hurt, and desperate appearance. She held the suspended disgusted stare as she surveyed her surroundings.

Brenda had resided at this public housing address since she was eight-teen years old. She had dropped out of school in the 9th grade when she was pregnant with her first child, and had lived with her mother until a section eight unit was available. The father of her three children was forty-five and had been in prison for the last two years for selling crack. Brenda hadn't seen her own father since she was five years old.

The ghetto girl had good manners. Always grateful for my assistance and after our errands she always invited me inside her apartment and offered me refreshments. One day I was lounging on her decrepit couch. As I breathed in the strong disinfectant fumes I saw an admirable joy arise on Brenda's jaws when she spoke of her great grandfather, Grady McCuin Jr. Her great grandfather was a veteran of the Second World War. As an air aviator engineer he trained with the first Air Force of black pilots at Tuskegee Institute. After the war, President Truman integrated the Air Force. Tuskegee was disbanded and he spent the remainder of his service at Fort Richardson in Alaska. Since no major airlines in the country were hiring black pilots before or after the war was over, the veteran went on to receive a bachelors in Electronic Engineering at UCLA. He returned to his birthplace Oklahoma City in 1953. When the VA began to offer home loans to veterans, many black veterans in Oklahoma were denied. Since he wasn't one of the fortunate blacks to receive a housing loan, and no one in the state of Oklahoma hired black engineers in 1953, Mr. McCuin worked for the Oklahoma City street department. Like many black men he had to get a second job. They lived in a dilapidated rental home on Northeast 9th street. He died five years ago, never owning a home.

Her mother, aunt, and her two older sisters were close, and Black Dickey was eager to be a pseudo member of the family. He wildly wanted to dive into the juicy goodies of this elegant giant.

Chapter Twenty-nine

The voluptuous mountain of a woman stretched her long legs and one Saturday afternoon I had a surprise knock at my door. Brenda had walked that mile up the road to my house.

Shelia and I had mangled the bed linen all night and my bedroom had a musty after sex funk. Since it was lunchtime I poured Brenda a glass of orange juice and using southern hospitable charm I opened the refrigerator door and invited Brenda to help herself. I dashed to the bedroom and ripped off the sex saturated bedding and doused coconut air freshener all over some fresh linen. I whirled an unknown exotic fragrance in the air and quickly dusted and wiped my computer desk, dresser, and the TV with lemon oil. I wanted to be prepared just in case.

And I was right. We discussed sex and then we did the dirty deed. Even though Brenda said she had only a few lovers and hadn't been sexually active in months she was afraid of the results of an HIV/AID's test. She was on the pill and with a whining beg Brenda said, "I want to feel your naked skin stroking inside me."

With our clothes on I approached her from the back. As Brenda leaned on the electric range Black Dickey scrolled between her but-hole and he began a slow wide roll. I sensuously licked the rear of her neck and unsuccessfully tried to capture the fullness of her oversized breast in both hands. My titillating exercises caused her to freeze and resist and then her bootie eased into miniature shudder twists. Brenda's marshmallow soft ass caught up to my rhythms and she added a little hump-funk to the beat.

To feel Black Dickey's penetration better and without losing tempo Brenda swooped up her silk skirt and ripped her draws down. Brenda's desires to feel sex's sensations were contagious. I unzipped and unleashed a neurotic Black Dickey and he was prepared to jam and twist himself right up her ass.

"Daddy don't!" I swiped Black Dickey down the side of Brenda's ass-hole and the audible cries of *Little Kayin*'s warning caused me to pause. I struggled with the lusting will of Black Dickey, muscling

him with both hands I mentally had to summon some of Mamma's strength. The judgment in Mamma's eyes came and my cravings halted.

We ended up butt naked in my bedroom. Brenda laid her long chocolate voluptuous frame on the mattress and she squinted like she was in pain when she saw me slip the sensitive ribbed rubber on Black Dickey.

Lurking over Brenda's chocolate body I scaled the five foot eleven inch beauty and made artful photographic delicious memories. As she inhaled and exhaled, I traced the rise and fall of her tummy up to her light nostril breezes and back down to her perfect upside down kinky haired triangle. I watched the lips of the opening of her pooh-nanny slightly draw breaths. With two index fingers I pulled apart Brenda's labia and examined the insides of her vulva. Musty smoked shades bled out of her outer labia tips and when I looked inside the color changed into pink, just like Loretta's had.

"Tehehe. What are you doing?" Raising her head off the pillow Brenda gawked at me as I stared up her twat. I don't believe the impatient giggling black woman had ever been observed carefully before she was fucked.

"I'm just admiring God's grand creation." I said smiling.

Brenda's hood, like my other four lovers, it resembled a wrinkled turkey's noodle. Curiosity caused me to wiggle the tender tissues and this automatically made Brenda's hips hump and gyrate a motion. Constant jiggles on the tissue triggered a flood of waterfalls that drench my fingers.

I decided I would torture the giant and excite one body part at a time. Without touching other boundaries of Brenda, I planted my tongue in the center of her big-girl tits. I drifted towards her left tit and with the tip of my tongue I measured tiny sample levels of sensitivity. Placing my whole mouth on Brenda's nipple I began to suck the bumps around her areola like a baby pumping for milk.

"Eke…ah!" Brenda oozed a breathless weak moan and began slightly switching her hips.

Getting my full nutritional supply out of the organ I continued slurping the huge organ and watched Brenda's wheezes increase with an emotional airiness. Brenda's hips began to surge mimicking the rhythms caused by a penis.

"Woo-whoa-woo!" Heaving a pleasurable sigh Brenda clasped both her hands behind my head. She bent her lengthy legs at the knees and began to waggle them in and out while she lunged her hips up gyrating them into an invisible penis.

"Woo-whoa-woo-w-e-e-e-e! Kayin you're going to make me cum doing that shit. "Woo-whoa-woo! Come on and fuck this pussy!" Brenda's stout back had joined the action and the bed-springs began screeching. She released one hand off my head and began squeezing tips of her other tit.

When I felt and saw Brenda was almost orgasmic, I stopped. I explained to the sexually frustrated young lady that I needed to get to know her whole body. After bringing the same result on her ear, neck, and naval, a miserable unsatisfied Brenda decided to take matters into her own hands.

"Shit! Screw you Kayin!" Still lying on her back Brenda propped her lengthy legs up and stuck two fingers to the top of her vagina and she immediately completed the mission.

"Woo-whoa-woo…woo-whoa-woo! Damn it!" Orgasmic sei-zures had the giant wide-eyed as her body pounced on the bed. Aroused in her erotic dance I decided to invite Black Dickey to her private orgasmic party.

"Whoa!" Shocked by the sudden shrill uncontrollably I shrieked. Talk about warm wet waters! Black Dickey fell into an ocean that was preheated and pulsating electricity. An inch away from kiss-ing, I acknowledge the goodness I was experiencing to Brenda's face. "Oh-my-God! I'm in heaven!" Bracing Black Dickey for the easy glide I passed her labia and there was little friction from her vaginal walls. Black Dickey plunged into the hot slushy slippery depths of her climatic motions. "Oh-my-God!" We said in unison.

"Oh God damn Kayin! Do me baby!" With both hands Brenda snapped a chokehold on my hips to keep them stationary. She be-gan bucking her hips and twisting her orgasmic vaginal muscles around Black Dickey while her juices drowned him.

"*Son, that's my great-great grand-daughter.*" I shuddered when I heard the declaration by the old dark skinned 89er. The quiver and his surprise visit caused my hips to delve deeper into Brenda's fluids with added power.

"Oh-shit! I c-a-n-'t s-t-o-p c-o-m-i-n-g K-a-y-i-n!" An orgasmic Brenda oozed the words out. She upped her beat by injecting a bizarre passionate rhythm to our grove and the newness made Black Dickey spurt his bag of juice.

Before our second round of intercourse I finger fed Brenda a piece of Aunt Betty's homemade pecan pie.

The way Brenda preferred to do doggie style was for her to lie flat on her stomach. I mounted on her back and Black Dickey slide down underneath her ass, entering her still sizzling hot twat. The girl wobbled her ass in wide stroked whirls. This was a new style for my chiseled body. I melted into the back of her malleable bare skin and the connection was soulfully spiritual. On each orbit that her hips swerved, every inch of my skin was turned on.

In my previous love making experiences there was a reason I never began doggie style the first time I had sex with a woman. I noticed with Loretta that Black Dickey was extremely sensitive to the nerves that extended between Loretta's but-hole and her vagina. I didn't want to prematurely lose my liquids. I didn't want to be perceived as an immature, awful or stingy lover. Maybe one shot will be all that I get with some women especially if the lady is impatient and if she believes first impressions are important.

I took control of the rhythms and drove long upward hard strokes that penetrated and stimulated Brenda's clitoris. After a bite of pie her sweet tooth had been nourished and after a stimulating whipping by Black Dickey her vaginal muscles were still pumped and her twat immediately started sucking up Black Dickey. Black Dickey's sensitivities trembled and his strokes uncontrollably picked up speed.

"Son, that's my great-great granddaughter you're humping." I was in the middle of busting one of my best orgasms ever. Appearing in my mirror, black as tar, displaying a solemn pitiful stare and I should add judgmental, there he was again. If he was in Brenda's ancestral tree I assumed there must be or should be an incest spiritual privacy law that would guard against kinfolk from being Peeping Toms. Shame and embarrassment gripped me tight. The grip was worse than the many times I had to stare into Trish's father's eyes, after I'd done his little girl. The orgasm fizzled out of a feeble Black Dickey.

"Son there has to be justice for my great-great grand children. You've got to see that they receive their rightful inheritance."

The totalities of my humiliating feelings were immediately replaced by fear. How the hell was I going to get that old Negro's land back? If white folks took the property from him back then, what makes that old fool believe I have any more power than he had? Shit! White folks here have already bamboozled me and most don't care to have an intimate meaningful dialogue with any black person. This is the reddest state and I knew these good old boys and gals in Oklahoma had a deaf ear to the reparation conversation.

All I could do for the old spirit was to care for his great-great grand daughter by offering my best. Outside of chauffeuring Brenda, I tutored her children and bought them books and clothes. For the little man of the house, I got him a calculator. I convinced Brenda to study for the G.E.D. test. And of course she was examined for A.I.D.S. The results were negative and I guess that could also be seen as her gift to Black Dickey.

Even as I watched the children's brains exercising, engaged in ideas and were learning, and saw their exuberant smiles whenever they received a present, I knew living in that area they would soon be seduced by drugs, gangs and introduced to negative behavior. The police and the justice system would start harassing them. Easily they would become victims because they wouldn't know the ways of the ghetto and white folk. I began to have nightmares of the little fellows laying in the rain and mud, cuffed, jailed and under suspicion, or convicted. I even heard guns blasting and a bunch of cops standing over the three bloody children's corpses. Since the white establishment of Jim Crow Laws in Oklahoma had already denied the ex-slaves and their children including me our 14th Amendment rights, they obviously were going to continue committing the same injustices to the newest recipients.

***

The air was cooler and the holiday season swept the usual superficial generosity into the hearts and on the faces of the white folks in Oklahoma City. Even though Black Dickey was soaking in three white vaginas and the activity unionized me instinctually with the oppressors, the laws and rules for him and the white twats were different. The heartland society of Oklahoma had already locked me up for being a black man. White folks fake smiles were supposed to be friendly seasonal greetings but the intimacy of actually knowing black people were still a mystery to them. Affection for black people was lost in their own selfishness—which is how I saw all their pretentiousness.

A week before Thanksgiving, Cherry made a decision to have a sex feast with Black Dickey at the Westin Hotel. She licked him up and down, devoured him in her mouth and ate his nutrients. I gained ounces tasting her from head to toe. We got drunk on wine and became exhausted in our sexual aerobatics. Cherry fell into a deep sleep and she started brutally snoring. Annoyed by her noise, I stumbled to the bathroom and showered. By the time I was clean and drying off I was halfway sober. I performed a sobriety test. As I touched my thumb on my nose I used the mirror to monitor my motions. Reflecting in the mirror I noticed Cherry's laptop on a desk behind me and beneath my reflection.

Birds were flying through autumn trees and golden brown leaves floated like feathers on the screensaver. The picture guided me to thinking what part of the furniture business was Cherry hiding behind those romantic fall scenes?

Brown's Bookkeeping was the name of a desktop link to an Excel document. I was curious, how much money was the largest furniture store in the state raking in? What digits are on the company's financial statements. Clicking on the link, dipping into the numbers and I saw that Brown's Furniture Store was generating more than half a million monthly in accounts receivable.

I took a tour of the Brown's sales projection ledger: accounts receivable, accounts payable, monthly invoice orders, and the ratio statistics of product sales. I immediately spotted disgusting discrepancies in what was actually moving and selling off the main floors, and what appeared to be over-purchasing. Cherry's excessive spending gave the warehouse a cluttered appearance. Some furnishings: queen beds, head boards, lamps, couches, dinette sets, sold quicker than other brands, and for the past six months Cherry had reordered the same amounts for everything. There were items Cherry automatically reordered and none of them were selling.

Six stockers, including me, were constantly unloading, stocking and moving the over-stocked pieces out of the way in order to get to the furniture that customers were actually buying. Unsold merchandise that Cherry was reordering monthly matched the unnecessary aches and pains logged into my back's memory.

I worked at the computer until the affects of alcohol had worn off and my body didn't wobble in the chair anymore. Sober enough to feel chilly from the 6 am moon breezes I decided to see if I'd logically represented the facts on a revamped ledger. On separate spread sheets I'd devised an ordering system that slashed overloads, or slow salable and un-salable items, and that equaled unnecessary shipments, and that saved the Brown's suppliers delivery time. Less disorder in the warehouse and this arrangement meant the loaders could use that time helping customers load their pick-up trucks. Most of all and the bottom line I was saving Brown's Furniture Store thousands of dollars.

5:15am on the dot and Cherry's alarm played a Jay-Z hip-hop tune. I heard Cherry's legs lazily shuffling in the sheets. Her eyes were shut when her feet hit the carpet hard.

"Good morning." Strutting towards the bathroom, Cherry touched me on the shoulder and her greeting was that of a lethargic drunk almost awake.

Tinkles were made in the toilet followed with a flush and spry sprinkles of the shower.

"Ah." Cherry moaned as steam breezed through the opened bathroom door. Black Dickey interpreted the 'ah' echo as a primitive morning mating call and he leaped in an ah-ha receptive way.

I crept into the bathroom and unfastened the glass shower entry; aware of my presence Cherry squinted through the spraying waters. Her lips curled into a smile when she spotted water drips beading and bouncing on a rock hard Black Dickey.

"Good morning sir." Black Dickey got more of a respective greeting than I'd received.

Cherry bent over backward and the water squirted directly on her spritzed hair. She spread her cheeks and a steam cloud formed a circle around the point of access to her goodies. With one hand she gripped Black Dickey and nuzzled him up her ass-hole.

"Ah-eke!" Cherry chimed and humped her butt bone into a rhythm.

I humped and dirtied and funked Cherry up with sweat and sex fumes and she howled like a wild dog. "Eke! Woo-whoa-woo!"

After our early morning delights, I scrubbed every inch of Cherry's hide.

Later while she was primping in the mirror I informed Cherry of the improvements I'd made with the bookkeeping system.

"Shit!" Disgusted Cherry stopped in the middle of stroking her hair to curse at me. She shimmed her tight sleek satin rose mini g-string panties up. Cherry walked up to me, and snatched Black Dickey and pointed a finger to the top edge of her panties. I saw her exposed vaginal hairs. "You'd better stick to what you do best."

In the coming months my back muscles became aware of one thing—they were less strained. Cherry had secretly adopted my categorization process and I believe she thought this ignorant Negro wouldn't even notice the differences.

***

Instead of the warm fuzzy nostalgic good time memories that escort the heart on holiday occasions, my first free festive season and the gloom of missing Mamma haunted me with a wretched aloneness. And my pitiful tortured seclusion in prison induced a neurosis. I showed symptoms of PTSD, Post-Traumatic Stress Disorder. This diagnosis was usually given to war veterans. Hand-to-hand combat, stabbings, humans being murdered in the worst way, believe me prison was probably, at times, worse than a war. I'd lived in constant fear for four years. I was as bad as an alcoholic without alcohol and no recovery program. To escape the devastating anguishes that were sucking a hole in me, I sought desperately to keep Black Dickey soaked inside the coziness of a vaginal hole. Black Dickey was the only part of my body celebrating. There were a few times in the middle of making love, the rage and fear would rise above the affection of pleasure and Black Dickey would peter-out.

The beginning of the New Year, white folks were back to themselves as distant as ever from the black community. I sensed the old spirit of Brenda's great-great grandfather inside my head challenging me to become more active with his wishes. I was an ex-con, barley surviving the life white folks had dealt me and was helpless to meet the old specter's overdue reckoning. I was afraid that if I tried anything, the dominant culture would take away what little freedoms I had. Bedtime and all alone, I took sleeping pills. The aim was to flee into a dead sleep and escape the old fellow's daunting haunts.

Like I already said, in prison time passes in slow motion. On the outside the cold dead days of winter quickly turned into the chilly breezy arrival of spring's lively green. March 18th was a cold blustery day and this was the anniversary date I was released from prison.

That morning, barely awake, I almost shit on myself when I rolled over on my back and spotted my old great-great grandfather squatted at the foot of the bed. He had a disgusting leer on his charcoal face. I snatched my legs into a bent position and waited for words to flow out of his lips. A sad disappointing stare was all I guess he seemed to believe was necessary. I blinked and the phantom was gone. He left me consumed with a disgrace and a dishonor that I didn't believe I deserved. Seconds later another guest appeared in the window. Brenda's great-great grandfather wore the same sickened mask.

Clearing my eyes, I leaped from the bed and landed on a burnt and mutilated banshee's head. Deadheads had covered the floor. Even though I knew the ghouls were translucent, every tiptoe I took I squirmed because it felt icky. I reached for my bed room door and the fried skulls took off in flight. The deadheads dangled off ropes that were tied to invisible necklines. Swiftly, the meaty skulls oscillated in circles around me. The swirling odor of blistered rotten human flesh became overwhelmingly intoxicating. I choked, coughed and ran from the room slamming the door. I entered the bathroom and finished what the spirits had activated—I shit. The whiff of my feces was like a welcomed perfumed aroma. Materializing and appearing next to me was my great-great grandfather smoking on his corncob pipe. He clicked a handmade chiseled cane on the bottom of the stool. I flushed and the old frontiersman dumped the ashes into the swirl of feces.

The haunting transparent heads waited until I hit the freeway before the gang emerged again. In the rearview mirror, on the back and side windows, and then they crowded the front window. Ninety miles per hour wasn't fast enough and the gusty winds couldn't blow them off.

All day at work, decayed heads materialize on the furniture like Jack O' Lanterns dropping down for a Halloween party. The two old timers, the kernels of Brenda and myself were also there. While transferring furnishings up and down aisles and around corners, I passed right through the condemning stares of the ageless corpses.

"What the hell do these deadheads want and expect from me?" By end of the shift I screamed in frustration. Are they waiting for me to tell the Brown's to give up their property and money because some old ghost told me the land was stolen from him over a century ago? Shit! They're not getting me locked up, placed in a loony bin or killed.

The spirits didn't bother me on the ride home and I figured we'd all put in a hard day's work.

Approaching home I spotted the top portion of Brenda's frame on the porch. Her bottom half was concealed by the stonewall of our raised flowerbed. Resting in a plastic lawn chair, Brenda had cuddled a red stocking cap down under her ears and was hunched down to keep the cool flurries off. Her body was warmed by a fake, long, three-quarter black leather looking coat that was made of rubber and it had a white collar that was cotton instead of fur.

To heat up her chills I fed the mammoth woman hot cocoa with a taste of Hennessy. Every inch I licked on Brenda's almost six feet of chocolate skin my taste buds were treated with an exotic flavor. Cocoa butter, coconut, banana, chocolate, and strawberries were moisturized into the fabrics of her squashy hide. Delicious and lusty turn-ons, her appetizers always made me salivate like Pavlov's dog. And like a bank robber seeking a safe place to hide, Black Dickey always found a secure hiding spot whenever he slithered among the slimy walls of Brenda's pooh-nanny.

"Eke! Woo-whoa-woo! Shit!" Gargantuan! The monster of all orgasms landed between Brenda's heaving hips. Hysterically she snatched a grip hold on my hips and heaved me from one side of the bed to the other.

"Look for the deed inside the paneling of an antique trunk at the foot of my great-great grand-daughter's bed!" Brenda's eyes widened and I thought she had heard the withered spirit of her great-great grandfather whispering. Instead she was traumatizing by the effects of the massive orgasm.

Sacrificing Black Dickey's appetites, skipping his usual second and third servings of sex, I hurried and got dressed. I was anxious to investigate the trunk. As the Camry's wheels rolled, I remembered once while making love to Brenda we'd rolled off her bed and bounced on the tattered crate before we landed on the floor. Undisturbed, Black Dickey was still stuck inside her and we were still hypnotic in our eroticism.

I decided to keep quiet about seeing the ghost of her great-great grandfather, a deed, or that I'd seen other spooks until I had tangible evidence; some believable backup in my bare hands. Even if I had verification I shouldn't be to eager to share these spooky and the mind-boggling hallucinations, with anyone.

Chapter Thirty

There was a rusty buckle glued to an old worn out lock. Time and changes in the temperature had smeared both into a neat weld to the seasoned decaying chest.

"Have you gone crazy nigger?" I believe that's what Brenda's astonished expression was probably saying, her big wildly confused eyes watched me pound on the precious antique crate with a hammer and I still hadn't explained why. But before she had a heart attack or brought me up on charges, I thought I should at least give Brenda some information. I told her what I believed was in the strongbox.

Scraggly mildewed clothes were on top of dead bedbugs, moths, silverfish eggs, and broken cockroach wings. Gingerly I dug through the muck with my bare hands. I felt grubby. The idea of finding a live mysterious living insect or creature was freighting. Finally, entrenched deep enough, I felt the crust of an old zipper on a side pocket. My eyes lit up when I saw what was inside the pouch.

Carefully I unfolded a crinkled, aged document. The paper was dingy but every word on the certificate was legible.

The document wasn't a deed; stamped on the heading was 'Government Patent'. It was a map navigating 160 acres, a section northwest of the city. Grady McCuin was on the certificate, and the date was 1889, the year of the famous land run. With the seal of the president and congress, the declaration was filed at the Federal Land Office in Oklahoma City. The Seminole Development Company did the survey of the land. Stuffed in the same fastened side pocket I counted more than five years of homestead receipts.

With this essential information, I told Brenda the fundamentals of the truth and watched the stunned broke ass welfare mamma's eyes have an orgasm. She wore the expression of a leprechaun that just found the pot of gold or did her gesture contain its own uniqueness. Maybe it was born deep into the gallows of a slave ship and this amazing gaze of joy and relief was finally weirdly appearing in her eyes.

"God damn! I'm. I'm. Am I rich Kayin? I am ain't I? What do I need to do? Help me please!" This time her trembling bones and bulging eyes were not the results of Black Dickey's magic.

We had found the patent, but living the tortured jail life and exposed to the evils of Oklahoma's civil rights of the past, I knew we needed more proof. Thank God for the Internet! This amazing invention could be our best friend. Since Brenda didn't have a computer we hopped in the Camry and skipped a mile back up the road to my house.

After several searches I located a library in Lawton, Oklahoma and that was the only place on the planet we could actually verify on microfilm the authenticity of the Oklahoma land run patent.

Brenda was full of melodramatic inquiries of how I'd come across this magical news. I told Brenda that I'd run across an ex-inmate and during our discourse, her family's name came up. He enlightened me to an old prison story that had been circulating since Big Mac opened. The tale was about her great-great grand father and a stolen deed. *That was my white lie to Brenda.* The possibility of an ancestor of my public house lover being the original owners of the Brown's property, the largest furniture store in the state, I wondered how this fact would be received by the white establishment, the people that claim to be in charge of the world's morality.

That night I saw a manic Brenda amused, enthusiastic and full of self-doubt. Her passions were rooted in the illusion of potential wealth and prosperity, and the destitute skeptic. This black woman had struggled with earth-shattering realities. How could she ever advance in an America that had been institutionally unwilling to share in an intimacy with people that had her complexion? And if she lived in the world as a rich black woman, how would she live? I wasn't ready to offer false hope by hopping into her imagined or true realities.

Trying to calm Brenda, I became aware of how lottery ticket winners felt when the sweepstake's office was closed and they had to wait until the next day to claim millions. Brenda and I sipped on Hennessy. And even though she was tipsy, she was still possessed by a feverish zeal. I transferred some of her excitement into sweaty four rounds of entertainment for Black Dickey.

When the birds chirped their first notes the next morning, I phoned the furniture store and left a message on the their machine, saying, I was sick. We were on interstate 44 headed south, 85 miles to Lawton before the light hit the skies.

We arrived in Lawton before the library opened and decided to wait and eat breakfast at the other Big Mac, Mac Donald's. Terror entered my soul when Brenda suggested the eating establishment.

"I'm buying me a house and getting my children as far away as I can from those awful projects." Brenda said as she munched down her second egg Mac muffin.

"And I'm going to send my kids to the best private schools too!" She said nodding her head in a womanly, African American, cultural matter of fact way.

Time seemed to stand still after we left the restaurant. It took forever for the old wrinkles on top of wrinkles white lady to turn the key and open the library door. Anxious, my hand got stuck in my back pocket while I was reaching for my wallet to pay the small fee to see and get a copy of the microfilm. As the black research student explored the mimeograph for Grady McCuin, her hand and eye coordination moved too damn slow. Brenda and I glared mean stares at her.

Brenda held one side of the copied document and I held the other side. We gaped with stupid stares tracing each word while tiny miracles of wonderment formed inside us. Grady McCuin, with the president's signature and the seal of congress was stamped on the document...we definitely had an original patent.

"We need a lawyer." A declaration of determination roared from the poverty stricken black woman.

And not just any lawyer...not just any lawyer this time! My previous experience of settling with an attorney without a reference or a work history had gotten me four years in prison.

Our state senator was a black woman and also an attorney. Celeste Washington had represented the black community for more than twenty years. Even though it was handily defeated, she had introduced a bill that sought eradication of Oklahoma's mandatory six years for citizens who are busted for the first time for crack cocaine. A lifetime NAACP member, the civil activist had fault hard to get monies and standards up for public schools that would equal a private education. Instead of permitting gentrification to occur in the old historical black neighborhood, where I began life, she'd orchestrated a coalition of black churches that bought Urban Renewal properties. The partnerships restored old houses, built new homes and sold them to low-income, first time homeowners. And before the state executed the last black woman—a year before the Supreme Court declared to murder a retarded person was unconstitutional—Celeste Washington had rubbed shoulders with Jesse Jackson to protest the state sanctioned murder. They both spent the night in jail. Her sentiments on reparations for blacks had been heard but dismissed by the state's legislature. Celeste Washington had delivered eloquent speeches on the senate floor demanding payback for slavery and all the Jim Crow Laws that deliberately, illegally denied opportunities and penalized citizens of the United States for the color of their skin.

Her voice was assertive, polite and strong yet femininely gentle. After telling her our story, immediately a fierce urgency ate up polite and gentle. Celeste Washington was excited to take the case. In fact when she saw the patent documentation she guaranteed victory. Decked out in a white floral Armani Collezioni asymmetric jacket and seamed pants, the slim 5' 9" fifty something caramel, cream sister stood behind her senate office desk with a larger than life appearance. Her cerebral system demanded that Brenda and I focus on her eyes and carefully analyze her strategy. When she unleashed her jacket, her arm muscles were sensuously chiseled. When she primped around the desk her butt stood out and up and her mid-sized tits perked. Almost gangster-like, aggressive and clear and in layman terms, she explained how the evidence that we had was ironclad.

"Those patents given during the 1889 land runs were perfect titles." Mrs. Washington exuberantly said, and proceeded to read us textbook arguments straight from her law references.

"Any Land Patent will always rule over a Warranty Deed. In **Wineman vs. Gastrell**: *'A grant of land is a public law on the statute books of the state and is notice to every subsequent purchaser un-*

der any conflicting sale made afterwards.' And **Summa Corpora-tion vs.** California said, 'forever that the Land Patent would always win over any other form of title.' No Land Patent has ever lost an appellate review in the courts."

Celeste Washington had a bold *in-your-face* confidence and it made me feel better about life just looking at her. The term mover and shaker epitomized how quickly she got things done and her aggressive nature belonged to her alone. Before the end of the day she'd done a historical background check on the land and discovered that in 1914 oil was gushing. And even today, six blocks north of the furniture store, the black gold still flows. Oil was the Brown's avenue into capitalist supreme status, and the by-product of being rich is that this family now owns the largest furniture store in the state. By the end of the day the mover and shaker Celeste Washington had set up a meeting with the Brown's and their lawyers for Friday afternoon.

Even though the senator was inspiring, the possibility of one of us getting payback from all that has been done and taken from the black race would surprise me. The cold-hearted history lessons in prison had destroyed my faith in a fair and just America. Either way Black Dickey knew a choice was being made. He was sadly aware that the time of diddling in Cherry's pink delights was probably nearing an end. And after Friday's showdown with her family Cherry's out of rhythm ekes, ahs and grunts and the painful passionate faces she made would only become jerk-off memories. My prison instincts and common sense had prepared Black Dickey for this reality.

I was back at work the next day and activating penitentiary 101, minding my business and cleaving to secrets. This was easy since the white employees at Brown's furniture didn't know me as a person anyway.

I slipped into Cherry's office in the middle of business hours. A shocked Cherry saw me wagging a rock hard Black Dickey in my hand and he was pointing in her direction.

"Kayin what are you doing? I'm working!" I'd shut the door but that didn't stop her from nervously instinctively gazing around to see if someone was watching us. "My father's in the building! Are you crazy?" I approached her pacing like an android. With my first robotic step her enraged edginess frightened Black Dickey but as I got closer they both changed. He was already stout and he bulked even bigger. Cherry took note of him cultivating right before her eyes. I let him go and the muscles in Black Dickey popped and pointed and begged for what he desired. Her anger and fear changed into *the pleasures of danger*. The risk of getting caught was arousing the animal instincts in Cherry. She leaped out of her cushioned black leather chair. Gawking and never taking her eyes off Black Dickey she rushed and maneuvered through her office furniture and made it to her door. She aggressively tried to lock an already locked doorknob.

"You're going to get me in trouble." Still with a tiny bit of trepidation, Cherry whispered a half hearted warning while kicking off her two inch heels, and climbing out of her black-laced panty hoses. She leaned over the desk and hiked the back of her crimson mini skirt. With gumption and grief I took my last view of an exquisite X-rated scenic piece of art.

Shaking and twisting her ass she muffled her orgasmic tones and all that restrained animal tension was transported into her hands and released. The phone was the last of everything to fall—notepads, pencils, files, books, and her laptop, Cherry's frenzies had cleared off her entire desk.

In her final moments of exhilaration I heaved a load of juices inside the walls of Cherry's contracting vagina. And I gazed at Cherry's overwhelmingly spent appearance, I silently said goodbye.

Thousands upon thousands of black men had been tarred and feathered, dragged and humiliated, castrated and lynched, falsely accused for what I had just finished doing. And I had doggie did white royalty. Cherry's twat was unique and every vagina heaven Black Dickey had entered they all offered him a different and special brand of animated ecstasies. Only a few generations ago ungodly unconstitutional laws were made to stop this natural human act. Even though what Cherry and I had was mostly shallow, in our orgasmic experiences I did feel an intimacy that had exposed me to an emotional place that was part of her soul.

As I drove away from the furniture store that evening, I saw a young Grady McCuin with his mule all alone on the barren landscape. Going home on the freeway, as I gazed out the side window, in the usual location of a Holiday Inn, there was a Native American woman kneeling by a clear running brook. She was bathing a baby.

***

That Friday afternoon, four white men draped in expensive business suits entered the senator's office. Three wore glasses and rigidly clutched to soft leather brief cases. They had the appeal of high priced lawyers. A bulky man entered. He was built like a bull and his suit fit too tight, he was probably a bodyguard. Seconds later the two Brown patriarchs strutted into the quarters. Clad suavely in winter scarves, top hats and coats—the two monarchs stripped down dispensing the warm veils to the huge security person. Impeccable, hand woven, tailored suits were beneath the top apparel. A person had to buy that unique fabric only if they were vacationing in that foreign country. God himself had personally taken the time to silken their shirts. Expensive watches and diamond rings, refined Italian and French shoes, from head to toe the Brown's wardrobes cost more than Brenda and my ancestors had earned in their lifetimes combined.

The man who'd hired me, the person that I'd never seen inside his own furniture store, was leering across the table at me. When the shit hit the fan, I guess the granddaddy of the vagina that Black Dickey had soaked part-time inside of, was still the financial overseer of the Brown's empire.

Symbolically, dignified with red-white and blue honor, the elder Brown and his son sat across from me as the perfect picture of the American family dream. Old man Brown's daddy, the original redneck cowboy, along with Oklahoma's earliest business owners, governors, legislators, and congressmen like 'Alfalfa' Bill Murray, instituted and built an aristocracy of hate all across the sooner state. In reality it was a greedy structure camouflaged to the uneducated and ignorant white masses as a superiority system. That political economic organization initiated a list of subservient deadly laws and humiliating attitudes against its dark citizens. These black people were un-liked, despised, and unlucky like the newly arriving immigrants to the United States and Oklahoma. The latest refugees, the English, Russians, Irish, French, Jews, Germans, and Italians, these newest citizens were able to foster relationships with the prairie's white societies and have their magical rags to riches storybook tales come alive. The pioneering wealthy white men and women of the state were responsible for reviving old southern ideas and those traditions trampled the notion of an intimate life, an endearing togetherness that may have formed between blacks and whites. They made sure that never happened. They championed the Jim Crow segregation laws and developed a psyche in the white community that has survived generations. In fact I'm sure I felt the residue of that attitude when I was arrested, convicted, and sentenced. The lack of concern for a black man's life lived in the hearts of the juror's that had placed me in prison. That's what I saw when I stared across the table into old man Brown's eyes.

The large loops in Brenda's new perm gleamed and her snow-white blouse gave the dark colored giant woman the appearance of a black Baptist dressed up on Sunday morning. Brenda's shaky eyeballs were an indication she was frightened by the powerful white men and her sweaty palms were the symptoms of a damaged, unworthy colored girl. I wore my indigo suit, and as Brenda and sat together, I was reminded of an image I'd seen in an old *Jet Magazine*. Lifted straight out of the pages of history, we looked like the black and white photographs on the pages. We were a characterization of the 1960's freedom fighters.

Celeste Washington, joined Brenda and I on one side of the conference table; opposite from us the lawyers occupied three chairs and the Brown's sat side by side. Psychologically the chair arrangement was even more unbalanced than the actual visual.

The old man's under-eyed, evil sneer at Brenda shattered all pretexts that this was anything but a typical business session. The scoff was grabbed out of the old souls of generations of southern racists. *"You're not my equal—you skank ass nigger!"* Brenda quivered from the stinging glance. The powerful white man's history and his presence pierced through every generation of Brenda's lack-of-enough-love like a butcher knife ripping into a tender tomato. Cold winters and hand-me-down Christmas gifts were the ragged pieces of Brenda's life. Her psyche was equipped with less than a high school education. Brenda's mother was born in poverty and then struggling paycheck to paycheck with even less schooling. Brenda had lived her life for twenty-three years and everyday of her life she'd witnessed inequality and the denial of civil rights had torn emotional holes into her family. She had every right to be furious at the Brown's. Instead the giant black woman trembled in the presence of the evil, an evil that was responsible for most of her shamefulness and her family's tribulations.

The elderly man's wicked egotistical scorn unleashed an echo of auditory illusions that filled my head and they began telling small horror stories. I tapped into a world jam-packed with millions of insincere yes sirs and undeserving yes ma'ams from a suppressed people. One story concisely explained itself: *Once upon a time there was a group of dark people and because of their complexion they were slaves. For over two and a half centuries, the slaves were often treated worse than livestock. Owners bought, sold, beat, and killed both their animals and slaves. But usually they didn't rape the livestock. Upon freedom, instead of receiving the tender loving care the dark folks desperately craved, these people were disenfranchised and made second-class citizens in the only country they knew as home.*

I offered Brenda self-assurance by squeezing her moist hand under the table. The gesture only gave Brenda a momentary calmness. Throughout the proceedings, a bashful Brenda that I'd never seen habitually batted her eyes as if she was trying to hide her worthless soul.

Of course, ahead of time, the senator had already prepared our guest a menu of the dinner she was serving.

"Gentlemen, let's begin. The organized stateswoman issued copies of the patent deed to each of the men. There was grumbling among the group and then, in rhythm, the lawyers held the document up to the light, giving the authenticity and terminology close inspection.

With all the dignity and shock of a New York businessman that suddenly finds out his junk bonds are worthless, Cherry's daddy puffed out his chest to half match his bulging midriff and shouted, "This is preposterous!"

The stale odor of animal's hair permeated over my shoulders; I turned and spotted a young Grady McCuin rubbing the forehead of his mule.

"The old man, he was born almost twenty years after his father took my land. I've heard his father tell him the legend. Handing down stories to their offspring on how they humiliated niggers, that's the way it was done back then. At dinner tables, and holidays like Thanksgiving and Christmas Day, sharing these precious gifts brought them laugher and joy.

And out of the angry eyes of the specter I felt a mysterious juice being pumped up my backbone. The sap straightened my tissues and my bone marrow seemed to rise and release an unrestrained vigor that briefly overwhelmed my insecurities and my Okie social brainwashing. With a strong, straight torso, the substance gave me the moral authority to gawk at the old Brown as an irate militant black man. The elder Mr. Brown shuddered and his bold pugnacious glare was tamed to mere white fear. His affect was just like all the previous experiences I'd seen a black man's fierce presence have on white men. In jr. high school the black mad eyes would cause white male and female teachers to quiver. And later those same educators would misuse the power of the pen with unprovoked failing grades and expulsions on black students. Those students didn't initialize the threat or deserved the demoralization.

"We'll study this matter and get back to you later senator." Sheepishly the elder Brown said. Briefly standing behind the Brown's a glimmer of Mr. McCuin and his mule appeared. And I thought my militant scowl was the reason for the old farts cower. Had he heard and possibly even saw the old 89er? Or was it guilt? He knew his wealth was built on stolen land. Old Mr. Brown rose and like a stone that makes ripples through a pond, the whole Brown clan was up and out of the room.

"We got them!" The senator said. She slammed her hands on the table, gawked at the door and triumphantly repeated the victorious song, "We got them!"

"I expected at least some resistance, an argument or more outrage, or who, where and the slightest inquisitiveness as to how the patent had gotten in our hands." This bad lady was ready and prepared for whatever went down. She cut her eyes at us with her own curiosity, how did we get our hands on the antiquated patent?

"These are big boys! They'll run to their big boy friends, the local judges, and gather opinions on how they'll have to rule. When they discover what I already know, they'll get a glimpse into an appellate decision." Celeste Washington tapped her ballpoint pen on a notepad and confidently stared into our eyes. "And we'll win there too."

"Our next move is to consider if Brenda's willing to settle or go to court, and if you're ready to settle for what amount." The civil rights leader glared only at Brenda. Brenda shuddered. Maybe she was intimidated by everything that this powerful black educated woman represented and that included the lawyer's self-esteem and her aggressive nature. And maybe the tremor was about the whole unnatural experience itself. Less than five days ago this welfare mamma was making love to me in a dilapidated bed in the projects.

I never contacted nor did I ever hear from anyone connected to Brown's Furniture Store for a long time. My suspicions that Cherry would stick to family loyalties were accurate. Was it immoral for me to treat Black Dickey to his last taste of her? Well, we both ended up acting in our own self-interest.

Old man Brown phoned Aunt Betty and fired her. "Fuck you old fucker!" And she slammed the phone down.

I didn't work for three weeks. I had a little money saved to eat on and a place to live. My extra expenses were the state ordered lab test, and the parole officer. Shelia mysteriously left my life that same Friday. It was almost as if there was a universal synchronicity conspiracy between the two white vaginas. Another expense eliminated. Expense? Black Dickey will tell you that Shelia was a necessary need. Her vagina was his food and his shelter, part of his Maslow's hierarchy. God allows the moon, stars, and the heavens to shuffle a person's life in mystifying ways. Shelia joined Cherry as part of my fantasies in jerk-off memory heaven.

My sexual relationship with Shelia had lasted a year. I'd ceased trying to understand Shelia's history. I didn't lecture her on the profession she'd chosen nor did I question her exploits with other customers. She didn't intrude on my life, didn't offer any suggestions, what I should or shouldn't do. I did find out I was the only one who could get some of her loving on credit.

We added, to our John and whore relationship, intimate steamy showers in the mornings. I would scrub suds up and down her labia and she began to gently wipe sex odors from my genitalia. We shared quaint quiet meals. I usually cooked and served or Shelia brought fast food over.

From the time Shelia and I met we were both like birds with broken wings. When Shelia changed her cell number and stopped coming around I didn't search for her. I would like to think that the natural cozy animal passions our bodies ravaged out of the others had healed her wounded limb and she was well enough to fly away.

A week later I was feeling secure and satisfied after Black Dickey had sweated several rounds inside Abrinna's tight twat. We relaxed, I became less guarded, and we talked. I decided to share Brenda's dilemma. Of course I left out the sexing part of the friendship.

Abrinna was the first white person that I knew that had willingly exposed herself to the African American world. She knew the politics and black history inside and out but the idea of reparations stunned her *Okie* thought process. The philosophy of payback for a crime has been welded into the American psyche since the self-righteous creators of the Constitution declared that our democracy was a foundation based on laws. The so-called *"Law"* was the reason the white folks said they'd locked me up.

"Do as I say don't do as I do" This is the philosophy white Americans apply when African Americans demand reparations. Reparations, this ideology was the ax that chopped the head off all the groundwork, all the culture we'd integrated into our bonding experiences. I believe she couldn't resolve or admit that for generations her ancestors were some of the people that had perpetrated crimes against a whole race of people. Even if they did nothing and were silent, they joined the pack and nurtured the racist seeds and are responsible for the separation that exist between blacks and whites today. Abrinna's forefathers were probably hard working folk that chose to play it safe by going along with society. They

were probably just like me before I was the recipient of these deep-seeded historical injustices.

"What about the money you receive monthly off your family's oil and gas leases?" I asked my Jewish lover. In her soft gray hurt eyes I could see the sensibilities of her southern conservative rational coming forward. *'Pull-yourself-up-by-your-bootstraps'*, this mentality was ingrained in the Okie psychic and was always applied to black folk whenever they were demanding their constitutional rights. I could see this moral philosophy working beautifully inside the Jewish woman's pretty little head. Fidgety, briefly she gazed at me with a pitiful stare and I saw her whole body had snarled up. Abrinna felt shame for me, for embracing the idea of reparations. Or she was shocked I had knowledge of her finances.

"Are you searching through my private documents?" A fiery Abrinna snapped. She folded her arms around her breast as if I'd raped her.

"You left the notebook of leases on the dinner table, and like any book, I opened it out of curiosity. Anyway that's not the point. Your family had opportunities to gain wealth because this state finally embraced them. Black people weren't even allowed to work in the oil fields. Have you ever in your life heard of a rich oil black man? Look at this house." Our eyes connected and we gazed around at her intergenerational wealth. At twenty-five Abrinna's house was paid for. She was living in a lifestyle, if you measured her assets against blacks who had worked two jobs all their lives she would put those Negroes to shame.

I hadn't allowed an intimate, emotional love to be the cornerstone of a relationship since Loretta. With Abrinna, I delved into weird delusional possibilities of *'us against the world'*. Maybe black and white could have bound us together if we were more than just babes in the multicultural process. I did dream of commitment or marriage and us having golden brown children. Maybe our bond would've been a part of a healing to hold up and show the Oklahoma world. I had a need for an illusion of *being in love*. But it was just a fantasy. Black Dickey was heartbroken that Abrinna's tight twat would also become another collection of his jerk-off daydreams.

The God that gave me carnal abundance, secure spots for Black Dickey to bathe in ecstasy-land, had almost abandoned him, but the gracious spirit had left the African Queen for Black Dickey to play with.

Chapter Thirty-one

My weekend get-to-gathers with Little Kayin had changed into anytime during the week and sometimes whenever Loretta had an appointment and no babysitter. My relationship with my son brought unusual rendezvous with Loretta. Occasionally Loretta would cook an intimate dinner at my house and we'd enjoy a rented movie with our son. The more time I spent with my son, I began to have bona fide natural warmth for my growing sperm cell and surprisingly with that expansion, the less I thought I was in love with his mother. But I still had dreams of *US* as a family. I was still guilty of needing to believe the idea that the love Loretta and I had created would rise from the dead. That fantasy dogged me while we watched cartoon movies with Little Kayin. As my son discovered new wonders and as the land of fantasy appeared in his eyes, I'd see Loretta admirably checking-him-out and I'd fantasize about *US* as a real family.

It was necessary that I inform Loretta of Brenda's situation. She needed to know why I was going to be late with next month's child's support: Would this tough-minded sister be receptive to my explanation, or Brenda's situation? Fear created a dream.

***

Loretta froze with a fork between her lips. She stopped chewing with a mouth full of steak. Tears flooded her eyes and she began to sniff and cry.

I knelled in front of her and she sobbed into the handkerchief I handed her.

"I'm so…so…so sorry Kayin…sorry I didn't wait for you! You have to understand my family; we've suffered the hardship of poverty for generations. We live in a community where most of our black men have been locked up at least once. And when a person goes to prison, that's a whole different story. Nothing but bad stuff happens for that person's future. If a black man survives prison, I've witnessed how devastating the experience can be for him! For years they usually suffer from untreated PTSD and usually they become

dead-beat unproductive creatures. Every night while I waited on you, a piece of me was murdered. And when you were released, I didn't know what sort of person I would be exposing my son to. Kayin you've grown into a better man." Her guilt brought her to her knees. With both hands she sheltered a torn face that was full of tears, shame, and regret.

I hugged one arm around her waist and the hand that I'd pictured wringing the skank ass whore's neck with, I used that palm to massage the back of her neck.

After Loretta had a good cry we embraced and rose together in one unionized motion. As we hugged our bodies found old familiar places, those tender loving spots. Would I evoke and arouse a memory of her and Black Dickey? Would she remember our passionate orgasms? If ever there was a time I wanted to exploit my prison sensibilities and abuse Loretta's vulnerability, this was certainly the opportunity.

***

In reality life never gets as good as a dream.

"You've never asked why I got married?" After enlightening Loretta to Brenda's difficulty, we sat around my kitchen table and Loretta never responded. She sipped on a cup of green tea and then posed the question that I'd never asked her.

Seconds passed and in silence we stared at each other. Impatient for an answer the career woman raised her eyebrows. *"Read my mind!"* My quietness screamed. *"Cause you got horny bitch!"* That was my abandoned heart's answer. What did she want me to say? I glared at Loretta and the gawk begged her to answer her own question.

"Kayin I chose you to be my first lover because I thought we had potential. We had the possibility to live a life better than our parents." Anxiously Loretta gazed at her watch and nervously sipped on her tea. Loretta's points of analysis in a conversation are always filled with short little tales and could end up as long stories. When she checked the time I guessed she was scrutinizing which version she would share, short or long.

"When I first saw you and your cousin Danny together, my heart took a nose dive. I saw our possibilities dwindling. And lo and behold the bastard took you down!" Loretta finished off her tea in one large gulp. She had made her first point.

"God damn it! Every family in America has a Danny in it." Pointedly with dark sarcasm I told her, "He's not a drug addict, and he's not a dealer, sweetheart. Danny's life has been even tougher than ours, we're supposed to ditch black people like him because they're not on the same road to success as us?" I thought I'd question her logic before she justified her common sense and added more delusional rationalizations as she made up her fairytale lifestyle.

Loretta leaped from her chair. I believe she was surprised I was defending Danny. Yeah, I was still mad at my cousin, but neither one of the ingrates showed up for Mamma's funeral. I heard the wisdom of my great-great grand father, *"They don't make too many like your mother anymore."* Loretta was responsible for the decisions she'd made.

"You don't use good judgement, Kayin that's your weakness. You're losing a job and placing your son's interests over some damn welfare mamma!" Loretta snatched her purse off the table and stomped out of the kitchen.

"Mel would never consider such a silly ass choice." While she was leaving, Loretta compared me to her husband. I guess this was her way to stab me in the balls and rationalize the choices she'd made.

I always thought Loretta selected me as a partner because I was a charming, hard working and an intelligent man with morals, and of course, easy on the eyes. Wearing Loretta down wasn't even the reason I got my first piece of ass. And somewhere in my insecure head I'd assumed Black Dickey's mastery of her vagina was the reason Loretta had stayed as long as she did. In escaping the ghetto, statistically, she'd made careful choices. I believe she was terrified of mingling with the people in our community that were unworthy or risky.

Reflecting delivered a memory of our first failed attempt at lovemaking. *"It's okay Kayin..."* It probably was okay and she could've lived a lifetime without ever exploding in ecstasy-orgasm heaven. Since Mel wouldn't do anything out of the ordinary he's, probably lousy in bed, I hoped.

Loretta and I were no longer virgins, literally metaphorically and the adversities of life had shown our true colors. Hard times had separated us from a single journey and made us into two different people. I'd always accepted Loretta's conservative ways as being a part of her personal make up. She's the hardest working person on the planet. I never would have thought that her busy bullheaded lifestyle was a by-product of terror and she used those shrew discriminating assets for her survival skills. She'd mastered *how to live in the white man's system.* Loretta was right. I was weak with generosity. I'd always tried to do the right thing. Mamma had described those concepts as virtues. It had been a long time since that good quality lived in my life daily. Incarceration and the realities of powerlessness had shoved this good feature to the side and made a huge space for self doubt and hate. Prison had altered my destiny and had given me reasons to grind my fingers into a fist and have maniacal thoughts of killing a man with my bare hands. The successful sisters and brothers of slavery and Jim Crow must have used better coping skills than Loretta and I.

If someone compared and subtracted today's inflation from the time the Brown's began pilfering and profiting from the oil in 1914 one could calculate the black gold had made them more than five billion dollars. Today, according to their accountants they were worth a whopping eight hundred million dollars.

Two months after we met in the senator's office there was a settlement. The first offer made to Brenda's family was for twenty million, then twenty-five million. And to avoid infinite legal entanglements, a happy-to-be-black-and-rich-in-America Brenda and her two sisters were advised by the senator to settle for a whoop-de-do sixty-six million dollars! Plus the Singleton family would receive twenty percent of the existing revenues of the oil pumped out of their great-great grandfather's land. This didn't change the reality that all those lost dollars could have provided opportunities to millions of African American families and they could've lived more of the American dream. And I thought about what life could've, would've been like for the African Americans that live in the most successful black neighborhood in America, Greenwood, Tulsa's black Wall Street.

The news spread over the plains and throughout the nation that a black woman had received reparations. Just like the O.J. Simpson broadcast inspired blacks that justice was possible for them in America, the same information made many white people angry, afraid, and led a lot of them to the conclusion that blacks were now special and their lives were targets for an unimaginable impossibility...***reverse discrimination.***

From the time the penniless welfare mamma received her pot of gold, every time I laid eyes on the exquisitely super-sized, delicious box of chocolates, she was always dancing in a daze. Money...can...make...you...happy! Our last love making performance was in a luxurious suite at the Sheraton. How do you give an orgasm to a person that's already sun bathing in erotica? It was easy. Every gyration, each dip and all of our fluent wiggles seem to easily satisfy and stimulate an even brighter heavenly radiance through Brenda.

After our passions were pleased I was given a check for five hundred fifty thousand dollars and that gesture brought a sparkle to my after sex glow. The buxom woman lay sweaty and spent across the luxurious king-size bed and graciously said, "It's a finder's fee. "

Time slowed down, three weeks of unemployment and I became nervous. Senator Celeste Washington to the rescue! When she called, and as she talked, I drifted back to our quaint around the table confrontation with the Browns. In her private office I was surrounded by the powerful and I was frightened and that unusual unique situation also energized my soul in a way that no other experience had. Well, we're not counting sex. As the dynamic senator spoke I was aroused the same way again. I accepted a job from her. Government contacts always lead to business associations. With these two alliances I founded a non-profit organization that would initiate the white Okie life into interactions with the African American experience. My dream of becoming an electronic engineer and working for a fortune 500 company, that life died in prison, and has never resurrected.

I paid the rest of Mamma's note on the house off and decided to change the deed into Aunt Betty and Danny's names.

Oklahoma has one of the cheapest real estate markets in the country. A hundred and fifty thousand dollars and a brother can own a small mansion. That's what I paid, cash. The house is the newest home located in the same block as my son and his mother's.

And lo and behold, I found out that money was the best aphrodisiac for attracting the honeys. The small fortune was my genie in a bottle, it granted me my childhood dream! I'd been in prison for four years, out working a decent blue-collar job for one year and I hadn't seen nor had I heard from my dream girl Trish. Right after I got the gold my fine ass home-girl showed up grinning like we were the best of friends and had been partying everyday. Trish had gotten a divorce, was still a year older than me and was still the most ravishing and erotically appealing female on the planet.

As children we'd played house and gyrated like we were making love. This was way before our energized hormones grabbed our bodies. And now, the Goddess that I fantasized, and immediately discovered jerking off, and as I grew into manhood, in my imagination we were always having lusty musty sex. In the flesh, she was finally stretched out butt naked across my king size bed. Under the same pubescent spell mixed with my sexual experiences and habits I began studying every stunning inch of this supernatural creature's body.

The same olive vein on the top of Trish's wrist was in the inner sides of her elbows and it made an artistic string along her neck. The emerald was under her armpits. The two grapes that had represented her tits had metamorphosed into delicious round tight melons, and the lime blood carrying vessels streaked through the areola circles around her nipples. I ruffled Trish's vaginal hairs, and under the dark black wavy fur I found the emerald seam again, it was still there.

I almost came just sliding Black Dickey into the entrance of Trish's juicy hole. We flowed into a natural rhythm. And just like when we were children, Trish was leading the way.

"Damn! I knew I should've tried some of this a long time ago." Lying on her back, staring deep into my eyes she gritted her teeth. I guess Trish's sixth sense was letting her body know our initial erotic sensations were real and she was preparing for the ride. As usual,

I performed all the sexual positions in my repertoire but the time and the elation of satisfaction was the difference. Our lovemaking began at 9 pm Friday night. I warmed up leftover pizza for breakfast and dinner. And our animal affection session wasn't over until 2 pm Sunday afternoon. If Trish didn't have an appointment to show a house—she had her own real estate agency—I'm sure our sex-recreational life would've lasted the whole weekend.

The solution for my anger at white people in one word from the spiritual council, was forgiveness. Like a sober alcoholic prays for a daily reprieve in order to stay sober, this was the pill I had to swallow to contain my rage. Blacks had been in America since sixteen hundred and nineteen (And fifteen thousand years before Columbus), and had labored day and night to defeat slavery and Jim Crow laws. *(And for a black person to marry someone white, in some states some of those decrees were on the books until the year 2000.)* It had taken that long for the white doors of humanity to creep and barley open. The next phase of the frontier for me was to see if I could possibly have a deeper relationships with white folks, and maybe they wouldn't feel like they needed to continue hurting me, and people that looked different from them. *"Diversity is a lifestyle."* That's what the spirits said.

When the tree leaves got old and changed to the color of brown, I was able to convince Danny that I had a plan to increase his janitorial service. In the most segregated and glorified edifices in Oklahoma's America, on God's day, Danny and I dressed in our Sunday best and we went to an old southern Baptist white church.

"Man, just look at all the little demon angels up in here. I'm going to sex the hell out of these little white bitches!" With his sneaky jive smile and while the parishioners stood and sang the opening hymn, *All For Jesus,* I could see Danny picturing all the young white women naked. As we integrated our African American personalities into that white congregation, a number of Danny's visualizations did come true and his business quickly multiplied.

As a black spot in the midst of large gatherings of white people, I still have lurid visions of dissected penises, rotten mutilated heads, black women being raped, colored children screaming in flames, and sometimes, I doubt God's plan for humanity. The reasons why white folks are out to get me and seem to have an internal need to harm my life continues to be a mystery for me. Often I've pondered this question, were their ancestors like vampires and instead of craving blood, did they have insidious desires to murder and dehumanize, and mutilate the genitals of black men? And it always shocks me when a scared white woman guards her purse when they see me. Sometimes, unconsciously, I find myself sheltering Black Dickey with the palm of my hand when I'm in that sea of white folk.

My probation was completed and the state had stopped collecting my urine samples. I was still an ex con and was sad of that fact. I was off parole and off paper in Oklahoma meant my privileges to vote were restored. I still drove the same Camry. I loved gray but painted it baby blue. I was changing. I was inventing a new me, a new life. Since I paid cash to the builder of my new home and since we're in a depressed market, in time my house will be worth more than half a million.

The stature of being president of a foundation offered opportunities for business deals here and there and at the end of the year I was easily worth over a million dollars. I needed that money and more for my son's future. I'll spend every penny to keep him out of Oklahoma's unjust justice system.

I still ask myself what Maslow would think of the society I lived in. Often, without a request from me, there's a stopover by new and old black souls with some demands. *"How am I doing Mamma?"* That's my daily question.

Someone once said past behavior is the best predictor of future actions.

***

May 27, 2009 as an African American teen-aged robber lay helpless on the floor a white Oklahoma City pharmacist emptied his gun into him. The security system captured the shooting on video.

***

June 01, 2009, an Oklahoma highway patrolman stopped and choked an African American ambulance driver while he was taking a patient, an African American woman, to the hospital. The Af-

rican American paramedic was cited for failure to yield at a light and was arrested. The African American woman's son caught this incident on video.

***

In my early morning jogs I'm no longer afraid to see Oklahoma's America for what it really was and is today. And I'm always questioning the humanity of the fine lady. I try to perceive people for who they actually are. In the November Presidential Election of 2008 Oklahoma was the only state in the country that McCain won hands down in every single county; all seventy-seven. With the pitiable odds of one in three against a black man doing prison time, the percentages probably triples for an ex-con and then doubles if you live in Oklahoma. I don't think of it in terms of if the bad boys come for me but when they come. I'll be ready with a new and improved better lawyer.

As I erotically make love to Trish I know my fantasies of her twat had lived in Black Dickey's head a long time, her pooh-nanny couldn't possibly be this damn delicious! And as soon as some bad circumstance develops in my life, I expect Trish to disappear. And I guess Black Dickey's already seeking pleasures, security and contentment; searching the planet for an old fashioned passionate dependable vagina.

About The Author

   Kenneth Bowens was born in Tulsa Oklahoma. Thirty-four years earlier, in 1921 the most affluent African American community in U.S. history, **Greenwood's "Black Wall Street"** was bombed and destroyed. The National Guard flew airplanes and dropped incendiary devices right down on Black Wall Street. Some folks believed that the fiery explosives were nitroglycerin shells. The Tulsa Police Department united with fifteen thousand white vigilantes and they machined gunned and killed three hundred and maybe as many as three thousand black children, women, and men. They looted and burned fifteen thousand homes, six hundred black businesses, twenty-one black churches, twenty-one black restaurants, thirty black stores, and two black movie theatres. Kenneth lived in Seattle, Washington for fifteen years, where he wrote two plays, and studied improvisation and acting. He's moved back to Oklahoma and lives in Oklahoma City.

www.ingramcontent.com/pod-product-compliance
Lightning Source LLC
Chambersburg PA
CBHW080843250626
47163CB00003B/428